THE
LIBRARY
OF
LEGENDS

Also by Janie Chang

Dragon Springs Road
Three Souls

THE LIBRARY OF LEGENDS

A NOVEL

JANIE CHANG

HARPER**AVENUE**

P.S.™ is a trademark of HarperCollins Publishers.

THE LIBRARY OF LEGENDS. Copyright © 2020 by Janie Chang. Excerpt from DRAGON SPRINGS ROAD copyright © 2017 by Janie Chang. All rights reserved. Printed in the United States of America. No part of this book may be used or reproduced in any manner whatsoever without written permission except in the case of brief quotations embodied in critical articles and reviews. For information in the U.S., address HarperCollins Publishers, 195 Broadway, New York, NY 10007, U.S.A. In Canada, address HarperCollins Publishers Ltd, Bay Adelaide Centre, East Tower, 22 Adelaide Street West, 41st Floor, Toronto, Ontario, M5H 4E3, Canada.

HarperCollins books may be purchased for educational, business, or sales promotional use. For information, please email the Special Markets Department in the U.S. at SPsales@harpercollins.com or in Canada at HCOrder@harpercollins.com.

FIRST EDITION

Designed by Diahann Sturge

Maps by Nick Springer / Springer Cartographics LLC

Library of Congress Cataloging-in-Publication Data has been applied for.

Library and Archives Canada Cataloguing in Publication
Title: The library of legends : a novel / Janie Chang.
Names: Chang, Janie, author.
Identifiers: Canadiana (print) 20200179462 | Canadiana (ebook) 20200179470 | ISBN 9781443456050 (softcover) | ISBN 9781443456067 (ebook)
Classification: LCC PS8605.H35625 L53 2020 | DDC C813/.6—dc23

Canada Council   Conseil des arts
for the Arts   du Canada

ISBN 978-0-06-285150-5
ISBN 978-1-4434-5605-0 (Canada)

20 21 22 23 24 LSC 10 9 8 7 6 5 4 3 2 1

To the memory of my father and uncle, who packed up their books and became refugees in their own country, walking more than a thousand miles to safety with their university. The evacuation of Chinese universities during a time of war was emblematic of the Chinese regard for education. It was one of the country's most remarkable achievements of intellectual and cultural preservation. It's also a chapter of history almost unknown outside China.

Though the country is broken, hills and streams endure;
And in the city spring comes again to trees and grasses.
But flowers shed fearful tears,
And desolate birds sing the sorrows of parting.
Beacon fires have burned for three months now,
And letters from home are worth ten thousand pieces of gold.

From "Spring View" by Du Fu (AD 712–770)

THE
LIBRARY
OF
LEGENDS

THE JOURNEY WEST

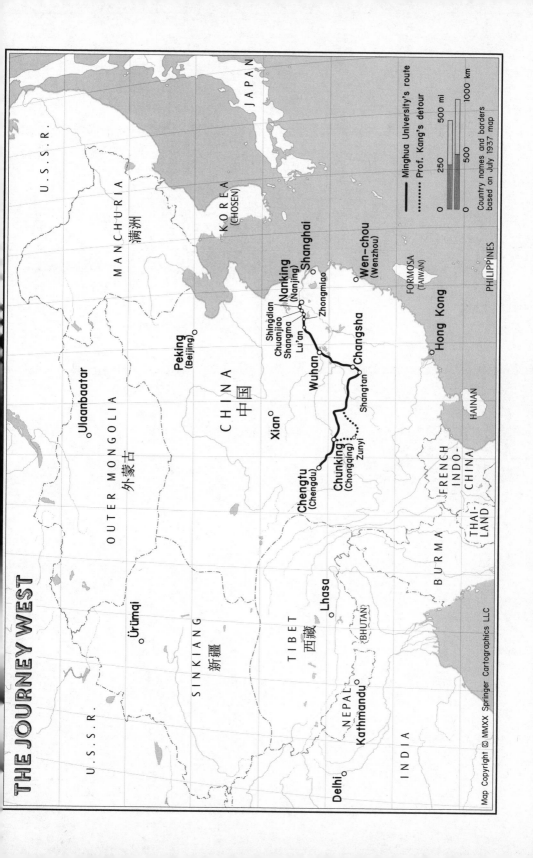

THE JOURNEY WEST

U.S.S.R.

MANCHURIA 满洲

OUTER MONGOLIA 外蒙古

Ulaanbaatar

Ürümqi

SINKIANG 新疆

TIBET 西藏

Lhasa

BHUTAN

NEPAL

Kathmandu

Delhi

INDIA

BURMA

THAI-LAND

FRENCH INDO-CHINA

HAINAN

Peking (Beijing)

Xian

CHINA 中国

Chengtu (Chengdu)

Chunking (Chongqing)

Zunyi

Shangtan

Changsha

Wuhan

Lu'an

Zhongmiao

Shindian
Chuanjiao
Shangma

Nanking (Nanjing)

Shanghai

Wen-chou (Wenzhou)

FORMOSA (TAIWAN)

Hong Kong

PHILIPPINES

KOREA (CHOSEN)

JAPAN

U.S.S.R.

—— Minghua University's route
········· Prof. Kang's detour

0   250   500 mi
0   500   1000 km

Country names and borders
based on July 1937 map

Map Copyright © MMXX Springer Cartographics LLC

CHAPTER 1

September 20, 1937—Nanking, China

The approaching aircraft were too far away for Lian to tell whether they were Chinese or Japanese. A moment later, she didn't need to guess. The spiraling wail of sirens churned the air. Then the bombs began falling, like beads slipping off a necklace.

She had been on her way to the train station. She'd gotten off the rickshaw to buy a steamed bun for breakfast. Now she stood outside the bakery as though rooted to the pavement, uncertain what to do. The nearest air-raid shelter was two blocks away, across from the railway station, its entrance already besieged. Even if she were willing to abandon her wicker suitcase, she would never reach the shelter in time.

A strong hand gripped her arm and yanked her through the bakery door.

"Get to the back room," the baker growled. But she

shook her head and dashed out, struggling back with the heavy suitcase. She had to save her books.

Inside, the baker and his wife were throwing damp cloths over trays of buns. He pointed to a storage room built against the back of the kitchen, sacks of flour stacked against one wall. The couple joined four small children squeezed together against the sacks. Lian hesitated, then slid her wicker suitcase under a worktable. But before she could run to the storage room, a shrill whistling pierced her eardrums, followed by the sound of explosions. The floor shuddered. Next she heard the sharp, rhythmic report of antiaircraft guns.

There was a roar of sound and then the world went silent.

LIAN HAD LEFT Minghua University early that morning, spending precious coins from her small cache to ride on a rickshaw that jounced its way through congested streets. Rickshaws and handcarts, handbarrows, wagons, and the occasional automobile. Nanking was evacuating. Every vehicle was piled high with trunks, sacks of food, furniture, and people. Invalids and the elderly, mothers holding children. Their expressions ranged from anxious to stoic.

Her own appearance, Lian hoped, signaled maturity and reserve, enough to dissuade the attentions of hawkers, pickpockets, and talkative fellow travelers. She'd pulled her hair into a tight knot, the severe style offsetting her least-favorite feature, a small chin that made her seem years younger than nineteen. At least her navy-blue Minghua blazer proclaimed her of university age.

The Japanese had yet to bomb the city's outlying districts. Minghua University's campus lay southwest of Nanking and was a haven compared to the frenzied scene around the railway station.

The university had begun emptying bit by bit as nervous parents instructed their children to come home.

Lian's home was Peking, where her mother lived. But Peking had been taken by the enemy earlier that month. She'd been frantic for her mother's safety until a much-delayed letter arrived. Inside, her mother had tucked in money for Lian's train fare. Peking was already lost when her mother wrote that letter. The Chinese army was in retreat and the Japanese were marching in.

> *Daughter, everyone expects the Japanese to reach Peking within days. I'm leaving tomorrow. I will meet you in Shanghai. When you get there, find the Unity Mission School and stay there. Tell them your mother is a former student. Tell them I'm on my way. They won't refuse you.*

But when her mother mailed the letter, the Japanese had not yet attacked Shanghai. Every day, newspapers printed photographs of Shanghai's streets, now cordoned off with barbed-wire barricades that separated Shanghai's International Settlement from the rest of the city. The Settlement was not Chinese territory. It had been ceded to foreign powers decades ago and the Japanese military couldn't enter. Now refugees streamed into the sanctuary of the Settlement, past gates guarded by Japanese sentries.

Lian was taking the Nanking-to-Shanghai train, which terminated at Shanghai's North Railway Station, safely located inside the Settlement. But how would her mother get to Shanghai? What if she couldn't get past the barricades? It was too late now for second-guessing or a change of plans. Her mother was on the road and Lian had no way of contacting her, let alone in a timely fashion.

These thoughts and a multitude of other worries spun hazily in Lian's head and slowly, slowly, she opened her eyes. Sunlight from a back window illuminated motes of white dust hanging in the air. No, not dust. Flour. The baker's family was sweeping the floor, coaxing snowy piles onto a large cloth, which they tilted carefully into a bin. Lian sat up and leaned her back against the wall.

One of the baker's children knelt down and spoke to her. Lian saw the girl's lips move, forming words. Words Lian couldn't hear. She shook her head in bemusement. The girl shrugged and went back to sweeping. Lian stood up slowly, still leaning against the wall. She noticed with detached wonder that she was covered in a fine film of white. She took her blazer off and shook it a few times until the fabric shed its dusting of flour.

Then she knelt beside the kitchen table and pulled her suitcase out. She staggered to the front of the shop, wondering why the suitcase felt twice as heavy as before. Outside, she put it down and peered at Shing An Road, toward the railway station. Murky smoke stung her eyes. All she could make out were large, inert shapes but her hearing was coming back and there was a muted sound of shouting voices.

Wreckage covered the road. Rickshaws in splinters, carts missing wheels, a wooden store sign lying broken on the sidewalk. A pile of fallen bricks where a wall used to be. Fragments of yellow-glazed roof tile littered the road like autumn leaves. A middle-aged woman sat up, then steadied herself against what remained of a lamppost. Her plump face streaked with grime, stout figure swaying, the woman stared up at the sky. She burst into tears and limped away, vanishing into the smoke.

Beside the lamppost, a toppled handbarrow blocked the sidewalk. It was surrounded by bundles, goods that had fallen off.

Then one of the bundles twitched and slowly crawled across the cobblestones toward a smaller bundle. And lay still again.

Lian pushed her knuckles into her mouth to block the scream rising from her throat, backing up until she bumped against the bakery wall. She had to get hold of herself. There were people in need of help. She had to do something. She picked up her suitcase and began walking uncertainly toward the station, into the smoke.

A mound of rubble heaved up and she jumped back in alarm, dropping her suitcase. Bits of brick and wood dropped away to reveal the undercarriage of an upside-down rickshaw. The two people who had been sheltering beneath it stood up. The young man who had pushed up the rickshaw carriage turned and surveyed the street. He was tall, with the lean frame of an athlete. Streaks of dirt obscured his features but his jacket was a familiar shade of blue.

The petite young woman beside him wore the tunic and baggy trousers of a servant. She gave the young man a handkerchief and he wiped his face. Then he dusted off his jacket with a jaunty air, not at all as though he'd just lived through an air raid. He smiled when he saw Lian, a grave and courteous smile that made her feel as though he was giving her his complete and undivided attention. In a far corner of her mind, she acknowledged that his smile would've been captivating if she weren't so numb, so overwhelmed by all the destruction.

He walked toward her, his first few steps a bit unsteady. He pointed at the enameled badge pinned to his jacket, then to the embroidered crest on her blazer with a grin of recognition, as if they were at a school social. The servant girl simply stood on the street, appraising the ruins around them.

"I'm Liu Shaoming, fourth year," he said. "Call me Shao."

Lian recognized him now. It would've been hard not to. Liu

Shaoming was at the center of an elite circle at Minghua, all scions of wealthy families connected either by kinship or business interests. Her female classmates considered him the handsomest man on campus.

"That's Sparrow Chen," he added, indicating the girl with a tilt of his chin. "She works on campus."

Sparrow's face was clean of dirt and soot, her features calm. Lian found the girl vaguely familiar, wide-set eyes in a face just verging on prettiness. Yes, of course. Sparrow was the one who cleaned the dormitory floors. How could she not have remembered?

"Hu Lian. Second year," she said. It was ridiculous, in this place and at such a time, that she should wonder how she looked, her cheeks streaked with tears from the stinging smoke, hair and clothing dusted with flour.

"We were on our way to the station," Shao said, "the ten o'clock train to Shanghai. You too?"

She nodded and turned away to look down the street. A light breeze was dispersing the smoke and she could see more of Shing An Road. And the railway station. It seemed undamaged, but twisted vehicles and shattered masonry filled the street in front of its arched entrance. The air-raid shelter and buildings across from the station had taken a direct hit and were now in flames. All those people, now buried under bricks and shards of glass.

"There were too many people trying to get in the air-raid shelter," Shao said, his gaze following hers. "Sparrow said we should find cover somewhere else. Good thing we did."

His next words were interrupted by an explosion from the direction of the shelter, making them both jump. There was a whoosh of sound, and flames rose from another building.

"Young Master," Sparrow spoke for the first time. "We must get out of here. Now."

"No, no, we should go help," Lian said, staring at the flames, the smoke. She picked up her suitcase again.

"That was a gas explosion and there will be more," the girl said, as patiently as if Lian were a child. "This street will burn to the ground before the fire trucks come. If they even come. We must get back to campus, let them know we're safe."

"Sparrow's right," Shao said. "Let's walk back to campus."

He reached down and took the wicker suitcase from her. "Let me take this," he said. "We left our luggage behind when we ran from the station."

When Lian didn't move, he took her hand. She followed him obediently and they made their way slowly through the ruined streets. Past crumpled vehicles flung against walls, homes collapsed into small landslides of shattered building materials. Past ragged piles of bloodied clothing, some moving feebly. Lian couldn't stop hearing the screams and desperate voices calling out for mothers, husbands, children. For help. *Jiu ming ah, jiu ming!* Save me, oh, save me!

"This is hopeless, Sparrow," Shao said after several blocks. "The streets are a mess. I can barely tell where we are."

"I know the way," Sparrow said. "Let me lead." There was a pure and shining quality to the young woman's voice, Lian thought.

"Sparrow and I grew up together," Shao said. "She was one of our house servants. She claims she got bored with Shanghai and that's why she came to Nanking. But I'm certain my mother sent her to keep an eye on me. Right, Sparrow?"

Sparrow looked over her shoulder and smiled.

Blinking tears from her stinging eyes, Lian thought for a split second that Sparrow Chen's silhouette glowed, shimmering with a clear light that gleamed through the murk. Lian wiped her eyes with a grubby sleeve and when she looked again, Sparrow's figure was quite ordinary, a petite shape clambering over the wreckage of a fallen roof.

All the way back, Shao talked. About his roommate, Pao, who had gone home the week before. About his two older brothers, one running the family's shipping business, the other working as an aide for a senior cabinet member in the government. About his home in Shanghai, a modern villa with formal European gardens in front, classical Chinese gardens at the back with two goldfish ponds and a pavilion.

Lian knew he was trying to distract her, but she barely heard his words as she stumbled along beside him, back to Minghua University. Back to the tranquil campus designed after American colleges, its green lawns edged with gravel walkways, and halls and dormitories of warm red brick. Back to a tranquility that could not possibly last.

CHAPTER 2

As Shao and Lian trailed Sparrow through the wreckage, Shao kept glancing down at Lian, trying to place her. It came to him only after Lian's hair came loose from its matronly bun and hung down to frame her face. Each year, Minghua University awarded scholarships to three students. The school newspaper always printed their photos. Lian was one of the scholarship winners from last year, her fees and expenses fully covered for four years. She was a literature major, if he remembered correctly. He recalled thinking at the time that she looked too young to be attending college.

They followed Sparrow's trim figure past neighborhoods blasted beyond recognition, through tangles of people and vehicles, along streets Shao didn't know existed, until finally the crenellations of Nanking's city walls loomed above them. They left the city through its triple-arched southern gate. After another hour of walking, Shao began spotting familiar landmarks. They were almost at Minghua University. He knew it would've taken much longer if not for Sparrow.

When they reached Minghua's gates, Shao insisted they all go to the school clinic. He only had a few cuts on his hands, which the nurse treated with iodine. There wasn't a scratch on Sparrow, who returned to the servants' quarters. The school nurse took one look at Lian's pale face and called an aide to take her into the ward. Lian would stay at the clinic for a night or more to recover from her shock.

Shao used the telephone in the nurse's office to call his father in Shanghai. His father was in a meeting, the secretary informed him, so Shao left a message to say he hadn't boarded the train. That he was safe and back at the campus. And what would his father like him to do now?

When the war began, some families had kept their children home, so they'd be together if they had to flee. Others believed their children would be safer at school in another city. Some, like Shao's father, had changed their minds partway through the semester and sent for their children to come home.

There was no single correct decision, Shao reflected. Only anxiety, leavened by hope. And now perhaps Minghua University would evacuate Nanking.

THAT NIGHT, SHAO lay awake on his narrow dorm bed, trying and failing to push away memories of the morning's horrors. He wished his roommate, Pao, hadn't gone home. But there was something else that prevented him from sleeping, something that prickled at the edge of his consciousness. Something to do with the letter from his father. It had arrived weeks ago, ordering him to come home.

But Shao had been reluctant to leave Minghua University. Professor Kang had asked him to lead a tutorial group, the first time he'd been given such a responsibility. The first-year students had been enthusiastic in their discussions and touchingly in awe of Shao, so he'd kept delaying his departure. Until the Japanese began their aerial attacks on the city.

Giving up on sleep, he lifted aside a corner of the blackout curtains. Overhead, a full moon glowed serenely behind a thin veil of clouds. Enough cloud cover, he hoped, that there wouldn't be any air raids this night. Dropping the curtain, he reached over to his desk and turned on the lamp. He found his father's letter and sat down on the bed. His father never wrote actual letters, just appended a few lines to the ones Shao's mother wrote. It was her monthly missives that kept Shao up to date with every birth, marriage, illness—and sometimes death—in their large clan. He scanned his father's words again, the handwriting elegant and spare, penned in a deep blue ink that exactly matched the border of his mother's stationery.

> *I know how much you want to stay at Minghua, but you must come home before it gets even more dangerous to travel. Your mother is worried. Leave before Minghua University evacuates Nanking. Buy a train ticket and let me know the date.*

His father had signed the note as usual with his seal, a red stamp with his name, Liu Sanmu, in traditional *li-shu*-style script. Unconsciously Shao picked up his own chop from the desk and rubbed his thumb across the cylinder of polished white jade, identical, but for the carved signatures, to the ones his father and older brothers carried.

Your mother is worried.

An oblique reference to his mother's state of mind was always a cause for concern and always effective at ensuring his obedience. She could be withdrawn one day, vivacious with wit and charm the next. Shao recognized his own impulsiveness as one of his mother's traits and always tried to keep it in check. He'd inherited little else from her. Like his brothers, his height, thick brows, and clean, square sweep of jawline were his father's.

He read his father's words for the third time and identified the sentence that bothered him.

Leave before Minghua University evacuates Nanking.

Not "in case Minghua University evacuates Nanking" but evacuation as a statement of fact. The Liu family owned *Xinwen Bao*, one of Shanghai's major newspapers. Shao's father was the paper's owner and editor in chief, privy to information from a wide network of contacts. Liu Sanmu was careful never to criticize the Nationalist government, not even in private. But in advising his son, he had let something slip.

His father didn't believe the Chinese could hold on to Nanking.

WHEN CHANCELLOR ZHAO called an assembly, Shao suspected it was to announce their evacuation. Some of the students in the large auditorium grumbled, especially the ones whose hometowns were now occupied by the Japanese. They wanted to stand their ground. Some of Shao's classmates had already dropped out and enlisted. Angry voices around Shao echoed his own hatred and feelings of helplessness.

The army would never let Nanking fall, it's our nation's capital.

I don't care what my parents say, I'm enlisting. I can join our defenses at the city walls.

Women are volunteering too. First aid, couriers, emergency services.

In Tientsin, the Japanese had bombed Nankai University, then set fire to what remained of the campus. During a press conference with foreign journalists, the Japanese press officer had insisted it had been necessary to target Nankai University because it was an anti-Japanese base. In fact, they considered all Chinese universities anti-Japanese bases.

When Chancellor Zhao took the stage, a respectful but reluctant silence replaced the clamor. The announcement was as they'd expected. The Ministry of Education had ordered universities to get out of the enemy's path. The government wanted students to continue their education in safety, far from the front lines. Schools must evacuate to cities inland where the government was setting up temporary campuses.

Minghua's interim campus, they were told, would be in the city of Chengtu, deep in central China. They would take only what they could carry on this journey of a thousand miles.

A traveling campus, Shao thought. *No, a refugee campus.*

Then Chancellor Zhao cleared his throat. "I know how badly some of you want to enlist and defend our country. But war threatens not just people and places. It destroys knowledge, culture, and history. If we want China to have a future, we must save our cultural and intellectual legacy."

"He's going to tell us to stay in school," the student beside Shao muttered.

Murmurs of protest rose from the audience then faded when Zhao held up a hand for silence. He paused to take a deep breath and Shao realized the elderly gentleman was trying to hold back tears.

"My dear young friends," the chancellor said, "I can't forbid you to enlist, but I ask you to consider that your educated minds will be the most valuable resource you can give our nation once this war is over."

Exiting the auditorium, the students were quieter and more thoughtful than they'd been fifteen minutes earlier. Shao found the chancellor's uncharacteristic display of emotion disturbing because it meant the situation was more dangerous than they'd all chosen to believe.

Outside, under the late summer sunshine, Shao suddenly felt as though he was seeing Minghua's campus for the first time, the flower beds and lush green lawns of the quadrangle, the neatly raked gravel paths shaded by sycamores. He had been awed by the stately halls of stone and brick when he'd first arrived. Now there was the distinct possibility he would never see this campus again, not the way it stood today. He winced at the memory of Shing An Road, the flames roaring above shattered buildings. He hoped their beautiful campus would escape ruin.

"Were you planning to enlist?" a voice beside him asked.

It was Wang Jenmei, a fourth-year student who made no secret of her sympathies for the Chinese Communist Party. Shao's roommate, Pao, had taken Jenmei to a movie once and found her too outspoken, her manners too casual. Too much of her conversation had been spent trying to persuade Pao on the benefits of a socialist system. Despite her bold beauty, Pao had never taken her out again.

Shao shook his head. "My father forbids it."

"The government is right about one thing," Jenmei said. "We must think of China's future after the war. We must protect our students."

"So the Communist leadership doesn't want students to enlist either?" he said, just to tease her.

"Most of China is illiterate." Jenmei waved her hand, an airy gesture. "Finding a hundred thousand raw soldiers is easy. But university students are much harder to come by. So yes, on this particular issue the Communist leadership agrees with the government."

She turned and ran lightly down the steps to the quadrangle. His eyes followed her shapely figure, her graceful movements. She joined a small group of students and immediately took over the animated conversation.

Shao couldn't help but contrast Jenmei with Lian. One so bold and confident. The other cautious as a bird. Lian had clung to his hand all the way back as they made their way through the chaotic streets. Once he'd glanced down and she had looked up at the same time. She had a kittenish face with a small chin. Her eyes were the same color as the smoky topaz his mother wore at her throat. That he should remember her eyes so clearly caught him by surprise.

Shao pushed his way past groups of clustered students. He was a tutorial leader and had to set a good example and get to the room on time, even if most of the students were still milling about outside. Across the quadrangle, he saw a slim figure carry a bucket and mop up the steps of the Faculty Building. As if she could sense him watching, Sparrow Chen turned around for a moment, then continued through the double doors, her bucket swinging.

CHAPTER 3

Lian had the dormitory room to herself now. Her roommate had gone home several weeks ago, taken away by her parents shortly after Peking and Tientsin fell. Lian cherished her solitude. Without a roommate the plain room felt like a sanctuary, a place where she could dispense with any pretense of enjoying her classmates' company, avoid the puzzling, intricate protocols required to feign friendship.

Lian dosed herself each night with syrup of poppies. The nurse had given her a small bottle to help her sleep. Even so, she woke up several times, jolted out of dreams that left cold sweat on her brows, ghostly images from the railway station curling like burnt paper at the edges of her mind. She turned over to try and sleep again but the silence disturbed her. Nanking was under blackout and nothing moved on the streets outside Minghua's walls. Not the familiar rumble of farmers pushing handbarrows on their way to market or the cries of night soil collectors. No laughter from revelers reeling their way home.

Yet there was something *about* the silence, an expectant stillness that felt like the hush of a theater audience waiting for the star performer to appear. Lian rolled over just as brightness flared at the window, outlining the blackout curtain. Its brilliance was not that of early morning. Awake enough to be curious, Lian got out of bed and raised one edge of the drapes. To the east, the barest hint of morning colored the horizon. To the west, the sky was steeped in darkness, dim hues of blue and gray flecked with stars, a low-hanging half-moon.

The light came from the courtyard below.

It was a girl. She stood with her back to Lian. Her head was turned up to gaze at the heavens and her slim silhouette gleamed with a cool, clean radiance. She lifted one hand to the sky as if in greeting. Then a scattering of clouds dimmed the constellations and light drained from the courtyard as the girl walked away, vanishing into the shadows.

Lian climbed back into bed and pulled up the blankets, wondering what she'd just seen, or if she had seen anything at all. By the time she fell back into sleep, it seemed to her that the shining figure was merely the memory of a dream, brought on by syrup of poppies.

AT HER FIRST class the next morning, Lian's instructor gave her a note. Professor Kang wanted to see her in his office. Lian hurried across the quadrangle, almost at a run, partly because she didn't want to keep the professor waiting, but mostly because she didn't know what to make of the attention from other students she encountered on her way. Students who knew her asked how she was feeling; the ones who didn't nodded friendly greetings. Her narrow escape at the railway station had given her new distinction among her peers.

She pushed open the heavy double doors of the Faculty Building and climbed the steps to the second floor. At the top of the staircase she paused, a moment of fatigue. One of the cleaning staff, a young woman, was mopping the floor. Lian recognized Sparrow Chen, and they exchanged smiles.

A half-dozen other students were also waiting in Professor Kang's office, leaning against the walls. One was Liu Shaoming. She berated herself for not responding to his friendly smile of greeting with anything more than a nod. There were two girls, Yee Meirong and Wu Ying-Ying, who were both second-year classmates. She also recognized Shorty Ho, whose round face and innocent smile belied his reputation as a troublemaker. The others Lian didn't know. When Professor Kang came in the room, they all straightened up.

Kang was revered, the dean of literature and a recognized authority on classics of the Tang Dynasty. Most professors at Minghua dressed in Western suits and ties but Kang kept to traditional garb, a long scholar's gown, high-necked, and always in a plain, dark fabric. With his wispy gray goatee and round cap, he wouldn't have looked out of place in an old woodcut. He was how Lian pictured a scholar from the imperial era of a hundred years ago.

Kang peered over the half-moons of his lenses.

"You're the last of our students whose parents wanted you home," he said, "but the situation has changed drastically over the past few days. It's no longer safe for you to travel. The university

is responsible for your care, so when Minghua University evacuates Nanking, you'll be coming with us to our wartime campus
in Chengtu."

"But what will I tell my father?" Shorty Ho asked. "He's expecting me on the weekend train to Hangchow."

"You can telephone," Professor Kang said, "or we can send a
telegram if your family doesn't have a telephone. Also, if you have
any money in bank accounts here, take it out. You'll need it in the
weeks to come."

"What will we need to buy, Professor?" Meirong said.

"Stationery and supplies," he said. "Small personal items such
as soap and toothpaste. The government will cover our food and
lodgings, but we shouldn't count on all the arrangements falling
into place right away. It's best if you also have your own funds."

When the other students left Kang's office, Lian stayed behind.
The professor gestured for her to sit on the chair by his desk.

"Sir, I can't go with you," she said. She leaned forward, hands
clutched in her lap. "My mother's on her way to Shanghai and
I'm supposed to meet her there. I have no way of contacting her. I
must get to Shanghai."

"You can't go on your own, not anymore," he said gently. "Do
you know when your mother will get there? Where she will be
living?"

Lian shook her head. "She was about to flee Peking when she
wrote to me. But she told me to go to a foreign mission, the Unity
Mission School, and wait for her there."

"When your mother wrote that letter, she didn't know the
Japanese would attack Shanghai," the professor said. "Nor that
refugees would be pouring into the International Settlement. The
refugee centers are overflowing. If the Mission can't take you in

and you can't afford to pay for a room, you'll be living on the streets. Our university is responsible for your safety. I can't let you go, my dear."

His words, so kindly meant, struck her like a blow across the face. The professor had voiced what Lian didn't want to acknowledge. That her mother was traveling alone at the mercy of a transport system in chaos. That her mother had to cross stretches of occupied territory before reaching Shanghai. That unlike her classmates from Shanghai, Lian and her mother lacked a fixed address there. Could Lian count on the Unity Mission to take her in? And for how long? She had no relatives or friends in the city, so even if she made it to Shanghai on her own, her small cache of funds would soon be spent.

Lian's chest felt hollowed out. "But what happens when my mother gets to Shanghai and I'm not there?"

"Write to your mother care of the Mission," Kang said. "Tell her you've evacuated with us to Chengtu. When your mother writes back, we'll assess the situation. If there's a way to get you safely to Shanghai from wherever we are, I promise we will."

"But how will she even know where to send a letter?" Lian said. She wouldn't cry in front of the professor. She was no longer a child.

"We'll be making stops along the way," he said. "There will be towns the Ministry of Education assigns for longer-term stays. They'll publish lists of those places as well as all the universities' final destinations so that families can know where to send letters and money."

Lian could only hope her mother knew to look for the lists. She never should've left her mother's side. She should've gone to university in Peking instead. Guilt and fear hardened into a lump just below her rib cage.

"Now there's something we need to do, and I'd like your help," the professor said, his voice brisk. "With the Library of Legends."

The Library of Legends. Her reason for coming to Minghua. Lian leaned forward in her chair, intrigued despite her distress. "Help with the Legends?"

"We're bringing the books with us," he said, "and I need volunteers to wrap them up for transport. Can I count on you?"

"Of course, Professor," she said. "How will the Legends be transported?"

"By wagon, donkey cart, handbarrow," he said. "On our backs if necessary. We're not leaving such a treasure behind."

CHAPTER 4

The army officer organizing their evacuation had advised the university to leave the campus after dark, when there was less risk of aerial attacks. The entire school couldn't all leave at the same time, so they divided into groups with students, professors, staff, and laborers in each. Army vehicles looped between Minghua's campus and the ferry terminal on the Yangtze River. From there, barges carried staff and students to docks on the other side of the river. Waiting riverboats and barges took them farther south and west, where they would continue the next leg of their journey.

The next evening, another group. Five nights, five groups.

If all went well, the professor hoped all groups would meet up within the week and from there, the entire campus could continue their journey together. Due to the war, only a third of Minghua's students remained. This made evacuation simpler, but it was still a daunting challenge to move some five hundred people.

Kang was leaving Minghua University with the fifth and final group. As the most senior member of faculty traveling with the group, the professor was in charge. He was also responsible for the university's most important possession. While every group included wagons with crates of library books, the fifth group would be bringing the Library of Legends with them. To his shame, sometimes the professor caught himself worrying more about the Legends than his students.

Out on the playing field, carts and wagons waited for the army trucks. The students would get into the trucks, the wagons would fall in line, and Minghua's last convoy would leave the campus. Inside the auditorium, nervous excitement rippled through the ranks of students. The professor paused for a moment to touch the crates before stepping out to the middle of the stage. He signaled his assistant, a graduate student named Shen, who hurried over and blew three times on a whistle.

"Attention," Shen shouted. "Attention. Professor Kang has something to say."

Kang regarded his audience with gentle, myopic eyes. "We begin a very long journey tonight. We have many miles of walking ahead of us and our country is at war. I cannot predict all the hardships we will face, but I know there will be more than we can imagine."

"We don't mind, sir!" a voice called from the audience.

"I want you to know our group bears a special responsibility," the professor continued, "because we carry with us something as valuable as your lives and just as irreplaceable."

He turned to Shen, who handed him a book. It was bound the old-fashioned way, a plain blue paper cover stitched to pages of soft rice paper. When Professor Kang held it up, some of the students nodded knowingly.

"This is a volume of the *Jingtai Encyclopedia*, a masterpiece of scholarship documenting China's art, culture, and literature," Kang said. "During the Ming Dynasty nearly five hundred years ago, the Jingtai emperor commissioned this work. The encyclopedia originally consisted of 11,000 volumes. We carry with us 147 volumes, the section known as the Library of Legends. The Library of Legends records our myths and folklore. It is all that remains of the *Jingtai Encyclopedia*. We are guardians of a national treasure."

There was an audible intake of breath.

"The Legends are part of our identity," the professor continued. "Now I have a task for each of you. I ask you each to carry one book from the Library so that you're responsible not only for your own safety but the safety of our heritage. I'm also giving you all the assignment to read the stories as we travel."

There was excited conversation as the students queued up. Shen handed out the precious books, each volume wrapped in brown paper. Some students put away the books in their rucksacks, others sat down to read, turning the pages with great care.

Three whistles again and a different voice called out for attention. Minghua's director of student services climbed onto the stage. His square, ruddy face shone down at the students.

"Students of Minghua!" Mr. Lee said. "Our group includes 114 students and 9 professors, 123 in all. Plus 16 servants and laborers. On this historic journey, we're not just a school. We're also comrades in arms."

There was scattered applause and the stocky man beamed

again. "Before we leave, let's give our group a name," he said. "It adds a bit of team spirit."

Suggestions came from all sides. *Minghua Departments of Agriculture and Literature Wartime Campus* was shouted down as too unwieldy. *Minghua Refugee Convoy* sounded too dismal. All agreed that using "Minghua" without qualification implied their group represented all of Minghua. In the end, *Minghua 123* won the vote, the "123" for the number of students and faculty in the group.

The clatter of idling engines and squeal of gears told the assembly that trucks had pulled into the campus. The professor walked outside to greet the young army officer who had been organizing their evacuation. Then a last roll call, and the vehicles rumbled out the gates. Riding at the front of the jeep with the young officer, Professor Kang resolutely resisted turning around for a last look at the campus he had come to think of as home.

THE PADDED VEST Professor Kang wore over his long scholar's gown kept out the night chill but couldn't hide his thin frame. One hand tugged absentmindedly at his wispy goatee as he gazed at the skies, then over to the barges where workers were unloading wagons and carts.

It was a moonless night but the stars shone brightly enough that he could see across the river, where crowds of fleeing citizens swarmed the same ferry docks that Minghua 123 had departed an hour ago. The exodus out of Nanking thronged all the roads leading to the Yangtze River. On the muddy banks, khaki-clad soldiers pushed back the crush of people, only letting through those with tickets for the ferry. Even from this distance he could hear frantic shouting, as men and women clamored to get their families across.

The professor turned at the sound of his name. The army officer was calling for him.

"The Japanese have escalated air raids over Nanking and the surrounding countryside," the young officer said. He was clean-shaven and not much older than the senior students. "They've been bombing boats used for troop transportation."

"And you think these riverboats might look like military transports to them?" Professor Kang said.

"The waterways are risky right now, sir," the young officer said. "Moon or no moon, some Japanese planes are following rivers, using them for navigation. Last night's group narrowly missed getting strafed. You should take a different route. I advise the road through the hills, under the cover of Laoshan Forest. It's a longer trek, but right now it's the safest option."

"And when we're back on the open road?" the professor asked. "Surely we would be safe. The enemy wouldn't attack civilians, would they, Captain Yuan?"

"There's always the danger that an overexcited pilot mistakes you for a military convoy," the captain said, "or they deliberately attack even though they can see you're civilians. It's been known to happen. Travel on moonless nights whenever possible. You'll get used to walking by starlight."

"I will take your advice," Professor Kang said. "Captain Yuan, can you tell me anything at all about transportation once we're farther inland? Any trains or trucks? Otherwise it's twelve hundred miles to Chengtu. We'll be on the road for months."

"You'll have to ask along the way." Yuan shook his head. "Others will be making those arrangements and quite frankly, you can expect the situation to change constantly. Use the military maps I gave you. They're very detailed. Towns, temples, water sources such as streams and wells. The towns are marked with population counts, so hopefully you can stop in places large enough to accommodate your group."

"Very helpful," the professor said, "thank you."

"I wish I could do more," Captain Yuan replied, "but universities all over eastern China are evacuating and transportation is tight. I'll see what I can do, but I must get back to my unit in Nanking."

"You've done more than enough already for your alma mater, Yuan." Professor Kang smiled and held out his hand. "It's good to see you again after all these years."

But the officer didn't shake the professor's hand. He dropped to his knees and touched his forehead to the dock three times.

"Teacher," he said, "in case we don't meet again, thank you for the honor of having been your student. May favorable winds attend your journey."

"My dear boy," Professor Kang said, no longer smiling. There were tears in his eyes. "You're the one who will need favorable winds. You and your comrades."

As the university's laborers hitched donkeys to carts and secured baggage onto handbarrows, the professor watched another overloaded ferry cross from the city side of the river. Dockworkers barely had time to put down the gangplank before the passengers surged off. Some rushed to the riverboats, pleading to get on. Some took the open road heading west. Others headed into the forest.

A man pulled a handcart loaded with trunks, furniture, his wife, and four children. An old woman with bound feet rode in a rattan armchair tied to a pair of bamboo carrying poles shouldered by two men, her sons. A young mother trudged by, a baby slung across her back, a basket of provisions on one arm. A boy followed, a toddler clinging to his back. The professor wondered what the woman had left behind so that she could bring three children.

Finally, the convoy was ready to move. The students lined up single file, each following the person ahead. Some of the carts carried lamps. They entered the forest, taking a road that cut through the hills of Laoshan Forest. Pine trees and foliage provided cover from the enemy, but between the darkness and the travelers ahead of them, the students made slow progress.

They faced a journey of more than a thousand miles, some of it through terrain that might be safe one day and enemy occupied the next. Yet from the murmured conversations Kang overheard, the students seemed more concerned about the distance they'd have to walk than danger from the enemy. For them, it was the greatest adventure of their young lives. They were so touchingly confident, believing they would all make it safely to Chengtu under the university's protection. The professor offered a silent prayer to the gods that it would turn out so.

CHAPTER 5

They finally emerged from Laoshan Forest just as dawn broke. The convoy halted and some of the students threw themselves on the ground and pulled out their canteens. Lian counted some twenty wagons and carts. The ones pulled by donkeys carried the heaviest items. One was stacked with pots and pans, another with fragile laboratory equipment. Three of the wagons carried books and reference materials the students would need for classes while on the journey. Their luggage was lashed to handbarrows and carts. Some staff members had brought their families, and children slept squeezed between luggage and rice sacks. There were several handbarrows and carts drawn by laborers, glad for the pay and a chance to evacuate with the university.

Like all the other students, Lian carried a canvas

rucksack on her back. She pulled out her volume of the Legends and opened the brown paper to look at the book again. *Tales of Celestial Deities.* She had wrapped this one herself several days ago. She looked around at the rest of the group, suddenly overcome by the knowledge that she and the other students were more than classmates now. They were caretakers of the Library of Legends, bound by a common duty. This realization lifted some of the numbness that had gripped her emotions since the terrible morning at the railway station.

"Surely the gods will protect us for looking after the Library of Legends," a voice beside her said. "I'm going to interview Professor Kang and write an article about the history of the Legends. It deserves a piece in our school newspaper. When we manage to print *Minghua News* again, that is."

It was Yee Meirong. She dropped down cross-legged on the ground beside Lian and smiled.

"Actually, there's already something about the Library of Legends's history," Lian said, somewhat apologetically. "By Professor Kang. It's printed up in a pamphlet available from the university library."

"Obviously, I didn't go to the library often enough," Meirong said. "All right then. I'll write something when we get to Chengtu about the further adventures of the Library of Legends on its epic journey out of Nanking."

"There are copies of the pamphlet somewhere in the book carts," Lian said. "I'll find one for you, if you like."

"Thanks. You know, Lian, there are only twenty of us girls in this group. We must look after one another." Meirong beamed, a smile so wide and sincere Lian couldn't help but warm to her. Meirong gave her a nudge. Mr. Lee was making his way up the line.

"Nearly there, nearly there," Mr. Lee called. "Let's move, Minghua 123, let's move! Just two more hours to Shingdian Village and we can eat and sleep."

There were groans but no words of complaint as students got up and slung packs over their shoulders. Lian adjusted the straps on her rucksack and fell into line, Meirong beside her. A laborer pushing a handbarrow came alongside them, the barrow's single center wheel rumbling over the rough road. One side was stacked with crates marked "Lab Equipment—Agriculture Department," the other side held a middle-aged woman with her arms around two sleepy children, legs dangling over the side. A professor's family.

Behind them, someone had pulled out a harmonica. Lian recognized the tune after just a few notes. A spirited march would've been more suitable for their situation, but perhaps the musician was feeling sad. She never thought a harmonica could play the "Blue Danube Waltz" so wistfully.

And despite her best efforts to push it down, a childhood memory surfaced. From before Japan took over Manchuria and turned it into a puppet state. From a time when her family had lived there in Harbin, a city she remembered as lively, the streets noisy with voices speaking a dozen languages, the scent of baked bread and roasting chestnuts warming the icy air. From the days when she had taken happiness for granted.

LIAN WAS NOT quite eleven years old that winter night. Her parents had come back from ice skating and couldn't stop laughing. Faces glowing pink from the cold, they sang at the top of their voices and waltzed through the courtyard of their home, gliding their feet as though still twirling on the frozen lake. Lian had been entranced. She stood with her *amah*, child and nursemaid equally bemused, giggling as they watched her parents spin.

Then her father ran over and swept her into his arms. "Your mother was the most beautiful woman and the best skater," he said, kissing her. "Everyone on the ice, Chinese and foreign, they all stared to admire her."

Whenever this memory of her parents surfaced, Lian could see their elegant figures dancing across the courtyard. She could see her mother's head thrown back in laughter, but her father's face was indistinct, a blur under the fur hat. She felt, rather than saw, his smile. The only way she could anchor his features in her mind was by looking at the framed photograph beside her mother's bed. The lock of hair that fell across his forehead, the well-shaped nose and high forehead.

A month later, on her birthday, everything changed.

Their cook had made panfried dumplings for lunch, her favorite. Lian carefully cut and set aside a piece of cake for her father, who had been away all week, but would be returning later that night, after her bedtime. Her mother had been wiping cake crumbs off Lian's chin, gently scolding her for making a mess, when the discreet jangle of bells told them the gatekeeper had let in a visitor.

Holding hands, mother and daughter hurried to the room in the main hall where the gatekeeper sent guests to wait. When her mother stepped over the threshold, the man standing by the elm wood chair bowed. Lian didn't recognize him, but in his old-fashioned scholar's gown of dark-blue silk he seemed quite elderly to her. He glanced down at her, and then looked at her mother.

"Lian, go back and finish your cake," her mother said. She stood very still, not taking her eyes off the man. She didn't ask him to sit.

Obediently, Lian left the room. But once around the corner, she crept to the window and peered in. She could see their faces in profile, her mother's and the man's, both still standing. The man's words were indistinct, his voice quiet but urgent. What he was saying made her mother stiffen, clasp her hand tightly on the chair back, holding on as if for support. The man strode across the room and took her mother's hand in his. He patted it awkwardly, hesitantly. Only after he left did her mother sink down to the chair, head in her hands, shoulders shaking.

Then her mother stood up and wiped the tears from her eyes. Lian abandoned the window and ran as fast as she could to the dining room. She had just finished the last mouthful of cake when her mother came in and sat beside her, apparently quite calm. Then she told Lian that her father had died.

The next day four strangers crowded into the same room. The men rested uneasily on the elm wood chairs, their backs straight and rigid as tombstones. They spoke, softly at first, then sternly. Her mother shook her head repeatedly, her gaze never flinching, her chin lifted slightly. Defiant.

A few days later, less than a handful of people stood with Lian and her mother at her father's funeral. It was early in the morning, the ground still hard, grass and leaves still crusted with frost. After brief murmured condolences, everyone hurried away, leaving Lian and her mother to watch the gravediggers pile soil over her father's cremated remains.

A young man climbed the path toward them, carrying a small wreath of white chrysanthemums. He wore Western garb, a heavy wool greatcoat unbuttoned over a dark suit. His hair, when he took his hat off, was cut very short, military style. Her mother lifted her chin and stared directly at the stranger.

"Your mistake, my husband's life," her mother said. Then she spat on the ground and took Lian's hand. They walked away from the grave, the stranger still standing there with his wreath.

That night, Lian woke to the sound of sobs and screams. Her *amah* tried to get her back to bed. "Don't go, Little Miss," she begged. "Leave her be."

But Lian struggled out of the nursemaid's grip. She ran along the hallway then paused, suddenly feeling like an intruder as she stood in front of her parents' bedroom door. It was shut, but light shone through the space between door and floor. The cries stopped, replaced by gasping sounds. It couldn't be her mother making those dreadful, strange noises. She had to see for herself. She slid quietly on bare feet along the hallway to the adjoining bathroom. The bathroom was dark, but the inside door connecting to her parents' room stood ajar.

Lian knelt cautiously beside the thin wedge of light and peered in. Her mother crouched on the floor, face veiled by her unbound hair. She rocked back and forth, something dark and bulky clutched to her chest, eyes fixed on the wall between two windows. The wall where her parents' wedding photograph hung in a black-lacquered frame. Then her mother began sobbing again. The gasping noises, Lian realized, had been her mother catching her breath. Her mother's sobs turned into cries. The howls of a wounded animal, of a woman on the edge of madness. No longer defiant.

Unable to move, Lian crouched mesmerized. Helpless to comfort her mother. Ashamed to be spying. Finally, her mother collapsed and the bulky object she had been cradling dropped to the floor with a thud. It was one of her father's old boots, scuffed brown leather.

Lian ran outside, her small feet scarcely feeling the cold. It had been raining all evening, but now light from a full moon gleamed on the courtyard's slate paving stones. Raindrops glittered from shrubs and trees, and she saw each one with perfect clarity, saw how precariously they clung to bare branches. When her *amah* caught up to her and wrapped her in a quilt, Lian didn't protest at being carried back to bed.

This was why Lian didn't object when her mother took them away from Harbin a week later, leaving behind the courtyard home, her school friends, and her *amah*. Why she obeyed without a word as they moved from one shabby Peking neighborhood to another. Why she never complained when her mother insisted on an idiosyncratic and secretive life.

"We must be invisible as foxes in hiding, Daughter," she said. "It's the only way for us to stay safe."

Lian didn't argue because she was willing to do anything, absolutely anything, never to see her mother like that again.

CHAPTER 6

Mr. Lee billeted them in an ancestral hall belonging to the largest clan in the village of Shingdian. Minghua 123 squeezed into all four of the buildings around the single small courtyard as well as the dining hall and servants' quarters. Lian was so tired she could hardly wait to fall onto the bedroll she'd spread out on the floor. She'd already forgotten what the cook had fed them. Steamed buns stuffed with something. Meirong was sound asleep, curled into a tight ball, blankets pulled over her head to block the sunlight streaming in through carved window shutters.

They would travel like this day after day, Lian realized as she drifted into exhausted sleep. Walking by moonlight and starlight, sleeping in temples and ancestral halls because in some towns those were the only buildings large enough to house them all.

Minghua 123 set out again after sundown for their second night on the road. Meirong walked beside Lian. Since sleeping beside each other on the floor of the ancestral hall, she referred to Lian as her roommate.

"There was so much knowledge collected in the *Jingtai Encyclopedia*," Meirong said, "all those volumes of poetry, epic histories, and scholarly essays. Why do you suppose the gods chose to save the volumes of legends and folklore instead of any other?"

"I thought it was the scholar-bureaucrat Yao and his descendants who saved the Library of Legends," Lian said. She was starting to feel comfortable with Meirong, with the way her classmate changed topics suddenly, her mind busy as a dragonfly darting from one thought to another.

"What I think is this," Meirong said, continuing as if she hadn't heard. "Maybe it's because legends are truer to our natures than serious literature. Maybe myths and legends reveal more about us than poetry or epic histories."

"Very perceptive, Miss Yee," Professor Kang said, as he walked up from behind. "Myths are the darkest and brightest incarnations of who we are. They slip into our dreams and underpin our reality. Perhaps that's why the gods judged the Library of Legends worthy of special protection."

Although the professor's age and status entitled him to ride on a cart, he always walked a few miles each day, using the time to chat with students up and down the line.

"Or it could be even simpler," he continued. "Maybe the gods are vain and want their stories remembered."

He strode ahead, chuckling to himself.

PROFESSOR KANG MADE his way up the line, past donkey carts carrying books, supplies, and laboratory equipment, past students walking together in twos and threes. Sometimes he spoke to other travelers on the same road. Some refugees walked bent beneath the loads they carried, some were stunned with grief and loss. Some were as loud in anger against their own government as they were about the enemy.

"I've seen this a hundred times before," a young female voice said. The professor turned to the glowing presence beside him. A glow he knew no one else could see.

"What have you seen before?" he asked.

"Forced migration," she said.

"In a country the size of China," the professor said, "there's always a catastrophe going on somewhere. And in its wake, a populace fleeing danger, hoping to reach safety."

Disasters were inevitable and China's history was rife with plagues and famine, floods and earthquakes. And there had been so many wars. Wars between petty kings and rival generals, bandit armies and invading hordes. More recently, revolution. People fled their homes only as a desperate act of last resort.

"This war is different, something else altogether," she said. "The sheer scale of destruction. This will change China because it will change its people. So many lives shattered."

There was a long silence as they continued walking.

"You mean the refugees," the professor said. "They'll lose their homes and family history when they leave the land where they were born and raised, where their ancestors lie buried."

"Right now, they mourn the homes and possessions they had to leave behind," she said. "But soon, even though they can't put it into words, they'll understand they've also left behind the places that defined them. Where they were known because of their families and professions. Where they had a place in the world."

"But once the war is over, they can return," Professor Kang said. "It's temporary."

"But that's just it," she said. "Many won't ever return. Others will go back to try and rebuild but their livelihoods will be gone. Shops and factories, livestock and farm equipment. How much of their past will they jettison to move ahead with their lives?"

"After the war, China will rebuild," he said. "The government will take care of its citizens. Look at what they're doing for our students."

"Your students are fortunate in that respect," she said. "As part of the university, their place in the world is still defined. They'll still have a purpose once they reach Chengtu."

"I just hope we can bring them safely to Chengtu," the professor said, unable to suppress a deep sigh.

"Then about this next town, Chuanjiao," she said, her voice serious. "We should only rest there one day. I know everyone is tired, but we need to get inland as quickly as possible."

"I'll make sure of it," the professor said. "Thank you for the warning. It's good to have heaven on our side."

"I'm not heaven," she said. "I'm only a Star. I can only help a little, just enough to keep our group safe."

The professor smiled. "It's good to have a Star on our side, Sparrow Chen."

It was on their way to Chuanjiao that Minghua 123 encountered death for the first time.

They were only four hours out of Shingdian and it was still dark when they saw the military trucks stopped on a cratered stretch of road that had been bombed during the day. Medics were tending to wounded civilians. Lamplight threw long shadows behind soldiers and civilians. Men and women crouched at the side of the road, keening over unresponsive shapes. A crew of exhausted-looking workers helped soldiers pile long bundles onto a flatbed truck. With a pang, the professor realized the bundles were corpses.

At first, Minghua 123 tried helping the injured but the army doctor ordered them to keep moving as quickly as they could. They had to get beyond the reach of Japanese aircraft. To linger meant more risk.

"The students' safety is your priority," the doctor said to Professor Kang. "I shouldn't even have stopped to treat these people. We're already short on medical supplies. The more we do here, the less we have for our soldiers."

"How far inland should we go before it's safe?" Kang asked. "How far can Japanese planes fly?"

"The range of those planes isn't the issue," the army doctor said. "It's the front lines you need to worry about. They shift all the time and if they shift farther west, the enemy will be able to fly deeper into the province. Consider yourselves always at risk. Until you get to Chengtu, anyway."

"How can we find out where the battle lines have moved?" Professor Kang said.

The doctor snorted. "If you find out, you're better off than we are. Communications are terrible, always late, and not even accurate. Just keep going west and south as fast as you can."

There was very little chatter among the students after the sobering sight of the injured and dead. The first they'd seen. Their journey was no longer an adventure. A few of the male students trudged with rifles over their shoulders, old equipment the army had given them, along with some rudimentary training, in case they ran into bandits. But the guns were all for show, just a deterrent. They had fewer than two dozen bullets between them.

"WE CAN'T BE that far from Chuanjiao," Meirong said. "The sun's already coming up. We should've arrived an hour ago."

"It's because we stopped to try and help those wounded refugees," Lian said. "And the wagons had to go very slowly through the fields since the road was bombed out."

Minghua 123 had also stopped at a village to refill canteens, a short break that had turned into a long rest. Daylight showed them a flat road and fields of newly harvested wheat, the short bristly stalks of pale gold standing straight up from the brown earth. The travelers walked over a small bridge, its stone balustrades carved in cloud and dragon patterns, a relic of a time when the village had been more prosperous. The stream below the bridge was just a thin trickle.

The long hours of walking had sapped their strength. Most of the students complained about blisters. What bothered Lian most was the ache of her hip bones in their sockets. Meirong plodded beside her, humming a tune Lian didn't recognize. Meirong's snub nose and habit of tying her hair in pigtails made her look much younger than her classmates. She was outgoing to the point of being occasionally annoying, in contrast to Lian, whose reputation was one of shyness, reserved to the point of being unapproachable. Or so Meirong informed her.

It wasn't shyness that made Lian keep her distance, though. Her life had been one of wary evasion. She'd followed her mother's lead, avoiding entanglements with people who might ask too many questions. Silence, discretion. A pretense of shyness, timidity. Her mother had schooled her in caution. She was more skilled at deflecting than befriending.

But that was before the easy camaraderie of Minghua 123, where keeping to oneself was impossible. With only twenty female students in the group, Lian was drawn into their circle. Her fellow students offered drinks from their canteens if they saw she'd taken her last sip and smilingly made room on a cart if there was an opportunity to ride, all without any hint of condescension or expectation of a favor to return.

Then there was Meirong's frequent and unaffected laughter, her sly humor. "I hope good grades are contagious," she'd remarked, "because if I walk beside a scholarship award winner for a thousand miles, surely mine will improve."

The cart in front of them stopped, jolting Lian out of her thoughts. Beside her, Meirong tripped and swore under her breath. From behind came panicked cries, the braying of donkeys being led off the road, the rumble of wagons rolling into the fields. Above it all, they heard an airplane approaching from the east, its engines droning; then it appeared out of the glare of the rising sun.

"Run!" Meirong gasped. She slid down the embankment and sprinted away into the rows of wheat. There was no shelter to be had between the rows of short stalks, but at least if everyone scattered, they wouldn't give the enemy a single easy target.

Lian raced after her, rucksack bouncing on her back, frozen feet slipping down the embankment. She fell facedown, hardpacked earth slamming the breath out of her.

"Here, let me help you up," a man's voice said. Still gasping for air, Lian looked up at Liu Shaoming's smile. Behind him, Sparrow Chen scanned the sky, one hand shading her eyes as she squinted at the horizon.

Shao pulled Lian to her feet and practically lifted her into the field. He set her down beside an irrigation ditch. Dry stems of wheat prickled her backside and stabbed at her hands.

"We'll be safe here," Sparrow said. She had a quiet voice, but Lian heard it very clearly despite the approaching rumble. It was sweetly pitched and cut through the throb of engines. It was the voice of someone Lian felt she could trust.

"Into the ditch, please," Shao said, as calmly as if they were entering a classroom.

Obediently she rolled into the trench. Farther along, Meirong was already crouched in the ditch beside some other students. They all sat with knees tucked, faces turned to the sky. Shao flashed Lian his bright smile again. She stifled a gulp and told herself her heart was racing because of the advancing Japanese airplane. Even though his uniform was covered in dust, it was evident that Shao's jacket was beautifully tailored. Cuffs of fine, cream-colored wool cloth peeped out from the jacket's sleeves. He radiated wealth and confidence. As if he were only sitting in the trench to keep her company. As if tragedy had never touched him and never would.

Everyone had fallen silent, as if they could hide behind silence. The reverberating drone had turned into a roar. Lian squeezed her eyes shut at the sharp, rapid reports that could've been strings of firecrackers going off. But these were not the cheerful percussive snaps heard throughout the streets during New Year festivities. These were menacing and purposeful.

Then it stopped. The sound of engines faded slowly, too slowly. And then the skies were quiet. Lian opened her eyes as voices called out, the shouts of families trying to find each other.

"Thank you for getting me off the road," she said, turning to Shao and Sparrow.

But Shao was already out of the ditch, jogging across the field toward the road. Sparrow had also climbed up and put a hand down to help Lian. She was slightly shorter, slightly thinner than Lian. In that moment, Sparrow looked almost pretty, her eyes bright, cheeks flushed pink from excitement. Lian wondered if anyone ever looked past the servant to see the girl.

Did Shao ever look?

Sparrow scrambled up the embankment and onto the road. Meirong was already there, waving at Lian to join her. Sparrow bent down to help an old woman collect food that had fallen out of a basket. She picked up some cabbages and turned to put them in the old woman's basket. Clouds drifted across the horizon, momentarily dimming the early morning light.

And for a moment, instead of Sparrow's waifish features, Lian saw an exquisitely beautiful young woman. A woman whose figure gleamed with a faint and barely perceptible glow. Something prickled at the back of Lian's memory, something from a dream. Then the layer of cloud shifted, and sunrise once again flooded the landscape. Lian blinked and all she saw was Sparrow, continuing up the road to join the rest of Minghua 123.

A perfectly ordinary servant girl. Who was running as if something terrible had happened.

EVERYONE FROM MINGHUA 123 seemed all right. The university's wagons and carts were back on the road and donkeys were being harnessed to their traces. A few of the handbarrows had tipped over but were being pushed upright. Lian and Meirong heard snatches of relieved conversation and couldn't see any casualties. They slowed to a walk.

Then, as they got closer to the last cart at the end of the Minghua caravan, Meirong tightened her grip on Lian's hand. The road beyond the last cart was pockmarked with bullet holes. The small stone bridge had been strafed. Students stood in a circle, some staring down, others looking away. Gaps between their legs revealed a figure lying still on the ground. A dark-blue uniform tunic and trousers, black shoes. A smear of blood. Before Lian and Meirong could get much closer, someone stepped in front of them.

"You don't need to see this," Shao said, gripping Lian's shoulder. Shorty Ho stood beside him, helping block their view.

"Who is it?" Meirong whispered. "Is he . . . ?"

"Mr. Shen is dead. The only one of us harmed," Shorty said.

Lian had known the teaching assistant only slightly, a polite nodding acquaintance when they passed each other in the halls. She hardly felt Meirong's hands clutched tightly around her arm, barely heard her friend speaking to Shao and Shorty. The victims they had seen on the road a few hours ago had been nameless and faceless. But now the dead had a name. Mr. Shen had been one of their own.

"Mr. Shen is the first of us killed by the Japanese." Shao's voice was rough with barely controlled hatred. Lian flinched even though she knew the hostility wasn't directed at her.

"The Japanese plane strafed the bridge and kept going," Shorty said. "Luckily for us it was targeting the bridge and turned back before reaching the end of our convoy. But Mr. Shen had fallen behind."

The circle of students parted as Professor Kang arrived, bringing with him two of the university's laborers. The two men wrapped Shen's body in a tarp, then lifted the bundle onto a handcart. One of them took the cart's handles and with a nod to the professor, pulled it up the road.

The professor said something to Sparrow, who had been standing to one side, not joining in, not moving. She nodded and walked away. Sparrow looked shaken, but then, so were they all.

"What will happen to the . . . to Mr. Shen?" Shao asked the professor.

"We'll be at Chuanjiao Monastery very soon," Professor Kang said. "I'll ask the monks to look after the burial."

"We're moving again," Shorty said. "The carts and wagons are rolling. Shao, let's go."

Sparrow returned carrying a small chalkboard with ropes looped through holes at the corners. Professor Kang knelt on the ground to write, his strokes quick and precise.

"Second-year literature students, please gather around," Professor Kang said. His voice was soft, but they all hastened to obey. Kang cleared his throat, then recited what he had written.

Though rainfall bends the river-grass, a bird is singing,
While ghosts of the Six Dynasties pass like a dream
Around the Forbidden City, under weeping willows
Which loom for three miles along the misty moat.

"'A Nanking Landscape' by the Tang Dynasty poet Wei Zhuang," he said. "Learn it by heart and consider its meaning. When you write your essays, remember the politics of his time."

He put his arms through the ropes and shouldered the chalkboard. They continued their journey, the elderly professor walking in front of his students, the day's lesson hanging down his back.

CHAPTER 7

Dispersed through the halls of Chuanjiao Monastery, Minghua 123 settled down to sleep. Professor Kang knew the students were distraught over the group's first casualty, but at the moment he had another duty. He kept vigil on a bench outside the room where monks were wrapping Shen's body. They would stay for a night at the monastery and hold a funeral for the graduate student.

He tried to read the book on his lap, *Tales of the City Gods*. While the Legends contained many tales of obscure deities, some long forgotten and no longer worshipped, City Gods did not fall into this sad category. Each city had its own much-venerated City God, the god who protected the city's boundaries and all who lived within. City God temples were always busy, drifts of incense smoke rising to the murmur of prayers for the city's prosperity, for the health and safety of its citizens. He turned the pages and found the story he was looking for, "The Nanking City God's Wife."

> A doctor had an only child, a beautiful daughter. One night she dreamed she had been given in marriage to Nanking's City God. In the morning the young woman told her family about the dream and they were frightened for her. When she died in her sleep that night, they knew the City God had claimed her as his wife. The good people of Nanking honored her with an altar in the rear hall of the City God's temple.

He closed the book when the Star sat on the bench beside him. "We'll leave right after the funeral service," Professor Kang said. "Right now, the least I can do is show respect while the monks make preparations."

"Why did Mr. Shen have to stop there?" she said. Her beautiful eyes were haunted and miserable. "If only he'd kept up with our group, he would've been safe. Even just another twenty feet closer and he would've been safe."

"You can't blame yourself," the professor said. "Heaven charged you with protecting the Library of Legends. We merely follow in the shelter of its slipstream. Shen's bad luck is not your fault."

"Tell the students to stay close to the carts," she said. "Tell them again and again. They must not fall behind."

"It wasn't your fault," he repeated. He wanted to hold her hand, give her a pat on the back, some reassuring gesture. But she was immortal, she was a Star. It would be presumptuous to touch her. It was enough for him, it had always been enough for him, that she was in this world. Sitting beside him on the same bench.

THE FIRST TIME the professor had seen Sparrow, she had been on her hands and knees polishing the floor just outside his office. He had opened his door to see a young woman bent over, rubbing the wooden planks with half a coconut husk. It was still daytime, but inside the long hallway with its narrow windows and dark paneling, it was dim enough for him to see her glow.

Professor Kang blinked. He saw Sparrow Chen, the servant girl. He also saw a shining form that conjured memories of perfect, long-forgotten days. His senses swam with visions of trees reflected in clear lakes, the fragrance of magnolia, the quick soft beat of golden feathers flashing between green banana palms. Then she had looked up, her features exquisitely and impossibly beautiful. Unquestionably not of this world.

How does one start a conversation with the supernatural?

"A Star," she said, in response to his questioning gaze. "From the constellation of the Purple Forbidden Enclosure."

Professor Kang's words came out in an awkward rush. When he was a boy in Soochow, he told her, his family had lived next door to a Fox spirit. He had been friends with the Fox until he left for university in Nanking. On another occasion in Soochow, he had been strolling beside a canal early one morning and glanced up to see the figure of the Goddess of Mercy painted on a cloud. As the cloud moved across the sky, she turned her head slowly from side to side, looking down on the city as though she was inspecting it. He had watched until high winds scattered the cloud and the Goddess of Mercy dissolved into the sky.

"Fewer and fewer mortals can see us now," the Star had said, her smile wistful. "Whether it's to do with an open heart or random chance, who can say. But then, who's to know why heaven allows any mortals to see us at all. I'm glad you're one of them, Professor."

Kang never pressed her for explanations, never asked what she was doing in the form of a young woman. Nor did he ask her what it was like, her home in the heavens. He didn't feel entitled to know. Just thinking of the Star, the fact of her presence, filled him with a quiet, incandescent joy. He was a small boy again, in the presence of wonder. He was grateful for whatever the Star chose to reveal but he never presumed to ask.

Over time she shared tidbits of her story. After a while, he patched together the fragments. He consulted the Library of Legends. When he could contain his curiosity no longer, he had to ask.

"Your story," he said, "it very much resembles the love story of the Willow Star and the Prince."

The Star seemed relieved. Glad, even. She said she didn't mind having someone in this life who knew her true identity. Especially since Shao wasn't allowed to know.

"It's one of the conditions set by the Queen Mother of Heaven," she said. "It's all a game to the gods. Someday Shao may remember who I am, what we meant to each other. Then I'll be allowed to take him home with me, back to the heavens."

Professor Kang shook his head. "But to do this through eternity, waiting through so many reincarnations, not knowing if you'll ever manage to make him remember."

"It's been interesting," she said. "I've lived among mortals for hundreds of years but still find your obstinacy hard to fathom. I used to think you were stubborn because of your tendency to hope."

At first, she had found humans' hopefulness endearing. Valiant even. Now she couldn't begin to count all the ways they managed to delude themselves.

"When the dragon winds of disaster rush at you," she said, "you always believe yours will be the one house left untouched by the storm. You invest in one dubious scheme after another, never learning from past mistakes. You trust that a husband might stop drinking or a lazy son finally discover ambition."

"So have you given up on us," he'd said, "we mortals and our many failures?"

"Worse than that, Professor." A wry smile. "I've learned to hope."

THE MONKS FILED out of the room, leaving the shrouded body on the table. They bowed to the professor as they passed.

The Star stood up. "Come with me," she said. "I have another duty. There's someone I must find."

The professor followed her through the monastery's many courtyards. Plaintive voices and sounds of muffled weeping seeped out from doorways and windows. In addition to the students, Chuanjiao Monastery sheltered other refugees, a constant stream over the past few months, the abbot had told him. The Star continued to the far end of the monastery and entered a small courtyard squeezed between two empty, dilapidated halls. The professor paused beside the first hall and peered inside the door. Stacks of broken furniture and empty crates lined the walls. A family lay fast asleep huddled in one corner, arms and legs thrown possessively over their belongings.

The door to the second hall was wide open. A man wandered in and out, muttering as he walked. His tunic of dove-gray cotton was streaked with ash, his trousers dirty at the knees. Despite his obvious confusion, there was dignity in his bearing. It was hard to tell his age; his face could've belonged to an exhausted thirty-year-old or a man of fifty.

"I'm sorry, so sorry," he murmured over and over to no one in particular. "I could do nothing. So sorry." The man made a circuit of the courtyard, then went inside the hall and came out to begin all over again.

The Star gestured Professor Kang to stay back.

She stepped in front of the man. He stared back at her with dull, unfocused eyes. The Star put her hands on his shoulders and slowly, his eyes cleared. He stood taller and his plain tunic shed its dirt and took on the unmistakable sheen of heavy silk, lengthened to a long robe with wide sleeves, elaborate bands of embroidery at the hems. Robes of state from another century. He was larger than any normal man, his bearing regal, features transformed by a long, magnificent beard.

"You're a Star," the deity said. "Which one?"

"The Willow Star," she replied. "And you're the Nanking City God."

"I couldn't do anything," the City God said, his handsome face miserable. "How can I protect the boundaries against machines that fly over walls? I had to leave, I couldn't bear watching the destruction anymore."

"You're not to blame," the Star said. "Airplanes didn't exist when the gods made you guardian of Nanking. Where are you going now?"

"I don't know." His voice faltered. "I've just been following some families from Nanking. Looking after them. They're going west. That's all they know. West."

"West is good," the Star said gently. "Northwest, actually. The

Kunlun Mountains. The Queen Mother of Heaven has opened the Palace gates."

The City God's eyes widened.

"It's time for you to leave," the Star said. "The Palace gates won't stay open forever. Can you find your way there?"

The Nanking City God nodded. Then he bowed to the Star, one celestial being to another. As he straightened up, his silk gown shimmered into transparency. He made his way out of the courtyard, the tall figure growing mistier until it vanished altogether.

"There will be other departures," the Star said, still looking at the spot where the Nanking City God had been. "Animal and guardian spirits. Minor deities. Creatures of protection. It's long overdue."

"If so many are coming out into the open I wonder that more people aren't seeing them," the professor said. "Well, even if others can see spirits, how would I know anyway?"

"There is one other person at Minghua who can see spirits," the Star said. "Hu Lian. But she's not quite ready."

"Ah," the professor said. "I did wonder."

"She loves reading the Legends but to her they're just part of China's mythology," the Star said. "Her mind finds ways to deny what her heart perceives. But perhaps, one day." She shrugged, a graceful lift of the shoulders.

Professor Kang nodded. One had to be open to gifts from the gods, otherwise a Fox spirit was just an animal, the Goddess of Mercy only a cloud. And a Star merely a servant girl. Beyond plain dumb luck, the professor couldn't say why he'd been given the gift to see supernatural beings. Yet he sagged under the recognition of what he'd just seen and heard.

China and Japan had been fighting for decades, battles both

nations politely described as "incidents." Now they were openly at war. Professor Kang realized he'd been hoping the gods might intervene. Perhaps not to end the war, but a small miracle of some sort to reduce the suffering.

But now he knew that prayer and pleas would not move the gods. Now he knew there was another evacuation underway.

CHAPTER 8

Minghua 123 left the monastery an hour after dark. Shao looked up at the night sky, grateful that only a tiny sliver of crescent moon added its light to that of the stars. The students wore white handkerchiefs knotted around their arms, the only tokens of mourning they could muster for Mr. Shen.

In retrospect, it was a miracle that Mr. Shen had been the only victim. There had been a short debate about changing the name Minghua 123 since they were no longer 123 people.

"If we change to 'Minghua 122,' then we exclude Mr. Shen," Shao argued. "Keeping our name the same pays tribute to his memory, that he is still part of our group."

"And do we want to change our group name every time some-one dies?" Shorty said. "It would be so demoralizing."

His words were shouted down and Ying-Ying slapped his shoulder. "How can you even talk about such things?" she said indignantly. "Implying that others in our group might die?"

"Don't yell at me," Shorty said. "I'm just saying what every-one's thinking." He rubbed his shoulder.

During their time at Chuanjiao Monastery, Mr. Lee had asked for volunteers. He appointed a dozen of the seniors, including Shao, as scouts. The scouts drilled Minghua 123 on the actions they would follow when under aerial attack. The feeling was unanimous that they should light as few lanterns as possible. They had to learn how to walk safely in the dark. They coordinated get-ting carts and barrows off the road, donkeys and all, giving prior-ity to the precious library carts. They practiced throwing tarps over the wagons to camouflage them. They knew to run for cover, scattering as widely as possible, heading for trees and ditches, out-croppings of rock, whatever might offer protection.

Whether this was of real use or not, Shao couldn't tell. Was there really anything they could do to be safe? But it was all they could do. It was all they had.

The property where they would stay was only a few hours' walk from the monastery. When they reached it, the walls of the vacant estate were surrounded by stands of bamboo, barely visible from the road. Minghua 123 would've missed it completely if not for their guide, a young monk who had accompanied them from Chuanjiao Monastery.

The students settled in quickly, the routine now familiar. There was a head count upon arrival. Then the search for sleeping quar-ters, the female students given first pick of rooms. Each group of roommates carried out another head count of the students in their room. Afterward, they ate. The cook, his assistant, and the kitchen cart had left a few hours in advance so that meals would be underway by the time the rest of Minghua 123 arrived.

Then at last, they slept.

MORNINGS WERE COLDER now and, like everyone else, Shao had slept in his clothes and spread his coat on top of the blanket. His eyes opened to coffered wooden ceilings painted in green and gold with figures of lucky animals. He counted off each one. Bats for good luck. Cranes for long life. Phoenixes for success. Horses for swift advancement. Bears for courage. And *qilin* unicorns for the birth of talented sons. He smiled, remembering his nanny, Amah Fu, and her stories. How she believed absolutely in the existence of supernatural creatures.

It will be an easy walk this evening, he thought. Their next destination was only a short distance away. Mr. Lee had told them Minghua 123 would rest at Shangma Temple for ten days, giving the professors time to teach a few classes before getting back on the road. Shao suspected the lessons were to keep their minds off Mr. Shen's death as much as anything else.

The fragrance of steamed rice drifted into the room, the kitchen staff already busy with breakfast. Most of his classmates were still sleeping but a few had tied up their bedrolls and were gone. Shao decided to take a walk around the property. He pulled his coat on and noticed a button had come loose. He pulled the button off and put it in his pocket. He'd have Sparrow sew it back on for him.

The estate felt curiously and pleasantly familiar. His father had taken him once to the outskirts of Shanghai where the Liu family's real estate firm owned an entire street lined with old-fashioned courtyard homes much like this one. The courtyard homes were soon to be demolished, making way for more fashionable foreign-style villas. Shao had tagged along behind his father and the architect as they inspected each of the properties. It was one of the few times he'd had his father to himself. Wandering around this old house brought back pleasant memories.

A bamboo garden flourished in one of the courtyards. Some grew thick canes striped in green and yellow, others stood only knee-high, their leaves as dainty as ferns. Weeds pushed up between paving stones. Another year of neglect and the courtyard would look like a wilderness.

A movement between the trees and he realized someone else was in the courtyard. Wang Jenmei, her voluptuous figure a contrast to the austere elegance of bamboo. If he'd known, Shao would've avoided this courtyard, but now it was too late. She had seen him and flashed a smile, one that invited him to join her. A smile that seemed to imply he was entering her domain.

"The floor too uncomfortable for sleeping?" she said. She lifted one shapely eyebrow, giving her words a slightly mocking intent.

"Not at all," Shao said, "there's just no point in oversleeping. I wanted to take a look around this old place."

"There's estates like this all over China, Shao," Jenmei said, waving her hand at the surrounding houses. "High walls protecting fine homes meant to house generations of a single family. Rather like yours, I'd guess."

"My great-grandfather built eight houses side by side on the same street," Shao said, "for his sons and grandsons and their families. I suppose that counts as one estate for one family."

"My family's home is three hundred years old," she said. "Three hundred years of ancestors under the same roof, same town, same street. Unlike your family, however, my grandfather and his sons lack ambition. Our wealth flows out the door, never in."

"But obviously they believed in giving you an education," Shao said, hoping to end the conversation. He'd made enough small talk to be polite. But she put a hand on his arm, stopping him from leaving.

"After this war, China will be different," Jenmei said. "Farmland and homes like this will belong to all the people. The Chinese Communist Party will make sure no one lives in luxury while others starve. Come to a Communist Students Club meeting, Liu Shaoming. Just one."

Shao shook his head. "You know my family. I could never join any Communist group." He smiled pleasantly as he said this. Minghua 123 was a small community and they had months on the road ahead of them. There was no need to create an uncomfortable situation. "I'll see you at breakfast."

He left the bamboo garden to look for Sparrow. He needed that button sewn back on.

SHAO'S MEMORIES OF his early childhood were vague, his days an interchangeable series of games and meals, of being put to bed by Amah Fu. Until the day Sparrow walked into his room. What Shao could recall was that he had been crying, throwing a tantrum over some now-forgotten indignity, when a small girl appeared at the nursery door. She walked straight to Shao, which startled him so much he stopped crying. He rubbed the tears from his eyes to take a better look, at her pale skin and wide-set eyes, her birdlike frame. Shao had been too young to explain to himself, let alone to an adult, how the sight of Sparrow affected him. It was as though his real life had begun and that Sparrow was part of the journey.

The Liu household's younger children mixed freely, masters and servants. All of them ran back and forth between the houses, all part of a single huge estate. They played together, seemingly heedless of the difference in their parents' positions until they were old enough for school. The Liu children attended private school. The servants' children did not.

Shao learned before then, however, that Sparrow was not his equal. His parents had been hosting relatives from Changchow and he had refused to play with his cousins, preferring Sparrow's company. For this, he'd been scolded by his mother. It was the first time his mother had ever raised her voice to him.

"You shouldn't spend so much time with the lower classes," she said, an angry frown marring her perfect features. "She's just a servant. Play with your cousins. You are their host."

As a child, Shao always assumed Sparrow's parents were family retainers, servants whose own ancestors had served the Liu clan for generations, their lives and well-being tied to their masters' prosperity. They counted on the Lius to arrange their marriages and funerals, to provide jobs in Liu family businesses. But Sparrow, he learned, was an orphan.

"I think your fourth great-uncle picked her off the streets," Amah Fu had said. She frowned, her broad forehead wrinkled in thought. By then she was no longer his nanny but still worked in the house. She paused for a moment from folding a tablecloth, then shook her head. "I don't know, but there was talk that Sparrow's mother was a maidservant who died. Unmarried."

That was all anyone could tell him about Sparrow. She never volunteered any information about herself. When asked, she'd only say she had no memory of her life before the Liu household or how she got there. Over the years, Sparrow took over from Amah Fu. In addition to her other household chores Sparrow cleaned Shao's room, mended his clothing, and always appeared when he needed her. Sparrow was the one constant in his life, always calm, always reassuring. It wasn't because of anything she said, it was how Sparrow made him feel. As if there was something else that mattered more, something more real than his father's indifference, his mother's melancholy.

His mother's moods darkened Shao's early childhood. That he was not the only one affected became clear one momentous day when Grandmother Liu tottered through their front door, actually making the walk from her mansion at the other end of the estate. Supported on each side by a maid, she entered the spacious foyer. Then his grandmother sat down on a small wicker chair and two burly house servants carefully lifted the chair up the circular staircase, the old woman's tiny bound feet dangling, her two maids trailing behind.

A silent crowd gathered at the foot of the stairs, her sons and daughters-in-law, her grandchildren and an assembly of servants. At the back of the crowd, Shao clutched Amah Fu's hand. His father waited at the top of the stairs, his handsome, square face downcast. He met his mother's irritated glare with a look of shame. The servants set down the chair, Grandmother Liu and her maids vanished down the hallway. Shao's father stood for a moment with slumped shoulders, then followed. Whispers drifted around Shao.

Do you remember the first time she tried to take her own life?
She doesn't realize how lucky she is.
Too spoiled. Too educated. No wonder the master turns to other women.

Soon after, Shao was old enough for school and worries about his mother became easier to push from his thoughts, supplanted by the excitement of new friends and teachers, books and sports. It became even easier when the Zhu family moved in across the street. The Zhu boys soon discovered how many playmates there were in the Liu estate and came over so often some of the elderly Lius mistook them for members of their own clan. By the time Shao finished high school, he and Zhu Pao had been best friends for years. Shao was closer to Sparrow, but that didn't count. Sparrow was only a girl and a servant.

Her devotion required no effort from Shao.

CHAPTER 9

Two scouts carrying lanterns led the way. It was their second night of walking and they would reach Shangma Temple before daybreak. None of them grumbled about traveling on a dark night, with only stars and a sliver of crescent moon to brighten the sky. It was far preferable to nights when the skies were clear, the landscape sharp and distinct beneath a full moon. Starlight brightened the outlines of clouds, picking out a ridge of hills no more than a mile away. Their destination, hidden in the notch of a valley, was not yet visible. They walked silently in a long uneven procession of twos and threes.

Fall was cold this year, unusually so. Even students from the northern provinces felt the chill. For many in Minghua 123, raised in coastal cities and temperate climates, it was pure misery. They wrapped up in every piece of clothing they'd brought, but even with faces and heads muffled, it still wasn't enough. Fatigue was to blame, demanding more from their bodies than they could spare.

On the road ahead, Shao saw a female student beside a donkey cart. Even if the lantern hanging from the cart hadn't lit her face, he would've recognized Lian. She was alone, Meirong nowhere to be seen. He walked faster to catch up. She offered a shy smile of greeting and the lantern enclosed them both in its wavering circle of light. They walked for a time in silence, then Shao cleared his throat.

"So, Lian, which volume of the Library of Legends do you carry?" he said. This had become a frequent question between students, some of whom had never even heard of the Legends before the evacuation. Some, especially the agriculture majors, made it clear they were reading their Legends book purely out of duty.

"*Tales of Celestial Deities*," she said. "And you?"

"Fox spirits, alas," he said. "*Tales of Fox Spirits, Volumes 100 to 140.*"

"I don't think there are that many . . ." she began to say, then they both laughed.

"There's a big collection of Fox lore," Shao said, "enough for multiple volumes. But not 140 of them. Just three, filled with variations of the same story."

"A poor but handsome young man falls in love with a beautiful mysterious maiden," she said, "and his fortunes improve dramatically. They live together happily until the day he discovers she's actually a shape-shifting Fox spirit. Whereupon he rejects her and all his fortunes vanish."

"In some stories the man accepts her for what she is," he said, "and they live together happily until he dies. Then the Fox disappears, presumably to find love with some other young man."

"I think the saga of the Library of Legends itself is wonderfully intriguing," she said. "It's amazing that even a single volume managed to survive."

"Yes, that's how I feel too," he said. "Did you read Professor Kang's pamphlet about the Legends? It almost makes one believe in heavenly intervention. That the scholar responsible for editing the volumes kept a copy for himself, and it stayed in his family for centuries."

"The reason I wanted to attend Minghua was because of the Library of Legends." Her words were eager, her voice passionate. "It's all that's left of the *Jingtai Encyclopedia*, from a time when China represented the peak of human civilization. Did you know about the Legends before coming to Minghua?"

"My father bought the Minghua University Press edition for his library at home," he said. "I used to spend hours reading the Legends. It's a relief to know that even if something happens to the books we carry, at least the stories inside them won't be lost."

"But to hold the originals in your hand," Lian said. "To read those stories in the actual handwriting of scholars who copied them out five hundred years ago. To see notes scribbled in the margins by the imperial scholar Yao himself. What enchantments those books must hold to have survived so long."

"That's exactly how I feel," he said. It pleased him to hear her voice so animated. To know she appreciated the Legends as much as he did.

"My father also owned a Minghua edition of the Library of Legends," she said, and her voice grew subdued. "He would've loved to see the real Library but . . . well, he died when I was a child."

They walked together in silence. It was a companionable silence. Shao liked that Lian didn't demand anything of him, that he didn't have to make polite, trivial conversation.

A lamp and footsteps. "Young Master, the other scouts are asking for you," Sparrow said, holding out a lamp. "They're going to confirm the arrangements for our stay in the next town."

Ahead of them, some students had detached from the main group, lanterns casting small pools of brightness along the road.

"Lian, let's walk together again sometime," Shao said, taking the lamp. "Sparrow, see you in town."

Sparrow didn't reply. She wasn't looking at him, but at Lian. A pitying look. A trick of the light, he thought. Then he sprinted to join the knot of scouts at the front of the line.

CHAPTER 10

Shangma Temple would be their refuge for ten days, giving them a much-needed rest. Built as a religious retreat, the Buddhist temple stood between hills far away from the main road. It was centuries old, a complex of buildings that included temples, a monastery, gardens, and a guesthouse for pilgrims. The path to the temple's main gate was a steep and winding climb, the first test of a pilgrim's devotion. An easier path for wagons and draft animals led to a side entrance. Terraced courtyards looked down on the stream that ran between two small towns called Shangma and Shiama, Upper Horse and Lower Horse, connected by a wide stone bridge.

During its years of prosperity, a steady procession of the devout traveled to Shangma Temple seeking

prayer and peace. They breathed in clean mountain air and re-
freshed themselves in the icy chill of Shangma Temple's waterfall
pool. The truly pious climbed even higher, to the hanging valley
above where they could worship at a small shrine.

But in recent decades the number of pilgrims coming to
Shangma Temple had dwindled and now only a dozen elderly
monks remained to look after the property. They lived in one
courtyard. The rest of the property, the guesthouse and lesser
temples, stood empty. The abbot had been more than pleased for
Minghua 123 to stay there in exchange for rice and money.

Professors inspected temples and halls to decide which ones
to use as classrooms. Servants boiled water for baths and laundry, beat quilts and mats on paving stones to rid them of bedbugs. Students cleaned the rooms where they would sleep, swept
out the halls that would be their classrooms, and unpacked
books to set up a makeshift library on brick-and-board shelving. All the students longed for rest, for the chance to study and
think about something else besides the war. They longed for the
illusion of normalcy.

HO LIFANG, KNOWN for so long as Shorty Ho that his classmates
had forgotten his formal name, reached inside his pants to scratch
his balls. He paused to glance at the doorway. They'd kept the
guesthouse's windows and doors open to air it out. He reached in
deeper for a really long, satisfying scratch. It felt like eons since
he'd taken a bath or put on clean clothes. There were nights when
he had slept with nothing but a thin mat between him and hard
earthen floors. The dirt on his clothes chafed his skin. Or maybe
it was lice. Or maybe the itch in his crotch signified fleas.

It would be his turn to bathe in an hour. And for the next ten glorious days, he would sleep in a proper room. The guesthouse didn't have any beds, but its floors were wooden planks, not the hard-packed earth or cold slate used for temples. He stretched luxuriously in anticipation and scratched some more. He heard footsteps in the corridor and quickly yanked his hand out. He groped in his rucksack for a book, then waved it at the classmate walking past. As though he'd been reading all this time.

He glanced at the cover. His volume of the Legends was *Tales of Dragon Lords*. He sighed and read the introduction.

> There are 128 dragon, dragonlike, or serpentine deities. Their element is Water. The Dragon Lords control all forms of water, from freshwater lakes and rivers to the sea. They determine rainfall and, therefore, floods. They can be benevolent or malevolent. As with most animal deities, Dragon Lords and their offspring can shape-shift, appearing as mortals when they wish to involve themselves in the affairs of mankind.

Shorty tried his best to get past the first page. The Library of Legends might be a national treasure, but it wasn't the sort of thing that interested him. He gave in to fatigue. His eyelids drooped and a soft snore escaped his nostrils. His hands let the book drop.

A cold breeze scoured the room. It ruffled the book lying open on his stomach and turned a few of the ancient pages, then paused. Had Shorty woken up, he might've found the book open at "The Story of the Dragon King's Daughter," a tale that hadn't been recounted for centuries within hearing of a waterfall pool. He might've stood by the window, closed the shutters, and, while doing so, admired the hanging valley above, a view of orange and gold autumn foliage. He would've glimpsed torrents of water that cascaded over steep rock faces before merging into a single waterfall that plunged into the pool beyond his window. And had Shorty been one of the few remaining mortals who could see, truly see, he also might've noticed something swimming down the waterfall.

PROFESSOR KANG WAITED on the stone bench. Two hundred years ago, a landscape designer had positioned the seat thoughtfully, just beyond the waterfall's spray. Shangma Temple had been built during an era when people set aside time to admire such views, to compose poetry while listening to birdsong and splashing water. Now his ears were attuned to other sounds, to the rumble of aircraft engines, the mechanical wail of sirens.

An undulating movement disturbed the curtain of falling water. Then a swaying shape emerged from the spray and swam toward the edge of the pool. It rose up, a column of white. The professor clenched his fists so tightly his nails dug into the palms of his hands, but he'd promised the Star he would do this. He stood up and slowly, warily, moved closer to the pool. He could hear his heartbeat over the sounds of rushing water.

When the creature turned around, it had become a woman. She stood swathed in silvery silk, shining out from dark rock walls like a pillar of glacier ice. There was a blue tinge to her pale complexion and the barest trace of a pattern on her cheeks that suggested scales. Her hair rippled down her back, its own dark waterfall. Her long robes swirled in the current, not quite covering the tail that supported her graceful figure.

The professor cleared his throat and bowed. "Noble Lady, I have a message for you."

The Dragon Lord's Daughter stared at him with unblinking, lidless eyes. "So. You can see me."

"Yes, Noble Lady," he said. He was speaking to a Water Dragon. A Water Dragon. "The Willow Star sent me with a message from the Queen Mother of Heaven."

"There are rumors in the wind, rustlings of news in autumn leaves," she said. "Is it true? The Palace gates are open?"

"Yes, it's true," he said. "The Willow Star asks that you go to the Kunlun Mountains as quickly as you can. Tell your kin. Tell everyone you know. The gates won't stay open forever."

And a moment later, a large white snake swam its way up the waterfall. Professor Kang sat down again. He listened to the splashing of the pool and waited for his pulse to settle down.

TOO RESTLESS TO lie still, Lian tiptoed out of the guesthouse. Minghua 123 was not the only group sheltering at the Buddhist retreat. Halls and temples held a few dozen refugees who had followed them to Shangma, hoping the monks would take them in. Some were on their way to relatives, hoping for a place to live until it was safe to return. Others had tagged along with Minghua for safety or perhaps for a sense of destination. Many had no idea where to go, driven only by fear and instructions from the authorities. They knew only that they had to press ahead, keep moving west or south, deeper into the heart of China.

Lian had walked beside some of these families, listened to them exchange news and rumors. In low voices they repeated what they'd heard about cities taken over by the Japanese. They debated the safest routes, which ones skirted occupied territories, which towns had refugee centers. Their voices grew heavy with longing as they spoke of their homes, of doors that opened onto laneways, of whitewashed walls and gray roof tiles. Of meals eaten at large round tables noisy with crockery and bickering children. Of springtime when fields glazed over with green, lush with anticipation of the harvest to come.

Parents whispered in dark corners, trying not to wake their children. They hoped for news that the Japanese had been repelled. They wanted nothing more than to retrace their steps and rebuild their lives. Yet they also knew if they returned it would be to piles of rubble. The houses where generations of their family had lived and died were gone. If their houses and shops still stood, they would've been looted, emptied of furniture and goods, and stripped of the keepsakes that had given their owners joy.

Lian recognized many of the refugees. The young peasant couple who shouldered carrying poles, the dangling baskets filled with their belongings and two children. The family that took turns, men and women both, carrying their grandmother on their backs, her bound feet tapping against their hip bones as they walked.

There was the young couple, once proud owners of a small shop. They had nothing now, both home and livelihood gone. They huddled in a corner, his hands around a steaming bowl of hot water. The bowl was beautiful, a fine blue-and-white porcelain. It was undoubtedly their own, a cherished piece they couldn't bear to leave behind. The husband passed the bowl to his wife but it slipped out of her hands and shattered on the slate floor. The woman began to weep, picking up the shards as though they were precious gems.

Suddenly, Lian could barely breathe, gripped by the knowledge that such scenes, and worse, were being repeated tens of thousands of times across China. She stumbled away from the guesthouse, her heart weighted with sorrow, loss, and rage. The young couple, those families, they would never be the same. China would never be the same.

She stopped running when she reached the waterfall pool. She sank onto the stone bench. Spray from the waterfall fractured sunlight into small rainbows. It was all ridiculously, inconsiderately beautiful. She was still sobbing when Liu Shaoming found her. He didn't say a word, just sat down beside her.

"I'm tired, that's all," she said. She shrugged, hoping the casual gesture conveyed how little her tears mattered.

"Everyone's tired," he said, "tired and sad. We wouldn't be human otherwise."

The look on his face was both grave and questioning, his entire attention was fixed upon her. If her mother had been there, she would've cautioned Lian against getting too close. But her mother wasn't there for comfort or caution. And what if her mother was wrong? Lian's classmates were friendly and kind, especially Meirong. And Shao had been nothing but courteous and thoughtful.

He put an arm around her and she allowed herself to lean against him. The vault of her heart opened, just a little.

CLASSES WERE BACK in session. Students sat on stone floors for their lectures then gathered to study in the library at rickety tables built from sawhorses and planks. All the chairs had been collected to use in the library, so they ate their meals standing up, holding a bowl and chopsticks. Shoveling rice into their mouths as quickly as possible so they could go back for seconds.

Like everyone else, Lian and Meirong walked to Shiama every day after classes, not to shop but to read the newspapers. Shiama, the larger of the two towns, had a post office. Its manager pasted up newspapers on the outside walls, papers from Shanghai,

Wuhan, and Nanking. They were always at least two days old, but it was better than nothing. Many of the townsfolk couldn't read, but during these extraordinary times, everyone deserved to know the news and there was no shortage of volunteers to read articles out loud. The students were only too glad to do so when asked. They read avidly, not just for news of the war's progress but also to gain some sense of which routes were still safe, which railways still available.

Lian devoured the headlines but was also drawn to smaller articles, descriptions of refugees on the road. Men and women swarming railway tracks, hoping to catch a ride that would save them hundreds of miles of walking. Families crammed into freight cars, those outside hanging on to doorframes and handholds, those inside packed together so tightly they stood upright despite their exhaustion. Reports of underequipped and undertrained soldiers being sent to the front lines. Photos of disheveled recruits in military camps outside the city of Changsha, some not even in uniform.

The papers from Shanghai shocked them. An editorial in *Xinwen Bao* left the students speechless.

> *Some of Shanghai's foreign residents treat the war as spectacle. Never before has a great metropolis given its residents a ringside seat at a killing contest involving nearly a million men. They stand on apartment roofs and watch as Japanese airplanes dive on our soldiers in the trenches. From the safety of Bubbling Well Road, guests at the Park Hotel's popular dining room gaze out through large picture windows and sip cocktails while commenting on the marksmanship of the Japanese batteries. One gets the impression the audience is*

disappointed their views of bloodshed are obscured by buildings and barricades.

"How can they be so heartless!" Meirong exclaimed, her face red with indignation.

"The white foreigners consider us inferior. Therefore, our suffering is insignificant," Wang Jenmei spoke from behind. The tall girl shrugged. "One million or twenty million dead, Chinese or Japanese, it doesn't matter to them."

Several of the townspeople dawdling around the newspaper wall drew closer. Jenmei noticed their interest and straightened her shoulders. She lifted her chin and her expression took on a dramatic intensity as she turned to face her small audience.

"There's only one way we can drive back the Japanese," she said loudly. "And that's if the Nationalist government would stop fighting the Communists. All Chinese must unite against our common enemy, regardless of our politics. Then we wouldn't need to beg for help from foreign allies."

There were murmurs of agreement. Jenmei's striking looks won her as much attention as her words. Lian pulled at Meirong's sleeve.

"I've heard that speech before," she said. "We should work on that assignment, the one where we pick a story from the Legends to research. It's worth twenty percent of the final grade."

"You go," Meirong said, "I'll come find you later."

But she wasn't looking at Lian. She was watching Jenmei, admiration for the older girl shining out from her face.

To LIAN'S RELIEF, only a few other students occupied the library. It was a half day, and most students were in town. Minghua 123's temporary library occupied the largest hall in the temple complex. The walls were lined with shelving built from bricks and boards. There weren't enough shelves, so open crates of books sat in rows on the floor. She settled into a corner and pulled some writing paper from her rucksack.

A girl at the opposite end of the hall caught Lian's eye and gave her a half wave before returning to her own work. It was novel to Lian, this unsolicited warmth. She still hid behind Meirong, who was gregarious enough for them both, but the niceties of friendship came more easily to her now. Lian had learned that a compliment could break the ice, a question encourage conversation.

She wished Meirong would stop teasing her about Shao just because he walked with her sometimes or sat beside her at the library on occasion.

"It's because we survived the bombing at Nanking West Railway Station," Lian said. "He's being kind, that's all. He treats me like a younger sister."

"That's how these things begin, Lian," Meirong said, wagging her finger. "Then it grows into something deeper. Don't deny it. You'd like to be more to Liu Shaoming than a younger sister."

Now, after crying on his shoulder by the waterfall pool, Lian did wonder how Shao truly felt about her. He had been so understanding, had known she didn't need words of comfort, only his shoulder to cry on. Then there was that look on his face, the thoughtful questioning expression that made her feel as though she could tell him anything.

She'd become alert to his presence. Unbidden, her ears sifted through the hubbub of chatter for mention of his name and her mind tucked away overheard scraps of conversation.

That Liu Shaoming. He's like a young god.

When Shao looks at you, you can tell he's really paying attention, not like other boys.

That servant Sparrow, though. What do you think she means to him?

Lian tried to concentrate on the pages of the book in front of her. She shifted to a more comfortable position on the rickety library bench.

"Miss Hu. May I sit?" The soft voice was cultured, smooth.

Mr. Lee, the director of student services, smiled down at her, a porcelain mug in his hands. His face was already thinner than it had been a week ago. His eyes, distorted behind the lenses of his wire-rimmed glasses, were disconcertingly bright, giving him an eager, predatory look.

Lian quickly stacked the books she had spread all over the table to make room. He sat down and put his tea mug on the table.

"You're from Peking, am I right?" he said in a whisper. He lifted the lid from his blue-and-white mug. The steam from his tea wafted up, wonderfully fragrant. "Did you hear from your family before we evacuated? Are they still there?"

"It's just my mother," she said. Her chest hollowed out, as it always did when she thought of her mother. "She wrote before the Japanese attacked to say she was fleeing Peking. I hope she's safely in Shanghai now. But I won't know until I get a letter."

"If she reads the bulletins," Mr. Lee said, "she'll see Minghua on the list of evacuated schools. She'll know the stops along the way, the ones where we will stay for weeks, not days. Her letters might reach you en route. And if not, there's always our final destination, Chengtu."

Lee didn't have to explain this to her. They all knew there was no easy way to get in touch with their families while on the road.

"I came to talk to you about Liu Shaoming," Lee said. "A fine young man from an extremely influential clan."

Shao was the last thing she expected Mr. Lee to bring up. She drew back slightly from the director of student services.

"The Liu family is connected to the highest levels of government," he continued. "It would be terrible for their reputation if Liu Shaoming joined the Communist Party."

"Why do you think he might?" she said. There were left-wing student organizations at every university and Minghua was no different. All the students were interested in politics, or at least pretended to be. Some only knew the names of important people on either side, could repeat a few slogans. A small number, such as Wang Jenmei, were truly serious.

"Students debate politics, of course. That's normal." He removed his glasses and pulled out a handkerchief. Spotlessly white, edged with a blue stripe. "But it would be quite the coup for the Communist Party if he joined. It would be humiliating for his family and by extension, the government."

"I don't understand why you're telling me this, Mr. Lee," she said.

"I think Liu Shaoming is fond of you," he said. He breathed on his lenses and began polishing them. "I want you to keep an eye on him. Let me know if he starts going to Wang Jenmei's Communist Students Club meetings."

"You want me to spy for you?" Her expression must've betrayed her feelings of shock. And disgust.

Mr. Lee put his glasses back on and leaned in to whisper even more quietly. "You will, if you don't want your friends to know your father was shot for being a Japanese spy."

She gasped. "He was a railway engineer. Not a spy."

"And Shao," he said. "I wonder how he'd feel about you if he knew. Come now, I'm not asking for much, Miss Hu. Just let me know if you think he's getting involved in left-wing politics."

Lian remained on the bench after he left, pretending to read, her eyes stinging. What had gone wrong? Her mother had guarded their privacy so carefully during their years in Peking, sacrificed friendships that could've made their lives less lonely. But those efforts had been in vain. They—whoever had given Mr. Lee his information—knew about her father. Which meant he knew their false identities. All her mother's caution, all her tactics, had been useless.

Hands trembling, she wrapped up *Tales of Celestial Deities* and stuffed it back in her rucksack. She tried to walk out the library doors calmly. Outside, the temple buildings were shuttered against the cold, the courtyards empty. Winter winds did not encourage lingering in the open. If only she could find a quiet corner, a place where she could think. Perhaps one of the smaller classrooms in the side courtyard.

But when Lian pushed open the heavy wooden door, Professor Kang was at the front of the room, writing on a chalkboard. The creak of hinges made him turn around.

"Miss Hu. You're not at the market." His voice was gentle, his smile open and kindly.

"I've been already. To read the newspapers," she said. "I . . . I wanted to spend some time reading my book of Legends. To work on my term paper."

"You're in Professor Song's class, aren't you?" he said. "Which book of Legends do you carry?"

"*Tales of Celestial Deities*," she said. "But I haven't selected a story yet for the term paper."

"Ah. That volume contains one of my favorite stories," he said. "'The Willow Star and the Prince.' Please stay here, Miss Hu. I'm finished." He gestured at the lines of poetry, elegantly written even though in chalk.

The professor closed the door softly behind him and Lian slumped with the relief of being alone. She sat on the ground. All she wanted now was to escape from Minghua 123, vanish into the mass of nameless and homeless. She wanted to find her mother, for the two of them to run away. They would become invisible as foxes in hiding. She had to warn her mother. If only she knew whether her mother had reached Shanghai.

CHAPTER 11

After her father died, Lian's mother got rid of their servants. The cook, the housekeeper, even her *amah*. Her mother told Lian she didn't need to go to school for the rest of the month.

"We're in mourning," she said. "Your teachers will understand."

There had been visitors, but none stayed long. One of them, the elderly man in the blue scholar's gown, had handed her mother a large brown envelope. Afterward, her mother seemed excited, almost exuberant. She went out on errands several times that week, leaving Lian alone in the house with strict instructions not to answer the door.

And then the announcement. "Little One, we're going to stay with friends of the family in Hangchow. We leave in a few days."

The day before they were supposed to leave, her mother took her visiting, farewell courtesies. She had never been to their homes before but Lian vaguely remembered some of the women, guests at her parents' parties.

"We're taking a long holiday," her mother said to each lady. "To Hangchow, where we have family friends."

Lian had never heard her mother mention anything about Hangchow before. But she said nothing, just ate the sweet biscuits they put in front of her and sat politely until each visit was over. There was something forced about it all, a brittleness to her mother's conversation, an avid gleam in the eyes of their hostesses.

Except at the last house, where the woman greeted her mother with genuine warmth. A woman taller than most, her complexion and features Eurasian. Many of Lian's classmates were Eurasian. This was not unusual in Harbin, a city with a large European population, mostly Russians who'd come to build the railways and then stayed. A servant took Lian to the kitchen, where a tabby cat and her kittens dozed contentedly in a box beside the stove. When the servant came to get her again, Lian stood up reluctantly, wishing she had cats of her own.

At the front door, their hostess was helping her mother into her coat. "I wish I could do more to help," the woman said.

"It helped just talking to you, Jialing," her mother replied. She clasped the woman's hands. "No one else understands what it's like to live in fear."

When they got home, her mother slammed the front gates shut and leaned her back against them. "You were very good, Lian," she said, her eyes shut. "Very obedient. Thank you."

"The lady with the kittens," Lian said. "Can we go back some other time? After we come back from Hangchow?"

Her mother didn't seem to be listening. "Oh, those women, Lian. They didn't want to let me in the door, but they didn't want to miss the opportunity to look me over either."

That was when Lian realized her mother was crying.

They boarded a train the following day. Once they'd settled in their compartment, Lian's mother locked the door. She wouldn't let Lian explore the rest of the train, not even walk to the dining car. Lian could only go out of their compartment to use the toilets. Lian read the few books she'd brought and gazed out the window at the wintery countryside, stripped bare of greenery.

Her mother lay down on the opposite seat, a wool shawl pulled over her legs, but her eyes were wide open. At noon the porter knocked on the door and Lian let him in to fill their teapot with boiling water from a huge kettle. Then Lian's mother roused herself and brought food out from their wicker picnic basket. They ate a small meal of hard-boiled eggs with rice, a dash of soy sauce to add flavor. They shared a tangerine.

"Let me show you something," her mother said, after putting away their food. She opened her travel case and took out a large brown paper envelope. She unfolded a document stamped with multiple red seals. "This is who we are now."

Lian frowned as her mother ran her fingers down the words and read out loud. *Hu Yinglien. Status widowed. Dependent, Hu Lian, daughter.* Her own name, "Lian," was the same. But their family name was "Jin," not "Hu." And her mother's name was "Beihua," not "Yinglien." And her mother's birth date was wrong. So was hers.

"Those aren't our names," she said, "someone made a mistake."

"It's not a mistake," her mother said. "We'll be using different names when we get to Peking."

"Aren't we going to Hangchow?" she asked.

"That's what I told everyone, Lian," her mother said, "so that if anyone looks for us, they'll go to Hangchow instead of Peking. Peking is a huge city. We'll be safe there."

All she needed to do, her mother said, was remember that their family name wasn't "Jin" anymore. From now on, she was Hu Lian. They would never go back to Harbin. Lian's mother poured a little hot water into a napkin and wiped tangerine juice from Lian's hands.

Lian sounded out her new name quietly. "Why are we Hu? Why not Chang or Lee?"

"Because 'Hu' sounds like the word for 'fox,'" her mother said. "It will remind us that we must be as cunning as foxes. We must be invisible as foxes in hiding."

For the first time since Lian's father died, her mother smiled with real warmth. There was even a look of mischief in her eyes. Lian still didn't understand why they had to change their name or hide away in Peking, but if it meant her mother smiled more, she would.

There were so many things they'd had to leave behind. The shelf of toys beside her bed. The kitchen table and the high chair where she perched to watch her mother and the cook wrap dumplings. The blue bicycle she rode around and around the courtyard garden. Her father's Library of Legends. There were just too many volumes. More than anything, she regretted leaving his books behind. She hoped she wouldn't forget the evenings curled up beside her father, his quiet voice reading the stories out loud to her.

In Peking, they moved into a poor but quiet neighborhood inside a maze of narrow lanes. In their new home, her mother's determined efforts to erase their previous life meant they lived a frugal and secretive existence. Instead of selling the house in Harbin and closing out all bank accounts, her mother had taken some of their money but left enough behind to support the fiction that they had intended to come back.

Her mother had been an orphan at a mission school run by Americans. In Peking she found work as a typist for an American tobacco company. She went to work with her hair pulled back in a matronly bun, wore dowdy, drab colors that made her look ten years older.

When Lian was thirteen, her mother began worrying about a neighbor. He was a widower, a dry goods merchant with two small children and a sickly, elderly mother.

"He's always hanging at the shop door, watching for me," her mother said as Lian set bowls, spoons, and chopsticks on the table. "I think he's a spy."

"All shopkeepers stand by their doors," Lian said. The man always rushed to the counter whenever she and her mother entered his store. She thought it more likely the man found her mother attractive. He was tall and large-boned, with a big nose and bold features that hinted of northern ancestry, perhaps Russian blood.

"No, no," her mother said. "He's been sent by the secret police. We must get out." Her porcelain spoon rattled against the bowl, her voice grew shrill.

"Then let's move," Lian said, putting an arm around her mother. "We'll move to the other side of town. We'll be invisible as foxes in hiding."

She suddenly felt very old.

Her mother maintained a veneer of calm to the outside world; she was disciplined when it came to concealment. But Lian learned to recognize the early signs of panic. The quick, nervous movements of her mother's hands. The way her mother's eyes darted around, searching for hidden terrors. After seven years and four homes her mother was still cautious, but less inclined to panic. Each change of address seemed to ease her mother's mind, as if each move put more obstacles between her and her demons.

When Lian won her scholarship to Minghua University, her mother made a small celebration dinner, all Lian's favorite dishes. River shrimp stir-fried with green peas, a hearty Harbin-style chicken stew, a simple salad of shredded cucumber in a sweet vinegar dressing.

Then after dinner, Lian's mother finally told her what happened seven years ago.

Her father had gone to Tientsin on business. He stayed with a cousin, the man in the long blue scholar's robe who had come to see her mother. This relative was the only one who still spoke to her father. The others had shunned him after he'd married her mother, an orphan with no family and no dowry. In Tientsin, her father had indulged in his hobby of browsing for antique books.

"Your father was shot down in the street," Lian's mother said. "A police officer thought he was the Japanese spy they'd been hunting. A young officer, who realized his blunder almost immediately."

But the authorities still accused her father of being a spy.

Her father's cousin had military connections and was able to unearth the truth. It was a delicate time for the Tientsin police. The young officer was nephew to the chief of police, whose career was on the brink after a series of highly visible and embarrassing mistakes. The family was ready to compensate Lian's mother if she promised silence. They threatened her if she made a fuss.

"But I've known people like that before," her mother told Lian. "Even if you cooperate, they don't trust you. Sooner or later, they find a way to get rid of you. We had to disappear."

Lian washed the last bowl. "Mother, if you want me to stay, I can attend Beida University instead and live at home."

"No, no. You must go to Minghua University," her mother said. "I've made you sacrifice too much already." Her eyes filled. "I know how much you've worried and watched out for me. But I'm better now."

"I don't mind staying," Lian said. "Peking is home now."

Her mother put a hand over hers. "Your father always wanted to see the Library of Legends for himself. He would've been so proud. I'm so proud."

BUT ALL THIS time, the authorities had known. Had been keeping an eye on them. The truth didn't matter since official accounts claimed her father had been a Japanese spy. Lian didn't want to give in to Mr. Lee's demands. But how could she face Shao and Meirong if they thought her father had been spying for the Japanese? Would they even give her a chance to explain?

She had thought herself indifferent to Meirong but now realized she was not. Meirong's sunny, uncritical friendship suddenly mattered very much. And as for Shao, she shuddered when she remembered the hatred in his voice whenever he spoke about the Japanese.

She had to do as Mr. Lee ordered. And all the while she had to behave normally. Pretend nothing was wrong, that she enjoyed the company of her classmates. The best way to act busy was to throw herself into her studies. Opening her rucksack, Lian pulled out *Tales of Celestial Deities* and began reading.

The Willow Star and the Prince

There was a prince, just a minor one. The Willow Star was only a maidservant in the heavenly court. But the plainest servant girl in heaven is still more beautiful than the loveliest mortal and when the Willow Star descended to visit the mortal world, they met and fell in love. But their happiness didn't last. The heir to the throne decided to purge the court of potential rivals and the Willow Star's Prince was executed along with other sons of the royal household.

The Star returned to her home constellation, crying so hard the stardust of her tears flooded the skies, obscuring both moonlight and starlight, making celestial navigation difficult for mortals. The Queen Mother of Heaven demanded she cease her crying. The Willow Star begged the Queen Mother to let her reunite with her lover. The Queen Mother agreed, with conditions. The Willow Star could join the Prince during each of his reincarnations, but she couldn't tell the Prince about their past. If she could make him remember their love, she could bring him home to the heavens.

As far as we know, the Willow Star has yet to succeed in this quest.

CHAPTER 12

Under a full moon, fears of enemy aircraft were never far away from Shao's thoughts. They were on the road again, bound for a fishing village called Zhongmiao near the city of Hefei. There, inside the borders of Anhui Province, they would be safe. However, by now, Minghua 123 knew "safe" was a relative term. Reports of battles moving south and west meant they would soon be within reach of Japanese bombers again.

Shao had been taking his turn at the rear of the convoy to make sure no one lagged behind. Now that another scout had taken his place, he made his way up the line, rummaging in his rucksack for the steamed bun he'd saved from the previous day. Then he remembered he'd already eaten it. He sighed. Hunger was no longer a novel sensation. Nor the cold. His hands, wrapped in rough woolen mitts, were chilled, and his lips were chapped from the cold wind.

A hand on his elbow interrupted his thoughts. "Would you like a bun, Young Master?" Sparrow said. "The cook's assistant gave me an extra."

Shao devoured the bun. The heavy steamed bread weighted down his stomach like lead. As if she knew what he was thinking, Sparrow poked him in the stomach, and he pretended to recoil, as though they were children again. Her face was still that of the girl he remembered, especially when her eyes crinkled in laughter. She reached in her pocket and pulled out a paper bag. Dried apricots.

Shao bit into one. It tasted of summer, sweet and intense. He chewed slowly, transported back to his childhood, to the orchard behind his grandfather's summer house in the Moganshan Mountains. He closed his eyes, remembering how the air had been scented with ripening fruit, pears, apricots, and peaches. The tickle of long grass brushing against his bare legs as he chased Sparrow through the trees. Both of them collapsing in giggles. She'd been allowed to go with his family on that trip, for some reason.

He took another apricot. "You can have the bag," she offered.

"No, that's all I need." He pulled his rucksack more firmly onto his shoulders. "Before we left Nanking, did you even guess what it would be like?" He gestured at the surrounding countryside. "That things were so, well, so *backward* in so much of this province?"

The names of the small towns where they'd stayed for rest stops were already fading from Shao's memory, yet what he had seen was lodged in his mind. Towns that hadn't changed in a hundred years, where electricity was still a rumor. Counties where a single family owned all the land, ruling what was practically a feudal system with tenant farmers toiling in the fields. Children and adults shitting over open troughs, faces emaciated from hunger and wasting illnesses. He saw a peasant population steeped in superstition, farmhouses where livestock and people shared the same quarters.

"Not just in this province," she said. "The poverty, the primitive rural villages, this is what conditions are like in most of China."

"I've been appalled so often, Sparrow," he said. "Every day, I still can't believe what I see." Only to Sparrow could he admit this. Because she understood, already knew, he'd been unprepared for the poverty. "I mean, the lice and skin sores, vermin-infested sleeping quarters—for us it's temporary. But these people, it's how they live. Will they ever see better days?"

"It's been like this for centuries," Sparrow said. "Human life has always been one of China's cheapest commodities."

"What did you say? 'Commodities'? Sparrow, where do you learn such words?" he teased, knowing that Sparrow read everything that came her way. Since working at Minghua she had even made use of the library, with special permission from Professor Kang.

"The poor exist in our cities as well," she said, looking prim.

"I know that," he said. "I'm not blind."

It was just that he'd never paid them much attention. Beggars determinedly staking out their small patches of pavement. Children squatting outside shop doors, selling cheap candies and cigarettes arranged on wooden trays. There were so many, and they were so persistent, so much a part of the streetscape. Sometimes he flipped a coin to a beggar or bought a package of mints off a tray.

Sparrow poked him in the ribs. "I think you're getting exactly the sort of education you need right now."

"You sound like Wang Jenmei," he said. "Are you going to lecture me on socialism now?"

She was silent for a moment. "You need to stay away from that one, Young Master."

"Don't worry, Sparrow," he said. "Even if I attend one of her meetings, I'd never get involved in her brand of politics."

"That's not what I mean." Sparrow shook her head. "Her skin is not as tough as it seems. Her feelings bruise easily. She doesn't like being disappointed."

"No one likes disappointment. I need to catch up with Shorty," he said. "On second thought, I will take those apricots. He may want some."

It was easy locating Shorty, who was whistling, something he often did while walking. Rather irritatingly, however, it was always the same tune, one from an American film. "Pennies from Heaven."

SHAO HAD COME to Minghua University because of Pao, his neighbor and best friend, whose father owned a fertilizer company and ordered Pao to study agriculture or chemistry, or both. He didn't care which university Pao chose. Pao decided on Minghua.

"Do you think I should attend Minghua, too?" Shao sat cross-legged on his bed. "It's far away, Sparrow. Four hours by train. My mother might not like that."

Sparrow squinted at the shoe she was polishing, gave it an extra wipe with the rag. "It's one of the best universities in China and your mother wants the best for you. She'd be proud to tell her friends you're at Minghua."

A small knot loosened in Shao's chest. "I'd like to live in a different city. Meet different people." Get away from his mother's melancholy. Away from under his father's thumb, just a little.

She started on another shoe. "If Pao's there, you won't have any problems meeting new people."

"I'll miss you, Sparrow," he said, in a rush of regret. She had never been exactly pretty, but at that moment, he thought the curve of her lips the sweetest he'd ever seen.

After the first few weeks in Nanking, when the excitement of settling in at university had worn off, a sensation of unease stalked Shao, a drifting aimlessness. As though he'd somehow strayed from the path he was meant to walk. Following Pao, he had majored in agriculture, telling himself that he, too, wanted to help China produce better crops. But he floundered.

Pao was sympathetic and unhelpful. He slapped Shao on the back and said, "Let's go hit some tennis balls and you'll feel better."

Shao woke one morning, drowsily aware that someone was sweeping the hallway outside his dormitory room. It was a comforting, familiar rhythm. Three long sweeps of the straw broom and then a short one to push all the dirt into the dustpan.

He sat up. Pao was still sleeping, snoring lightly. Shao pulled on his dressing gown and threw open the door. "Sparrow! What are you doing here?"

"I wanted to see Nanking." She was dressed in the dark-blue tunic and trousers worn by all Minghua servants, from grounds-keepers to cooks.

"But why did you leave Shanghai? And my family?" The Liu servants counted themselves fortunate. It was unheard of to leave the Liu household voluntarily. "Did my mother send you?"

"They're not my family. My place is with you, Young Master." Sparrow walked down the staircase, broom and dustpan in hand. She paused at the landing and gave Shao a wide, sweet smile that made her look almost pretty.

Shao shut the door and sank back on his bed. The untethered sensation was gone, in its place a feeling that he and Sparrow were part of the same journey, that all was well, now that she was here. When he was a boy, that feeling had come over him frequently when he was with Sparrow. But as he grew older, he'd dismissed it, as he did now, the sensation washing over him quickly and draining away. He told himself it was just because Sparrow had turned up suddenly, reminding him of the first time he'd seen her at his nursery door. It was just because she had always been part of his life.

A week later, Shao changed majors. Whatever he was searching for, he knew it wasn't to be found in crops or soil, weeds or drainage. Literature and the classics were how he would search for purpose.

THE YOUNGEST AND oldest members of Minghua 123 traveled on wagons and carts, perched wherever there was room to squeeze on between luggage, crates, and baskets. Female students and servants could also ride for a brief respite from walking. It was Lian's and Meirong's turn to ride. They sat with their legs hanging over the side, their backs resting against sacks of rice, knocking each other every time the cart bumped over a rut.

Lian had spent the earlier part of the evening keeping an anxious eye on Meirong. On their last day at Shangma Temple, Jenmei had announced she was heading up a student newspaper: the *Minghua 123 News*. She scheduled a "walking meeting" to discuss plans while on the road to Zhongmiao. Meirong had volunteered immediately and even offered to work as coeditor alongside Jenmei.

Lian had trailed the walking meeting at a safe distance. She watched Meirong's spirited gestures and obvious enthusiasm with dismay. The others in the group were mostly second-year students like Meirong. Jenmei had a way of attracting young admirers.

Now Meirong was dozing, almost asleep, while Lian sat miserable, wide awake. How could she keep Meirong away from Wang Jenmei? What if Mr. Lee demanded she spy on Meirong as well? Lian had been avoiding Shao, certain that her every word and gesture, her false smiles, even her downcast eyes, would betray her. She had even been avoiding Meirong.

Her sense of belonging, always tentative at best, had evaporated, leaving nothing more than a dim remembrance of warmth. When she looked at them now, her classmates seemed to shine with duty and patriotism, so united in their camaraderie they were like a family. They looked out for each other. They trusted each other. She wanted to stop caring about Meirong and Shao, stop caring about all the classmates who had so inexplicably become friends.

On days when Lian couldn't bear any more of Mr. Lee's scrutiny, the only reason she didn't run away from Minghua 123 was because she had no idea where to go. If she had learned anything since leaving Nanking, it was about the hazards of wartime travel. Her mother could be anywhere. On a train heading straight for the coast or on a meandering route that might take weeks or months before reaching Shanghai. She had to wait until she knew her mother had arrived in Shanghai—or some other destination.

Only then could she make a decision.

Fatigue prevailed over misery. Lian wrapped her arms around her knees and put her head down with a sigh, letting the motion of the cart rock her into drowsiness as the road passed through open fields. The cart followed the wide curve in the road to pass a large pond, the ruined shell of a farmhouse behind it. There were people camped inside and around the farmhouse's walls, refugees too tired or too poor to find a better shelter.

A cold wind carried sounds from the encampment. Coughing and sneezes. A child's whimper. With the approach of morning, the full moon was starting to fade, but its image still shone out from the pond, a perfect reflection on that tranquil surface. Three figures moved to the water's edge. Two were ragged, a man and a woman bundled against the cold. The third, she somehow knew, was Sparrow. Their conversation carried across the waters of the pond.

"Don't take too long." It was Sparrow's voice. A voice that gleamed. "The gates to the Palace will only stay open for a year."

"We'll tell the others," the woman replied, "but not all are willing to leave."

The conversation made no sense at all to Lian.

Sparrow held the woman's shoulder for a moment, a gesture of farewell. The man put his hand out and Sparrow gave it a quick squeeze. He seemed to be wearing a fur mitt, badly made. Or else his hand was deformed. Sparrow continued to the front of the Minghua convoy, where the road vanished into the shadows of a bamboo forest. The couple stood motionless at the side of the field, shoulders hunched against the cold. When the cart rolled past, Lian caught a glimpse of their eyes. Yellow and shining with glints of green. The eyes of wolves. Or were they foxes?

She put her head down on her arms and fell asleep.

ON THEIR FINAL approach to the fishing village, Minghua 123 stopped to let a detachment of soldiers march by. Lian and Meirong moved off to stand in the fields while soldiers and military vehicles took over the road. The officer leading the soldiers was on horseback. He looked tired, his chin dark with stubble. The scouts carrying rifles stood at attention as he rode past. The officer saluted them gravely in return, as if they weren't just students holding outdated guns.

Meirong tugged at Lian's sleeve. "I wish you'd join the newspaper project," she said, "then we could work on it together. I know you think Jenmei might slant the articles to favor a left-wing point of view, but all she wants are well-written articles, regardless of ideology."

Lian forced a smile. "I'm not a journalist."

"We need all kinds of help," Meirong said, "not all of it to do with writing. I mean, you could just do the copying. Copy the finished articles onto newsprint. Then we'll paste up the news sheets on walls."

"On walls where?" Lian asked.

"Wherever we're staying, like at the post office in Shiama. Any town or temple," Meirong said, "wherever people can see it. And we'll also need copies for ourselves, so that when we're settled, we can publish our writings. We badly need volunteers to copy two sets of everything. One to paste up on walls and one to keep."

"I'll think about it," Lian said, "but you know I'm taking the Honors program and the assignments are quite heavy."

"We're a traveling campus in the middle of a war, Lian," Meirong said. "Our instructors will excuse anything. You could do half the work and still pass. And while working for *Minghua 123 News*."

Meirong gave her a wide, confident grin before breaking into a run. She caught up to the *Minghua 123 News* group, which was re-forming again at the front of the line.

"Not much farther to go now." Lian turned with delight at Shao's voice, then looked down, hoping the heat in her cheeks wasn't too obvious. She kept walking, but he didn't say anything more, just kept pace beside her, seemingly content to walk in silence.

Then he gave her a quick nudge of the elbow. "Look who's coming our way."

Coming back from the front of the line, Wang Jenmei approached with the easy stride that made her every move graceful and leisurely.

"Shao, Lian, good morning," she said in greeting. "Why don't you attend a Communist Students Club meeting sometime? It doesn't mean you're committed. Everyone else in Minghua 123 has come at one time or another."

Lian shook her head. Some classmates had attended once, just to be polite, and regretted it. Jenmei wouldn't leave them alone now.

"I promised my father not to get involved in politics," Shao said.

"You mean, not the socialist kind of politics," Jenmei said. She seemed amused rather than hurt at this rejection. "If it makes you feel better, you can attend a Nationalist Students Club meeting to balance things out. How about you, Lian?"

"I'm really not interested," she replied. Kept her eyes on the road ahead. "I also promised not to get involved in politics."

"Well, dear classmates," Jenmei said. "At some point, you must decide what you stand for."

She strolled away and Lian couldn't help notice how Shao's eyes followed Jenmei's lilting, seductive walk. All the students had lost weight from poor food and constant marching, but Jenmei had somehow become both leaner and more shapely.

"Shao, would you ever attend one of those meetings?" Lian said, hoping her voice didn't betray anxiety.

He paused before answering. "When we were still in Nanking, I would've said no, not ever. But that was before all this, everything we've seen. So much poverty. This isn't how it should be in a modern republic."

"China is a huge country," Lian said, "with a huge population. It takes time to modernize the entire nation. Once this war is over, once we're able to rebuild—"

"I agree with the Communists on one issue only," Shao interrupted. "The war would be over sooner if we put all our efforts into fighting the Japanese. Why are we also fighting the Communists? They're Chinese, too. We shouldn't be killing our own people."

A shout from students at the front of the convoy made everyone strain to look ahead. They were within sight of Zhongmiao Village. Bathed in sunrise, whitewashed houses hugged the shoreline of a wide green lake. Small boats moved through rippling water, fishermen setting out for a day's work. The village looked tranquil, untouched.

BY THE SHORES of Chaohu Lake, Zhongmiao Village was only a four-hour walk from the city of Hefei, a distance that now seemed to the students quite a reasonable distance for a day's travel. Behind the village were hills covered in forests. The students learned there were scenic caves and hot springs nearby, and some were already making plans for excursions.

Their new lodgings were in a factory at the western corner of the village. Minghua 123 called it their "factory campus." The owner had stripped out all the equipment and moved his manufacturing business to safety farther inland. The government then took it over to house universities. It was undeniably ugly, a collection of drafty buildings arranged around a large work yard of brown earth packed down as hard as concrete, the entire area enclosed by a brick wall topped with shards of broken glass. As if to compensate, the factory stood on a rise with a magnificent view of the lake.

Two warehouses, still smelling of raw cotton, would be their classrooms. Minghua 123's library went into the third and smallest warehouse. Now emptied of machinery, the long factory building became both barn and storage room. The kitchen and dining hall were just large enough for their needs. At the far end of the yard were the workmen's quarters, a dozen bunkhouses laid out in two rows on either side of a boardwalk, bathhouse at one end, outhouses at the other. These buildings now formed the men's dormitory.

The large triple courtyard house, once the owner's, was for faculty, families, and the female students. The traditional halls felt comfortingly familiar, tugged at memories of childhood holidays with elderly grandparents, of crossing courtyards to knock on an indulgent auntie's door. Even the factory owner's undistinguished rock garden, second-rate by any reckoning, offered solace.

There was no way to partition the warehouses into classrooms, so professors lectured as quietly as possible, their students sitting huddled in a circle around them, some on low stools, most on cold bare concrete.

One night a student chalked some words above a bunkhouse door: *Hall of Idle Pastimes*. The indignant residents soon scrubbed it off, but a day later, each bunkhouse sported a name. *Hall of Contemplation, Moon Viewing Pavilion, Gallery of Refined Pleasures*. Names that echoed memories of homes and gardens left behind. Someone nailed a wooden plank to the first bunkhouse, giving the boardwalk between bunkhouses a name: *Scholars' Lane*.

The ugly oblong of industrial ground bolstered Minghua 123. A month of routine and studies, of feigning normal school days, while trying to forget they lived in exile.

CHAPTER 13

The men's bathhouse didn't have running water. Rain barrels just outside the door collected water and inside were three shallow wooden tubs. A brick stove heated metal pails of water and a long wooden table held washbasins. By now the students considered this the height of luxury. The boys drew straws for the first shift. Shao, Shorty Ho, and Shorty's best friend, Chen Ping, won the first draw. Towels thrown over their shoulders, the three grinned at their envious classmates and strolled through the door of the bathhouse, hands raised in mock victory.

"Ten minutes," shouted a student at the end of the line, "or we'll come and tip you out of those tubs."

"Keep that door shut," Shorty Ho hollered back, "you're letting the cold air in!"

Shorty Ho pulled off his tunic and then his cardigan and sweater, his undershirt. He poured hot water into the shallow wooden tub, added some cold water from another bucket, and climbed in. Doubled up, knees to chest, the water just came to his hips. He ladled warm water over his head and groaned with pleasure.

It was amusing to Shao how much Shorty Ho had changed. He was no longer the fashionable, swaggering urbanite. Now he layered on clothing with more concern for warmth than style. He had shaved his head to discourage lice. Instead of his usual two-tone leather wing tips, he sported cloth shoes with straw sandals tied over them. The students' leather shoes, made for sidewalks and classroom hallways, had fallen apart after constant walking on rough roads. As replacements, students bought the traditional cloth shoes available in every small town, the soles made from layers of cloth glued and sewn onto stiff cardboard. Then they tied straw sandals over the shoes, a trick learned from other foot travelers they'd met. The sandals kept cloth soles from touching damp earth and slowed down wear; they were also cheap to re-place, only a penny for three pairs.

"The factory owner must've been a good employer," Shao said, rubbing soap on his face, "to provide sleeping quarters and bathing facilities for his workers."

"I can't believe you're that naïve," Chen Ping said. "The owner charged them rent and took it out of their wages. He probably charged them for hot water, too. And the workers counted themselves lucky to have jobs at all."

"You don't know that," Shao said. It was a mystery how someone as serious as Chen Ping had become such good friends with Shorty. Yet other strange friendships had developed on this journey. Lian and that talkative Yee Meirong, for instance.

"I do. Our family owns cotton mills," Chen Ping said, pulling a sliver of soap out of a mesh bag. "It's how things are done. Don't you know how your family business operates?"

This mildly reproachful comment stung Shao. The Liu clan had so many business interests. His father's newspaper. Real estate. There was a tin mine somewhere up north. His older brother Tienming ran one of the shipping firms. But Shao had never taken an interest in any of them.

"Five minutes left!" a voice shouted from outside the bathhouse door. "And don't use up all the hot water!"

The three finished washing and quickly got dressed. They emerged into the cold air, skin pink from hot water and scrubbing. A clothesline had been strung between two bunkhouses and they hung their towels up to dry.

"Look at the cuffs on my shirt," Shorty remarked to Shao, "disgusting. You've managed to keep your clothes pretty clean."

"What? Oh, it's Sparrow," Shao said. "I think she washed a few of my things."

"As good as a personal maid, eh?" Shorty said. "I don't suppose she'd be willing to do my laundry?"

"Ask her yourself," he said, suddenly irritated with Shorty. "I'm going to help put away library books."

But in the library warehouse, the shelves were already stacked, and volunteers were giving the books a final dusting. All that was left to do was put away the empty crates. Shao picked up the last two crates and carried them to the factory building. There, a dozen students had gathered, perched on empty carts and wagons, listening intently to Jenmei. He set the crates down.

"All of us come from big cities," she said, "cities transformed by contact with the West. Foreign movies, international newspapers, schools that gave us the education needed to qualify for university. Even the poorest scholarship students among us are better off than the peasants and villagers we meet on our travels."

From the quick turn of her head, he knew Jenmei had seen him.

"But we know nothing about the rural population. The government is counting on us to shape China's future," Jenmei said. "The vast majority of Chinese are rural. How can we shape China's future, how can we help our countrymen when we're ignorant about the lives of peasants a few miles outside our cities?"

In a rush of understanding, Shao realized Jenmei counted herself as one of the ignorant, as unprepared as the rest of them for the poverty they witnessed every day. Jenmei looked at him with a self-deprecatory smile. In the set of her shoulders Shao recognized purpose, enough to anchor a life. Resolve and determination he had yet to discover in himself.

IN THE COURTYARD house beside the factory, the women of Minghua 123 were also busy with laundry and baths. The weather had turned sunny. Lian, Meirong, and a dozen others leaned against the smooth wooden railings of the veranda, towels wrapped around newly washed hair, the sun warning their shoulders. Some girls had rinsed their hair with an infusion of simmered *bai bu* roots, easily available from herbalists. Others had been lucky enough to get hold of rubbing alcohol, which they had massaged into their scalps.

Even though Minghua 123 traveled with their own sheets and blankets, it had been impossible to stay free of pests. No matter how much they swept and mopped the floors of the inns and halls where they stayed, they couldn't get rid of fleas and bedbugs. There were times when Lian thought bare floors were cleaner than the beds, mattresses stuffed with straw or kapok cotton that bred new generations of pests, all of which migrated to blankets and clothing.

"And now lice. How mortifying," Meirong said. "I wish we could wear crew cuts or shave our heads as the men do." Most of the girls, Lian and Meirong included, had already cut their hair to blunt, chin-length bobs.

"Has it been an hour yet?" one girl asked. "Should we keep the towels on for another ten minutes to be sure?"

In reply, Meirong pulled off her towel. She hung her head upside down and began combing out damp hair. Specks like black sesame seeds fell to the ground.

"Who's next for the steamers?" one of the servants shouted from the courtyard kitchen.

Lian and Meirong folded their sheets and blankets into neat squares then joined the line by the kitchen door. They placed the bedding in deep bamboo baskets that the servants would stack over large tubs of boiling water. An hour of steaming was the only way to be certain of killing bedbugs and their eggs.

"After this, a few nights of peaceful sleep," Meirong said, "and then those little demons will jump back on and we'll be scratching again."

"Clean hair, clean sheets," Lian said. "What a luxury. Almost makes me want to stay here in this ugly campus."

"A few weeks here means we might get one more steaming session before moving on," Meirong said. "Lian, come with me to the library for a minute, before we go work on the newspaper. I need to find Ying-Ying. She borrowed one of my textbooks again. Took it right out of my rucksack and *then* asked permission."

Inside the factory gates, Lian automatically looked around for Shao. And for Jenmei. Fortunately, they were at opposite corners of the yard, Jenmei talking to some girls, Shao surrounded by classmates. Shorty, Chen Ping. They all looked conspicuously clean. Then Jenmei strolled across the yard to join Shao's group. She said something and the two laughed. They broke off from the group and sat together on a bench beside the bunkhouses. Lian suppressed a jolt of dismay.

"You go inside the library and find Ying-Ying," she said to Meirong. "I'll stay out here in the sun and let my hair dry a bit more."

She tried not to stare too obviously as Jenmei leaned closer to Shao. The look on his face was thoughtful and searching. The look that made Lian feel she had his complete attention. Would Shao become one of those students who melted away in the evenings, attending those not-so-secret political meetings?

"That Ying-Ying," Meirong said. She came out of the library waving a textbook. "She's the most absentminded person I've ever met. Now, to the newspaper office. You promised to help." Meirong was determined to make her take part. Lian could no longer refuse without being rude.

Somehow Jenmei had managed to cajole Professor Kang into giving *Minghua 123 News* its own bunkhouse to use as an office. To Lian's surprise, Sparrow was inside, standing at a long table built from sawhorses and boards. Her right sleeve was rolled up and she held a calligraphy brush.

"These are the stories that have been approved," Meirong said, after greeting Sparrow. She handed Lian several sheets of paper. "Now we need them copied onto newsprint."

Meirong put a stick of ink and an inkstone in front of her, then poured a little water from a beaker into the inkstone's well. Silently, Lian began grinding the ink.

"I don't think Jenmei has done any work at all this week," Meirong said, looking irritably at a stack of writing. "She promised to give these articles a final review before we started copying. I need to go remind her."

The door slammed shut behind Meirong. Sparrow glanced up from her writing and looked amused. Lian had never noticed the young woman's eyes before. They were as dark as the waters of a forest pool, yet luminous as though a lamp shone in their depths. A pointed chin lent determination to her features. Slim, steady fingers guided the brush in neat columns of beautifully formed characters. Her hands were delicate, not rough and red as Lian would've expected from years of scrubbing floors.

"Your calligraphy is exceptional, Sparrow," Lian said, looking over her shoulder. "How did you learn?"

"From a classical scholar," Sparrow said. "The Young Master's fourth great-uncle. When I was a child, I cleaned his study and afterward he would give me lessons. He taught me to read and write. And eventually, calligraphy."

"Fourth Great-Uncle must be a very kind man," Lian said, "taking the time to do that."

"He had retired," Sparrow said, "so I suppose tutoring a servant gave him something to do."

They worked across from each other in quiet concentration. Over the weeks and miles, students and servants had become more familiar with each other. Professors even chatted with laborers as they walked along the road. But Lian realized she'd never had a conversation with Sparrow, nor had she ever seen Sparrow gossip with any of the other servants. Lian stole a glance at the servant, who had known Shao since he was a boy, and probably knew him better than anyone else.

"Sparrow, do you think Shao would join the Communist Students Club?" she said.

The young woman wet her brush on the inkstone. "His family

forbids it," she said. "But the Young Master is not with his family right now. I suppose he might attend a meeting or two out of curiosity."

If only out of curiosity, then there was no need to report to Mr. Lee. But what if the director of student services thought she was holding back? What if he punished her by telling Shao about her father? Shao would despise her.

And so would Meirong, she realized with an unexpectedly sharp pang of distress.

THAT EVENING, AS the dining hall filled with hungry students, Lian looked around but couldn't see Meirong. Food went quickly. If anyone was even a few minutes late, they'd be lucky to scrape a spoonful of rice from the bottom of the pot. She had last seen Meirong back at the newspaper office. That's probably where she was, Lian thought, too absorbed in her work to realize how much time had passed. Lian hurried across the yard, cursing Jenmei under her breath. If Meirong was overworked, it was from trying to please the senior student. But when Lian got to the newspaper office, the bunkhouse windows were dark. The next place to look was the courtyard house where all the women lived.

Then she paused at the sound of voices from inside the bunkhouse. Soft laughter. One of the windows now betrayed a small gleam of light. Silently, Lian moved closer and stood on tiptoe to look in. A candle on a saucer flickered. There was a dish of dried apricots on the table beside the saucer. A hand reached in from the darkness and took an apricot. Then another candle flared, brightening the space. Jenmei leaned down and fed a dried apricot to someone sitting on the floor. Shao.

Mesmerized, Lian watched as Jenmei knelt on the blanket to face Shao. Under the quivering flame her expression was rapt, adoring. She moved her face close to his, but he leaned back slightly, his smile as uncertain and wavering as candlelight. Jenmei took his hand and placed it on her cheek. This time, when she leaned forward, he didn't resist her kiss. And when she finally pulled away from him, Jenmei's expression was no longer adoring but something else. Triumphant.

Lian backed away from the bunkhouse, fist jammed in her mouth. She ran all the way back to the dining hall, where she found Meirong eating dinner.

"Where've you been, Lian?" her friend asked. "It's a good thing I saved a bowl of food for you."

AFTER DINNER, LIAN returned to her room. Lights and noises filtered through her window shutters, servants bustling about finishing the day's chores, families putting children to bed. She lit a lamp and sat beside it to read but the printed pages may as well have been blank. All she could see were two dim figures under the flicker of candles. Had she been the only one who didn't realize what was going on between Jenmei and Shao?

She'd been so sure that Shao's feelings for her ran deeper than mere kindness. At the same time, she'd never dared hope for much. After all, he belonged to one of Shanghai's great families. Her daydreams had been modest, laughably naïve now that she thought of it. Walks along the lakeshore. Moments of quiet conversation. Nothing as deliberate, as brazen, as Jenmei's advances.

When her roommates came back, Meirong wasn't with them.

Lian joined in the small talk while the two other girls got ready for bed; they chattered for what seemed an interminably long time before they finally got under the covers. Silence fell over the courtyard home and deep even breathing filled the room. But Lian stared up at the ceiling, listening until the door opened and shut with a soft click of the latch. Then the scuffle of shoes being removed and the bed beside hers creaked.

"It's really late," Lian whispered, "where've you been?"

"I did it, Lian, I went," Meirong said. "I went to the Communist Students Club meeting. Jenmei made so much sense." She spoke in a low voice but Lian could hear the quiver of excitement. More than excitement. Jubilation.

"Oh no, Meirong," Lian said. She had been afraid of this. "Please, you mustn't join them."

"It was just one meeting," Meirong said. "It *is* late, isn't it? I'm tired."

"Who . . . who else was there?" Lian couldn't help asking.

"We promised Jenmei we wouldn't tell," Meirong said, yawning. "Safer that way."

Lian waited a few moments, then whispered, "Meirong, was Shao there?"

But there was only the soft exhalation of Meirong's breath, the shadowy rise and fall of her chest.

LIAN DIDN'T WANT to see Shao or Jenmei, on their own or together, didn't want to hear the gossip. She ate her meals quickly and returned directly to the courtyard house to study there instead of at the library. She avoided her classmates even more now, slipping easily into practiced isolation. She would hover at the periphery of a group, offer a few words of conversation, and then slip away. She kept her distance so unobtrusively none of her classmates, even Meirong, seemed to notice.

But Mr. Lee noticed.

When Lian left the dining hall after breakfast one morning, she and Ying-Ying passed Mr. Lee crossing the yard. They exchanged greetings but before he sauntered away, Lee tossed a comment to Lian, a casual passing thought.

"You seem rather solitary these days, Miss Hu. I'd like to see you spend more time with your classmates. More time with the newspaper, perhaps?"

His tone was amiable and no one but Lian would've caught the menace in those words. Lee continued across the yard, his sturdy figure and ponderous walk unmistakable, his shadow a stain on the ground.

"You *have* been rather a hermit these days, now that I think of it," Ying-Ying said. "Will you do more with the newspaper?"

But the last thing Lian wanted was more opportunity to rub shoulders with Jenmei. She couldn't bear to watch her draw Meirong further into the Communist Students Club or endure the sight of Jenmei with Shao.

"I was thinking I'd volunteer for Professor Kang," she said. "He needs help with the Library of Legends." The library was always busy. If she spent time there, Mr. Lee couldn't accuse her of being solitary. Not for the next little while.

CHAPTER 14

Lian used a wide, soft brush to dust off the book's cover. *Tales of Enlightened Mortals Who Became Immortal.* She turned carefully to the first page. The students had temporarily handed in the Legends they'd been carrying so that volunteers could inspect every page for damage. At some point the entire Library of Legends would have to be stored in a safe place. Professor Kang had taken advantage of their long stay to order boxes from the coffin maker in Zhongmiao Village. Built to exact measurements, they'd be strong, nearly airtight, and easy to stack.

"Miss Hu," Professor Kang called from the other end of the long worktable. He beckoned her over.

"About your term paper," he said. "There's something you should see in the caves above Huilong Nunnery."

"Why, what's in the caves, Professor?" she said.

"There are some Ming Dynasty murals that tell the story of the Willow Star," he said. "Sparrow says she's interested so you can go together, if you like."

"But what about you, sir?" she said. "Won't you come with us?"

"I understand it's a steep climb," he said, "otherwise I'd love to see them. Perhaps you could make some sketches to show me."

An opportunity to see ancient wall paintings. A chance to get away from the campus for a day. Away from Shao and Jenmei. And Mr. Lee.

AFTER A NIGHT of rain, the air was still and the skies clear. An hour of walking took Lian and Sparrow off the main road onto a quiet trail that led up a hill, layers of pine needles soft underfoot. Openings between the trees gave them glimpses of Chaohu Lake, its green water and the pale sandy crescent moon of shoreline beside Zhongmiao Village. Lian breathed in the bracing resinous scent of pine, free of anxiety for the first time in days.

A plain brick wall and open wooden gates marked the nunnery's entrance. The pebbled path beyond the gates was tidy, swept meticulously clean of pine needles. A nun in dove-gray robes put down her broom when she saw Lian and Sparrow. Head shaven and smooth-skinned, it was hard to tell her age, but when she smiled her greeting, Lian thought the nun might've been nineteen or twenty.

"We've come to see the Willow Star murals," Sparrow said.

The nun pointed to a bench by the wall to indicate that they should sit, then vanished up the pebbled path. Fifteen minutes later, an older nun came out. She was lean and wiry, her face a withered oval, her plain gray gown stained at the hems. One veined hand carried a covered bowl. She looked them over, her eyes resting speculatively on Sparrow.

"It's a steep walk," she warned, pointing at a narrow track leading away from the nunnery gates. "Twenty minutes to get up there. The cave is also a temple. We ask for donations."

Lian dug into her rucksack but Sparrow stopped her. "Professor Kang gave me money," she said and handed the nun a silver coin.

Lian and Sparrow followed the old woman up the hill, a steep ascent as warned. The track would've been wide enough for two had the shrubs and trees on either side been trimmed. They walked beneath rhododendron and pine, stout trunks of loquat and slender canes of bamboo. Yellow poplar leaves lay scattered on the path in front of them like gold coins. They brushed against branches still dripping with last night's rain and soon their hair and shoulders were damp.

Then the air-raid siren sounded.

"The trees are too dense up here," Lian said, heart pounding. "We can't see the beacons. We won't know if the bombers are really coming."

"We're safer here than in the village below," the old nun called back with a dismissive wave of her hand. "They're not interested in a small place like Zhongmiao, anyway, not when Hefei is so close."

"Keep walking, Miss Hu," Sparrow said. "There's nothing else we can do."

Lian tried to peer through the canopy of trees as she walked. Aircraft roared overhead and branches rattled as though a storm had rolled in. The nun set a brisk pace and was already far ahead; she hadn't even bothered to pause when the airplanes flew by. She probably walked this steep trail every day.

The path ended at a small clearing. The limestone cave's opening had been widened to a rounded arch, protected by a shallow portico roofed with orange tiles. The glazed tiles were barely visible, covered in moss and smothered beneath a tangle of the same vines that draped the cliffs above. Ducking her head as she entered, Lian found herself inside a high domed cavern.

There was an altar table in front of a narrow recess in the rock wall. There in the niche, lit by a pair of oil lamps, a statue greeted Lian's gaze with a sneer. The Goddess of Mercy's features were as bland as rainwater, but some of the gilt on the statue's upper lip had flaked away, just enough to twist the benevolent smile.

The nun placed her bowl on the altar and lit a handful of incense sticks. Then she knelt on a cushioned stool to pray, silently rocking back and forth. A ginger cat came out of the darkness to settle with a supervisory air on the stool. A shadow twitched in the corner but the cat didn't pay any attention to the small rat crouched there.

Prayers finished, the nun stood up. She gave the cat a scratch between the ears before putting the bowl on the ground and taking off its lid. The cat jumped off its stool and began to eat with dainty bites. The rat came out of its corner and dipped its head into the bowl. The nun chuckled in delight, pointing at the animals to make sure Lian and Sparrow noticed the two creatures, sharing a meal side by side. She lit a pair of oil lamps and gave them one each. She beckoned and they followed her to the entrance of a passageway.

"Keep your hand on this rope and you won't get lost," she said, pointing.

Two ropes were tied to a metal ring attached to the wall. One was thick and braided, the other thinner and twisted. The nun put a hand on the thinner rope and pointed again to make sure Lian knew which one to take. She started down the passageway and Lian followed, keeping her hand on the rope, which was strung through a series of metal rings. Soon the only sounds were the nun's tuneless, repetitive humming and the shuffle of their feet as they moved deeper into the caves. At one point the passage forked and the thin rope ended, tied off on a spike, while the heavy one continued around the corner. On the other side of the fork, another metal ring held the next length of thin rope and they followed it down the second tunnel.

They emerged into an oblong chamber, its ceiling too high for the small oil lamps to illuminate.

"The Willow Star and the Prince!" the nun announced, swinging her arm in a wide arc. "Look, look at the paintings!"

Lian lifted her lamp. The curved limestone walls had been whitewashed to provide a background for the murals. A series of paintings, each inside a black-lined border, covered the longest wall of the cavern. Even in the dim light and from several feet away, Lian could see how rough they were, the figures crude and stiff, the colors tawdry. She stepped closer and it was obvious that the outlines of older images had been traced over inexpertly with a thick brush, the shapes filled in with solid colors, no shading or highlights.

Some of the background had been spared, however. Lian moved along the wall and found faint details. A delicate clump of irises and gentian, a pair of waterfowl standing atop a rock. The original artist had taken clever advantage of the uneven rock surface so that a goose's body jutted out while its neck and head pulled back in surprise. A horse's muscular haunches bulged and a rabbit peeked out from a hole in the limestone.

"These are not the originals," Sparrow said, turning to the nun. "When were they painted over?"

The nun looked offended. "The paintings are renewed when-

ever we can afford an artist. Anyway, the pictures aren't important, it's the story that matters."

Sparrow smiled. "You're right. It's more important that the
legend survives. We thank you for its preservation."

There was a sweet, melodious quality to her voice when she
said this and Lian saw the nun's eyes widen. Lamplight played
across her elderly features, which softened as though she were a
girl again.

"The murals are from the later decades of the Ming Dynasty,"
the nun said, her expression neutral once more as she addressed
Lian, "but they say the story of the Willow Star is from before the
Tang Dynasty, so the legend itself could be a thousand years old."

The nun took Sparrow's lamp and walked over to the first
panel of the mural. The light revealed the outlines of a lake. Beside
the lake, a horse paws at the ground, its reins loose. Feet planted in
his stirrups, the horse's rider stands, a young man with his mouth
open in admiration. His eyes are fixed on a girl bathing under the
shade of a willow. Her nakedness is hidden by the tree's flowing
branches, her hair elaborately dressed with ornaments of stars.

"You can see why she's called the Willow Star," the nun said.
"This is their first meeting." She gestured farther along the wall
at another panel where the Prince and the Willow Star sit in a
garden pavilion, a chessboard between them. The nun moved to
another panel where the Prince kneels on the ground, the execu-
tioner's sword about to touch his neck. In the next panel, the Willow Star is prostrate before the Queen Mother of Heaven, whose
hand points at the Wheel of Rebirth.

"Here the Star is deciding whether or not to take the Queen
Mother's offer," the nun said. "All mortals must drink the Tea of
Forgetfulness between reincarnations to erase memories of their

previous lives. So it's impossible for the Prince to remember her, yet the Star accepts the offer so that she can be with her Prince during each of his lives. Her love is eternal and unconditional."

She moved along to the next mural, the colors brighter, painted by a different hand.

"Now this painting is only two hundred years old, added during the Qing Dynasty," the nun said. "The Willow Star and the Prince during one of his reincarnations."

"This isn't mentioned in the Legends," Lian exclaimed. She set her lamp down on the cave floor and pulled a notebook out of her rucksack. "The story in the book ends by saying that the Willow Star hasn't succeeded yet in getting the Prince to remember. There wasn't any mention of what happened during their reincarnations."

Two young women are pictured running through the streets of a town. It's raining heavily and they appear to be following a red lantern that hangs in the air, leading the way. One woman is richly dressed, the other wears more simple clothing, but stars are woven into the long braid that hangs down her back. There are three lines inscribed beside the mural.

> In this reincarnation they are born into the same wealthy household, the Prince a cherished daughter, the Willow Star her maidservant. The Prince escapes an unhappy marriage with help from the Willow Star. Mistress and maid grow old together.

"Oh, this is a real find," Lian said, pencil scribbling rapidly across her notebook. "It's so tantalizing and so frustrating not to have more. Do you know any other tales of the Willow Star and the Prince?"

"I only know what's here," the nun said. "Stay and look at the paintings as long as you like." She handed the lamp back to Sparrow and caught hold of the thin rope. Soon there was only the shuffle of her cloth shoes fading into the passageway.

"I promised to sketch the murals for Professor Kang," Lian said. "The lamps should be good for another hour, shouldn't they?"

"I'll let you know when we need to leave, Miss Hu," Sparrow said. "And I'll hold up the lamps for you."

"It makes me want to cry when I think how many stories have been lost from not being written down," Lian said, pulling a sheet of plain paper from her rucksack.

"But tales alter over time, anyway," Sparrow said. "In the marketplace or their own homes, storytellers shape narratives to suit their audience and the times. They add and remove details, even change the moral of the story. Yet each version is authentic."

"Sparrow, that's astonishing." Lian looked up. "You could research and write an entire thesis on that subject."

A peal of laughter, and lamplight wobbled. "Too much work," Sparrow said.

"The Willow Star made a bad bargain," Lian said, turning back to her sketching. "Why did she ever agree to such impossible conditions?"

"She was only a maidservant negotiating with the Queen Mother of Heaven," Sparrow said. "Perhaps she believed her love was strong enough to overcome impossible conditions."

"And she's been enduring life after life for a thousand years," Lian said.

"But she's immortal," Sparrow said. "Maybe immortals feel the passage of time differently than we do. Maybe a hundred years to her is only the blink of an eye, a single beat of the heart."

"But still, it can't be easy," Lian said. "She's at the Prince's side through all his lives, watching him grow up, marry, raise children. Watching him fall in love with mortals."

There was a long silence. "I like to think," Sparrow said, "that while the Willow Star is on Earth, the Prince can't fall in love with anyone."

"The poor Willow Star," Lian murmured, finishing her sketch of the last mural.

"But she has hope. And therefore persistence," Sparrow said. "The persistence of water, no matter how small a trickle, eventually wears a path through rock. And eternity is more porous than rock."

They walked back along the path, the scent of leaf mold rising up as their footsteps disturbed the ground. Lian peered through the shrubs for a view of the fishing village and to her relief the village's one main road looked peaceful, the houses intact. There was no sign that enemy aircraft had done anything more than fly over. Zhongmiao's small fleet of fishing boats was sailing back to shore. A strong wind had come up and gusts rippled the lake's green surface.

Impulsively, Lian grasped Sparrow's hand. "Thank you so much for coming with me to the caves. I'm glad we got to know each other better."

Sparrow squeezed her hand in return. "I'm glad too," she said. "I'd like to think of us as friends."

LIAN FELL ASLEEP almost immediately that night. When she dreamed, it was of stone-paved streets in a strange city, rain streaming from roof gutters, storefronts shuttered against the storm. Windbeaten branches tapped against whitewashed walls and there were no streetlights anywhere. Two women with cloaks thrown over their heads were hurrying through the rain. Their gowns were in an ancient style. She followed them as they ran along streets and over bridges until, finally, they reached a neighborhood of high walls and imposing gates. The two women stopped at the entrance to a grand mansion, a set of double doors lit by a large red lantern that hung from the roof of a shallow portico. As if she sensed Lian's presence, one of the women paused and turned around.

And even though what Lian saw were the figures of two women standing in the rain, she knew one of them was actually the Prince. And that the Prince was Shao. The other woman, the one who had turned around, shone like a sliver of crescent moon. It was Sparrow Chen.

"I'd like to think of us as friends," she said, looking straight at Lian. Then the two women vanished through the doors.

CHAPTER 15

Food was something the students talked about constantly, especially while eating their meager, unimaginative meals. Some mixed large spoonsful of chili sauce in their rice and noodles just to have something tasty. Cook Tam had been hired just before Minghua 123 left Nanking and many of the students doubted his credentials. Others, more forgiving, pointed out the kitchen didn't have much to work with. They complained, but knew they were lucky to have anything to eat at all. They were especially lucky that Zhongmiao was a fishing village, so Cook Tam was able to serve fresh fish every week. But they still couldn't help reminiscing about their favorite dishes.

"Roast pork with crispy skin," Shorty Ho said, looking down glumly at the salty boiled peanuts sprinkled over his rice. They ate lunch standing around the dining tables since all their chairs and benches furnished the library. "River shrimp fried with scallions. My mother's sticky-sweet Eight Treasure Rice Pudding."

"Chicken cooked with chestnuts in a honey-soy sauce," said another. "Salt-and-pepper eel. Or just a fried egg."

Shao longed for many foods now, but more than anything else he craved fresh fruit. Oranges especially, the sweet juicy segments and fragrant peel. At New Year's, his grandmother would give out oranges to all the children. But they weren't allowed to eat them until she had taken out her ivory-handled knife and sliced each one into eight segments. When she handed Shao his cut orange she would say, "Here, have a duck, have a duck!" Then the old lady and the boy would giggle together in delight at this private joke because he had once confided to her he thought oranges more delicious than roast duck.

The other thing Shao missed was the news. He had never done without a daily newspaper. But Zhongmiao was just a small fishing village, a place where few could read. News arrived by word of mouth, more rumor than news by the time they heard. For Minghua 123 this was unacceptable, so Old Fan, one of their laborers, made the four-hour walk to Hefei every other day. He left in the morning and returned late in the afternoon with a bundle of newspapers. Sometimes Cook Tam went along to replenish their supplies. On such occasions they would take a handbarrow, Old Fan pushing, Cook Tam riding in comfort. Sometimes the cook sent his assistant, a scrawny young man nicknamed "Bantien," which meant "Half the Day," because the cook complained it took half the day for the assistant to achieve anything.

Shao could always tell by the number of students loitering in the yard whether it was time for Old Fan to return from Hefei. When he appeared at the factory gates, the large man was always besieged by students eager to snatch a look at the headlines, entreaties to let them see the front page before he delivered the papers.

"It's your professors who pay for these newspapers, Young Masters," he would say, swatting them away. "You can read the news when the professors are finished."

But on this afternoon, when Old Fan and Bantien walked through the yard, both were untypically silent. Old Fan gave a copy of *Xinwen Bao* to Chen Ping, the first student who stopped him. Chen Ping unfolded the newspaper and cried out in dismay.

"Shanghai has fallen!"

The shout brought students running. The battle for Shanghai had dominated front pages since August. The Battle of Jiangyin to prevent Japanese warships from moving up the Yangtze River. The Battle of Luodian, a suburb of strategic importance. The heroic, doomed defense of Sihang warehouse, which the government had hoped would spur support from Western allies.

And now the November 8 issue of *Xinwen Bao* reported that the army's central command had given the order for a general retreat from Shanghai. Chen Ping read the front page out loud to a circle of grim faces. When Chen Ping handed out pages of the newspaper, Shao took the middle section, searching the columns until he found the editor in chief's essay, his father's words.

Outside the International Settlement, streets are cratered and buildings leveled. Japanese sentries patrol empty neighborhoods, their soldiers looting among the ruins. Inside the Settlement, an estimated 500,000 displaced persons have taken refuge, filling camps and hospitals. There are also refugees who have not been counted, the ones being housed and fed by relatives. It's common for twenty people to squeeze into rooms meant for a family of six.

Foreigners who once belittled the Chinese family system as feudal and nepotistic are now thankful our tradition of duty to family has prevented worst-case scenarios. We hope they now understand our resilience as a people and a nation. China is worth supporting. China is worth more than words of sympathy. China needs her allies to take action.

A muted atmosphere settled over the factory campus in the wake of losing Shanghai. Shao leaned against the back wall of a bunkhouse. In the yard, students drifted together in small, subdued groups to huddle over the newspapers. Some of the female students were weeping.

"I knew Shanghai might fall, I just didn't believe it actually would." Jenmei came to stand beside Shao. She leaned her head on his shoulder. Shao hoped everyone was too preoccupied to notice. "Your family should be safe, though; they live inside the International Settlement."

"Yes, we do," he said. "But my father goes in and out of the Settlement on business quite often to see the situation for himself. It's a constant worry to my mother."

Jenmei patted his arm, her eyes sympathetic, her full lips curved in a soft smile. Then she slipped her hand into his. Just as gently he pulled his hand away from hers.

"Jenmei," he said, keeping his voice low, casual. "I've been thinking."

"You've been avoiding me for days, Shao," she said. Her smile twisted, became slightly mocking. "Don't feel embarrassed about what happened between us. I don't hold myself to bourgeois notions of romance and neither should you. It was just an expression of physical desire. We shared a kiss or two, nothing more."

But there had been more. The smooth curve of her body from

neck to back, the hollows at the base of her throat. The insistent pressure of her arms. Yet even as he listened to her murmured endearments, he'd felt detached. He'd sat up, moved away. And she had taken his refusal as a gesture of chivalry, that her virtue mattered to him. That she mattered to him.

There were only twenty girls in Minghua 123, a ratio so lop-sided hardly any of them lacked admirers. But the romances were innocent, the girls treated with utmost deference. They were fellow scholars, young women from good families. Shorty Ho, who had developed a huge crush on Ying-Ying, would never think to lay a finger on her, never do anything to harm her reputation. Instead, he sent her poetry. All of it his own, all of it terrible.

"Alas, I can't help my bourgeois notions," Shao said, trying to keep his tone light. "You're a classmate and deserve my respect. I apologize. I won't let it happen again."

"Well, don't let this keep you from attending meetings," Jenmei said. Her smile grew brighter even as her eyes narrowed. "It gives the younger ones confidence to see a senior student there."

"I'm sorry, Jenmei," he said, shaking his head. "It's not what I'm looking for."

"What are you looking for then?" Her smile was too wide. "Have you found it with your little maid? A servant who doesn't deserve respect? Or that timid little Hu Lian, always hiding away from others?"

"Sparrow is a friend, a member of my household," he said, both angry and astonished that she would bring a servant into the discussion. "And Lian is a friend. I don't understand you."

"No, apparently not," and she sauntered away, tossing her hair so that it fanned out in the wind before settling again on her shoulders.

AFTER THE FALL of Shanghai, the school newspaper received a flood of submissions ranging from fiery, patriotic opinion pieces to wistful memoirs of favorite spots in the city. Even Shorty Ho dropped off two pages of heartfelt prose. Meirong spent long hours sifting through the pile and handing out stories for volunteers to copy.

"You're spending too much time on this newspaper," Lian said. "You do too much."

"Oh, Lian, you can say it," Meirong said. She squinted over a submission. "You think I follow Jenmei blindly. But there's lots of debate at our meetings, we all ask questions."

"Communism is officially forbidden by the government," Lian said. "What if Minghua decides to actually enforce the rules?"

"Our professors are very tolerant," Meirong said. "Anyway, the worst thing they could do is expel us. Or send us to a camp for reeducation."

Lian sat beside Meirong and Ying-Ying for a few minutes. When more students entered the newspaper office, she got up quietly to make her way next door to the courtyard house. She couldn't be part of it anymore, the cheerful teasing, the sharing of confidences. Not when she worried that Mr. Lee might expand her spying activities. Not when just a glimpse of Shao or Jenmei brought a hot flush to her cheeks.

Outside the factory's front gate, campfires burned against the brick wall. When travelers saw the handmade sign for Minghua University, many came in to beg for shelter. Even after some of the students reported cash and small items being stolen, Professor Kang still allowed travelers to camp inside the walls, but with added precautions. Two of the laborers stood guard on Scholars' Lane while two more watched the gate.

Lian walked past bands of travelers cooking their meals on charcoal braziers. The flickering glow cast cruel shadows on gaunt faces. She felt suddenly and irrationally fearful. She turned her eyes away as she hurried past and breathed a quiet sigh of relief when she reached the double doors of the courtyard house. The old gatekeeper who used to work for the factory owner bobbed his head at her and returned to his pipe.

The sound of conversation from the courtyard made her pause. She'd hoped for a bit of solitude. There were people in the courtyard garden, screened from her view by shrubs of rhododendron and tall bamboos. Lian moved quietly along the brick walkway that bordered the courtyard, then stopped when she recognized the speaker's confident tones.

"The meetings aren't just for students, you know," Jenmei said. "If anything, it's working-class folks like you who need to learn about the rights you'd have in a socialist country."

She sounded harsh, almost accusing. It wasn't the persuasive, playful voice Jenmei normally used when coaxing people. Lian stayed out of sight, backing into the corner of the courtyard, a dark shadowed space between two houses. She peered out from behind the wall but still couldn't see past the bamboo.

"Thank you, Miss Wang, but it's not for me." A second voice, clear and lilting. Sparrow.

"Your young master attends these meetings," Jenmei said. "I thought you followed him everywhere. You followed him from Shanghai to Nanking. And now on this trek across China."

"I've no interest in politics, Miss Wang," Sparrow said. "Please excuse me, I have duties."

"Wait, Sparrow, wait," Jenmei said. "You know him better than anyone. How can I win him to our cause?" The plaintiveness of her voice, so different from a moment ago, made Lian think Jenmei didn't really mean the Communist cause.

There followed a long pause. "He's searching for something you can't give him, Miss Wang," Sparrow said.

"And what is that something?" Jenmei said, her voice bitter.

"Do you give it to him? Besides washing and mending his clothes, what else do you do for him?"

The sound of a slap. And then a gasp, a shocked intake of breath.

Lian shrank deeper into the shadows, heart pounding. Jenmei ran from the garden, wiping a sleeve across her eyes. At the brick path, she paused to straighten up, then strode into the forecourt, self-assurance in the swing of her hips. She called out to the gatekeeper, a cheerful greeting. No one could have imagined she'd been in tears a moment ago.

In the courtyard garden, behind the shrubbery, light moved. Sparrow, holding a lamp. The glow vanished in the direction of the laundry room, and Lian's heartbeat slowed to a normal pace. So much of what she'd overheard worried her. Jenmei had been angry at Sparrow, hostile and accusing.

But of more immediate concern, Jenmei had said Shao was attending meetings. In a place as confined as the factory campus, how could Mr. Lee not know this already? Was he testing Lian, waiting to see how long it would take for her to report this?

Unbidden, her mind conjured their figures in the bunkhouse again. Candlelight caressing bodies. Lips touching.

MR. LEE HAD TAKEN to dropping by the newspaper office every day. Although the students working on the paper were pleased he was so interested in *Minghua 123 News*, Lian knew his visits were to check on her. One day, as soon as she moved away from the table to leave, so did he, nodding at the student he had been chatting with, giving another a friendly slap on the back. He followed her out the door, staying a few feet behind until they were near the center of the yard, no one close by.

"I'm glad you took my suggestion of spending more time with

the school newspaper," Mr. Lee said. "That makes it easier for you to keep an eye on things. And are you? Keeping an eye on things?"

"Yes, I am," she said, still unsure of what to do. He turned toward the bunkhouses.

"Mr. Lee, wait," she said, and he stopped to let her catch up. "What happens to Shao if he gets involved with the Communist Students Club?"

"Nothing. His family's too important." His voice was kind. "We would take Wang Jenmei out of school, that's all. She's the bad influence, not Liu Shaoming."

"Would she go to one of those reeducation camps?" she said.

"Perhaps," he said, his eyes intent. "Is there something you want to tell me?"

"Liu Shaoming has been attending her meetings," she said. Her words came out in a rush. "I wasn't sure until last night. And I don't know how often he's been."

Not waiting to hear his response she hurried to the library warehouse, books clutched tightly to her chest. She'd done it, but there was nothing to worry about. Shao's father ran one of Shanghai's biggest newspapers, his family owned banks and ships. They were the confidants of top government ministers. Nothing would happen to Shao. But Jenmei might be expelled. The meetings would stop and there wouldn't be any more spying to do.

And there wouldn't be any more trysts by candlelight.

"WE ALL KNOW what the Nationalists want for China," Chen Ping said. "But maybe I should hear some other points of view directly. Not through a newspaper politically biased toward the government. How can I defend or denounce either position without knowing the facts?"

Shao knew Ping's interest in politics was purely academic, but he didn't want his friends to have more to do with Jenmei than necessary. She'd intrigued him at first, her strong will, her confidence. She brimmed with purpose. Lacking any of his own, he'd envied her convictions.

Her attentions had not gone unnoticed by his friends.

"She's been waiting a long time for you to get within striking distance," Shorty said. "Lucky for you I'm not taller. I know she'd find me irresistible."

Jenmei had become more outspoken, recruiting students and even servants. Although she promised members anonymity outside the Communist Students Club, Jenmei was using the fact that Shao had attended a couple of meetings to induce others to join. He didn't like that. When he'd distanced himself from her, Shao hadn't thought she'd be the sort whose feelings were easily hurt. He should've seen through her façade. He should've listened to Sparrow's warnings.

"Don't waste your time, Ping," Shao said. "Not tonight at least. We need to get ready for the morning." Their time at the factory campus had come to an end. They were leaving Zhongmiao Village the next day.

Shao packed all but the few items he would need in the morning. He climbed into bed by the dim light of the one lamp that still burned inside the bunkhouse. Most of his dormmates were already under the covers, getting in as much rest as they could before the long walk. The students couldn't wait to get to a larger city. They were desperate for mail from home, and not just because they needed to know their families were safe. Out of touch, unable to draw on bank accounts, they were running low on cash and Shao was no different. He had lent a great deal of money to his classmates, never expecting to be paid back. He'd heard that professors were emptying their own wallets, giving Cook Tam money to buy food for Minghua 123.

He turned over and closed his eyes. He had to sleep. They would leave at first light.

BUT MINGHUA 123 did not leave at first light.

Instead there was shouting and commotion, fishermen from the village clamoring at the factory gates. The disturbance spread to the courtyard houses, where servants knocked on professors' doors and called out in urgent hushed voices. Lian and Meirong threw on their clothes and ran out to the courtyard.

"Stay here," one of the professors said, hurrying past, ashen faced. "Tell everyone to stay here. Do not leave the premises."

But if the professors wanted to keep rumors at bay, it was a forlorn hope. The servants who opened the gates already knew why the fishermen had come running up from the lakeshore and the news soon spread. A student had been found dead at the edge of the lake. Drowned. The factory yard filled with anxious young men and women. They scanned the factory campus to look for their closest friends, reassure themselves.

The murmurs in the yard began to echo one name.

The faculty members and Mr. Lee returned, a somber parade. At any other time, it would've been a comical sight, the normally dignified academics in various stages of dress. Professor Zhang wasn't wearing his socks and bare, bony ankles showed above his shoes. Professor Song's head was still covered with the round crocheted cap he wore to flatten his hair while he slept.

Without being told, the students gathered closer. There was no need to call for silence. Professor Kang cleared his throat.

"There's no easy way to break the news," he said. "The fishermen found a student drowned in the lake. We've identified her as Wang Jenmei."

He waited for the cries and gasps to die down. "Mr. Lee and I are going to Hefei to get the police."

A shocked silence. Then the air began rustling with whispered speculations. And something else. Fear. But only after the donkey cart took Professor Kang and Mr. Lee out of the factory gates did the whispers rise to a fever pitch of noise.

Drowned, the fishermen said, her head held underwater.

Murdered for her politics. It must've been the Nationalists.

The villagers brought her body to the coffin maker's shop.

Like everyone else, Jenmei's roommates had been busy packing the night before and gone to bed early. She often returned late and they assumed she was at a meeting. They didn't wait up.

Lian backed away from the crowd and leaned against the wall of the library warehouse. All of Minghua 123 was milling about in the yard. She caught sight of Shao at the far side of the crowd with his friends, his face grim. Meirong was sobbing, her face pressed against Ying-Ying's shoulder.

Anyone who saw Lian would think she had tucked her hands inside her sleeves to keep warm. But she did it to hide their trembling. Had her words condemned Jenmei? Was this a warning to students? Was this all it took to pronounce a young woman's death sentence? Suddenly, she wasn't so sure anymore that Shao's family, their wealth and connections, would keep him safe. She wanted to ask Mr. Lee what had happened. But she knew she would never muster the courage.

Just the thought of speaking to Mr. Lee made her choke. He had lied, said Jenmei would only be expelled, perhaps sent to a reeducation camp. Had he been the one who killed Jenmei? Lian ran behind the library warehouse. One hand pressed against the wooden planked walls, she vomited, trying to disgorge her fear with every heave. But even as she retched, she knew Jenmei's death would never relinquish its hold on her. All she managed to empty onto the hard soil was last night's supper and none of her guilt.

Lian straightened up, caught her breath. She had to behave as normally as possible for the next little while. It wouldn't be difficult, it was all right for her to appear nervous and shocked. Frightened, even, because everyone was distressed.

She returned to her room at the courtyard house, where several other girls were already sitting on their beds talking. Meirong sat with her arms wrapped around her knees, silently crying. Lian wanted to put her arm around Meirong, say something comforting, but she couldn't. Whatever she said would come out stiff and stilted.

"Why does this feel so awful?" Ying-Ying said, her hands twisting a grubby handkerchief. "I didn't know Jenmei that well. I knew Mr. Shen better because I went to his tutorials. But I wasn't this upset when Mr. Shen died."

"It's because she wasn't killed during a Japanese air raid," Meirong said tonelessly, "or from any of the risks we've faced together during our evacuation. She was murdered."

Murdered. Lian clenched her fists to hide their trembling. Jenmei was dead and it was her fault.

CHAPTER 16

All the books and chalkboards had been packed up, but the faculty did their best anyway to give the students a day of classes while waiting for Professor Kang and Mr. Lee to come back from Hefei. They lectured from memory, organized discussion groups, and assigned short essays. Anything was better than idle time, time for talk that inflamed fear and speculation. For the next several hours, the routine of an ordinary school day dulled the horror of Wang Jenmei's murder.

In the late afternoon, the students rushed out to the yard, drawn out of their classes by the rattling vibrations of an engine in poor repair. A dusty black police car drove through the gates and two military policemen climbed out, followed by Mr. Lee and Professor Kang. From the sergeant's irritated demeanor,

Shao could tell he considered this trip to Zhongmiao Village highly inconvenient.

The sergeant made a tour of the campus with Mr. Lee and Professor Kang. He went to the courtyard house and the room where Jenmei had slept and came out with a bundle of papers and notebooks. Then they all climbed back into the black car and drove down to Chaohu Lake. Some of the students followed at a run, trailed at a more sedate pace by a servant driving one of the donkey carts. Fishermen helped lift Jenmei's covered body onto the cart, which then set out for Hefei. Professor Kang rode back to Hefei in the police car and Mr. Lee stayed behind.

From start to finish, the policemen's visit had taken less than an hour.

Cook Tam and his assistant unpacked some equipment from the kitchen wagon and made an unusually substantial meal, fresh lake fish steamed with ginger and soy sauce, plenty of rice, and pickled vegetables. Students scraped leftovers into tin lunch boxes for the next day, not trusting they'd have time to eat on the road.

"The police sergeant yelled at the coffin maker," Shorty said, over a second helping of rice. "He was angry they had brought the body into the shop instead of leaving it by the lake. Disturbing the crime scene, he called it."

Already they were referring to Jenmei as "the body."

"The fishermen were being kind," Chen Ping said. "They didn't want to leave her just lying there."

"The sergeant kept complaining it was pointless and a waste of time to investigate since the body had been moved," Shorty said. "But I got the feeling he was glad of an excuse."

Shao cupped his hands around a mug of tea. He hadn't trooped down to the lake with the others. Jenmei was dead. Murdered. It was horrible. He felt ashamed of the rush of relief, the moment of lightness he'd felt when he first realized he would never have to face her again. Her knowing smile, the proprietary way she put her hand on his arm. Her determination to lay claim to him, mind, body, and ideology.

"The villagers asked Professor Kang to pay for a priest to exorcise the spot where Jenmei was found," Shorty said. "They're afraid her drowned ghost will haunt their waterfront."

"I don't believe in spirits," Shao said. "But I'm sure the professor will do it to make them feel better."

"The professor will do it," Chen Ping said seriously, "because he doesn't want Jenmei's ghost to wander the lakeshore for eternity."

AFTER DINNER, THE students assembled in the former library warehouse. Mr. Lee's jovial smile was missing. To Lian's eyes, he seemed genuinely distraught. Most of the girls were in a huddle at the center of the space, holding on to one another. She stood behind them, wary of what Mr. Lee might say, not wanting to catch his eye. She looked around for Shao and found him at the very front of the gathering.

"Professor Kang is staying overnight in Hefei," the director of student services said, "where he's arranging for Wang Jenmei's burial. He must deal with some officials and contact her family. What I want you to know is that our plans haven't changed, only delayed by a day. Unpack only what you need to use tonight. We leave for Lu'an tomorrow as soon as the professor returns."

"Sir," one of the senior students called out, "what about the investigation into Jenmei's murder? What will the police do?"

Mr. Lee shook his head. "There won't be an investigation. We're at war with both Japan and the Communist Party of China."

He didn't need to say more. Jenmei had been an outspoken Communist. The military police had no incentive to look into her murder. Whoever killed Jenmei had nothing to fear. It might've been Mr. Lee, it might've been an outsider. It could even have been some other member of Minghua 123. But they would not be apprehended. They could do anything. To Jenmei, to Shao. To her.

The students dawdled, delayed going back to their rooms for the night.

"Do you think the murderer was one of the villagers?" one of the girls said.

"In such a small place?" Ying-Ying scoffed. "It must've been an outsider, a Nationalist agent who slipped in and out to do the deed. Think of all the refugees who've camped here."

Lian didn't mention the unthinkable. That the murderer might still be among them.

"Those military policemen hardly spent any time here," Meirong said, finally speaking. "The murder of a left-wing student hardly matters to them. What's the purpose of a university if we can't exchange ideas? If Jenmei was killed just for talking about her beliefs, they might as well kill us all."

"Please, Meirong," Lian said, looking around. "Don't say such things."

"I won't let this affect the newspaper," Meirong said. "*Minghua 123 News* is Wang Jenmei's legacy. Lian, can you put in more time?"

"Of course," Lian said. Not because she wanted to, but at a time like this, how could she refuse Meirong?

She left the warehouse with her classmates and crossed the yard to return to the courtyard house. There was no doubt in anyone's mind that Jenmei had been killed for her politics. The murder was a knife stab of a reminder—as if they needed reminding—that China wasn't just at war with the Japanese, but also fighting a civil war.

Lian's eyes were drawn to the entrance of the dining hall where Mr. Lee stood, surveying the yard. Cook Tam emerged from the kitchen and joined him. They spoke, their heads close together. As she turned back to her friends Lian felt, rather than saw, the two men gaze in her direction.

CHAPTER 17

Minghua 123 were on the road again by midmorning. Every so often they heard the buzz of aircraft but, mercifully, always from far away. The Japanese weren't interested in Hefei at the moment and Minghua 123 was taking advantage of it. Walking in daylight was much faster and they had to make up for lost time. They were glad not to be traveling at night when the air was colder, the wind even sharper. It was a quiet exodus as the students trudged their way west, skirting the southern edge of Hefei.

They lodged in the buildings of a small Buddhist temple, its halls barely large enough to hold all of Minghua 123, let alone the other refugees sheltering there. The students had a long five days of walking ahead of them but no one cared. They just wanted to leave Jen-mei's murder behind.

PROFESSOR KANG CLIMBED the low rise of a path on a small hill beside the temple. A three-quarters moon cast its light on the road below. The path led him to a lookout point with a stone bench, put there for admiring the view. A granite stele stood beside it. The stele was inscribed with a date, fifteenth century. He ran the list of emperors through his head and placed it during the reign of the Yongle emperor. The professor sat on the bench and lit a cigarette, careful to hold it away from the book on his lap. *Tales of Fox Spirits, Volume 100.*

He thought of Wang Jenmei and Shen. Tallied up against the number who had died so far in this war, against the deaths to come before the war ended, they did not even merit footnotes in history. If Minghua University survived, the two students might find their way onto a commemorative list of students and faculty lost during the war. If someone took the time to write a narrative about the evacuation, succeeding generations might learn how they'd died, where and when.

But Jenmei and Shen were no longer his charge. What Professor Kang worried about now was how to avoid losing more members of Minghua 123. Hunger and fatigue were already taking their toll. Students caught colds and never got better. The students took their studies seriously, reading by the light of cheap oil lamps that smoked and irritated their eyes, so several had eye infections and would need attention when they reached a town with medical care. They were malnourished, another reason so many were prone to illness. Winter had set in and fresh vegetables were scarce. Professor Kang and his colleagues had given what money they had to Cook Tam for food. He hoped the government and their promises of cash would catch up to them in Wuhan, the next big city on their route.

Professor Kang waved a hand in greeting when he saw the Star, her lithe form glowing as she came up the path. The acrid scent of cheap tobacco wafted around the stone bench and she lifted one eyebrow. He wasn't smoking, just letting the ashes fall to the frozen ground.

"I tried to buy this, just one cigarette," he said, stubbing out the cigarette. "I met a man from Soochow on the road. He could tell by my accent I'm also from Soochow. When he learned I was a professor, he insisted on giving it to me. The smell reminds me of my rebellious youth, when I smoked mainly to annoy my grandparents."

She sat on the bench beside him. It was the first time they'd had alone since Wang Jenmei's death. Despite the glow that radiated from her, he could tell she was tired. He remembered how upset she'd been after Mr. Shen's death. How she had felt somehow responsible.

"This was murder," he said gently. "There was nothing you could've done. You've led our group to safety."

The Star nodded but didn't look much happier. The professor gestured at the expanse of fields below, bisected by a road that extended from east to west.

"Even the humblest of country temples somehow manage a good view," he said. "I'm not a greedy man but I confess to a certain pleasure at seeing the landscape from above, horizon to horizon. It makes me want to own it all, as far as I can see."

"Animals feel safer when they can sight predators from afar," the Star said. "Humans like high ground for the same reason. To see enemies coming from a great distance."

"And as the machines of war increase in speed and brutality we want to own more and more of that distance to keep them at bay," Professor Kang said. "May I ask how your . . . comrades are doing?"

"Word is spreading now," she said, "and most know it's time to leave. There's some resistance, of course, especially from the ones who've inhabited earthly forms for a long time."

"But they return to a paradise," the professor said. "Surely that must be a comfort."

"It's comfort of a sort," the Star said, "but what purpose will they have in that paradise? They've been guardians of rivers and lakes, forests and fields. Of a single tree or a humble hectare of land. Even if no more than a half-dozen farmers pray to them for a good harvest of beans, they've had a purpose."

Her brightness shone on the book of Legends. *Tales of Fox Spirits, Volume I.*

"I see you've been reading, Professor. It's not necessary to bring out the books anymore. The pages of the Library conjured up spirits, woke them up to begin the exodus. Now the exodus has gained momentum. Look, over there."

She pointed at the road below where a procession was coming into view. It was a vision of gaiety, the merrymakers holding red lanterns, banners fluttering from long poles. Every now and then, there was the snap and sparkle of firecrackers. The revelers carried cymbals and wooden clappers; they walked alongside musicians playing bamboo flutes.

The shadows they cast under moonlight were of foxes, bushy tailed and slender legged.

"Fox spirits," the Star said, "young ones. They can't just walk. It has to be a game. These spirits are dancing all the way to the Kunlun Mountains."

When he looked again, the dancing figures belied the parade's apparent festivity. He sensed melancholy beneath a determined effort at exuberance. Thin reedy notes floated up to his ears, a tune that spoke of loss and departure. The professor and the Star watched in silence until the cavalcade of young Foxes vanished behind the hills. Every now and then the professor thought he heard the faint clash of cymbals, until finally the landscape was silent once more.

"The only supernatural beings I've noticed leaving have been guardian spirits, benevolent immortals," the professor said. "May I ask, what about the other creatures described in the Library of Legends? The demons and ghosts, the evil spirits?"

"Death, suffering, and brutality run unchecked in this war," the Star said. "Why would they leave when the pleasures they enjoy are all right here?"

The professor sagged at the harsh truth of her words. They sat in silence for a while, then she touched him lightly on the sleeve.

"In all this time, you've never asked me," she said, "what happens after the Palace gates close."

"I'm guessing we'll be left to find our own way," Kang said, after a moment. "No matter how badly we do it."

"You guess correctly," the Star said. "When the Palace gates close, the gods and guardian spirits will leave your skies. The constellations will shine as before, but they will be just what your scientists say they are, flaming balls of gas and rock. People might continue to pray, but whatever boons or burdens follow will not come from the gods. They will be of your own making."

"If I may ask, what about you?" he asked. He could hold back no more. "Once the Library of Legends is stored away safely, will

CALGARY
PUBLIC
LIBRARY

Forest Lawn Library
Self Checkout
November,07,2020 11:20

39065155911504   2020-11-28
Adult paperback - Forest Lawn - 2019
39065155910407   2020-11-28
Adult paperback - Forest Lawn - 2019

Total   **2 item(s)**

You have 0 item(s) ready for pickup

To check your card and renew items

go to www.calgarylibrary.ca

or call 403-262-2928

you also go to the Kunlun Mountains? As you say, the Palace gates will close."

"I haven't decided yet," she said. "I've grown less certain since we began our journey, Professor. More attuned to the human passage of time. More affected by human emotions. I know the Prince will never remember me." She sounded very sad and very lost.

"Don't lose hope," he said. "Eternity is porous. How many times have I heard you say that?"

"But I don't have eternity anymore," she said quietly. "Now there's less than a year of your time before the Palace gates close. I must come to a decision."

NIGHT HAD FALLEN by the time Minghua 123 reached the town of Lu'an. The principal of Lu'an Middle School met them at the school gates, apologetic. There weren't enough billets for all the students and faculty.

"No problem, no problem," Mr. Lee said, "our senior professors can lodge with families. Everyone else can sleep in the assembly hall. We're used to camping."

But they didn't manage to sleep. Air-raid sirens woke them and the students scrambled for the school's shelter. They huddled there until the all clear sounded then returned to the assembly hall. Nothing else disturbed the night, but the students were too tense to rest.

The next day, sirens sounded as soon as the morning mists cleared. Their time in Lu'an extended from a day to several more. They couldn't go on the road, not while the town and its surrounding areas were under attack nearly every day. Minghua 123 remained in Lu'an Middle School's assembly hall. When attacks came, they shared the bomb shelter with the school's pupils and teachers, the ones who had dared come to classes that day. When air raids caught students out on the town, they ran to the public shelters, but these were so crowded and claustrophobic they made every effort to reach the school and its large bomb shelter. Professor Kang had the wooden crates holding the Legends brought there. It gave the students some comfort. The Library of Legends was their talisman, their lucky star.

Airplanes roared overhead, sometimes on their way to other targets, sometimes to drop bombs. And sometimes the aircraft flew by for one final pass to release propaganda leaflets, sheets that floated down like giant feathers. They landed in streets and courtyards, sometimes swirling in the hot currents above blazing buildings, drifting until heat scorched them into ash.

The air raids were short, usually lasting no more than an hour before the all clear sounded, but they felt ten times longer. The shelter's wooden buckets that were used as chamber pots filled quickly as nervous bladders emptied. Their stench permeated the shelter, uncomfortably warm from the heat of so many bodies.

AFTER WAITING OUT several raids, Lian could gauge how far away the bombs were by sound, the whistling noise as they fell through the air, and by the shudder of the shelter's ground and walls with each explosion. Some of the students studied, or at least pretended to, opening textbooks under the quivering light of a few dim bulbs strung across the ceiling. They took turns reading out loud from the Library of Legends to the boys of Lu'an Middle School. So far, the boys had heard from *Tales of the Horse Gods*, *Tales of Forest Spirits*, and *Tales of Magical and Benevolent Creatures*.

All of Minghua 123 joined the town's cleanup brigade. As soon as the all clear sounded, the male students helped put out fires and cleared the streets of wreckage. They helped homeowners salvage furniture and belongings. They searched for survivors, carried away the injured and the dead. The female students hurried across town to volunteer at the hospital.

Lian followed behind Meirong as they picked their way through debris-strewn streets, barely keeping up as her friend clambered over piles of rubble. If there was one good thing about being trapped in Lu'an, it was that they'd been so busy that Meirong hadn't had much time to mope. In helping others, she'd regained some of her liveliness.

Lian felt a hand on her back and turned to see Shao's smiling face, framed between a pair of chubby legs, a toddler riding on his shoulders.

"Is he hurt?" she said. "We're heading for the hospital."

"No, he's fine," he said, "but his father is busy putting out fires and asked me to take him to his mother. She works at the hospital."

"Would you like me to carry you?" Meirong asked, lifting her arms up. The child shook his head and clung to Shao.

"The residents of Lu'an used to joke about feeling left out of the war," Shao said. "They said they felt slighted because Japanese bombers never 'paid their respects' to the town."

"They must be feeling very honored now that the Japanese visit so often," Meirong said.

Shao laughed, which made the little boy laugh too. The child jiggled up and down. "That means he wants me to go faster," Shao said. "See you at the hospital."

Meirong grinned at Lian, looking for a moment like her mischievous self again. Lian shook her head at the insinuation and stuck her tongue out. She had vowed to stay aloof but while she did her best to keep her distance, she couldn't stop caring about her friend. She was responsible for Jenmei's death. And, therefore, Meirong's sorrow.

As for Shao, she wanted very much to know if he mourned Jenmei. What had Jenmei meant to him? Lian alternated between wanting to avoid his company and studying him surreptitiously for signs that might reveal his feelings.

From up the street, the little boy squealed with delight as Shao broke into a trot.

CHAPTER 18

The principal of Lu'an Middle School told Professor Kang about a nearby temple whose walls were decorated with a pair of calligraphy scrolls attributed to the Ming Dynasty artist Wen Zhengming. Whether or not the scrolls were really Wen Zhengming's work, the professor enjoyed chasing down such literary relics, so he made an outing of it. The laborer Old Fan, who had somehow attached himself to Professor Kang, insisted on going along. It was his duty to protect the professor, the stocky servant said.

The scrolls turned out to be a disappointment, the calligraphy as mediocre as the lines of verse. But the walk had been pleasant, the temple no more than an hour down the road from Lu'an.

"Either they were forgeries," Professor Kang said to Old Fan, "or Wen Zhengming was having a bad day."

But Old Fan's head was cocked, listening for the now-familiar sound rolling in from the eastern horizon. From the direction of Lu'an, air-raid sirens began their wail. Old Fan took the professor by the elbow, guided him quickly to the side of the road, then helped him down the embankment into the fields. A few scattered groups of people, farmers on their way back from the market in Lu'an, also slipped down the verge with practiced agility. The roar of airplane engines came closer and the two men settled into a ditch. The ground at the bottom of the trench was cold and hard, which Professor Kang deemed better than muddy and wet.

At first he thought they were the only ones in the ditch. Then he saw a small, motionless figure some twenty feet away. It looked like a child, a girl. The professor frowned. He began crawling along the trench but Old Fan tugged at his ankle.

"Please, Professor," he said. "Keep still until the planes have gone away."

So the professor remained beside Old Fan and pressed his back against the side of the trench, looking up as the planes passed overhead, going on to Lu'an. Then came the explosions. He sighed, thinking of the townspeople's terror, the destruction.

Then he heard another rumbling, which at first he thought was more planes. But there was something wild in that pounding. He squinted toward the horizon and blinked. A herd of horses thundered toward the field. The ground shook. They were larger than oxen, larger even than elephants, long maned with coats sleek as satin, hooves shining like polished brass. Every ripple of their strong haunches, every toss of their necks made him yearn to gallop with them, to feel the sheer joy of running. They were heading north. As the horses neared the ditch, the professor saw that some carried riders, the most beautiful men and women he'd ever seen. Riding bareback, dressed in bright silks, the Horse Gods' long hair flowed behind them like banners.

One of the Horse Gods stopped beside the child and leaned down, laughing. "Come with us, Little One," he said, holding out his hand. "Let's go for a ride."

The little girl sat up with a delighted smile and the Horse God swung her up in front of him. A moment later, the hoofbeats faded and all Professor Kang saw was an empty field. Beside him, Old Fan scanned the sky. He showed no signs of having seen anything unusual. He clambered out of the ditch.

"That was loud, but it didn't last too long," Old Fan said. "Shall I help you onto the road, sir?"

Professor Kang looked along the ditch. He'd seen the Horse God take the girl away, but the small body was still there, still lying in the ditch. He moved along the trench toward the little girl. She lay curled up on her side, one thumb in her mouth. He took the other hand and felt for a pulse but there was none. She was dead. Gently he put her hand back. Something pale and round rolled out from the curve of the frail body. A turnip.

"Old Fan," he called. "I need you to carry this girl to Lu'an with us. She deserves a burial even if we don't know her name."

"That's my sister." A child's voice. A bedraggled girl looked down into the trench at the professor, blank eyes in a gaunt face. "My little sister," she added, as if to clarify. She picked up the turnip and tucked it in her tunic.

"Where are your parents?" the professor asked.

She shook her head. He understood. Either they were dead, or they had left the two girls behind. Families started out bringing all their children. But after weeks of walking and running out of food, the weakest children died. Parents abandoned daughters so that sons could eat. Some, too exhausted to carry their children anymore, left behind the smallest ones who couldn't walk. There were always orphans at refugee camps, children picked up by kindly strangers or by workers from the camp. They were mostly girls, some still babies, starving and lice infested.

He would take her to the orphanage in Lu'an. Which was already overcrowded. There was nowhere else.

"Did you see horses?" he asked, unable to help himself. She just gazed at him with the same blank look and shook her head again.

They got back on the road to Lu'an, Old Fan carrying the dead child, Professor Kang holding the older sister by the hand.

CHAPTER 19

The prospect of staying in a big city and comparing stories with other students lifted Minghua 123's spirits. The city of Wuhan, their next destination, had transformed into a hub for military and civilian evacuees, including universities. From Wuhan, they might even catch a train to Changsha, where the rest of Minghua University waited for them.

They were six days on the road from Lu'an to Wuhan when Professor Kang returned from a meeting in the village of Fanzhen with a smile of satisfaction. The army was moving a detachment of soldiers to Wuhan by riverboat. The officer in charge had agreed to take some of Minghua's students. They just had to get to the wharf, only a few miles from the village.

Minghua 123's female students would take the boat, which was scheduled to reach Wuhan just a day or two ahead of the main group. It wasn't that much faster, but it meant the girls wouldn't have to walk the whole way. Minghua 123 unanimously voted for Professor Kang and another elderly professor to accompany the girls, and to save them from the long walk.

The antiquated tugboat sailed that night. There was no moon, a good omen. The tugboat stayed close to shore, so weighed down an occasional wave splashed over its bow and wet the deck. The two barges it towed were equally overburdened, soldiers and supplies sharing the space with equipment, students, and the Library of Legends, stacked in their new crates.

The Bashui River's current ran deep and swift between narrow banks. Here they were more likely to meet bandits than Japanese patrols. The army captain in charge assured the students that bandits in this area were ragged gangs of deserters and petty thieves, unlike the gangs up north, their members hardened soldiers who used to fight in warlord armies. Bandits on this river would never dare take on a boatload of real soldiers. The engines' steady reverberation was louder than any conversation, but the passengers remained quiet all the same.

Lian leaned on the railing of the second barge, a wooden platform built on a shallow hull, half the deck covered by a brown canvas canopy for shelter against sun and rain. She watched the river, its currents swirling under starlight. Soon they would sail out of the Bashui and into the wider waters of the Yangtze River. Everyone had found a place on deck to settle for the night but she couldn't stop pacing, her mind as restless as her limbs.

Mr. Lee hadn't been the same since Jenmei's murder. He was still cheery and affable, but she could tell he was more nervous now. She shivered, not wanting to think how he might've had a hand in Jenmei's murder. There hadn't been an opportunity for him to approach her alone; she'd managed to avoid that so far.

She hoped that in a big city like Wuhan, with so many arrangements to make, he would have other distractions.

Then there was Meirong. She had recovered some of her outgoing personality. But there were nights when Lian still heard her sobbing. She didn't know how to comfort her. She wished she didn't care so much, but once kindled, the warmth of her feelings for Meirong proved difficult to extinguish.

Then there was Shao. Just picturing his face gave rise to a confused tangle of emotions. She ran one finger lightly along the railing, wondered what it would feel like to run her finger along his arm. Stars spilled across the sky, like glittering dust emptied from a celestial bucket.

"So many poems about the moon, but what about the stars?" Professor Kang said, breaking into her thoughts. "The moon comes and goes through its cycles but the stars always shine for us, constant and true. We should honor them more."

"I've never thought of it that way," she said, "but you're right. We always have starlight."

"Your classmates are sound asleep," the professor said, gently chiding. "You should rest, too, Miss Hu."

Lian sat down beside some crates just inside the canopy's shelter and pulled a blanket around herself. The others rested leaning against each other or curled up on thin sleeping mats. She allowed the motion of the boat to lull her into lethargy, turned her head for a view of the night sky, then fell asleep to the whisper of willow branches brushing the canvas above.

She dreamed of another boat ride, something pulled from a childhood memory. Instead of the cold, summertime. A canal with willows hanging overhead. Her mother's arms around her, a soft rhythmic splash behind them, the boatwoman singing to keep time as she pushed on the oar.

Then she was back on the barge, holding on to the rail to keep her balance. Large waves splashed over the stern of the deck, frothing as if a huge creature churned the waters beside the hull. Something surged up from the depths, a long sinuous shape with silver fins and a broad tail. It flashed through the current, following the barge for a moment before it launched away, slicing through the waves. Shining and scaly, terrible and beautiful. The River God gleamed, reflecting starlight from its scales. The silvery body surged up, a brilliant arc of light. Then vanished into the depths.

SUNSHINE WOKE LIAN. She peered up at daylight drifting through branches of soft green needles. Moored in a bend of the river, the boats had sheltered beneath a dense stand of swamp cypress, their trunks jutting up from the shallows along the shore. They would stay here until nightfall. The fragrant smell of steamed rice tickled her nose.

And from the front of the barge, an unexpected sound. A child's giggle.

She was called Duckling. She was three years old and the most enchanting little girl anyone had ever seen. The child had slept quietly in her father's arms all night and now she tottered on deck enjoying the attention. The female students had nothing to do except read and chat while the boats waited out the day. They happily fussed over the little girl. They gave Duckling candies and dried fruit, sugar to sweeten her soy milk, even a doll hastily sewn from towels and handkerchiefs. Ying-Ying found some red yarn, which she crocheted into ribbons. She braided Duckling's fine hair in two pigtails, red ribbons tied to flutter at the ends.

Duckling's bright face never dimmed, only grew more delighted. She walked unsteadily, laughing whenever a wave made the barge pitch, even if it made her fall. Duckling was so irresistible she even made Professor Kang laugh. The little girl quickly learned the songs they sang to her, mimicking their words without understanding them.

Little Duck, Little Duck,
Sing the moon, dance the stars!
The skies shine out from the pond tonight,
Come with us, Little Duck!

"It's actually a song about little frogs," Meirong said, clapping her hands in time to the tune. "But 'little duck' works just as well. And she loves hearing her name in the words."

Duckling's father was equally cheerful, a young soldier named Fung. He was probably the same age as the students, too thin for his uniform, forehead already weathered by seasons of labor under the hot sun. He watched his daughter's antics, beaming with pride at the students' praise for her sweet nature and happy smile.

Fung's detachment was made up of peasants from Shaanxi Province. They spoke a quaint and rustic dialect the girls found difficult to understand. Ying-Ying, whose grandmother came from Shaanxi, was best able to converse with the soldiers.

"They suffered several bad harvests and his wife died last year," Ying-Ying said. "When Fung joined up he had the choice of leaving the girl behind with an uncle or bringing her along. Well, he really wasn't supposed to bring her along but he did it anyway."

The army promised to feed and clothe him. To Private Fung this seemed a better future than life on a barren farm. He didn't want to leave his daughter behind with relatives who could barely feed themselves. They had no incentive to look after a girl who wasn't even their own and if he sent them his army pay, they would probably spend it on food and clothing for their own children. After losing so many family members to hunger and disease, he preferred taking his chances with the army.

Fung kept Duckling out of sight the best he could. His captain chose to ignore the little girl. "She's her father's problem," he said in curt reply to Lian's timid question. "If he wants to bring her along, so be it. But they get no special treatment."

Fung joked with his comrades, all of them raw recruits. They were in high spirits, lively as though gathering for a festival instead of fighting a war.

"They think it's an adventure," Lian said. "But then, at the start of our journey, we also believed we were on an adventure."

"We weren't actively marching into danger, though," Meirong said. Across the deck, Duckling, finally tired out, was being passed from lap to lap. "Doesn't he realize what it will be like on the front lines?"

"Oh, Meirong," Ying-Ying said. "Don't you think I tried to tell him? I said we could take her with us and look after her. That he could come to the Chengtu campus after the war and find her."

But Fung had never seen war. He'd never been away from his family's impoverished farm. All he knew was that he'd been given a new uniform of smooth khaki, the finest garments he'd ever worn, and that for the first time in her young life, his daughter was getting enough to eat. He was pleased the students had all fallen in love with Duckling and laughingly ignored their entreaties to let them take her.

"*Waah, waah,* she's all I have," he said. "She's my family. We stay together. Did you hear her just now? She's learned all the words to your song."

Four nights later, they reached the wharf in Wuhan. A courier paced beside his horse, waiting to greet the boats. He ran aboard as soon as they tied up, waving a cylindrical message holder. The army captain opened the leather holder, read the order, and flung down both in disgust. He shouted at the soldiers, who began moving equipment off the decks. Then he strode on board the barge and spoke to Professor Kang before storming off again.

"The captain asks us to stay out of the way and let the soldiers disembark first," the professor told the students. "They must march quickly for Henan."

"But Henan is north," Meirong said. "Even farther north than where we got on the boat. Why didn't they just leave for Henan in the first place?"

The professor looked sad. "My guess is that Henan has suddenly become very important and in need of soldiers."

They hugged and cosseted Duckling the entire time Fung and the other soldiers unloaded equipment from the barge. The girls stuffed as much food into Private Fung's knapsack as it could hold. When it was Lian's turn to hand over Duckling to the next student, she did so reluctantly. Her arms felt empty without the little girl. Duckling's laughter, so delightful a day ago, now broke her heart.

Within an hour, the barges were unloaded, and the detachment of soldiers formed up. At the very back of the column, Private Fung stood at attention, one hand stiffly at his side, the other holding Duckling's hand. When the column began to move, he swung her onto his shoulders.

The students called out her name and Duckling turned to beam at them, waving and laughing. Private Fung also turned to wave, a jaunty flourish that matched the wide grin on his face. The last they saw of Duckling was a small figure riding on her father's shoulders, red ribbons bobbing.

Many of the girls wept as the soldiers vanished around the bend. Even in that final moment, Lian hoped Fung would come to his senses and leave Duckling with them. *They are both just children*, she thought, wiping away hot tears. Father and daughter, marching to their deaths.

CHAPTER 20

A half-empty boarding school in Wuhan had been assigned to Minghua 123 for their stay there. The cramped dormitory rooms, their narrow beds meant for middle schoolers, seemed palatial. The boarding school's two dozen remaining pupils were teenage boys who had been cut off from their hometowns when war broke out. Their teachers were in the midst of planning their evacuation to Hunan Province in the south. Some of the boys had shyly asked the Minghua students about their experiences on the road.

Lian soon realized almost everyone in Wuhan was a newcomer. Thousands of troops poured into the city, adding to tens of thousands of refugees. Journalists from all the major papers waited in tea shops and outside government offices, exchanging rumors while scribbling out stories. It was, she had to admit, exciting to be in a big city again.

In Wuhan, food was still plentiful and street vendors offered cheap fare far tastier than Cook Tam's unimaginative meals. When Lian and her classmates strolled through Wuhan, they always bumped into other students. Sometimes her classmates even ran into friends and relatives, traveling with their universities. They eagerly exchanged news and stories, shared meals.

"No radios, telegrams, or telephones," one of them said over spicy noodles, the first really good noodles Lian had tasted since leaving Nanking. "One village where we stayed told us we were the first refugees they'd ever met. They didn't even know we were at war."

There were so many students in Wuhan, from both universities and middle schools, the government organized special events for them. The rally they were attending was sponsored by the Ministry of Education and attendance was mandatory.

"Would anyone even notice if we didn't attend this rally?" Meirong complained as they pushed their way to Wuhan University. "I've heard about them and they sound like a boring waste of time."

Wuhan University's own students had evacuated weeks ago. Their splendid campus now housed government offices. Students were already gathered on the huge playing field, some of them shivering after standing outside in the cold for so long. Lian felt the wind pierce through her coat. She wrapped her scarf more tightly around her collar and pushed her hands deeper into her pockets.

"There must be more than two thousand students here," Ying-Ying said, looking around.

They saw some of their classmates huddled at the edge of the field and elbowed through the crowd to join them. Shorty shouted and waved his arms at Ying-Ying when he saw her.

"Must you bellow like a street vendor?" Ying-Ying said. She tossed her hair at Shorty. "You're an embarrassment to our school."

"But it's my specialty," Shorty said, sounding hurt. Ying-Ying aimed a mock slap at his head, then allowed him to take her hand. They jostled for a better view of the stage, forming a tight cluster. Lian felt someone tug her hair and looked up to see Shao. He winked at her.

The speakers crackled with static and the opening bars of the national anthem blared out. Then a troupe of musicians came onstage to perform some patriotic songs and dances. Next a small orchestra made up of students played a Western piece, something classical. Finally came the real reason for the rally. A uniformed officer came to the microphone and began his speech.

"The Japanese bomb civilian targets to intimidate and demoralize." The speaker's words thundered through the open area, amplified to reach the far end of the field. "But this does not weaken our resolve."

Lian thought of what they'd already seen, the tired and the homeless, the sick and the hopeless. Refugee centers short on food, shelter, and medicine. Old men and women sitting listlessly on straw mats. The woman who had given birth on the muddy banks of the Yangtze. When they saw her, the current was coaxing her unresisting body into its waters. None of those people had gone to war but it had devoured them just the same. So many deaths, rendered anonymous by the sheer number of victims.

"China is a vast land and our military takes advantage of this. Our government and armies move inland strategically. Not to retreat, but to force the Japanese to stretch their resources across greater and greater distances."

Shao took her hand. "Your mother will be all right," he whispered, giving it a squeeze.

She gave him a quick, uncertain smile but did not pull away. She felt her hand grow warm in his.

WHEN THE RALLY ended, most of the students milled about on the playing field, introducing themselves, mingling and exchanging stories.

"I want to stay for a while," Meirong said to Lian. "Make some new friends from other schools and hear about their travels. It's all good material for *Minghua 123 News*. Unless you want me to walk back with you?"

"No, no. You stay," Lian said, glad to see her friend's extroverted nature surfacing. "I'm a bit tired and I need to mend my blouse." Lian didn't want to make any more new friends. Nor did she want to remember how warm and protecting Shao's hand had felt over hers. Because she was certain it meant more to her than it did to him.

Back at the boarding school, she stood for a few minutes beside the radiator in the dormitory's entrance lobby to warm up. Sunset angled its way in the windows, casting long striped shadows through the staircase banister. Lian reluctantly moved away from the radiator and trudged up the stairs to the room she shared with three others. As soon as she entered she saw the envelope on her bed.

Come to my office at six o'clock this evening.

It was from Mr. Lee. Her hands felt numb with cold again. What more did Lee want from her? And he wanted to see her at a time when everyone else would be in the dining hall.

Lee's office was on the second floor of the school's small administrative building. Lian pushed open the front door at the appointed time. Electricity to the campus was shut off at night to enforce the blackout. The entrance lobby was dark, but light from an open door sliced down the staircase. The wooden staircase creaked with her every step. She knocked at the door.

"Come in, come in," the director of student services called out.

Mr. Lee's desk faced the door, the window behind him taped over with newspaper. Other than a desk and chair, the office was bare. A door to the right of the desk, slightly ajar, connected his office with the one adjoining. A kerosene lamp cast the only light in the room. It was cheap, a clear glass chimney on a red-painted metal base, the sort that foreign oil companies gave away for free.

She took a deep breath, willing herself to meet his eyes.

"This is really the first chance we've had to chat since Zhongmiao Village," he said. "What do you know about Wang Jenmei's death?"

She gasped. It was the last question she had expected. "Nothing. I don't know anything. I thought you . . . would know what happened."

"And why would I know anything, Miss Hu? Do you think I'm a murderer?" He smiled as though joking, and his eyes flicked for a moment to the adjoining door. "Did you see anyone unfamiliar following our little convoy?"

"There were unfamiliar people every day," she said, keeping her voice steady. "People who walked with us on the road. The ones who camped at the factory campus."

"Very true." Mr. Lee regarded her over his glasses. "But there might've been someone you spoke to while you were on the road. Someone you might run into again. If you remember or notice anything, you'll let me know. Shut the door when you leave."

Lian wanted to bolt out the door, but restrained herself. She wouldn't betray her fear to Mr. Lee. By the time she reached the ground floor she was shaking so much she sank to the ground, back pressed against the corridor wall. She had to calm down, behave normally.

But how could Mr. Lee even think she knew something about Wang Jenmei's death? More confusingly, didn't *he* know?

Floorboards creaked and the door opened. Mr. Lee was coming out. She stood up and edged along the wall, deeper into the darkness of the corridor, away from the stairwell. Her fingers touched a doorframe. She didn't dare push the door open in case its hinges were rusty. She pressed herself against the door, hoping the shallow niche of the doorframe and its shadows were enough to hide her.

The staircase creaked with footsteps. Then she heard Mr. Lee speak and her heart lurched. He knew she was still there. But almost immediately another voice replied. A man's voice. Lee wasn't talking to her. There was someone else. There were two men coming down the staircase.

"I don't believe she knows anything about the murder." Mr. Lee sounded slightly anxious.

"Perhaps it was someone sent by the Juntong," the second man said. "Will the girl continue to cooperate?"

Juntong. The Nationalist Party's military intelligence agency. Lian shuddered.

"Anyone suspected of conspiring with the enemy would be torn apart," Lee said. "She doesn't want people to know her father was a Japanese spy. If we need her, she'll do as I say."

"Well, we can't ask for much. She's not trained." Lian thought the second man's voice sounded familiar.

"I know, sir"—Lee's voice was apologetic—"but she was the

best I could do on short notice after Shen was killed. But do you really think the Juntong planted an assassin in our midst?"

Lee had called the other man "sir." Someone more important. And Shen had been the previous student informant.

"If they did, then Wang Jenmei was more of a threat than we realized," the unknown man said. "Someone murdered that student and didn't bother informing us. Someone took action because we didn't. Wang's death was a warning, to us as well as to the students. We must be even more vigilant."

"Sir, just one more thing," Lee said.

The building door opened and slammed shut. Footsteps on the concrete outside. Lian pushed open the door she had been leaning against and tiptoed into the room. Across from the door, sheets of newsprint defined the rectangle of a window. Feeling her way to the window, she peeled aside one edge of the newspaper and peeked out. Lee was walking away, in the direction of the dining hall. The other man paused to light a cigarette. He took a long drag and strolled away. His burly figure, still wearing a white apron, was familiar.

Cook Tam was the man Mr. Lee had called "sir."

CHAPTER 21

It seemed as though they would never get to Chengtu. There were so many schools on the move, so many students. Housing, funds, food, and transportation were all difficult to organize. The government was building classrooms and dormitories in Chengtu, but at least three other universities were already on their way there.

"It's all taking longer than planned," Mr. Lee announced. "We'll meet the other Minghua groups in Changsha and stay a couple of months. We can celebrate the New Year there."

The students in the dining hall erupted in wild cheers at the prospect of reuniting with the rest of their classmates.

"There's more, there's more," he called over the

noise. "We're going by train to Changsha. Courtesy of the military. Boxcars for ourselves and our belongings."

They cheered even more, quieting down when Mr. Lee waved his hands for silence.

"One more thing. A family on the train has very generously offered to let our female students and older staff members ride in their private car." He cleared his throat. "Let me assure our young ladies it's perfectly safe. You'll ride in compartments with the women of the family."

Meirong gave Lian a nudge. "At this point, I'm willing to compromise my virtue if it means sitting on soft benches for the next hundred miles."

The bustling atmosphere in Wuhan had been good for Meirong. She'd made new friends from other universities and spent so many hours chatting with journalists that her classmates now teased her about changing her major to journalism.

"I just might," Meirong said, looking superior. "Once our school is all together again, I just may transfer to Professor Mah's Journalism Department."

Lian took comfort in Meirong's improved mood. And in the memory of Shao's warm hand over hers. But would she ever shed her guilt over Jenmei? Or the fear that clenched her heart every time she saw Mr. Lee, and now, Cook Tam? Or her dread of an assassin so mysterious even the two men she feared didn't know where that danger lay?

THE WUHAN RAILWAY station was mobbed. Lian and the other girls were able to get on board their train only because an army officer took them through the cordon of soldiers. When they finally climbed aboard the private railcar, a young woman their own age greeted them, her smile one of genuine delight. She wore a stylish wool suit, long hair twisted up in a knot. Her face was bare of makeup but her brows were carefully shaped, her nails buffed to a shine.

"My name is Wei Fanling. Please make yourselves comfortable," she said. "We're all family and we already know everything about one another. We've been dying for new companions."

Lian, Meirong, and Ying-Ying shared a compartment with Fanling and three other girls, all cousins. They were fresh and neatly dressed, making the Minghua students self-conscious of their shabby clothing and blunt-cut hair, the straw sandals tied over their shoes.

"Don't apologize," one of the Wei girls said. "You're so much braver than we are, enduring so much to continue your education while we ride in comfort."

The cousins bombarded them with questions. Their sincere, unaffected interest made conversation easy. The Wei family had traveled all the way from Anhui Province. Their grandfather had decided it was time to evacuate Anhui. After Changsha, the train was going to Chengtu, where the Wei cousins were going to attend West China University.

"But why didn't you head directly to Changsha from Anhui?" Meirong asked. "It's so much farther to come up to Wuhan and then go west."

"The direct route by rail was too dangerous," one said, "and this was the only way we could all travel together."

Fanling interrupted. "It's because General Wei is our uncle."

The general had arranged all their travel, giving his family priority on civilian transportation when possible, troop transportation if nothing else was available. This circuitous route was the result.

The Wei girls were delightful company but now that she knew, Lian felt uncomfortable riding in a railcar commandeered for a general's family. From the way Meirong and Ying-Ying quieted down, she could tell they felt the same. The Wei girls chattered on, oblivious to their unease. They gasped upon hearing of Minghua 123's run-ins with Japanese aircraft, shook their heads in sympathy at accounts of walking at night for long miles with nothing but starlight overhead, of the cold and hunger. But they'd never suffered through any of it.

"Did you know the nickname for West China University is 'Mistress College'?" one of the Wei cousins said. "Warlords used to send their mistresses to this university. They wanted sophisticated, beautiful hostesses to show off. The warlords donated a lot of money to the university so their women could attend school in style. That's why the campus is so beautiful."

"Our dormitory is like a palace," said another. "Don't get off in Changsha. Stay on the train and enroll at West China when you get to Chengtu."

"We can't abandon our school after all we've been through," Ying-Ying said.

"Anyway, your school sounds too fancy for us," Meirong said. "We prefer listening to lectures in drafty temples while sitting on hard slate floors."

"You'll love Chengtu when you finally get there," Fanling said. "The climate is so temperate, the air so soft and warm. Promise you'll come find us at our university when you get there."

FROM THE ROOF of the railcar, Shorty had a view of the road beside the tracks. Normally, rail travel from Wuhan to Changsha wouldn't have taken more than six hours, but the locomotive had been damaged during an air raid, and the conductor stopped every hour so his engineer could make sure the repairs were holding. Each time they stopped, the railway tracks were besieged by people hoping to climb on for a ride. Soldiers on the train had to stand guard and wave their rifles to push back the crowd.

Shorty noticed that a few still managed to clamber on at each stop and once they did, the soldiers turned a blind eye.

"They sleep, eat, shit up there," one soldier told him. "They don't dare get off in case they never get back on again."

"We lose a few when we go through tunnels," his companion said. "On the last trip, some of them fell asleep sitting up. They got knocked off even though the conductor blew the whistle several times to warn them."

By now Shorty could tell from the activity around the locomotive that their train was getting ready to move again. He reached down and thumped the boxcar door. It slid open and the two classmates who had been riding on the roof with him climbed down the handholds to go inside.

"Next shift," he shouted. Their boxcar was crammed with cargo and badly ventilated. They'd agreed to take turns sitting on top of the car to free up enough space so that the students inside could actually sit down. Shorty didn't like closed spaces and was taking an extra shift on top.

When the train began moving again, he sat facing the back of the train. It was better to have the rush of air at his back rather than blowing down the front of his padded vest. The steel panels of the railcar roof were slippery, but he pushed his feet against the raised edge of a metal seam and felt more secure.

The three students shared the roof with six men from the town of Changchow, all members of a carpenters' guild. The men had bribed soldiers to let them get on the roof; they were also riding south to Changsha, chasing work. The carpenters deferred to the students, who were legitimate passengers, but they defended the roof fiercely, demanding money from those who tried to climb on. "We paid to sit on this railcar, eh," they shouted. "Pay up or stay off."

The rocking motion of the train was soothing. The tracks passed through a forest dense with bamboo and pine. Tall yellow stalks and dry leaves waved above Shorty, splitting the sunshine into strips of light that flashed over the railcars, a rhythmic and hypnotic effect that made him sleepy. He jerked up, knowing how easy it would be to roll off the roof. When the train emerged from the shadows of the forest, Shorty blinked up at a sky no longer blue but fading into dusky sunset, shades of pink and amber staining the horizon.

He watched the forest recede, fought off drowsiness. *Just for a few moments*, he told himself as his eyelids closed and his mind strayed into the realm between sleep and waking.

If he hadn't closed his eyes, if he had been one of those who could truly see, he would've noticed jeweled glimmers shining out from the forest's depths and the fluttering of bamboo leaves that had nothing to do with a train rushing past. He would've witnessed a giant bird rise out from the forest canopy, its crimson head crowned in feathers like silver spikes. Then the flurry of lapis-blue wings and the flash of gold tail plumes as the phoenix shot into the sky. Then another. And another. Until an entire flock of phoenixes soared to circle above the bamboo forest. When they were all airborne, the birds veered northwest and vanished into a saffron-gold sunset.

A DOZEN SENIOR students from the first four groups that left Nanking ahead of Minghua 123 greeted them at the Changsha train station. They were there to guide the new arrivals to their lodgings.

Lian and the other girls followed the senior assigned to take them to the boarding school that housed all Minghua's female students. They were anxious to get to the dormitory but they couldn't help slowing down as store signs and enticing smells caught their attention.

The huge influx of refugees had transformed Changsha, and its enterprising citizens rose to the challenge of profiting from the flood of new arrivals. Every block was noisy with the pounding of construction work. Private homes hung out signs for room rentals and restaurants overflowed. Restaurants put signs on the sidewalk touting their house specialties.

"Pork belly steamed with pickled vegetables. Rice noodles with stewed beef," Ying-Ying read. "Oh, look! Bean curd and red peppers."

"I'm tired of steamed buns," Meirong said. "Let's come back here as soon as we've put away our luggage and get something nice to eat. Eggs cooked in spiced soy sauce."

"In Changsha, food is still cheap and plentiful," the senior called over his shoulder, "but expect prices to go up as the war goes on."

"All I can afford are sweet potatoes," Lian said with a sigh. They hurried to catch up with him.

"We've been here for weeks," he said, "and our classrooms are at Hunan University, across the bridge. We share the campus with two other universities."

They were being housed at Hande Girls Boarding School. Because of the war, Hande had closed its boarding school and kept it open only for day students. When they reached the school dormitory, classmates waiting at the entrance greeted them with cries of welcome. There were hugs and tears.

"I'm so happy to see you!" A tall girl with a long ponytail threw her arms around Meirong. "So the Literature Department is finally here! And the Agriculture Department, too?"

"Finally is right," Meirong said. "How long have you been in Changsha, Tan Wendian?"

"A month," Wendian said, tossing back her ponytail. "Too bad your group missed the last boat. You really fell behind. But you're in time for the Lunar New Year. The celebrations begin in two weeks and we're decorating the dining hall at Hunan University. There's an interuniversity team planning all the festivities."

"With so many universities in town, there's lots to do," another girl said. "On weekends and after classes, the streets are full of students. It's like Wuhan, but with fewer military uniforms."

"What about air raids?" Ying-Ying asked.

"We get them, but so far they're not very frequent and anti-aircraft defense is very well-organized," Wendian said. "We get plenty of warning. Come see your rooms and then we'll treat you to noodles. We've been here long enough to get money from our families."

"We bumped into so many students on the way here," Ying-Ying said as they trudged up the staircase. "How many schools are here?"

"The big three—Beida, Qinghua, and Nankai," Wendian said. "They were the first to arrive, so they got the best accommodations."

"Did everyone in your group get here safely?" Ying-Ying asked.

"Do you remember Huang An? He caught dysentery and died before we could get him to a hospital," Wendian said. "And thirty of our boys enlisted after Shanghai fell. What about you?"

"We lost a graduate student, Mr. Shen, when a Japanese plane strafed the road we were on," Ying-Ying said. Her voice dropped to a whisper. "And Wang Jenmei was murdered."

Wendian gave a little cry, then covered her mouth with her hands.

"We think it was political, a Nationalist agent," Meirong said, looking at Wendian. "Because Jenmei was leader of the Communist Students Club."

"It happened when we were in Zhongmiao Village," Ying-Ying said, "not far from Hefei. She was killed the night before we were supposed to leave. The local police didn't do much to investigate."

"Hefei is run by a fairly moderate faction of the military," Wendian said. She seemed to have regained her composure. "Here in Changsha, it's different. If Jenmei had been murdered here, I wouldn't have been surprised at all. The left-wing elements here keep a low profile."

"So how does one get in touch with left-wing elements in Changsha?" Meirong said. She saw Lian's horrified expression and rolled her eyes. "I'm joking, Lian."

"It's no joking matter," Wendian said. "The problem isn't the military. In fact, the military liaison officer for universities is very tolerant. The problem is the Juntong."

The dreaded military intelligence agency. Lian glanced over at Meirong and was glad to see her friend's sober expression, all teasing gone. It was a good thing Wendian knew so much about the situation in Changsha.

"Oh, and there's a big assembly tomorrow morning," a third-year girl said. "Mandatory for all students. Some general making a speech because of Nanking."

"Why, what about Nanking?" Meirong said.

"You don't know?" Wendian exclaimed.

While they'd been chatting on the train with the Wei cousins, Nanking had fallen. The Japanese now occupied China's capital city.

IN THE MORNING, a stream of university students crossed the bridge to Hunan University. The sports field was the only space large enough to hold them all and a stage had been erected in front of the stands. General Chen of the Eighteenth Army, one of the nation's most respected military leaders, would be addressing them.

Stern and handsome, General Chen stood at attention while the national anthem played. The microphone screeched as an aide adjusted it, then the general stepped up.

"Out of China's five hundred million people, we can recruit enough soldiers," he said. "But China has only forty-three thousand university students. Students, you are our nation's treasure. You are the ones we need to rebuild after the war. You are China's last drop of blood. If we lose you, we squander our future. Do not enlist. Evacuate to safety with your schools. Complete your education. It's your duty to the nation, to your families, to your own destiny."

But by the end of the day, fifty-one students and eleven servants from Minghua University had enlisted. Four more, all from the coastal town of Ningbo, decided to drop out and travel home together. They were worried about their families. Ningbo was south of Shanghai and Lian wanted very badly to join them. But the only way her mother could contact her was through the university. She had to wait for her mother's letter.

CHAPTER 22

In Changsha, university life felt almost normal to Shao. The buildings at Hunan University were reasonably warm, the electric lighting miraculous. There were lectures in real classrooms with real desks and chairs. There weren't enough classrooms to accommodate all the universities at the same time, so room rotations and long idle periods between classes stretched school days into the evening but no one minded. It was a relief, no, a pleasure, getting back to a routine of classes and study. Although they'd tried to keep up with their courses while on the road, how much studying could they really manage after eight or twelve hours of walking? How could they concentrate on lectures or take notes when their hands were numb from the cold, their stomachs growling with hunger?

Between classes Shao worked on assignments and

met with his tutorial group, which had reassembled. They met in quiet corners and corridors. Their eager questions made him smile, and there was new urgency to their discussions. The war made them search for answers in literature of the past since present-day news only brought uncertainty.

Shao ran into several friends from Shanghai, all in Changsha with their universities. Some had been in Changsha for many weeks; they'd already received letters from home. Flush and generous after cashing in money orders, they treated the new arrivals to cheap meals at Changsha's many small restaurants. Shao was learning to enjoy the region's distinctive style of cuisine, generously seasoned with mouth-numbing chilies.

"My tongue's still on fire," Shorty said, breathing in cold winter air through his mouth.

"I need to wash my face," Shao said. "Those noodles made me sweat more than a basketball game."

"Liu Shaoming! Shorty Ho! Hey, stop!" A uniformed soldier was puffing up the hill after them, waving madly. "Ping! Chen Ping!"

"I know that voice," Shao said, squinting. "But not that face."

"It's Wei Daming," Shorty said. "Thirty pounds lighter. And in a medic's uniform. And here, in Changsha."

"Daming! You dumb ox!" Shao shook the younger man by the shoulders. "What are you doing here?"

Daming's face shone with exertion from the climb, but his wide grin almost split his face in two. "I heard there were Minghua students billeted at Yali Middle School, so I came to see if I could find some of the old gang."

"Are you here to enroll?" Chen Ping asked.

Daming threw back his head in laughter. "What university would take me? Even if I hadn't been expelled, I would've flunked out. But the army was glad to take me."

"But a medic," Shao said. "How did you qualify for that?"

Daming laughed even harder. "Apparently, it was because I could read. They handed me the field surgeon's manual."

"Where's your cousin?" Shorty said. "Both you and Jin Ming were expelled for that prank."

The smile faded. "Jin was killed, old friend. I had to write my aunt and uncle. I really hope the postal system takes its time with that letter."

The cousins had been expelled from Minghua partway through the second week of classes. Daming and Jin hosted a farewell dinner at a favorite restaurant in Nanking, spending lavishly on food and drink for their friends. The next morning, they woke up in a hotel room with queasy stomachs and sharper minds. The gravity of their situation made their stomachs roil more than the bottle of brandy they had drunk so freely the night before. They knew what awaited them back home in Shanghai. Their fathers' wrath, their mothers' tears of shame. The disapproval of elderly relatives.

"Jin remembered our great-uncle in Anhui Province, a general," Daming said. "We bought train tickets, rode as far as we could, then walked the rest of the way to the front lines to enlist in his regiment. We thought if Great-Uncle wrote to our parents praising our patriotism, they might not be so angry with us for getting expelled."

"And did he write to praise your patriotism?" Shorty said.

"No. He gave us a tongue-lashing for getting expelled. Then told us that for the family's sake, he would try to keep us safe."

General Wei assigned Jin and Daming to the field hospital, where a doctor gave them medical manuals to read. They followed behind doctors and medics, helped out in the hospital tents. It all seemed like a big adventure. Then came their first battle.

The wounded poured in, lifted on stretchers, carried in blankets, helped in by their comrades. Some were reduced to screaming animals from pain, some were shocked and stupefied, others mercifully unconscious. Daming worked in the operating room, a small shack beside the main hospital tent. They ran out of morphine and Daming held down patients as the surgeon dug bullets out. He bandaged sawed-off limbs, stitched wounds. The air-raid siren howled but the surgeon kept operating.

Then a blast and darkness. Then silence.

He struggled up to see the roof and two walls gone. Tattered canvas flapped outside but there was no sound. A soldier, mouth open and contorted, screamed in the silence. Daming stood up but his legs felt as though he was pushing his way through a bog. He stumbled out and knew that Jin, that everyone in the hospital tent, was gone. That he was lucky he hadn't been sliced open by shrapnel.

It had rained while he was unconscious and the ground was soft. He skirted around small ponds of muddy water, bomb craters that had filled up. But it was a beautiful morning. A high wind fanned thin white veils of cloud across a clear, clean blue sky to skim the mountaintops. He remembered that so vividly.

Daming's great-uncle had been sick with remorse. "I should've sent the two of you back to Shanghai the minute I saw you," he said, glaring at Daming. "I should do that now before I have to write another one of these letters to the family."

"I'm not a very good field medic but the army can't afford to be picky right now, sir," Daming said. "Please, Great-Uncle, I'd rather stay and do my duty than go home."

"Hmmm," General Wei said. "I understand. I'd rather face the Japanese than Jin's mother."

He assigned Daming to oversee the transport of wounded soldiers from the front to hospitals inland. Now Daming spent his time shuttling back and forth on trains and trucks.

"I'm in the thick of it," Daming said. "Great-Uncle offered me a way out but I didn't take it. And it wasn't just because of Jin's mother. Call it patriotism or hatred of the Japanese, but I wanted to do something useful for once."

Then he brightened and slapped Shao's shoulder. "I'm taking a trainload of soldiers to the hospital in Chunking, but not for another two days. Lots of time to catch up."

When Shao took Daming back to his dormitory, there were loud cheers and greetings.

"Wei Daming! Have you come back to drag down the class average?"

"Are you staying for New Year celebrations?"

All through the evening, Daming sat in the dining hall, the center of attention. Some professors stopped to greet him, his misdeeds long forgotten. Everyone wanted a firsthand report on conditions at the front.

"Morale couldn't be better," Shao heard him proclaim. "Everywhere the troop transports go, long lines of men are waiting to enlist. Very soon the factories that moved inland from other cities will be manufacturing armaments. The Japanese don't stand a chance."

"Will Daming come to our New Year celebrations?" Meirong said. She nudged Shao and he moved over to make room on the bench for her and Lian.

"Trust me, he'll be the last to leave every party," Shao said. "And for the next month he'll be rotating between Changsha and Wuhan. I'm sure we'll see more of him."

"Do you think he'd be willing to tell his story for our newspaper?" Shao realized that Meirong was rather in awe of Daming.

His friend was no longer the thoughtless boy who'd been the despair of his family and professors. His lean face, though cheerful as he joked with friends, held the haunted look of someone older, someone who had seen too much. Shao looked over at Lian and she returned his smile. But her eyes also held the same haunted look. Perhaps they all did.

Shao's dormitory was unusually quiet when he returned. His roommates were absorbed in reading. Reading letters. He rushed to his bed and almost laughed out loud. A bundle of letters tied with string lay on the covers.

The four letters from his mother he skimmed quickly. There was one from a favorite cousin, others from friends in Shanghai. Another one from the Liu family's accountant, brief instructions attached to a money order. He lay down and returned to his mother's letters, this time reading each one more thoroughly. Gossip, weddings and births, illnesses, the death of one elderly great-uncle. His father had penned a few lines at the end of each letter, repeating admonishments to take care of his health.

When the dorm lights went out, Shao closed his eyes and put one of his mother's letters to his nose. It held the faintest traces of freesia and bergamot, a blend created especially for her by a perfumery in Shanghai's French Concession. The proprietor had brought out tray after tray of small bottles for his mother to sniff. He fell asleep and dreamed he was a boy again. They were in his mother's car, the chauffeur taking them through streets shaded by tall sycamores, a street of villas and brick walls. His mother's lace gloves lay crumpled on her lap, her face was hidden by a veiled hat. She pulled out a handkerchief and the scent of freesia filled his dream.

HANDE GIRLS BOARDING School, where Minghua University's female students were lodged, stood across the river from Hunan

University's large campus. It was a forty-five-minute walk from Lian's dormitory to the classrooms, a short distance for students now accustomed to walking eight or ten hours each day. Morning and evening, a procession of university students dominated pedestrian traffic on the bridge, heads and faced wrapped up against the cold. Early morning temperatures hovered above freezing and the wind picked up humidity from the river, pushing chilly damp air through their clothes.

Since coming to Changsha Lian hadn't seen much of Meirong, who came from the same town as Wendian. The two had been friends even before university, so Lian told herself it was normal they'd want to be together after so much time apart. Lian walked to and from the campus with any students who happened to be heading out at the same time. But on this evening, she deliberately fell behind so she could walk across the bridge alone. She had to think what to do next.

Finally, she had received a letter from her mother.

When she first saw the letter on her bed, Lian had resisted the urge to rip it open. First, she studied the envelope. The postmark was smudged but it had been mailed from Shanghai. Her mother had reached Shanghai. Lian examined the back of the envelope. There was no return address. She looked around at the other girls, all absorbed in reading their own mail. One or two were crying.

Lian slit open one edge of the envelope and smoothed out the sheet of onionskin paper.

My precious daughter. With luck, this letter has reached you in Changsha. I was overjoyed to find your letter waiting for me when I arrived at Unity Mission. You're not in Shanghai, but it's actually better that you're with Minghua. Now that I know you're with your professors and classmates, I want you to stay with them. You're safer with your school. They'll make sure you have food and lodgings. The last thing I want is for you to travel across the country all the way to Shanghai.

Unity Mission could not take me in, but I may have found a spot at another refugee camp where I've offered to do typing in exchange for a bed. It's best if you don't write to me at Unity anymore. The refugee camp is so busy and chaotic, your letter would get lost or thrown out. The bulletins list Chengtu as Minghua's final destination, so I will send my next letter there when I'm settled, care of the university. Hopefully you'll be safe in Chengtu by then.

She didn't doubt Mr. Lee had already read the letter. That he read the letters of any student he didn't trust. Her mother didn't know about Mr. Lee. Didn't know that all their years of living under false names had been for nothing. How could she warn her mother that the past had caught up with them?

The whole time they'd lived in Peking Lian had accepted, without quite understanding why, that they were in danger should their true identities be revealed. She understood now that there were people who would trample over another's life to save themselves. To save their reputations. These were the forces her mother had been helpless to counter. As helpless as Lian herself had been when Lee confronted her.

When they were in Nanking, Professor Kang had promised he'd find a way to get her to Shanghai. But only if her mother sent for her. But now, even if her mother did send for her, Lian couldn't ask for help from her school anymore. Mr. Lee would know. She couldn't risk it. He might forbid her to leave. She had to behave normally. She had to plan. She had been saving all her allowance money from the government. She had to buy maps and food for the journey.

Lian paused at the center of the bridge and leaned against its stone parapet. The river currents rippled with starlight. Minghua University would leave Changsha in a few weeks. There would be more stops in more towns, more nights of sleeping on temple floors until they finally reached Chengtu. Every mile they traveled brought them closer to the safety of Chengtu.

Every mile took her farther from Shanghai.

UNSTEADY FROM TOO much drink, Daming took a deep breath and leaned over the bridge's stone parapet, wondering if he was going to be sick. It was the first night of January and he'd just left his first New Year party. Four more weeks to go until the Lunar New Year, each week more festive than the one before as the calendar closed in on the Year of the Tiger. Despite the threat of air raids, there had been parties all over Changsha. New Year festivities carried on whether or not there was a war.

Since Nanking's defeat, scores of wounded soldiers had struggled into the city by truck and train. The railway station had become a target for enemy bombers. There had been more air raids in the last week than the past two months combined. There was talk of moving the universities out of Changsha.

Daming had taken a few days' leave from shuttling the wounded, spent the time pretending he was a student again, as carefree as when they had been in Nanking. He pulled the bottle of *moutai* out of his coat pocket. He'd won the coveted bottle off Shorty with the toss of a coin. Above him, thin clouds sailed quickly across the sky, pushed by a high wind. The Hsiang River flowed beneath the bridge, its currents black and smooth as a goddess's hair. There were supposed to be two River Goddesses who watched over the Hsiang, the wife and daughter of an ancient king.

A procession by the riverfront caught his eye, red lanterns held high by revelers costumed in ancient garb, dancing their way toward the riverbanks to the music of cymbals and reed flutes. He listened to the music echoing up from the shore and smiled. He recognized the old tune. "Full of Joy." He tapped his hand on the stone balustrade in time to the cymbals. Three cymbal clashes at the end of each refrain. *Pang pang pang.*

When the parade reached the riverbank, it didn't stop. The red lanterns continued moving into the water. Mesmerized, he watched the revelers balance on the river's surface, still dancing. From the waters the figures of two women in shining robes rose up to join them. Behind the women, huge riparian creatures emerged from the river, silver fins like rows of daggers along the spines of serpentine bodies, eyes the size and shine of pewter plates. Led by the two River Goddesses, the procession of revelers and river guardians descended into the depths. The red lantern lights moved downriver, growing fainter and fainter until they disappeared into darkness.

Daming lifted the bottle of *moutai* to his lips then paused. He held the bottle out and dropped it over the parapet, an offering to the river guardians.

AFTER YET ANOTHER New Year's party, Shao had rolled out of bed late. But with luck, Daming's train would be running late, too, as the railways tended to these days. He looked around the station and headed for the far end of the platform. Soldiers guarded a cordoned-off area where troops were waiting to board. More soldiers stood guarding the line of railcars that extended along the tracks, preventing people from climbing on. If there was any room left, they might let a few people on to hitch a ride.

But it didn't stop people from trying. A man broke away from the crowd and ran onto the tracks. The soldiers hauled him back onto the platform where he sprawled in a tangle of limbs. His leather shoes were cracked, his tunic greasy with stains. He clutched a bundle in his arms. He picked himself up and began berating the soldiers.

"Don't treat me as if I'm worthless," he shouted. "I'm a refugee now but I'm an educated man. I'm still that man! You should show respect!" He hobbled away, holding his bundle tight.

Spotting Daming, Shao called out to him, and Daming waved the soldiers to let him through.

"They don't care anymore," Daming said, who had also been watching the man. "That train he tried to board is taking soldiers to Henan, straight to the enemy. But refugees like him have nothing left to lose and they're tired. They just want to stop walking. Some will get off at the next town, or the one after that, hoping to catch another ride."

"We're leaving Changsha soon," Shao said. "This place is getting too many visits from Japanese bombers these days. They're moving us to a small town called Shangtan."

"So is Professor Kang more concerned about the Library of Legends or his students?"

They both laughed.

"Listen, old friend," Daming said, "I've told you a few things. That the war is going pretty badly for us. We have more soldiers but the Japanese are far better equipped and better trained. It's meat against machines. As an officer, I should've been more discreet. Given you more confidence in our military."

"I understand," Shao said. "Don't worry. I won't say anything."

"I've never thought about patriotism or politics at school," Daming said, "never joined any anti-Japanese rallies or cheered for the Nationalists."

"You were always an idler, Daming," Shao said. "You only came to college because you thought the parties would be good." He gave his friend a playful punch on the shoulder.

"I'll be shuttling between Changsha and Wuhan for the next little while," Daming said. "Maybe we'll be lucky enough to meet up again, old friend."

Shao made his way to the station exit, pushing past uniformed men. They held their rifles awkwardly—the ones who had rifles. Daming had told him that due to equipment shortages, some Chinese regiments were still waiting for guns. In the meantime, they drilled with closed umbrellas. The soldiers joked, trading friendly insults and scuffing their cloth shoes on the platform's tiled floor.

More than anything else, the cloth-soled shoes broke Shao's heart. These soldiers only had khaki uniforms and thinly padded coats, poor protection against the winter. They were defending a poor country, fighting for generals who knew China had more men to spare than weapons.

CHAPTER 23

After another week of heavy bombing, the universities were leaving Changsha. They couldn't wait until the end of the month, no matter how badly they wanted to celebrate the New Year in a big city. Changsha was no longer safe. Minghua University's interim destination was the town of Shangtan.

"It feels as if we'll never get to Chengtu," Ying-Ying said. "Wouldn't it be heaven to live and go to class in one place until the war is over?"

"After Shangtan, Chengtu," Lian said. "We're halfway there." And perhaps in Chengtu there would be another letter from her mother.

On the second day of their journey, they set out at nightfall from the village where they had rested. The students were eager to make good time and carried their supper with them, two steamed buns each. At the edge of the village, Lian spotted Meirong leaning against the wall of a house, strapping a new pair of straw sandals over her cloth shoes. Meirong looked up and smiled.

"I think I've had my penny's worth out of these straw shoes," Meirong said. "Fortunately, at this price, I have spares."

"Do you want to walk together?" Lian asked, as nonchalantly as she could.

Meirong shook her head, then looked up from tying her sandals. "Lian, I don't want you to think I've become less of a friend," she said. She lowered her voice. "It's just that, well, after we got to Changsha I joined the Communist student movement for real. I'm leading Minghua's Communist Students Club now."

"No! You mustn't!" Lian couldn't hold back her gasp of dismay. "Think of what happened to Jenmei."

"I knew you wouldn't like it," Meirong said, "and I didn't want you to worry or have to lie if anyone asked. I'd walk with you today but I can't. I'm meeting a comrade from one of the other student groups. He's walking partway to Shangtan with me. A walking meeting. We'll be hanging back at the very end of the line."

"Why are you doing this, Meirong?" Lian said.

"I'm carrying on Wang Jenmei's work," Meirong said. "I'm going to make sure the Communist movement at our school grows stronger."

"Meirong, please don't do this," Lian begged.

"I've been very careful, Lian," she said. She finished tying her sandals. "More careful than Wang Jenmei. She was too outspoken. And, of course, I trust you not to say anything." She flashed Lian a bright smile and squeezed her hand. "I'm glad you know. I didn't want any misunderstandings between us about our friendship."

Lian caught up with the convoy and joined the middle of the

line. She walked beside one of the library wagons, just behind Ying-Ying and some other girls. She turned for a last look back at Meirong, who was swinging her rucksack back onto her shoulders. As she set off, an old man behind her picked up the discarded straw sandals.

Lian hoped Mr. Lee wasn't aware of Meirong's activities. But even if he didn't suspect her, it didn't matter. With Meirong's joining the Communist cause, her friend wouldn't confide in her as before. Meirong had her own secrets now. Between the two of them, their secrets could fill a cavern. Their friendship could never be as before.

She wished her mother had given her a forwarding address for mail. Even if she sent a letter to her mother at Unity Mission, even if a kind person was willing to hold it, her mother wouldn't be going back to the Mission. And if she did, she wouldn't think of asking about a letter. Lian could only hope for news once they got to Chengtu. Until then, she couldn't leave. Not yet.

Some students had stopped by the side of the road for a quick drink, a bite of food from their lunch boxes. The moment he saw her, Shao said something to the classmate beside him and left the group. He was leaving his friends to walk with her. She recalled the warmth of his hand over hers and her heart quickened.

No, she couldn't leave. Not yet.

CHAPTER 24

Shangtan was small but blessed with good feng shui, protected by hills behind and the Hsiang River in front like a natural moat. Tucked at the foot of steep hills, Minghua's new campus was a difficult target for air raids. They had been assigned to army barracks left behind when the unit at Shangtan deployed.

"We'll be very safe here," Shao told Lian as they approached the town. "Apparently Shangtan is prone to fog from the river, which also discourages air raids."

Arranged in rows around a parade ground, the barracks were drafty and only just large enough to house them all, but it was far better than sleeping on the floor of a temple. The outhouses were a long walk down a muddy slope, but it was better than tramping into fields with a spade in one hand and a crumple of paper in the other. Signs at opposite corners of the parade ground pointed toward two bomb shelters dug into the hillside.

As soon as each group of students settled into their barracks, they went to the mess hall, where the kitchen staff ladled out their supper, stewed pork with vegetables over rice. There was actually a long table and benches for sitting. Lian took a bite of dinner, ravenous after the long walk. She put her bowl on the table and looked around. Shao was with some of the senior students. Ying-Ying and Wendian waved at her to join them.

"Lian, where were you?" Ying-Ying asked. "Professor Lan walked with us for several miles and we had such a good discussion about war and its portrayal in classical literature."

"Have you seen Meirong?" Lian said. "Do you know which barracks she's in?"

"I haven't seen her since noon," Wendian said. She didn't sound concerned. "She was walking at the very back so she'll be one of the last to get in."

But there was another roll call after supper and everyone except Meirong was accounted for. No one remembered seeing her during the final few miles to Shangtan. A trickle of foot travelers were still making their way into the town and Mr. Lee posted two scouts to wait at the top of the road. So far, no one they'd asked had seen a student matching Meirong's description.

"What if Meirong sprained an ankle or fell ill on the road?" Lian said. A small group of them had gathered by the barracks gates.

"We can't leave her out there," Wendian said, clearly worried.

"I can take some scouts," Shao said. "We can carry rifles."

"None of you are to leave the town, not now that it's dark," Mr. Lee said. "Absolutely not. There are bandits in this area.

Ruthless, unpatriotic deserters. And those rifles don't have any ammunition."

"The bandits don't know that," Shorty said.

"Look." Ying-Ying pointed. "One of the scouts has come back."

The scout ran toward them, a policeman hurrying up the hill behind. When the scout caught sight of Mr. Lee, he ran even faster.

"Yee Meirong has been arrested," he said, panting. "They've taken her back to Changsha, to the police station there. The policeman wants to see Professor Kang."

PROFESSOR KANG FOUND transportation to Changsha the next morning. Lian pleaded to let her go with him. The other girls contributed some clothing and toiletry items for Meirong, which Lian tied up in a large square of cotton. She put all the cash she had saved inside her tunic pocket.

Their transportation was a jeep. A corporal was taking two deserters to the military jail in Changsha; he'd happily agreed to the professor's request, glad for some extra company and conversation. He gave Professor Kang the passenger seat beside the driver, while he sat in the back with Lian and the deserters. The jeep jolted over potholed roads, the driver pressing on the horn at any excuse. It was thirty-five miles to Changsha and the jeep could've gotten there in less than two hours if only the roads were less crowded. Lian thought of how long it had taken them to walk that distance. Two nights.

The deserters crouched on the floor with their knees up, hands tied together. They were no older than Lian, dirty and despondent. The young men didn't say a word, but the corporal talked the entire time.

"You stupid turtle eggs," the corporal said, addressing the two. His tone, however, was amiable. "Went off to join the bandits, did you? You'll be shot for deserting now. Instead of dying in glorious battle you'll be executed as cowards. A shame to your parents and your ancestors."

One of the young men sniffled. Snot dripped from his upper lip down to a receding chin.

"They're not bad boys, Professor," the corporal said. "I know these two here. Farmers, sons of farmers. They hide in the mountains and when the army leaves town, they sneak back to work their fields, see their families again. But they should've done that before they enlisted. Leave home, they're just missing. Leave the army, they're deserters. But they're none too bright, these boys."

The jeep hit a pothole and the deserters, unable to brace themselves, bounced and fell against each other.

"We make this trip to Changsha once a week, with or without deserters," the corporal said. He hauled one of the boys to an upright position. "Your Mr. Lee asked us to pick up Minghua's mail at the Changsha post office every week. And also take your outgoing mail to the post office."

"I hope he compensates you for the inconvenience," Professor Kang said.

"Ha ha, cigarette money, that's all," the corporal said with a laugh. "Happy to help our universities. But I tell you, mail delivery is not very reliable at the moment. When the folks in Shangtan find out I agreed to this, I'm going to be taking all sorts of mail to the Changsha post office, not just yours."

When they reached Changsha, the jeep stopped at the police station to let the professor and Lian get out. The corporal climbed in again, in the seat beside the driver. As they drove away, Lian could hear him berating the deserters.

"Those poor boys," Professor Kang murmured. He looked down his glasses at Lian. "Our military liaison, Colonel Chung, is a good man. Let's talk to Miss Yee first, let her know we're trying to free her. Then when I know what's needed, I'll go see the colonel."

The police in Changsha let them in to see Meirong but would only allow one visitor at a time. When Professor Kang came out of the holding room, he went straight to the senior police officer.

"Miss Yee says you have her rucksack," he said.

"We took it to look for antigovernment materials," the officer said.

"It contains textbooks that are university property," the professor said. "We need those back, nothing else."

The officer reached into the cabinet beside his desk and pulled out Meirong's rucksack. "There were papers in there, we took those."

"I just want the university's property back," Professor Kang said, his voice mild.

The officer unbuckled the straps on the rucksack and emptied its contents on his desk. Some pencils, notebooks, two books. A sandalwood comb. A brown paper bag of dried apricots. Professor Kang picked up the two books. One was a textbook, the other Meirong's copy of the Legends. The rest he put back in the rucksack, which he handed to Lian.

"I'm going to see Colonel Chung now, to sort this out," he said to the policeman. "I will return shortly. This young lady has brought clothing and some personal items for Miss Yee. Please let her into the holding cell."

The small room was windowless, airless. When Lian entered, Meirong opened her eyes. She was sitting on a wooden chair, one wrist cuffed to the armrest. She had tilted the chair on its back legs so that she could lean her head against the wall behind. The front legs of the chair thumped on the floor when Lian hurried over to her. There were dark circles under Meirong's eyes.

"Lian. I was so happy when Professor Kang told me you'd come with him." Even though she spoke barely above a whisper, her voice sounded rough.

"How are you?" Lian said. "Here's your rucksack. And I brought you some clothes, toothbrush, soap . . ."

Meirong shook her head. "Take them back with you," she said. "I won't get to keep them anyway."

"Why did they arrest you?" Lian said.

"They found out," Meirong said. "They know I'm involved with the Communist movement. I was only an hour out of that little town when they arrested me."

"Was your comrade . . ." Lian faltered.

"He never showed up. I think he's been arrested too," Meirong said. Then her voice dulled. "Lian, they want to send me to a re-education camp. To make me an example. A warning to students."

"A reeducation camp," Lian said, trying to sound cheerful. "They're like a kind of school."

Meirong shook her head. "Wang Jenmei told me about them. More like a forced labor camp with interrogation and torture."

"The professor will get you out before then," Lian said. She couldn't let Meirong see her anxiety. "He's gone to see Colonel Chung. He says the colonel is friendly and helpful. He'll be able to do something."

"But he probably doesn't outrank military intelligence," Meirong said, "and it was someone from the Juntong who arrested me. Here"—Meirong reached deep inside her tunic and pulled out a small cloth wallet—"take my money. I won't be needing it."

"Yes, you will," Lian whispered. "What if you need to bribe guards, buy favors? Nicer food?"

"Oh, Lian." Meirong's laugh sounded almost normal. "The camp guards will take away everything I have anyway. I'd rather you have it." She lowered her voice to a whisper. "And when you have a chance, talk to Wendian. She's part of my cell. They need to lie low for a while. And tell them not to worry about me. I won't give them away. But there could be spies inside Minghua."

Lian squeezed Meirong in a tight embrace. How could she tell Meirong that she was one of the spies? But not the one who had betrayed her.

"COLONEL CHUNG PROMISED to do what he could for Miss Yee," the professor said when he and Lian were headed back to Shangtan. "Unfortunately, the odds are not in her favor. The Juntong confiscated papers from her rucksack and found articles written by left-wing activists. The best the colonel could do was lend us this car and driver to take us back to Shangtan."

The professor leaned back with a sigh, rested his head against the crocheted antimacassar of the seat's headrest. He had been energetic and forceful all day. Now he held the two books to his chest and closed his eyes. He looked like a tired old man. Tired and defeated.

Lian realized she had been taking him for granted. Everyone had. They hadn't appreciated the enormity of what Professor Kang and the rest of the faculty had taken on, shepherding a campus of young men and women through a war-ravaged land, all the while trying to keep their studies on track. And on top of all that, safeguarding the Library of Legends. She felt a rush of affection for the elderly man.

Lian leaned her head against the window, wondering what else they could do to help Meirong. But she hadn't slept all night for worry, and the motion of the car lulled her to drowsiness. When she woke, the car was driving along the main street of Shangtan, and Professor Kang was tapping her shoulder. She sat up.

"Professor Kang, if I can get transportation, can I go to Changsha on the weekend to see Meirong?" she asked.

The old man shook his head. "Let's wait and see if Colonel Chung is successful. If not, they'll have taken her to the camp by the weekend. In which case I'll try and arrange visits. But that's all we can do. It's out of my hands."

When Lian got to her dorm building, the other girls were sitting on beds, talking. The chatter stopped when she came in. It was a long time before she stopped crying and could answer their questions.

LIAN HAD PROMISED Meirong she would warn Wendian, but it wasn't easy getting her on her own. The barracks were cramped, opportunities for privacy rare, and Wendian always seemed to be part of a group. It was as though she was avoiding Lian, ignoring her pleading looks.

But Friday finally came, a half day when the students were free to roam Shangtan. Lian caught sight of Wendian's long ponytail bobbing along the street and followed her to a bookstore, the students' most popular destination. Wendian paused by the entrance and when she saw Lian, she moved along to the next store. They fell into step and continued on toward the market square.

"Meirong has a message for you," Lian said, looking around before she spoke. "She says you should all lie low for a while."

"It was Mr. Lee who gave her away to the Juntong," Wendian said. "I'm sure of it. Everyone knows the director of student services is usually a government spy."

"I didn't know that," Lian said.

"Oh, Lian, there are always spies." Wendian sounded sad rather than scornful. "There are even Chinese spying for the Japanese, did you know? They scout out towns, draw maps, identify targets for bombing raids. What else did Meirong say?"

"That you're not to worry," Lian said, "that she won't give you away."

"She'd die sooner than give us up." Wendian was silent for a moment. Her eyes brimmed with tears. "I wish I'd gone to see her, too, Lian, but I was afraid."

"It could've been risky," Lian said. "You were right not to go."

"We can fight back." Wendian wiped her eyes with a sleeve. "We're not helpless." She tossed her ponytail over her shoulder and walked away before Lian could reply.

But Lian did feel helpless. There had to be a way to get Meirong out of that jail, out of the reeducation camp. Could she plead with Mr. Lee? Did he have enough influence? What about Cook Tam? But she wasn't supposed to know about Cook Tam.

Perhaps if Meirong was willing to say she'd been naïve, led by Jenmei, the authorities would let her go. Meirong could be so stubborn, but if she could just see Meirong one more time, talk some sense into her, ask her to lie about her ideals. Give them up just long enough to persuade her captors.

"Miss Hu?" A gentle hand on her arm. It was Sparrow. "Professor Kang asked me to find you. He has news about Miss Yee."

"Maybe Colonel Chung has freed her," Lian said. "Maybe he wants me to go with him to Changsha and get Meirong."

Lian ran until she got to the barracks room that was both office and sleeping quarters for Professor Kang. She knocked on the door and the professor's voice called out immediately for her to enter. Mr. Lee was there, too. The director of student services looked resigned and unhappy, not threatening. But Lian knew right away from the expression on the professor's face that the news wasn't good. Professor Kang cleared his throat.

"Colonel Chung wasn't able to persuade the Juntong," he said. "Yee Meirong is being taken to a reeducation camp."

"Can we visit? Take her food?" she said.

"The camp is in a very remote location," Mr. Lee said, "a hundred miles away from any town. Even if we got permission, it would be extremely difficult getting there to visit."

"Of course, we'll keep trying to get her released," the professor said, "but apparently she isn't helping her own case."

No, of course not. Meirong's vow to honor Wang Jenmei's legacy only added to her determination. Even in death, Jenmei still had influence over Meirong.

There had to be something she could do for Meirong. Who never complained about the hardships of the road, who never asked to be her friend but just assumed they were. Meirong, who was so incurably stubborn. Lian couldn't leave Minghua, not yet. She had to ask Mr. Lee if he'd been the one to report Meirong. Beg him to intervene. And she had to do it before she lost her nerve.

LIAN HAD ASKED to see Mr. Lee in private and now he stood behind his desk, looking out the window even though there was nothing to see. It was dark outside and the glass panes only threw back their reflections.

"Miss Hu. What can I do for you?" He turned to put his cigarette carefully on the ashtray and a long stick of ash broke off. He turned back to stare at the window.

"Meirong. Did you give her up to the Juntong?" she said.

"I like young people," he said to her reflected image. "That's why I took this job. But the war. War changes everything, you know."

"You could've intervened," she said, "you could've talked to her, warned her."

"So could you," he replied, his back still turned.

"I didn't know she was in so deep. But she would've listened to you. You have authority."

"Do you really think so, Miss Hu?" He turned around and tapped the remaining ash off his cigarette, ground it out. "Do you really think either of us could've convinced her?"

Lian was silent for a moment, acknowledging the truth of this. "Meirong wasn't a danger to you. She was just idealistic."

"I don't know who could've given her name to the Juntong. It wasn't me," he said. "There were a lot of people in Changsha, a lot of mixing around with other universities, with strangers."

"But can you help get her out? Intervene? Please."

He shook his head. It was as she expected. He couldn't go against the Juntong's decision.

"I won't spy for you anymore," she said.

"You're upset," he said, turning back to the window. "Why don't you take some time to think things over? Let's talk another day. I know you want to visit your friend at the camp. I'll see what I can do."

Lian left Lee's office, shaking at the unfairness of it all, at her utter helplessness. The clear skies above, the glorious moon and starlight, they all mocked her. They traveled their arcs each night, untroubled by the woes of mere mortals. All she'd gotten from Mr. Lee were vague words about visiting Meirong.

From the corner of her eye, she thought she saw movement in the shadows outside Lee's office. But she turned her head away in case it was Lee coming out to speak with her again.

CHAPTER 25

Shortly after sunset, mists rose from the riverbank and clung to the hills above Shangtan. A
noise like sails snapping their sheets in a strong
wind made some of the townspeople latch their window shutters, wondering if a storm was on its way.
Above the cliff walls behind the barracks, a waning
crescent moon shone on leathery creatures climbing
out of hollows in the rock. They clung to the cliff face
for a few moments before taking flight. The giant bats
circled overhead before turning north, wingspans as
wide as those of an albatross.

Other sounds reverberated in the forested hills surrounding Shangtan. Gnarled mountain pines groaned
as though bracing for an earthquake. Sailors would've
likened the noise to the creaking of masts in a strong
wind as tree spirits tore their way out of ancient trunks

that had been their homes for centuries. Covered in moss, with resinous pine needles stuck to their scraggly hair, they dragged large veined feet through the forest floor and turned north. Now bereft of their spirits, the trees shuddered then settled into silence. They were unchanged, as tall and thriving as before, but the small creatures living beneath their roots suddenly felt more vulnerable. Rabbits and bamboo rats immediately began tunneling deeper burrows.

THE STAR BROUGHT a kettle of hot water to Professor Kang's office. The professor took out two small cups and put a frugal pinch of tea leaves into a teapot. They waited as the fragrance of fine *longjing* tea intensified.

"Lu'an is famous for melon seed tea so I bought some while we were there," the professor said, "but this variety of *longjing* from the Lion's Peak region is still my favorite."

The Star settled on a stool across from his desk. "I'll pay attention to what the local stores carry," she said, "and hopefully find you some more."

The professor poured, inhaling deeply in appreciation. The Star took the small cup and did the same before blowing on the surface of the tea and taking a sip.

"About the Library of Legends," the Star said. "When Minghua goes on the road again to Chengtu, you must take the books to the caves near Zunyi. That's where the Legends must be stored."

"But the university is going to Chengtu," Kang protested. "Shouldn't the Legends stay with us?"

"The Library must go to the caves at Zunyi," the Star said gently but firmly, "where they'll be safe until this war is over."

Each time the professor thought of leaving the Library behind, it was with a sharp stab of loss. But he knew they had been lucky.

The Library of Legends was intact. Minghua 123 had lost only two of its members. Three if you counted Yee Meirong.

The Star finished her tea and pulled a well-worn shirt out of her bag. She threaded a needle and began patching the elbows. The needle slid in and out of the fabric, her fingers barely seeming to make an effort.

"I'm guessing that's one of his shirts," he said.

"I accepted long ago that he might never recognize me," she said. "I've been happy just to be a part of his lives."

She finished sewing and slid her needle into a square of red felt. She folded the shirt and tucked it inside her bag.

"Let's go for a walk," she said.

Professor Kang put on a heavy coat and they went out into the winter night. It was silent, too cold for the rustle of nocturnal animals, all hibernating in their burrows and dens. Too early yet for frogs to sing from the mudbanks. The only sound was that of the Hsiang River lapping against its shores.

When she finally spoke, the Star sounded weary. "I've been down here too long, Professor. Learned too many human traits. Forgotten how things work in heaven."

"Is there something in particular you've forgotten?" he asked.

"When I asked the Queen Mother of Heaven to bring back my Prince each time to a life of comfort," she said, "it was because I couldn't bear to think of him coming back as a beggar or a starving peasant. So he's always reborn as a person of privilege. To a wealthy family. Sometimes royalty. But even so, he never seems truly happy in any of his lives."

"Perhaps it's because he misses you, even while not knowing it," Kang said.

"No," she said. "There's something else, something more. I just haven't figured out what."

They continued along the riverbank. He gazed up and imagined how the landscape might appear if he were looking down from the constellations, the river's watery path curling north to Changsha, continuing on until it flowed into Dongting Lake.

"I can feel it, you know," the Star said, "the exodus of immortal creatures. Each day I quell the urge to follow them north, to resist the polar pull of the Kunlun Mountains. He is all that keeps me here."

He. The Prince. Shao. The professor sighed.

SO MANY OF his classmates had rushed to enlist after Nanking fell. Shao did consider joining up. He had wavered, changed his mind a dozen times, and only Sparrow knew of his indecision. But if he'd had any thoughts of enlisting, they'd faded with his mother's last letter.

> The only place as safe as the foreign Settlement in Shanghai is the protection of your university as you move west. The only thing that keeps me from falling into despair is the knowledge that you are safe.

He couldn't enlist. His mother already worried enough about his brothers. More impatient and less tolerant of their mother's anxieties, they no longer lived in Shanghai. His eldest brother, Luming, was with the government in Chunking, aide to a cabinet minister. When the war began, his second brother, Tienming, had gone to the port town of Wen-chou to run the family's warehouses and shipping business. His mother's sanity depended on knowing Shao was with Minghua. She probably pictured students strolling cheerfully from one picturesque rural town to another, staying at quaint inns, dining on interesting local dishes. She had no idea what they had seen and faced.

He set his lamp on the floor beside his cot and sat down cross-legged to read. The arrangement Mr. Lee made for getting their mail to and from Changsha worked remarkably well. For the second weekend in a row, a package of letters had arrived for him. Some more than a month old, but at least they were getting through.

His roommates had set up a trestle table where they studied by the light of shared oil lamps.

"Shao, your lamp!" one of them called. "We need it here."

He waved off the request. "Right after I read my letters."

Unexpectedly, there was one from his brother Tienming. His brothers never wrote. It was his mother who wrote to each of them, passing on all the family news. His brother's letter had been posted from Shanghai, not Wen-chou.

> *Younger Brother, I hope you're safe and in good health. I heard from Cousin Wenfei at the Ministry of Education that Minghua University is on its way to Changsha, so that's where this letter will probably reach you, providing the situation doesn't change.*
>
> *You should know our mother is very ill. I have been going back and forth to Shanghai because of this. She won't allow us to tell you and she would never ask it of you because she says your education is too important and the journey back too dangerous. But I wanted you to know so that you're not taken by surprise should the worst come.*

Shao had to find Sparrow, talk over what to do. It would have to be first thing in the morning, as soon as Sparrow had finished her chores.

"Shao, can I borrow your fountain pen?" Chen Ping stood over him. "I've misplaced mine."

"Yes, yes," he replied, patting his pockets. "Here. But it's low on ink, let me find my ink bottle."

"No need," Ping said. "I only need to write a very short letter to my father."

"He is well, I hope," Shao said, out of politeness.

"Yes. I just found out he remarried. I'm writing to congratulate him." Ping couldn't hide his bitterness. "My mother died only last year, you know."

Shao straightened up. "Yes, I remember."

"I didn't even realize she was so seriously ill until it was too late," Ping said. "I'll never forgive myself for not seeing my mother before she died."

CHAPTER 26

Lian paused to button up against the damp chill of a winter breeze. Beside her, Shao pulled on his gloves, expertly mended along the seams. She pointed at a student hurrying across the parade ground, a scarf of mismatched wools wrapped around his head and shoulders.

"Shorty used to be such a dandy," she said. "He asked Ying-Ying to knit him that scarf from odds and ends. Who'd guess now that we're the academic elite of China? We look just like poor folk."

"And we're just as itchy." Shao scratched his arm, where clusters of tiny red spots formed a rash.

"Lice or fleas?" she asked sympathetically.

"Probably both. I'll have Sparrow buy some alcohol or *bai bu* roots at an herbalist's."

"One of your tutorial students told me about the talk you gave the other day," Lian said, as they walked across the quadrangle. "You told them to use their knowledge to lift up the poor folk and fight for democracy."

"Yes. We need to pay more attention to the rural population once this war is over," Shao said. "They grow our food but can barely feed themselves. Their labors aren't rewarded properly."

"And in the meantime," Lian said, taking one of his gloved hands, "Sparrow mends your clothes for nothing."

Shao looked genuinely astonished. "Does she?"

"Do you even notice all the ways she looks after you?" she said. "A wife couldn't do better than Sparrow." She winced at her thoughtless choice of words but Shao didn't seem to notice.

"I must thank her," Shao said. A pause. "You know, Lian, it was better when you were shy and talked less." But he was smiling and for a moment she forgot about Meirong.

"Hey, Hu Lian." A voice called from behind. It was Wendian. "A moment of your time."

"Go on," Lian said to Shao. "I'll find you in the library."

Wendian caught up to Lian and gripped her arm. Hard. "Were you the one who betrayed Meirong?"

"How can you say that?" Lian said, confused and astonished. "Meirong was my friend."

"You and your secret meetings with Mr. Lee," Wendian said. "I saw you leave his office last night."

"It wasn't . . . that wasn't a secret meeting." Lian groped for words, tried not to let guilt wash over her face. "I was asking Mr. Lee if there was anything he could do to help Meirong."

"Don't play the innocent, Lian," Wendian hissed. "I heard what you said. Watch yourself. I've taken care of Lee and you'll be next."

She stalked away, anger in the set of her shoulders, the gait of her walk.

Lian desperately tried to remember. What had she said to Mr. Lee? She had begged him to do more for Meirong. What had Wendian overheard? Lian's hand came up to cover her mouth, stifling a gasp of horror.

She had told Mr. Lee she wouldn't spy for him anymore. Was that what Wendian overheard? And what did Wendian mean about taking care of Mr. Lee?

ON SATURDAY MORNINGS, the jeep bringing mail from Changsha always came before noon. Lian could tell by the number of students milling around the barracks entrance that it had arrived. She walked a little faster, shoulders hunched against the light drizzle. She pulled her knitted hat lower over her forehead. Perhaps there was a letter from her mother. With a new address. A fixed address. She longed for some good news. She was still shaken by her encounter with Wendian the day before, unsure what to do about her warning, which had been ambiguous but definitely hostile.

She had to find an opportunity to get Wendian on her own. Speak to her again, convince her that she had never spied for Mr. Lee. She would lie, say that he'd asked her to spy for him and she'd refused. Perhaps Wendian would calm down.

Closer to the gates, she noticed the students were strangely silent. She hung back, not sure what was happening. Professor Kang and Mr. Lee got into a jeep, Mr. Lee moving awkwardly. His hands were tied behind his back. The vehicle drove away, canopy up against the rain.

Lian hurried over to Shao.

"What's going on?" she said. "Why are Mr. Lee and Professor Kang going off with the military police?"

"Mr. Lee's been arrested," Shao said. "On suspicion of spying for the Japanese. The professor has gone to Changsha to vouch for his innocence."

Lunchtime conversation was loud, some students arguing for Mr. Lee's innocence and others claiming they'd always had their doubts. Rumors abounded as the students pieced together what they'd overheard and observed.

"When the military police arrived," Shorty said, "they searched Mr. Lee's office and found maps hidden behind a bookcase, maps marked with targets for bombing."

"But that doesn't mean anything," Ying-Ying protested. "The maps could've been there before we came."

"It's all hearsay until the professor returns," Shao said. "Let's not jump to conclusions."

The entire campus had been on edge after Meirong's arrest. And now Mr. Lee. Whether or not Lee was guilty, they could be certain of one thing: the Juntong's interrogation techniques were not gentle. Lian couldn't stand hearing any more speculation. It made her worry all the more about what Meirong might be facing.

After lunch, she walked past Wendian, who was seated at a table by the mess hall door. She seemed to have been waiting for Lian because she got up and followed her outside, where the morning's drizzle had cleared the skies. Lian turned around to face Wendian.

"I went to see Mr. Lee because I wanted to ask whether he could do more to help Meirong," she said, not waiting for the other girl to speak. "Be reasonable, Wendian. Why are you blaming me for Meirong's arrest? She's my friend."

Her closest friend. The dearest friend she'd ever had.

"Because I heard you quite clearly, Hu Lian," Wendian said. "I heard you say you wouldn't spy for him anymore. Well, 'anymore' is too late."

"I refused him." Lian kept her voice as steady as possible. "I never did anything he asked. Meirong met so many people in Changsha, it could've been anyone."

"What about Wang Jenmei?" Wendian smiled, but it was more of a sneer. "Who in that little fishing village could've been responsible for betraying her? Lee is gone. You're next."

PROFESSOR KANG RETURNED from Changsha late in the afternoon. Shao pushed his way into the mess hall. The windows were foggy from humidity and the warmth of so many bodies crowded inside, everyone anxious to hear the professor's news.

"Mr. Lee will not be coming back to us," the professor said. "He's been cleared of all wrongdoing, but he's resigned from Minghua. He will be returning to his family in Nanchang. And there is a serious matter I wish to put before you."

The Juntong had arrested Mr. Lee after they received an anonymous note addressed to the senior officer in Changsha. The note had come in the bag of mail that the army jeep carried every Friday afternoon from Shangtan to Changsha.

"I'm aware the note might've come from anyone," Professor Kang said, "especially since many who live in Shangtan are making use of our mail arrangements. I know we're at war and tensions are running high, but I trust that you, as educated young men and women, will make sure of the evidence before accusing anyone. I don't need to tell you how much harm this has caused Mr. Lee. It's beyond mischief, it's malice. And it wasted valuable police time."

Then the wail of air-raid sirens drowned out the rest of his words. The Japanese were finally paying their respects to Shangtan.

Shao scanned the parade ground for Lian. She had been upset over Meirong, that was to be expected, but lately there was something else. The way she seemed to only half listen, her attention diverted elsewhere. The wary look in her eyes, even when she smiled at him. He caught sight of her, moving with the crowd toward the air-raid shelter at the north corner of the barracks. He found her inside crouched against a wall, arms wrapped around her knees, head down. He sat on the ground beside her and looked around the shelter.

Sparrow was already there, in a corner with some of the servants. Everyone around her buzzed with excitement and nerves, but Sparrow made Shao think of a calm pool of light. Chen Ping and Shorty came in, then Professor Kang, followed by laborers carrying crates of books. As the door clanged shut on the shelter, the roar of aircraft engines told him the bombers were almost directly overhead.

The Japanese had extended their raids beyond Changsha. It took just a short diversion for Japanese planes to reach Shangtan. Tucked against the hills, their campus was one of the more difficult targets, but today the fog had cleared. And seen from above, it was clearly a military barracks.

"Don't be scared," Shao said. Lian's slim body was shaking. "If bombs fall here, they'll land on the barracks, not on the air-raid shelters. We're dug right into the side of the hill."

"It's not the bombs that frighten me." Her voice was so forlorn. In that moment, all he wanted was to protect her.

"Then what is it?" he said. "What's frightened you?"

Lian looked around. "Stay behind with me after the all clear," she whispered.

The air raid was brief, no more than forty minutes. The shelter emptied quickly. One of the servants propped open the shelter door and a welcome gust of cold fresh air blew in. Soon it was just the two of them sitting on hard concrete.

Lian fidgeted, then finally spoke. "It's Wendian," she said. "She blames Mr. Lee for Meirong's arrest and she blames me, too."

She whispered as though afraid of being overheard, even though they were the only ones still in the shelter. Shao put an arm around her shoulders and pulled her close.

"I don't understand," he said. "Why would Wendian think you or Mr. Lee are to blame for Meirong's arrest?"

"According to her, every director of student services is a Nationalist spy," Lian said. "She thinks he reported Meirong after she took over as leader of Minghua's Communist Students Club."

"Oh, we all knew it was a good bet Lee was put here to keep an eye on us." He frowned. "But why does Wendian think you had anything to do with Meirong's arrest?"

"Because she knows I was spying on my classmates." She turned her head away. "Mr. Lee recruited me to spy, Shao. He threatened to expose me if I didn't."

Shao scoffed. "What's there to expose? You're a scholarship student."

"You don't know how my father died." Her eyes met his, pleading. "He was shot by a police officer who mistook him for a Japanese spy. The police admitted their mistake, but not publicly. Officially, my father died a traitor and everyone believes the official story."

Her face taut with misery, she told him how her mother had gotten new identity papers, changed their names, moved to Peking. That Lian had agreed to Mr. Lee's demands out of fear that she'd be shunned for being a traitor's daughter. That Cook Tam was also at Minghua to spy on the students.

"I don't know who betrayed Meirong," Lian said. "Mr. Lee said it could've been anyone, perhaps someone Meirong befriended in Changsha. But I'm sure Wendian was the one who sent the anonymous note accusing Lee of being a Japanese spy. She said she'd taken care of him."

"If she did, that was clever," Shao said. "Accusing Lee of being a Communist would've been ludicrous. But there's so much hatred when it comes to the Japanese no one would stop to think." He didn't voice the worst part of it. Before Mr. Lee managed to clear his name, he would've suffered horribly at the hands of the Juntong.

"And then Wendian told me I was next," Lian said. "I'm sure she'll have me arrested."

Unlike Mr. Lee, however, if Lian was arrested, she would not be released quickly. Shao knew this. Her father's past would be dragged up and reevaluated, this time to denunciate Lian. Like father like daughter, they would say.

"You don't have to believe me," she said.

"I believe you, Lian," he said. He did believe her. And he wanted to help. "You know, although he's in Shanghai, perhaps my father can do something. I'll ask him whether he knows anyone who can get Meirong released."

"Shao, is that possible?" Her eyes brightened. "Does your family have that much influence?"

"I should've thought of it sooner," he said. "I'll write to him."

"Write two letters," Lian said. "Mail takes weeks. Mail gets lost. We need to be sure at least one letter gets through. I'll take the second letter to your father in Shanghai."

"Lian, you can't mean you would go on your own," he said, taken aback.

"What if your father needs convincing?" she said. "What if I need to plead Meirong's case with him? This could be the only way to help her. Don't you see? I have to make sure your father says yes."

He tried again. "It's madness for you to travel to Shanghai alone."

"I have to go anyway," she said, jumping up. "I need to leave before Wendian carries through with her threats. I've been wanting to leave, to find my mother. I've saved money, I've bought maps. Just write those letters, please, Shao."

All this time he'd thought of her as the girl he'd guided through the streets of Nanking, silent and helpless. Now she stood, jaw clenched and narrow shoulders pushed back. Defiant and determined. Now he saw the steel in her. She would go on her own if need be to save her friend. To find her mother.

"I want my mother," she said, and this time a note of longing crept into her voice. Her brown eyes were bleak, but her chin was still defiantly lifted.

He couldn't let her go alone. "I want to see my mother, too," he said, getting to his feet. "We'll go to Shanghai together. The two of us."

Her face grew radiant and she threw her arms around him, then shrank back quickly, as if startled by her own impulsiveness. He tilted her face to his and she looked up at him, lips parted. The softness of her mouth and the warmth of her quivering body pressed against him stirred something, a yearning that felt familiar. It was nothing like what he'd felt with Jenmei, excited yet uneasy. Jenmei, with her knowing smile as she wound herself around him.

"The two of us," he repeated. "And Sparrow."

"WE MUST PLAN for the worst case," Sparrow said, coming straight to the point. "If Miss Hu is accused of being a spy, then we'll be accused of helping her escape. We'll be arrested if caught."

They were having dinner in the village instead of the mess hall. The noodle shop resounded with customers' shouts, the serving staff's responding cries, and in the background, the constant clatter of crockery. Here, they could speak in private.

"I know. Best case, Wendian does nothing," Shao said. "But we must leave anyway because of Meirong. That makes it a question of when. When is the earliest they would come to arrest Lian? We must get out before then."

"The earliest they'll come is Saturday morning," Sparrow said, "so we must escape no later than Friday evening."

"Why Saturday?" Shao said. She seemed so certain.

"Because the mail jeep comes on Friday," Sparrow said. "If Wendian puts a note in this Friday's outgoing mail, the Juntong in Changsha will get it Friday night or the next morning. Saturday morning is the earliest they would come to arrest Miss Hu."

"Which was when they came for Mr. Lee," Shao said, understanding.

They stepped out of the restaurant to the creaks and groans of rusty metal hinges. Street vendors were closing down stands, watched by stray dogs hoping for some final uneaten scraps. One sat down and scratched vigorously, making Shao wish he could scratch the rash on his own leg.

"The most important thing is to get as far away as possible in the first two days," he said. "After that, it'll be safe to travel more openly. With so many refugees on the road, the Juntong would have a hard time tracking us down."

"We'll need a few things," Sparrow said, "and food for the journey. I'll buy what we need while you're in class."

There had never been any question in Shao's mind that Sparrow would come. And Sparrow hadn't seemed surprised when he told her. But he'd experienced a moment of discomfiture when he first told Lian that Sparrow was coming. As if he and Sparrow should've been the ones running away together.

Briefly, the thought crossed Shao's mind that without Sparrow, they wouldn't get to Shanghai.

THE LAST DAY of the Lunar New Year had come and gone. The intensity of bombing raids had forced Minghua to keep their festivities subdued. But as if to compensate, Professor Kang reflected, February arrived with warm breezes and for the past several evenings there had been flocks of avian spirits crossing the sky. Like truant children, he and the Star often slipped away from Shangtan as evening fell to walk along the river. The airborne spirits flew into the west at sunset, making them difficult for his mortal eyes to see. Kang took great pleasure in watching their flight. The professor had seen poison feather birds, rainbirds, and three-legged greenbirds. Miraculous creatures he never would've noticed without the Star's prompting.

They paused at the river's edge, where the promise of spring hung from bare branches misted in pale green. Stems of new grass pushed through winter debris and the air carried a fresh, indescribable scent.

The Star gave him a nudge and he looked up. Silver-crested birds soared overhead, long scarlet legs trailing below white bodies. The professor strained his eyes to watch as they wheeled to the northwest, until the arc of white vanished against a drift of clouds.

"Cranes, or at least they look like cranes," the Star said. "They were human once, sages who became immortal through attaining enlightenment. Now they take the form of birds for their journey."

Unexpectedly, the Star put her arm through his as they strolled along the river, something she had never done before. Tall water reeds stirred in the evening breeze and dry grasses brushed against his ankles, leaving tiny burrs on his trousers. Beside them, waves lapped over stones polished smooth by flowing water. It was as though war had never touched his life. He savored the moment, lingered in its tranquility.

"Our paths must now diverge, my friend," the Star said.

Somehow he had been expecting this.

"Don't worry about the Library of Legends," she said. "On your way to Chengtu you need to make a detour to the town of Zunyi. Once you store the Legends in the caves outside Zunyi your duty of care will be over."

"But you're leaving?" he said. "When?" A stab of sorrow. One that would bury itself in his heart, he knew, as deeply as the loss of his wife and child, scars now decades old.

"I'm leaving tomorrow. I'm helping Shao and Lian escape," she said. "You don't know anything about it. But be aware that Tan Wendian is a very angry young woman who's been playing with lives. She's one reason why we must leave."

"I will pretend complete ignorance," Professor Kang said. "Do you need a map?"

The Star laughed, as he thought she might. He knew, because she had told him that after thousands of years of looking down on China, she could picture every city, hill, and river, swaths of forest and expanses of desert. Even new highways and railway tracks were easy to navigate because they connected cities to other cities. If she ever felt lost at night, she only had to look up and her sister stars gave her guidance. It was one of the precious fragments of insight he'd managed to glean over the years.

There were so many unfinished conversations, let alone the questions he'd never asked. Now he cursed his reticence.

"Something I'd like to bring up," he said, clearing his throat. "I've been thinking about what you said, that the Prince never seems truly happy. I think it's because he lacks purpose."

The Star looked at him, brows furrowed.

"When a man lives a life of good deeds, he earns a better life in his next reincarnation," he said, in a rush to explain. "He might be richer or happier in his family life. When he does evil, his next reincarnation punishes him with poorer circumstances. But life after life, the Prince has been reincarnated to much the same status as before. It means he's done nothing good or bad in each life to tip the scales enough either way to merit change. He neither advances nor worsens. It means he's lived a passive existence *every single time*. How is that even possible?"

"With intervention from the Queen Mother of Heaven, I suppose," the Star said slowly. "She promised me he would enjoy a good life each time. But even the Queen Mother must abide by the Wheel of Rebirth."

"So she can't meddle with his reincarnation," the professor said, pausing to face the river, "but she can meddle with his life so that he's reincarnated to a life that's no better or worse. She can do this by suppressing emotions and motivation. Traits that propel us to kindness or evil. Traits that fuel purpose."

"Purpose." The Star turned her face up to the sky. "I understand. The guardian spirits are leaving, but some do so unwillingly. With nothing to protect, no prayers to answer, they lack purpose."

Professor Kang knew this was his last conversation with the Star. That he would now live with the absence of wonder. He reminded himself that he had seen the immortal. That before she left, a Star had taken him by the arm. It was enough. It had to be enough. As if she could hear his thoughts, she turned to him.

"You've been a good friend, Professor," she said. "May favorable winds attend your journey, for all the days of your life."

THE JOURNEY EAST

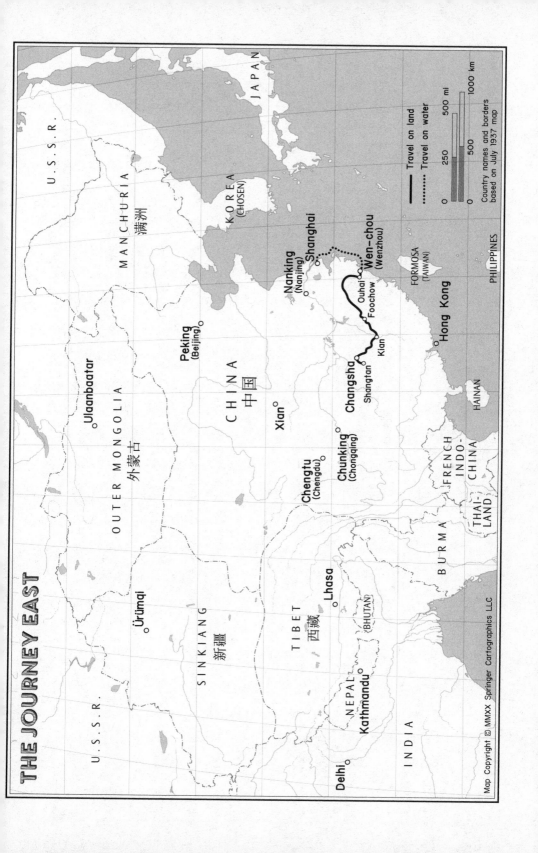

THE JOURNEY EAST

U.S.S.R.

U.S.S.R.

MANCHURIA
满洲

JAPAN

KOREA
(CHOSEN)

Ulaanbaatar

OUTER MONGOLIA
外蒙古

Peking
(Beijing)

Shanghai

Nanking
(Nanjing)

Wen–chou
(Wenzhou)

Ouhai

Foochow

Ürümqi

SINKIANG
新疆

CHINA
中国

Xian

Changsha

Shangtan

Kian

FORMOSA
(TAIWAN)

Hong Kong

Chengtu
(Chengdu)

Chunking
(Chongqing)

HAINAN

Lhasa

TIBET
西藏

BHUTAN

FRENCH INDO-CHINA

BURMA

THAI-LAND

PHILIPPINES

NEPAL

Kathmandu

Delhi

INDIA

Travel on land
Travel on water

0   250   500 mi
0   500   1000 km

Country names and borders
based on July 1937 map

Map Copyright © MMXX Springer Cartographics LLC

CHAPTER 27

On Friday, most students used their afternoon of free time to stroll around the streets of Shang-tan and its market square. They browsed secondhand stores and shopped for used books and clothing to replace what had worn out. They treated themselves to meals from sidewalk kitchens. The more devout offered incense at the town's temples.

Shao and Lian left the barracks in ordinary clothes, nothing that marked them as students of Minghua. They loitered in the market, watched a fortune-teller shake his bamboo canister, customers crowded around intently as the wooden fortune sticks spilled out onto the cloth-covered table. Stalls all around echoed with spirited haggling. Shao nudged Lian toward the stall selling baskets. The lane beside it led out of the square toward the riverfront, where they would meet Sparrow.

The rattle of fortune-telling sticks started up again and abruptly stopped. The wail of air-raid sirens churned the air. The market grew chaotic as stallkeepers gathered up their wares and stores emptied. Shoppers dashed in different directions, some going straight to the shelters, others running to collect their families. Shao pulled Lian down the lane and they began running toward the river.

"What if they bomb the riverfront like they did the other day?" Lian asked, panting.

"Let's find a place to wait and see what happens," Shao said. They cut through an area of bombed-out buildings, a neighborhood destroyed during the first bomb attack. They stumbled over a wrecked house, carved shutters, and chunks of roof tile. The sirens' howling continued unabated. Shao glanced up the hill for the warning beacons and saw both lights were extinguished. The planes would be overhead any moment. He pulled Lian into the shelter of a wide brick arch at the mouth of a long, low tunnel, its roof partially collapsed.

"What sort of bomb shelter was this?" she asked.

"Not a shelter. I think it used to be a kiln," he said, pointing at shards of pottery scattered around the yard.

The planes roared above them, polished metal bodies gleaming, their red sun insignias clear and unmistakable. Almost immediately explosions rent the air from the direction of the marketplace. Bursts of flame shot up. Shao took Lian's hand and they ran toward the river to where Sparrow waited. The river glinted bright gold, reflecting clear skies and a setting sun. He never doubted Sparrow would be there. Even if the riverfront were being bombed, she would be there. Still, he heaved a sigh of relief when Sparrow's figure detached from a stand of willows.

Sparrow looked deceptively boyish. She had exchanged her

dark-blue servant's garb for khaki trousers and a short, padded jacket. She'd brought supplies with her in canvas bags she'd sewn straps onto, improvised rucksacks for their journey. They'd left their Minghua rucksacks behind to give the impression they were still in Shangtan.

It was Sparrow who had suggested doubling back to Changsha. The city was teeming with new arrivals. They'd just be anonymous faces in the crowd, not worth a second glance.

"Wei Daming goes back and forth between Wuhan and Changsha," Shao said, when Sparrow brought up the idea. "He might be able to help us with transportation. If he's in Changsha, he'll be at the hospital." The thought made him feel better, to get help from someone they could trust. It would be an adventure.

The three fugitives followed the riverbank away from the town, entering the heavily forested hills as soon as they could. They went in just deep enough to keep the road in sight while remaining unseen. Twice they heard voices and the snap of twigs. They froze and the voices moved on. Bandits roamed the woods, mostly just young men trying to avoid military duty. But they were also hiding out, hungry and desperate. The three continued through the night, Sparrow leading the way.

At sunrise, they concealed themselves in a copse of red pine, under the dense cover of wide, fragrant branches. They slept until noon, when Sparrow shared food from her bag, balls of sticky rice wrapped around pickled vegetables.

Lian opened a map. "I'm afraid it doesn't show the roads all the way up to Changsha," she said. "I wasn't planning to travel in that direction when I bought these maps."

"It's all right," Sparrow said. "If we keep the road in sight, we'll get there."

"We haven't gone as far as I'd like. It's slow when we have to beat our way through the underbrush," Shao said. "Should we try the road for a while?" The rash on his skin still irritated him and he hadn't slept much.

They peered through the trees. The road below was busy with foot traffic in both directions. At the sound of a vehicle horn's repeated honking, the stream of people parted. A jeep came around the bend, followed closely by a second one.

"Saturday morning," Shao said, "and that second car was the military police. They're on their way to arrest you, Lian. Wendian did turn you in."

"We have an advantage, though," Sparrow said. "Yesterday's aerial attack went on for a long time, the longest so far. A lot of students were in town when the planes came. People might think we're missing because we're injured. Or dead."

They walked until the sun set, then sat down to eat while there was enough light to see. They continued through the night, following Sparrow, who never hesitated. Wherever the forest canopy parted, the sky above them was awash with stars. They reached Changsha in the early morning hours.

THE HOSPITAL HAD run out of rooms and patients lined its hallways. Stretchers crowded the corridors. Some soldiers didn't even have blankets or mats; they were just lying on the floor, crimson pooling on the tiles beneath them. The stench in the hospital was terrible, urine and putrefaction overlaid with the chemical tang of bleach. A row of patients sat slumped in chairs lined against one wall. A hospital worker was handing them mugs of hot water.

Lian apologized as she stepped over a bandaged soldier, then realized the man was unconscious. A nurse at the far end of the corridor was directing stretcher-bearers. Shao and Sparrow went over to find out if she knew Daming.

Lian wrinkled her nose and, with a sigh, decided to follow them. She stopped, feeling a tug on her trouser leg. A soldier on the ground reached out to her. His legs were bandaged stumps, his face drawn with pain. He tried to speak but could only point at his mouth and the teapot beside him. She kneeled down and held the spout to his mouth, pouring in a dribble of weak tea until he nodded and closed his eyes, exhausted.

She had to go outside, breathe in some fresh air. But as she passed the row of chairs, one of the patients clutched at the hem of her coat. She looked down at a swollen, discolored face. Both the man's eyes were blackened and one hand was bandaged down to the fingers.

She recoiled. It was Mr. Lee.

"I must talk to you," he said, standing up slowly. "Please, Miss Hu. Let's talk where it's more private."

She jerked her coat away from him, ready to flee.

"Please. I don't know what you're doing in Changsha and I don't want to know," he said. "I just need to tell you something. About the dossier I have on you. On your family."

She followed as he dragged his chair around the corner to another, narrower corridor. It was mercifully empty. He sat down, wincing.

"Don't worry about the file on your father," he said. "There's nothing in there to incriminate him. Not anymore. Not for the past few years. I was just trying to frighten you."

Mr. Lee kept records on as many students as he could. He always checked up on family backgrounds and when the files for Minghua's scholarship winners arrived, Lian's was unusually thick. Whether it was the work of an overzealous clerk or a lazy one who hadn't bothered removing outdated documents, the file contained far more than he'd expected. He read her father's history with interest. He'd been so intrigued he'd made inquiries of his own about the man who'd shot her father. He learned that the officer had been a lieutenant, the chief of police's nephew. And that the young lieutenant had died three years ago.

But of more direct consequence to Lian and her mother, Tientsin's all-powerful chief of police had been arrested for fraud. A litany of crimes and indiscretions had come out during the trial, including the cover-up over her father's death.

"The trial was held behind closed doors," Mr. Lee said. "It was an embarrassment to the police. They didn't publicly confess to their wrongdoings, but they did update their records. Your father's file is clean, his innocence documented."

When Lian arrived at Minghua under her false identity, Mr. Lee guessed she didn't know her father's name had been cleared. Thus when Mr. Shen was killed and Lee needed another student informant, Lian's secrets made her the easiest to intimidate.

"I had to improvise," he said. "I'm very sorry."

"Is there anything else?" she said. Lian didn't know what she wanted to do more. To sink to the ground in relief or slap him.

"No. Nothing more." He paused. "I'm sorry. Truly sorry." He closed his eyes.

"If you really mean that," Lian said, "forget you saw me today."

"I gave them years of loyal service," he said, eyes still closed, "and it meant nothing when an anonymous source sent in a false accusation. Don't worry. You were never here."

Lian couldn't stay in the same building with Lee anymore. She ran out the hospital door. Outside, she sat on the stone steps, one refugee among hundreds milling about the grounds. She tried to still the roil of emotions churning her insides.

All those years of hiding. All those years of living in dread, of seeing her mother's eyes cloud over with suspicion at every new face who entered their lives. She put her head between her knees. Once she found her mother, she would tell her there was no more need to worry. But how would her mother feel, to know all her precautions had been useless?

"There you are, Lian," said Shao at her shoulder.

He and Sparrow sat down on the steps beside her. Sparrow had found a nurse who knew Wei Daming. They were expecting Daming at the hospital in two days with the next trainload of wounded.

"We should stay off the streets as much as we can," Shao said. "Avoid running into anyone we know."

"It's already happened," Lian said. She repeated her conversation with Mr. Lee.

Shao swore. "He can identify us."

"I think we should keep to our plans," Sparrow said. "Mr. Lee doesn't know all three of us are here. And it doesn't sound as though he's eager to help the Juntong. We're still better off in a crowd."

They used some of Shao's money to rent an overpriced room above an herbalist shop. Shao was irritable, restless. And scratching a lot. The herbalist sold Shao some balm for his rash.

"Just flea bites," he said, inspecting Shao's arm. "Nothing to worry about."

They weren't the only ones lodging above the shop, so Shao stayed in the room to watch over their belongings while Lian and Sparrow went out to buy food. Changsha had been the right decision. Its streets were congested with new faces, refugees and workers, soldiers and reporters. No one paid them any attention.

Lian and Shao even bought tickets to a film the next evening.

It was one they had seen months ago in Nanking. But that didn't matter. In the darkened theater, they shared a paper bag of salty dried plums and for an hour, Lian forgot she was a fugitive. When she gasped during a suspenseful moment in the film, Shao put his hand over hers. She didn't pull away.

DAMING WAS DELIGHTED, then confused, to see them. He would have more time to talk after he'd made sure his patients were settled, and they arranged to meet later that evening at a food stand around the corner from the hospital.

"But don't tell anyone we're here," Shao made him promise. "You'll understand when we tell you, but it's a life-or-death situation. I'm not exaggerating."

When Daming arrived, Shao had already ordered large bowls of noodles with spicy tofu sauce. Lian and Shao looked around guardedly from time to time. Sparrow was her usual serene self, quietly spooning up the spicy soup.

"Shanghai," Daming murmured, drumming his chopsticks on the table. "Shanghai, Shanghai. Let's see. What's the best way to get there? I've heard the fastest route is to the coast and then by boat to Shanghai."

"But how?" Shao said. "Isn't Hangchow Bay under Japanese blockade?"

"Yes, but you can get on a foreign-registered ship," Daming said. "A lot of Chinese companies have reregistered their ships to fly foreign flags. And there's always smugglers. We use them regularly."

"Our military does business with smugglers?" Lian couldn't hide her shock.

Daming snorted. "How do you think our inland cities get their imported goods? How does this hospital get the supplies and medicines we need?"

"So let's go to Wen-chou, Young Master," Sparrow said. "Your family owns warehouses and ships there. Your brother Tienming is there."

"I never considered going around the coast," Shao admitted. "Only overland and as directly to Shanghai as possible. But you're right. Tienming goes back and forth regularly from Wen-chou to Shanghai."

"Wen-chou is still Chinese territory," Daming said, "so I might be able to get you on trucks heading that way. Or at least get you partway there."

"But wouldn't we have to travel through some occupied areas?" Lian said.

"It's a matter of reconnaissance and intelligence," Daming said. "And it really depends. The boundaries keep moving, as you know. Civilians can bribe Japanese soldiers to let them through. In other places, the enemy is spread so thin it's possible to slip past patrols."

"Sounds too easy," Sparrow said.

"And in other places you'll be shot on sight," he admitted. "Let me see what I can do. Let's meet tomorrow at the hospital, same time."

"We understand the risks," Shao said, clapping Daming on the shoulder. "If you can get us a ride even partway, we're forever in your debt."

AT THE HOSPITAL gates the next evening, Daming looked pleased with himself.

"We don't have any transports that go all the way to Wen-chou," he said. "But I got you a ride to Kian. If you can walk from there to Foochow, I've a friend at the hospital there. He can try to get you a ride out of Foochow. It's all here in this letter of introduction, just give it to him."

"Anything is better than walking the whole way," Lian said. "We're very grateful."

"I still have a few things to do," Daming said, "but there's plenty of time before the trucks get here. They won't set out until it's dark. Come with me on my rounds, Shao."

Shao followed Daming as his friend moved between rows of stretchers, wounded men lucky enough to be transferred to a hospital far from the fighting. The soldiers were quiet; some even looked up and smiled when Daming walked past.

"I haven't any real medical training, as you know," he said, so softly Shao could barely hear his words. "I feel like an imposter. I worry that men have died because of me. But now I'm not sure how much of a difference I'd make even if I were a real doctor. Sometimes all you can do is sit with them and hold their hand, so they're not alone when their souls depart."

Daming crouched down over an unconscious solder. He picked up the young man's wrist and touched it, checking for a pulse. He did this so gently, with such gravity, that Shao felt as though he were intruding on a sacred ceremony.

Outside, two covered trucks pulled up to the hospital gates. The driver of the second truck jumped out and shook hands with Daming, then took down the tailgate. They helped Sparrow and Lian climb into the back of the truck.

"Be careful, Shao," Daming said. "I signed you a pass but it doesn't mean every soldier on patrol will honor it. There's always the risk you'll be captured and forced to enlist. And you may need to hand out a few bribes. I hope my doctor friend in Foochow can get you closer to the coast."

"Thanks so much, Daming," Shao said, shaking his hand. "You take care of yourself."

"I'm off to Wuhan tomorrow," Daming said, "then I'm heading for the front. I've told my uncle I can't do this shuttling back and forth anymore. We've lost too many medics on the battlefields and that's where I should be. Good-bye, old friend."

Daming stood on the hospital's front steps as the truck pulled away. His straight back and slow wave of the hand made Shao think of his grandfather, the way the old man always insisted on seeing guests off, waving courteously until they were out of sight.

CHAPTER 28

S hao wished the trucks would drive faster, but they traveled with the headlamps turned off to avoid being noticed by the enemy. He couldn't help his impatience even though he knew they were extremely lucky to get a ride. Hopefully their luck would hold. With only the three of them, it would be far easier to hitch rides and find places to stay. Not like Minghua 123.

The two soldiers riding up front eventually stopped peering through the back of the cab to stare at the three of them. Sparrow sat by the tailgate on top of plump sacks musty with the scent of raw cotton. Lian and Shao huddled under their blankets, leaning against the side.

"Daming really did well for us," Lian said. "Here we are lying comfortably on bales of cotton. This truck could've been filled with charcoal or cans of tung oil."

The truck swayed and Lian fell against Shao. He resisted the urge to pull her closer. But what did it matter? It was just three of them here. He put an arm around Lian and he felt her slowly relax until she was leaning her head on his shoulder.

"I'm so grateful you came with me, both you and Sparrow," she said. "You're putting yourselves in danger doing this."

"Between the three of us, we'll get there," he said. "And look on the bright side. You won't need to hand in a term project."

"I'm rather sad about that," Lian said. "It would've been a good paper. The Willow Star and the Prince. I could've added some new firsthand research to a little-known legend, thanks to those cave paintings. I wish you could've seen them, too, Shao."

The truck bumped along and eventually Lian slid down to sleep, back curled against the sacks. Shao pulled the blanket over her shoulders. He was tired and his flea bites itched. Every bone in his body ached as though he was coming down with fever. The rough road didn't help. But it was also restlessness. Perhaps it was because he felt ill, but it seemed as though the finest of threads was unraveling in his mind, memories slipping by just beyond his grasp. Like trying to remember a dream after waking up, trying to piece together images that melted away the same moment they appeared. He rolled into a sitting position and clambered over to Sparrow, who was leaning out the tailgate, her face turned up to the night sky.

"Sparrow, I'm so sorry you're caught up in all this," he said. "And I'm angry, too. You should've stayed in Shanghai in the first place, like the good servant you're supposed to be."

"You should be glad I came, Young Master," she said. "I've a far better sense of direction than you." He gave her a mock punch to the arm, saw the silhouette of her shoulders shake with laughter.

"A week ago, I was a university student," he said. "Now a fugitive. All because of some misguided impulse to help Lian." He said this jokingly.

"You're doing this because it was the right thing to do," she said. "Miss Hu was truly in danger and so is Yee Meirong. And you're worried about your mother."

Sparrow put her head out the truck to look up again. Shao looked out too. Overhead, a quarter moon glowed behind a thin haze of cloud that obscured all but the brightest stars.

Ten bone-jolting hours later, the skies still the muted gray of early morning, the truck let them off outside Kian, a town set in a river valley. The provisions in Sparrow's rucksack would see them through the next few days and they wanted to avoid the town, so they set out immediately toward the hills, which were dense with pines and alders.

"This road winds between the hills," Shao said, squinting at a map. "If we walk at night, we can avoid Japanese airplanes and just as importantly, our own soldiers."

When they traveled with Minghua 123, they had taken major roads that passed through towns and large temples, places with enough room to accommodate a large group. Now he searched the map for less-traveled roads to take them away from Kian, roads where they would meet fewer people. As the sun rose higher, they spied plumes of smoke rising from distant ridges.

"Charcoal burners," Sparrow said when Lian pointed at the smoke.

They were encountering refugees on the road now, a bedraggled stream leaving Kian. Some stared at them, but without any curiosity. Most didn't bother giving them more than a glance, too tired to do more than put one foot ahead of the other.

"How are you today, Granny?" Sparrow asked an elderly woman. She rode on a handbarrow piled high with sacks and wooden chairs. The man pushing it was bent with age.

The old woman squinted. "It's a good day. It's his turn to push."

She burst out laughing and her husband chortled with mirth. The two looked at each other fondly. Shao couldn't help smiling. What did it feel like to love someone for decades, as this couple still did?

Sparrow continued walking ahead of them, chatting every so often with some of the travelers. She paused at the side of the road and waited for Shao and Lian to catch up.

"We'll be safer walking at night," Sparrow said, "and we must avoid villages between here and Foochow. Apparently, the army is sweeping through, conscripting soldiers. The only men on the road are either very old or still quite young, have you noticed?"

"Then we need a place to hide and rest during the day," Shao said. He'd never felt so tired.

"We'll find something along the way," Sparrow said. She sounded very certain.

"THAT MUST BE Foochow," Shao said. In the distance, farmland was interrupted by scatterings of houses, and beyond lay a landscape of peaked roofs. A light haze rose from the city, smoke from charcoal fires.

"Probably just another two hours to get there," Sparrow said. They cut through a field, keeping to a windbreak of poplar trees.

"Take a big step here," Lian said, "it's a ditch."

Despite this warning, Shao tripped and fell. "I'm fine, I'm fine, I wasn't watching." He got up and knotted his scarf more tightly around his neck. He'd stumbled a lot over the past six days. "Getting colder, isn't it?"

On the final mile to Foochow Shao could no longer deny something was very wrong with him, something more than hunger and fatigue. His legs were unsteady, and he went off the path into the shrubs twice, heaving up his last meal.

"Stomach cramps," he said, wincing. Sparrow found him a stick to lean on and he was able to keep walking. The first houses were coming into focus now, smoke rising from chimneys.

"Is it malaria?" Lian asked Sparrow. "Should we get some quinine or *qinghao*?"

"I don't think it's malaria," Sparrow said, "but definitely some sort of infection, something serious. That herbalist in Changsha didn't know what he was talking about. We need to get you indoors, Young Master. We have enough money for a room somewhere."

"It's just a cold," Shao said, trying to suppress his shivers.

Sparrow put a hand on his forehead. "You're running a fever. It's more than a cold."

"I'm fine," he snapped.

When they reached the first house on the outskirts of Foochow, however, Shao was beyond arguing. He could barely put one foot ahead of the other. He was dimly aware of being helped indoors, of falling into a pile of straw, shaking from chills. And then he slept.

SHAO HEARD SNATCHES of conversation, low, worried voices.

"I'll go into town and look for Daming's friend." That was Lian. "Where's the letter of introduction he gave us?"

Then he was retching again. Spewing what remained in his stomach. He was soaked in cold sweat, every bone and muscle ached, and his head was in a vise. His bowels gave way and a foul stink filled the room. He whimpered from the humiliation.

He woke up. Someone was spooning a bitter liquid into his mouth.

"It's from the army doctor in Foochow, Daming's friend." Sparrow's voice. "Drink it all."

Shao tried keeping his eyes open but his head lolled on the mattress. Or perhaps it was just straw bedding. But it was all right. Sparrow was taking care of him. He felt a warm, damp cloth wipe between his legs, smelled his own shit, and vomited again.

He was shivering. Someone pulled up the blanket he had kicked off and warmth enfolded him again. He fell asleep from sheer exhaustion, but his dreams were fitful.

Daylight entered through the shutters of a narrow window. The room was small, with clay jars stacked against its walls. He lay on a pile of straw heaped on a low brick platform. The air smelled sour, musty. He pushed himself up and looked around. A charcoal brazier smoldered in a niche, its smoke rising through a hole in the roof, its glow lighting the corner. Slowly, he grew aware of the noise of crockery, the smell of cooking grains, voices outside. Lian and another woman, chatting amiably. He sat up slowly just as Sparrow entered, sunlight filling the doorway behind her.

"Where are we?" Shao said. His throat felt parched but otherwise, he felt nearly back to normal.

"On the outskirts of Foochow," Sparrow said. "A woman and her daughter let us stay. We're in their storeroom. Miss Hu slept in the kitchen. Here, drink this. Real medicine."

More of the bitter liquid. Shao sighed and swallowed obediently. "Is it safe to go into Foochow?" he asked, remembering.

"Foochow seems safe enough now." Lian came into the storeroom. "The army recruiters have moved on. I found the doctor,

Daming's friend. He gave us those drugs and travel documents. There's a truck we can get on tonight. Are you well enough to walk?"

Sparrow put down a bowl of hot boiled millet. Suddenly, even this peasant food smelled tempting and he began spooning it down.

"I'm glad you're better," Lian said, putting her hand on his for a moment.

But all he felt was shame. Shame that she had seen him in a disgusting state.

THE TRUCK WAS parked at a wharf on the Fuhe River, near the eastern side of Foochow's town walls. The soldier driving the truck waved them to get on, not even bothering to look at their documents. They huddled together under the canvas awning, perched uncomfortably on wooden crates. The road was rutted as a washboard and the truck seemed to drive over every bump. Still queasy from fever, Shao hung his head over the tailgate several times to retch.

They traveled through a valley, timbered hills rising up on all sides. They reached a roadside inn at nightfall. If not for the rough wooden tables and stools set up in the yard, it would've looked like a rather run-down farmhouse. But someone had cared enough to plant ornamental shrubs in the yard. Dogwood and rhododendron waiting for spring, shoots of forsythia struggling to show green.

The innkeeper, elderly and unkempt, came out to greet the driver. He glared at the three passengers.

"Not enough food for everyone," he said and hawked a gob of mucus onto the dirt. He looked accusingly at the driver. "Usually it's just one of you."

"Don't worry, old man," the driver said, "my friends don't expect you to feed them. Just bring me what you have."

"We have our own food," Sparrow said. "But may we have some hot water?"

He spat again and stomped inside.

The room had a hard dirt floor, and the thin coat of whitewash on its walls was streaked here and there with mildew. Part of the floor was paved with brick, obviously an area where guests could roll out their blankets and mats for sleeping.

The driver sat down immediately at the one table. The old man threw more wood into the brick stove and barked at the woman who stood stirring a pot. She ladled its contents into a basin and set it down on the table in front of the driver. Boiled millet with a stew of chopped salt pork and vegetables.

Sparrow spoke to the woman, who banged a kettle onto the stove. Lian handed out steamed buns stuffed with pickled vegetables, gave one to the driver, who ate his in two gulping bites. All Shao wanted was a bowl of hot water. The old innkeeper hovered beside the table, and the driver pulled out some coins. Sparrow gave the old man money as well as a small packet of tea leaves, which brought a broken-toothed smile to his face.

"I'll sleep in my truck," the driver said. "You young folks sleep inside where it's warmer."

"Lie down and rest, Shao," Lian said. "There's no telling how much walking we'll need to do once this truck driver drops us off."

Shao squeezed her hand and smiled, although he'd rarely felt more miserable. He'd come with Lian so she'd be safe. Instead, he'd become a burden. His senses felt battered and the mere thought of the road ahead exhausted him. As soon as he pulled the blanket over his shoulders, he fell asleep.

CHAPTER 29

The inn and the forest around it were so quiet Lian could hear the faintest of breezes rustling through bamboo. It was no use, she couldn't get back to sleep. And Sparrow was gone. Wrapping a blanket around her shoulders, Lian went outside to the yard. Sparrow sat at one of the tables, her face turned up to the sky. When she saw Lian, she pulled out one of the stools. Lian sat down with a sigh.

"My mind is so restless," she said in reply to Sparrow's inquiring look. "Beyond getting to Shanghai and asking Shao's father to help Meirong, I don't have a plan. I don't know where to begin looking for my mother. I don't even have a place to live."

"There's more than enough room at the Liu estate," Sparrow said. "They'd be happy to have you as a guest."

To live in the same house as Shao. Their budding yet unde-
fined relationship. The scrutiny of his wealthy family and their
servants. Lian shrank at the thought. And for how long could she
impose on them?

"My mother's probably found somewhere to live by now," she
said.

Then she noticed Sparrow wasn't paying attention. The servant girl's head was cocked to one side, as though listening. A
moment later, Lian heard it, too, the sound of hooves. But not
the heavy clopping of horses or donkeys. Something lighter and
quicker was cantering toward them. Not just one, a herd.

When she saw them, Lian gasped. Sparrow put a warning
hand on hers. "Hush," she said. "*Qilin* unicorns."

They were dainty creatures, their deerlike bodies lithe and
sleek, manes fluttering bright as flames along their necks. The *qilin*
slowed to a trot, their long, tufted tails curved proudly over their
backs. Their leader, a black *qilin*, paused and the herd stopped.
The black *qilin* lifted one hoof, the single antler at the center of its
forehead burnished by moonlight. It tipped its head toward the
table. Sparrow stood and bowed in response. The leader delicately
sniffed the night air, then lashed its tail as if making a decision.
Then the black *qilin* leapt into the forest and the herd followed,
sprinting through the undergrowth. A moment later, the road was
empty.

But in the wake of their passage, trembling limbs of dogwood
and rhododendron put out their first blooms, forsythia shrubs
sprouted gold blossoms, and white mist poppies pushed tendrils
of green above the ground.

Lian could see all this because the yard was illuminated by
a soft glow. And this time, Lian knew she was awake. And she
knew also that she had been awake all those other times when

she had seen Sparrow Chen shining in the dark. Sparrow, who was not a servant. Sparrow, whose exquisitely beautiful features smiled at her.

Sparrow, who was the Willow Star. How could she not have seen?

THEY TALKED ALL night.

"You're an immortal," Lian said. "Surely you have powers? Or are you not allowed to use them?"

"I have no powers, Lian, only immortality," the Star said. "I'm just a celestial maidservant. No one prays to me, I've no obligations and no rules to obey except for my agreement with the Queen Mother of Heaven. My only advantage is that my sister stars guide me as we travel."

Lian couldn't be privy to all the secrets of the gods. But the Star told Lian about her three sister stars, also maids-in-waiting to the Queen Mother of Heaven. About the exodus taking place, the immortals and guardian spirits leaving China. About the promise she'd extracted from the Queen Mother of Heaven, that in each reincarnation the Prince would lead a privileged life, male or female, always born into wealth because the Willow Star couldn't bear to think of him suffering.

And about the unexpected consequences of this promise.

"He lacks purpose," the Star said. "And without purpose he's never been truly happy in any of his lives. Professor Kang helped me see that."

"Has he ever loved you, even if he didn't know who you were?" Lian said. "In all those lives, were you ever married or lovers?"

"Ah. Another detail unknown to scholars," Sparrow said, with a wry smile. "To give him lives of privilege, I bargained away any possibility that he would ever fall in love with me in mortal form. Yes, there were some reincarnations where we were married. Arranged marriages where he was kind to me and that was all. It was enough."

Lian closed her eyes. The Star might have lived beside her Prince in each of his lives, but she had never been more than a companion, a good friend. A loyal servant.

"I know," Sparrow said, as if reading her thoughts, "it was a bad bargain. But I was only a maidservant. How could I outwit the Queen Mother of Heaven?"

"Do you also go through the Wheel of Rebirth?" she asked. "How do you remember all your past lives?"

"I'm immortal," Sparrow said. "I'm not required to drink the Tea of Forgetfulness."

"What will you do now?" Lian said. "Will you go to the Kunlun Mountains with the other immortals?"

The Star didn't answer. Sunrise crept over the hills and light drained away from her. She stood up and was once again just Sparrow Chen, a house servant walking back to the inn.

Lian touched the flowering stems of forsythia, the pink-tinged buds of rhododendron. She remembered the shining single antler on the foreheads of the qilin. She thought over everything the Star had told her. And although they never spoke of it directly during the hours they'd talked, she didn't have to ask.

Shao had never been, could never be for Lian. Or anyone else on this earth.

CHAPTER 30

After the inn, they rode with the same truck driver for another six hours to the next town. There was no military there, no motor transportation at all. But Shao's money worked wonders when it came to getting a ride on a donkey-drawn wagon, where they bounced on hard wooden bench seats, squeezed between laborers on their way to repair a railway line.

Then came another ride in another truck. And another bout of fever.

Shao came to lying on a hard floor. A hard floor that bounced. A rush of cold air across his face opened his eyes. He squinted up to see stars and realized they were in an open truck, the warped boards of its sides barely higher than the seats. One good bounce and any passengers not holding on would've been thrown off those benches. Sparrow and Lian sat with their backs against the cab of the truck. The skies were clouded, the moonlight hazy. He felt a blanket being pulled over him.

Crusted with sleep, his eyes refused to open fully. Sunrise. Or was it sunset? They had to find shelter for the night. Or was it daytime when they had to hide away? He pushed himself to a sitting position on his elbows.

The truck had stopped at a crossroads. Lian and Sparrow were talking to a group of peasants. Most were men but there were a few women in the group. Donkeys and carts, handbarrows laden with baskets and sacks. The peasants' wide hats of woven bamboo cast eerie shadows on the hard dirt road. Their leader rode majestically on the back of a large water buffalo, looking down at Sparrow, nodding at her words.

"We'll give you a ride though it's out of our way," a low growling voice said. "As far as Ouhai, but no farther."

"Thank you, King of Beasts," Sparrow said. It was her voice, he was sure of it. But also different. A sweet, shining sort of voice.

Then as Shao's eyelids closed, the peasant talking to Sparrow changed. Now he loomed above her, twice the size he had been a moment ago. A savage face framed by long, fiery locks of hair, mounted on a tiger the size of an ox. Behind him, the peasants and their animals were gone, replaced by a procession of tigers, wolves, and leopards. Giant apes pushed handbarrows piled high with burlap bags wrapped around the roots of young saplings. A portable forest of cypress and gingko, golden larch and pink cassia.

And Sparrow. He could only see her back, but her entire figure shone with a cool, unearthly radiance. He wanted to shout out, warn Lian and Sparrow about the wild animals, the savage man. But he collapsed, exhausted. Doubting what he'd seen. Certain he was delirious.

Someone lifted him as easily as though he were a leaf and set him down. Laughter and crude comments, rough voices. A blanket thrown over him. He felt the air sweep his cheeks, the rolling rumble of wooden wheels beneath his aching body.

WHEN SHAO OPENED his eyes again, he was able to sit up. He was also ravenous and thirsty. There was a bowl of tea on the table beside him, tepid but quenching. The door opened, and Sparrow entered, carrying a plate that she set down on a wooden stool by the bed.

"Where are we?" he asked, eagerly reaching for the steamed bun she handed him.

"In Ouhai's finest lodgings. We're only four hours from Wen-chou," she said. "You've been sleeping for two days, so I hope you're all rested and ready to go."

"Of course. As soon as I've eaten."

"I wasn't serious," Sparrow said. "Get some more rest. We don't need to leave just yet."

"How did we get here?" Images tumbled in his mind. Giant tigers. Apes pushing handbarrows. A wild man with eyes like fire. Leopards and wolves. He shook his head.

"Some peasants were kind enough to make a detour for us," she said. "They put you in a cart." She took away the empty plate and a minute later, Lian came in.

"Hot soy milk," she said. "Think you can keep it down?"

"I thought I was coming to take care of you, Lian," he said, taking the enamel bowl. "But in fact, it's been Sparrow taking care of us, hasn't it? She defers to us and then takes care of everything in her own way."

THEY REACHED WEN-CHOU just before noon. The shops were open and tempting odors wafted out from restaurant doors, but they made their way directly to the waterfront to find Liu Shipping Enterprises. The three fugitives were dirty and their clothing smelled. The gatekeeper at Liu Shipping would've chased them away, but Shao's educated speech and air of authority gave him pause.

When the manager came out, he frowned at Shao. "You claim to be a member of the Liu family?" he said. "Liu Tienming's younger brother?"

Shao reached into his tunic and brought out a cylinder of white jade. He handed it to the manager. "My brother has the same one for his personal seal," he said. "We all do. I'm sure you've seen him use it to sign documents. Go ahead. Look at the name on the seal."

"No need, no need, Young Master," the manager said, giving it back. "Now that I look at you more closely, the family resemblance is strong, very strong. I'm sorry for my rudeness, sir. My name is Mah. Your brother isn't here. He's in Shanghai this week."

They followed Mah across the yard to a long wooden building. Inside, the manager shouted at two clerks who scuttled away to fetch more chairs.

"How often does Tienming travel back and forth to Shanghai?" Shao asked.

"He used to go every month and only for a few days each time," the manager said, "but your mother's illness has changed all that. His schedule is quite erratic now. On his last trip he stayed a month."

"He takes one of our own ships?" Shao asked.

"Yes, we have one that makes a regular Shanghai-to-Wen-chou run. Our ships are all registered now with a partner company, a Portuguese firm. So far the Japanese have respected the foreign flag and don't interfere."

"When does the ship sail again?" Shao said. "I need to get home, Mr. Mah."

"It returns to Wen-chou later today," Mah said, "and sails for Shanghai the day after tomorrow. When everything's on schedule, it's an overnight trip." He looked apologetic. "The *Dong Feng* isn't our fastest freighter."

"Where does my brother live?" Shao said. He felt a swell of confidence. For the first time in a long while, he was speaking from a position of authority. "My friends and I need rooms."

"Your family owns a fine house here," Mah said. "I'll send word to the, ah, housekeeper to get some rooms ready for you."

"We also need a doctor," Sparrow said. "Mr. Liu has come down with a fever."

"So unfortunate." The manager shook his head. "I'll send for a doctor to go to the house after lunch."

After months of privation and now, a housekeeper. Private rooms. A doctor. "How can life be so normal in Wen-chou?" Shao said.

"The question is, how much longer can life go on as normal?" Manager Mah replied. "The Japanese are busy right now holding the north and the east while they bomb central China. We're only a small port, not worth their notice, not yet anyway. So we take advantage of it while we can."

After sending a messenger to the house, Mah insisted on order-ing lunch. It would give the housekeeper time to get their rooms ready, he said. The restaurant next door sent over soup noodles with fried pork chops, a mixed vegetable stir-fry, and sesame-sprinkled buns. Lian and Sparrow quickly finished their portions, but Shao could only manage some noodle broth.

Rickshaws took them to an old-fashioned courtyard house. When they arrived, the gatekeeper bowed, then rushed inside. They heard his excited shouting.

"Mrs. Deng, Mrs. Deng! Ah Guo, Ah Guo! Come out! The master's younger brother is here!"

Almost immediately a man past his middle years came out of the interior courtyard. He wore a plain tunic and trousers of dark blue, obviously a servant. The woman following close behind was dressed in a long skirt and old-fashioned jacket with a high collar. The cut and fabric were too fine for that of a mere servant. She was also exquisitely beautiful.

"I'm Mrs. Deng," she said, with the slightest of bows. "The housekeeper. We have three rooms ready for you. Also hot baths."

Beside him, Shao heard Lian's quick intake of breath. He couldn't blame her. He had to force his eyes away from Mrs. Deng. He'd never seen anyone as lovely as his brother's housekeeper. If that's who she was.

"Put Miss Hu in the best room," Shao said. "And it doesn't matter which ones you give to me and Sparrow."

"If you'll follow me, Miss Hu. Young Master, Ah Guo will take you to your room." The housekeeper bowed again. "I shall come back for the other young lady." She walked across the small court-yard, the lines of her skirt emphasizing the graceful sway of her hips.

Shao followed the manservant to a house on the eastern side of the courtyard.

"How long have you worked for us, Ah Guo?" Shao asked.

"Twenty-seven years," the man replied, opening the door to

a plain but tidy room, "ever since your grandfather opened the shipping business and bought this house."

"How long has Mrs. Deng worked here?"

"Just two weeks," Ah Guo said. "Master Tienming brought her from Shanghai." His expression never changed.

IN THE AFTERNOON, Ah Guo brought the doctor to see Shao. Sparrow and Mrs. Deng were already in the room, but the man-servant hovered about the doorway possessively, the very picture of a family retainer. Dr. Mao was middle-aged, with a pleasant, square face and a cheerful demeanor that made Shao feel better just talking to him. Dr. Mao examined Shao's rashes and asked about his symptoms, examined the label on the now-empty medicine bottle from the army doctor in Foochow.

"He was right to give you antibiotics," the doctor said. "You have a form of relapsing fever, mostly commonly carried by lice and ticks. Your condition has been exacerbated by exhaustion and poor nutrition. You need antibiotics and bed rest. But I must warn you about the drugs you're getting."

Many patients with relapsing fever felt worse for a brief spell after their first large dose of antibiotics, the doctor explained. They often fell into a shaking chill, accompanied by more fever, sweating, and a feeling of extreme fatigue. But once that was over, Shao could expect a rapid and dramatic recovery.

"Drink lots of water, eat plenty of nutritious food," the doctor said. "And you must continue to get lots of bed rest. My guess is that you'll be in bed for another week."

"I'll make sure of it, Doctor," Sparrow said.

The doctor nodded. "If you send someone to Dr. Yan's office in the morning, I will have some antibiotics prepared for you."

"Where is Dr. Yan, sir?" Ah Guo said.

"He's taking a short holiday," Dr. Mao said, "and since he's been kind enough to let me stay with him while I'm in Wen-chou, the least I could do was act as his locum. Reminds me of my days at medical school."

He laughed as though it was a huge joke, eyes bright in his square face. Shao felt himself chuckle in response to the infectious laugh.

When the door closed behind the doctor, Shao sat back in his chair. The exhilaration of having reached safety drained away and suddenly he felt deeply exhausted again. Sparrow looked at him as if she could sense it too.

"Get back into bed, Young Master," she said.

Shao sighed and climbed under the blanket. "Where is Lian?"

"Still sleeping. And you should be too."

"That housekeeper, Sparrow. I think she's my brother's mistress. What do you think?"

But his voice was indistinct, slurring with fatigue. He was asleep by the time the question left his lips and didn't hear Sparrow's soft reply.

"She may be more than that, Young Master."

IN HIS DREAM, life had been a misery since the day of the wedding. No matter how hard Shao tried to please them, to carry out their every wish, they could not be won over, any of them. They were kinder to their own servants. Surely, not all in-laws were like this. Life had become unbearable. Now it was time to escape. Outside, rain streamed down from the roofs of the houses around the courtyard. Shao hurried to the far end of the kitchen garden and opened the back door, stepped out into the lane. In the dark, a waiting figure stood, a wide and loving smile on her face. She held out a cloak to fend off the rain. Together they made their escape, running through the water-slick streets of the town, arm in arm, until a familiar red lantern hanging above familiar double doors told them they were home. Really home.

When Shao woke up, it was morning. He was shivering but it was from a memory of the dream, of making his way through cold, windy streets in rain-soaked garments. The room was warm and there were clean clothes folded on the table beside him. His brother's clothes.

Shao crossed the courtyard to the central hall where the sound of voices led him to the dining room. He greeted Lian, who was nearly finished with her breakfast and chatting with Mrs. Deng. As soon as he entered, Mrs. Deng stood up and bowed, indicating the chair beside Lian.

"Please, sir," she murmured, then vanished through the door. She returned with a tray and set down a large bowl of congee and a smaller bowl of hot soy milk. The condiments were already on the table, pickled vegetables, shredded pork, and salted duck egg.

He waved her to sit down. "Don't interrupt your breakfast." He tried hard not to stare at her, at the fine silky hair that hung over her shoulder in a single loose braid, her complexion as smooth and glowing as a child's. Her every small movement as graceful as the flight of swallows in the evening sky.

He turned instead to Lian, who met his gaze briefly then looked down at her food. The hollows under her eyes were gone. Her face was scrubbed, her cheeks pink. The high-collared vest she wore over a long-sleeved dress gave her an old-fashioned look at odds with her short hair.

"Mrs. Deng lent me some of her clothes," Lian said, "while mine are being laundered."

"Please keep them," the other woman said. "They have never fit me very well."

Mrs. Deng's clothing, while obviously of good quality, was what a woman his grandmother's age might wear.

"I've been telling Mrs. Deng about the Library of Legends," Lian said. "She's very knowledgeable about folktales."

Her voice was overly animated, her smile too bright. As though she were a different person now, someone who didn't want to be in his company. How could he blame her? She had seen him at his lowest, covered in filth, babbling out his delusions. A liability for most of their journey.

"Mrs. Deng," he said, "is your husband also an employee of our company?"

"I am widowed," she replied. "Your brother Tienming was kind enough to make me his housekeeper." She shrugged. "I'm also his mistress."

The news didn't surprise him at all. The new Republic of China frowned upon concubinage, but in many cases, the practice of multiple wives and concubines had simply adapted to keeping women as mistresses. Many of his father's friends kept separate households, lavishing as much money and affection on their illegitimate children as those by their wives. He was a little surprised at his brother, though. Tienming was absorbed in running the family businesses under his care. He'd never shown any interest in taking a mistress. Tienming's children seemed to give him and his wife enough common ground to maintain a cordial, if somewhat distant, marriage.

"May I ask how long you've known each other?" he said.

"We met just a few weeks ago in Shanghai," Mrs. Deng replied. "But he was very persuasive. And I liked the idea of living in Wen-chou."

A few weeks. His brother must be thoroughly infatuated to have made her his mistress so quickly. Yet here she was in Wen-chou instead of with him in Shanghai.

"Why didn't you go to Shanghai with Tienming?" he asked.

"I don't like Shanghai." Another nonchalant shrug. Then she looked at Sparrow, who had just entered the room. "And who would've been here to welcome you?"

Sparrow held up a brown paper package, firmly bound with string.

"Good, you've got the drugs," Shao said, reaching for the package. "I'll take some and we can get on that ship tomorrow."

BUT MERE HOURS after taking the drugs, it was clear that Shao couldn't leave his bed, let alone leave the house to get on the next sailing. He lay tangled in damp sheets, unconscious and tossing, drenched in cold sweat. Shao felt a large hand on his forehead, fingers on his wrist. Dr. Mao. A hearty male voice assuring him that all would be well. It would soon be over.

The room, when he opened his eyes, was dim, the shutters closed. He turned his head and saw Sparrow and Mrs. Deng sitting at the small round table in the corner, heads close together. Sparrow was writing something. Lian stood behind, looking over her shoulder. Sparrow brought a piece of paper to his bedside. She spoke, words his muddled senses couldn't understand. Sparrow had his jade chop in her hand and pointed at the paper. A letter. He nodded, not sure what she wanted, but it was Sparrow, so he agreed and fell back into sleep.

Shao woke for brief spells, aware that Sparrow stood over him. Sometimes it was Sparrow and once, through half-closed eyelids, he saw Mrs. Deng holding a basin beside him as he vomited. But Sparrow was always there, changing his clothing, mopping his limbs with a warm, damp towel. Sparrow holding the spout of a teapot to his lips so that he could swallow some water. The room seemed brighter whenever Sparrow was there.

Light made him force open his eyes. Lian was not in the room, but Sparrow sat at the corner table with Mrs. Deng. They were the source of the light. And yet the young woman he knew as Sparrow didn't look waifish or plain at all. Her lovely features caught at his heart, a face so strangely familiar, so beloved. Was it really Sparrow?

"I came down to reason with you," he heard Mrs. Deng say. "Circumstances have changed. All creatures of legend are going home. The Queen Mother wants you home. Come back, dearest Sister. Give up on the Prince. He's had dozens of chances, hundreds of years."

Her voice was unlike anything he'd ever heard, sweet as the tinkle of jade bangles on his mother's arm.

"Hundreds of years is but a blink of the eye to us," Sparrow said. "I hardly feel as though it's been that long." This Sparrow was as exquisitely, delicately beautiful as Mrs. Deng but there was something about her, something more than beauty that moved him. He knew her from some other place. But where had it been?

"But when the Palace gates close this time, it will be for all eternity," Mrs. Deng said.

"I just need a little more time," Sparrow said.

"You've already spent too much time down here," Mrs. Deng said. "You've become tainted by abhorrent human traits. Jealousy. Rage. What you did to that young woman, even though you know he could never love her."

"She was out to seduce him. I couldn't have that." Sparrow's voice was cold.

"His entanglements have never bothered you before," Mrs. Deng said. "You know he can never truly love anyone while you're on this earth. You've changed, Sister. But it's not too late, if you come home."

There was a long silence.

"You do understand," Mrs. Deng said, "that he'll never attain enlightenment."

"What do you mean?" Sparrow's voice was startled.

"Mortals strive to live a good life so they can advance with each reincarnation until they reach perfect enlightenment," she said. "But because of your agreement with the Queen Mother, the Prince never finds purpose, so he never does any good, never advances."

Another long silence.

"This will be over soon, Sister," Sparrow said. She reached across the table to hold the other woman's hand. "One way or another."

Shao didn't understand anything of this strange conversation. But dreams seldom made sense. He couldn't bear so much brightness, so much beauty. He closed his eyes and slept.

SHAO GOT UP feeling stronger and more optimistic than he had in weeks. He opened the shutters and cold, bright sunshine flooded the room. There was a pile of clothing neatly folded on the bedside dresser, his brother's clothes. There was also a note from Lian on top of the pile.

> *Shao, I'm sorry to leave ahead of you but each day delayed is another day that Meirong suffers and another day I could be looking for my mother. The first thing I'll do is see your father to tell him you and Sparrow are safe in Wen-chou. Without your seal as proof, your father might*

not agree to see me so Sparrow put your seal on a letter of introduction she wrote—you were unconscious but Sparrow said it would be all right to do this.

He dressed and stepped outside to the small courtyard. The fragrance of steamed rice told him it was lunchtime. In the dining hall, Sparrow was laying the table for three.

"I saw the note," Shao said. "When did Lian go?"

"The ship sailed yesterday. Manager Mah made the arrangements," Sparrow said. "Miss Hu was very insistent that she get on board."

"How will we find her once she gets to Shanghai?" he said. "She's going to look for her mother and who knows where that will take her."

"She'll be at my flat." Mrs. Deng came into the dining room, a tray in her hands. "I've given her the key." At his look of surprise, she added, "Your brother let me have it, to use whenever I'm in Shanghai."

CHAPTER 31

The freighter pushed its way through the waters of the East China Sea, the waves brown with sediment from the many rivers that emptied out along the coastline. Weighted down with coal and barrels of tung oil, the *Dong Feng* sailed so slowly Lian feared it would take longer than two days to reach Shanghai. But apparently, they would reach the port on schedule.

Her courage wavered at the thought of finding her way through Shanghai's streets on her own. But she hadn't wanted to stay in Wen-chou any longer than necessary. Now that she knew, she felt like an imbecile for ever thinking that Jenmei had been her rival for Shao's affections. It was Sparrow and Shao, it had always been the Willow Star and her Prince, for hundreds of years. She had no business getting between them. As if she even could.

"It's cold out here," a voice beside her remarked. "And the dining room is serving lunch now. Don't you want to eat?"

Lian glanced at the man leaning on the rail beside her. "I dare not eat, Dr. Mao. I don't want to get seasick again."

She had run into the doctor the day before when she was leaning over the side of the ship in a state of misery. He had given her powdered gingerroot then stayed to chat. But whether it was the ginger or his conversation taking her mind off the nausea, she'd been grateful for the relief.

Dr. Mao had fled from a small town outside Shanghai called Pinghu, now occupied by the Japanese. Since arriving in Shanghai Dr. Mao had set up his practice again. So far, most of his patients were from his hometown, fellow refugees who couldn't afford to pay much. He had come to Wen-chou to buy drugs. His friend, the absent Dr. Yan, had told him prices were better in Wen-chou because he could buy directly from the boats smuggling medical supplies.

"Some of the drugs are for my own practice," Dr. Mao said, "and some I'll take to the German Lutheran Church's refugee camp. I volunteer there, as do many of my former professors from the Shanghai German Medical College."

"What do you know about the camps?" she asked. "Are there many? I suppose the Red Cross would be a good starting point to find information."

"Surely you don't need to stay at a camp," he said, a note of concern coming into his voice.

"Oh, I have a place to live, thanks to a friend," she said. "But the camps, well, I'm looking for someone."

"Shanghai, Shanghai! We're almost there!" an excited passenger shouted out.

The ship had entered Hangchow Bay. Passengers crowded the port side railing, pointing at the shoreline as the freighter surged through the bay's muddy waters. Lian stood at the bow, scarf wrapped around her head and chin tucked into her fur-lined collar. Soon the waters turned even muddier as the freighter swung into the mouth of the Yangtze River and steamed its way toward Shanghai. The river traffic grew heavier at the confluence of the Yangtze and Huangpu Rivers, a sign that they were just around the bend from Shanghai.

The other sign that they were closer to Shanghai was the grim debris being carried out to sea. Human corpses, some wrapped in shrouds, others just floating naked. Lian turned away with a gasp at the sight of a child's bloated body.

"River burial is the cheapest," Dr. Mao said. "Poor families who want to do the right thing for their loved ones say a few words, burn a stick of incense, then slide the body into the river."

"Aren't there any cemeteries? Crematoriums?" Lian said.

"Shanghai's crematories burn day and night these days," he said, "and the poor can't afford it. Every morning, cleaning squads pick up the bodies of those who've died overnight on the streets and in camps. Disease runs rampant in some of those camps. Last week it was cholera."

"Tell me more," she said. "Tell me what to be prepared for."

"Chinese coming in or out of the Settlement are searched by Japanese soldiers," Dr. Mao said. "Even when cars belonging to foreigners drive through checkpoints, their Chinese drivers must get out and bow to the soldiers."

Rents were exorbitant, with landlords renting out by the room. Families of eight or nine crowded into one small space, cooked on charcoal braziers out on the sidewalk, emptied their chamber pots in the sewer drains. The doctor was lucky to have a room to himself, a single room he used as both office and home.

Dr. Mao fumbled inside his coat and pulled out a card. "I

must get my baggage now, but if you are ever ill, Miss Hu, please come see me."

LIAN PUSHED HER way down the gangplank to the wharf, where the grand European buildings of Shanghai's famous Bund dominated the waterfront. She ignored the shouts of vendors, touts offering cheap lodgings, promising well-paid jobs. She was no gullible country peasant, ready to be swindled. She walked away quickly from the wharf with a display of great assurance, both arms firmly wrapped around the carpetbag Mrs. Deng had given her. It was new and more than adequate to hold her few belongings, but Lian missed her rucksack.

The city looked so normal. Men in business suits hurried along the sidewalks. Women in high-heeled shoes strolled together arm in arm, some wearing Western-style coats and hats, others the formfitting *qipao* dresses that Shanghai women wore so alluringly.

Cars and rickshaws advanced through busy streets, hampered by traffic at every intersection. Restaurants and shops welcomed expensively dressed customers both Chinese and foreign, banks carried on their business behind polished brass doors. But when Lian looked more closely, some buildings were pocked with holes from stray bullets and sandbags were still stacked beside walls.

Then there were the sights Dr. Mao had warned her about. Shacks built in alleyways using whatever materials could be found: packing crates, tar paper, bamboo taken from fences and scaffolding, even branches torn from trees in public parks. Destitute families huddled in doorways and niches. Any vacant ground, including plots of grass and flower beds, was occupied. Some of the younger refugees were still energetic and enterprising, selling and bartering what little they had. Others had subsided into resignation, waiting for heaven's will to do its worst.

From time to time, Lian paused to consult Sparrow's hand-drawn map. Just to be sure, she asked two young women whether she was on the right street. They were beautiful and stylish, wearing short wool coats over flowered *qipao* dresses, leather pumps adorned with bows.

"Yes, this is Hankow Street," one said. "Honan Road is just another ten minutes via the Number Eleven Bus."

"Is it really necessary to take a bus?" Lian said, dismayed. She didn't know how to use the Shanghai bus system. It was one more obstacle to face.

The young women burst into laughter. "It's a local expression that means to go on foot," the other explained, not unkindly. She pointed two fingers down and wiggled them to mime a walking motion. They walked away arm in arm, still giggling. They stopped to speak with a man, their smiles flirtatious. It occurred to Lian they might've been prostitutes.

She walked slowly, taking note of landmarks in case she had to retrace her steps, but Sparrow's map proved accurate. From the corner of Hankow Street and Honan Road, she looked across the street to the offices of *Xinwen Bao*, the newspaper where Shao's father worked. The newspaper that Shao's family owned, she corrected herself.

She opened the door of *Xinwen Bao*. Rows of desks filled the space behind the reception counter, some empty, others crowded with men reading out loud and talking over each other. A haze of cigarette smoke drifted near the ceiling.

"I'm here to see Liu Sanmu," she said to the clerk. "I have a message from his son."

"Which son?" he said. He looked her up and down. "He has so many."

"It's from his youngest son, Liu Shaoming," she said and pulled the letter out of her pocket. She pointed at the seal stamped on the envelope and the clerk put his pen down.

"Wait here," he said and vanished up the staircase. A few moments later he came down the steps and beckoned her to follow.

The door to the office was open. The man inside came around the desk and held his hand out. Shao's father was extremely handsome, and the family resemblance was very strong: a lean, square jaw and high forehead. Lian gave him the letter. He opened the sheet and frowned.

"This letter isn't in my son's handwriting," he said.

"Sparrow wrote it because he was too ill to sit up," Lian replied. "But he's on the mend now and quite safe at your house in Wen-chou."

Liu Sanmu looked up from the letter. "Well, at least he's seen a doctor. And Sparrow is with him. But why did you all leave Minghua University?"

"He left because he's worried about his mother," she said, "and I left because I need you to save my friend."

SHAO'S FATHER PACED up behind his desk, looking out the window. Lian fidgeted in the chair across, taking a gulp every so often from the glass of chrysanthemum tea he had poured for her.

"One of the challenges is identifying just the right person," he said, turning to Lian. "I don't have any contacts who can pull strings with the Juntong."

Lian understood. The indispensable connections nurtured by families for personal and business advantage ran on the exchange of favors. Shao's father didn't know anyone at the Juntong who owed him a favor. Or else he did but was unwilling to spend the favor on her, a girl whose family could offer nothing in return. If only Shao were here, pleading Meirong's case to his father.

"Mr. Liu, it was Shao who suggested asking you for help," she began.

He held his hand up. "I didn't say I wouldn't help. I need to find someone who knows the right person. Leave it with me."

"Thank you so much," Lian said. "Please convince the authorities in Changsha that Yee Meirong is just young and idealistic. She rushes in without thinking. But now she's had a scare and she'll know better. Please do whatever you can, Mr. Liu. I've heard terrible things about those reeducation camps."

"Well, my son risked his life to help get you to Shanghai so it must be important to him," he said. His expression softened. "Don't worry, I'll look into this. My family does have some influence, Miss Hu. It's only a matter of finding the right contact. Your friend will be released as long as she hasn't done or said anything rash in the meantime."

That was exactly what worried Lian and she bit her lip. Meirong could be so very outspoken. But all she said was, "Whatever you can do for her, I'm in your debt, Mr. Liu."

"I'm the one who is in your debt, Miss Hu," he said, "for looking after my son all the way from Shangtan to Wen-chou. You're a good friend, and not just to this Yee Meirong."

"You should thank Sparrow," she said, standing up. "She's the one who looked after both of us, I'm embarrassed to admit."

"Where are you staying, Miss Hu?" Mr. Liu said. "How can I contact you if there's news?"

She didn't want him to know she was using Mrs. Deng's flat. Not until Shao was back in Shanghai and could vouch for her right to be there.

"I'm staying with friends," she said. "But I can come by every week. Every Thursday? But I don't want to bother you if there's no need. Perhaps you could leave a message with your clerk downstairs if there's news."

IT WAS WELL past noon by the time Lian found Mrs. Deng's flat, on the third floor of a building near the western end of Connaught Road in the International Settlement. The street was a busy mix of apartments, restaurants, and shops.

"I only lived in that apartment for a week before coming to Wen-chou," Mrs. Deng had said when she handed over the key. "But it's clean and there's food in the pantry. Rice, flour, cooking oil."

The Star's sister had come down to Earth as soon as Sparrow, Lian, and Shao decided they'd go to Wen-chou. She found Liu Tienming in Shanghai and put herself in his path.

"That was quick work, Sister," Sparrow said.

"What incredible luck," Lian said, "that Shao's brother found you an apartment so quickly. And at a time like this when rooms in Shanghai are so scarce."

"That wasn't luck. The Lius own property all over the city," Mrs. Deng said, "and this apartment is one of them. I believe someone's mistress lived there years ago and it's been empty since. So Liu Tienming reserved it for my use whenever we're in Shanghai. He doesn't like hotels."

Lian couldn't fathom such wealth. To own property that didn't need to earn its keep. To have a flat sitting empty, casually available for the convenience of a mistress. To have servants who arrived at a moment's notice to clean rooms and stock the pantry. Mrs. Deng urged Lian to use whatever was there.

"I won't be returning to Shanghai," she said, waving off Lian's protests.

There was an elevator in the lobby but a nanny was herding

several children in. To avoid their inquisitive eyes, Lian took the stairs to Mrs. Deng's flat. Mrs. Deng. What else could she call the Star's sister? It felt strange enough addressing a celestial being as "Sparrow" but that was what the Star said to call her. It was her name in this life, she'd said.

How frustrating it must be for Sparrow, to live an immortal yet powerless existence.

Lian turned the key and pushed open the door to a dim, high-ceilinged space. To quiet. To serenity. Long velvet drapes covered tall windows and muffled street noises. She pulled the drapes open to bring in the sunshine and saw the room's gracious proportions. There was hardly any dust on the parquet floors and the large crystal chandelier reflected back sunlight.

The living room was furnished traditionally with elegant lacquered tables, chairs of bent elm wood, and inlaid cabinets. Beside it was a small formal dining room with a round table and six chairs arranged below a smaller chandelier. The tiled bathroom held a white porcelain tub, a marble counter lined with soaps and fragrant oils in glass bottles of European manufacture, luxuries she had only seen in shop windows. There was a small kitchen equipped with an empty icebox and a two-burner stove connected to a gas bottle. There was rice and flour in the pantry, jars of pickled vegetables, bags of beans, and dried fruit. Mrs. Deng had stocked all the basic necessities. There were even boxes of foreign biscuits and tinned meat. It was more than what her mother's pantry in Peking contained, most days.

Feeling like an intruder, Lian peeked in the main bedroom, took in the four-poster bed and matching armoires, their carved and gilded ornamentation. Inside were beautiful clothes in both Chinese and Western styles, all new. Possibly not ever worn. Stylish suits and casual skirts. Cocktail dresses and evening gowns. A wardrobe purchased by a man besotted.

The second bedroom was much smaller and to Lian's eyes, more comfortable. She put her bag down beside the bed, a modest traditional platform of rosewood with drawers built under the bed. The window looked down on a lane between buildings and she opened it just enough to allow some air in, then sat on the edge of the bed.

She had done as much as she could for Meirong. The relief of having found Shao's father and the flat gave way to fatigue and the reality of her circumstances. She had a place to live, but not very much money. Shanghai was a city in turmoil, and her mother could be anywhere. She would rest for a moment, then go to the Red Cross and begin her search. She couldn't wait to tell her mother that her father's name had been cleared. That there was no longer any need to live like fugitives.

She lay down on top of the bedcovers, just for a moment. When she woke up, it was morning.

LIAN BEGAN THE day at the Unity Mission refugee camp. The American woman there did recall Lian's mother coming to pick up the letter from Minghua University.

"We were already overcrowded, my dear," she said, apologetically. "We didn't have a place for her to stay or enough food. I remember her. We suggested she ask the Red Cross."

It took Lian an hour to walk from the Unity Mission camp to the Red Cross office on Ming Yuan Road, then another two hours to wait in line. She had to start somewhere, get something useful, to begin her search. She was not leaving without information.

But the young woman seated behind the desk looked up at Lian and closed her eyes for a moment, as if exhausted. Then she looked at the stack of papers on the table in front of her. Lists and lists of lists. The young staff member, surely not much older than Lian, was one of a dozen sitting behind tables arrayed along a ground-floor corridor of the Shanghai Red Cross office. If not for the guards at the door letting people in and out, the tables would've been stampeded by supplicants.

"I want you to understand the situation," the Red Cross staffer said. She put her elbows on the table and looked up at Lian. "To find one woman, your mother, will be very difficult."

"I'm prepared to go to every single camp to find her," Lian said. "Please, what I need is a list of the camps' names and addresses."

"There are more than one hundred fifty camps in the Settlement," she said. "But those are just the ones registered with the city. There are also camps run by small churches, commercial guilds, and native-place associations. They don't bother registering with us."

Lian's heart shrank at the thought of searching through so many camps. What if her mother was at one of the unregistered shelters?

"You'll have to make your own copy of the lists," the young woman said, "I can't spare the time." She gave Lian a wry smile that showed she was sympathetic. "And here," she said, handing over another list, this one typed in English, with Chinese notes in the margins, "these are the refugee camps run by foreign churches."

Lian scanned the list. "My mother said she was looking for work at a camp typing up reports."

"Why didn't you say so?" the staffer said, taking back the first set of pages. "That narrows it down. Only the foreign camps use typewriters."

THE NEXT DAY, Lian only managed to visit two camps. She didn't want to spend money on rickshaws or buses. She had bought a map, but Shanghai was such a big place. And her list had grown longer. At the second camp she visited, the French nun at the desk spoke perfect Chinese and asked to see her list.

"Here are some other foreign refugee camps and reception centers," the woman said, adding more names and addresses. "Some are privately funded and others are attached to mission schools and orphanages."

When Lian got back to the flat that evening, she ate standing up in the kitchen, a bowl of soup noodles from a small restaurant around the corner and a handful of dried fruit. She had bought vegetables, a block of tofu, and two eggs. She would use what was in the pantry very carefully. She understood how to be frugal. It was the only way she knew how to live.

Her mother had taken secretarial work in Peking with an American company. Lian now realized her mother's English and typing skills must've earned her a relatively good wage. Yet they'd always rented cheap rooms and her mother's only good clothes were the ones she wore to work, plain and modest. People said her mother spoke English with an American accent. Lian circled a few names on the list that seemed American. The American Baptist Mission camp. Yale University Mission. The American Society of Friends Mission. She would try those first. She should've thought of this sooner.

She sat up in bed and studied the list more closely, trying to remember the tidbits her mother had mentioned of her early years, the mission school that had educated her, giving her a way out of poverty. But her mother had never talked much about her past. When Lian thought about it, her mother had always lived under a veil of secrecy, even when they'd been happy.

CHAPTER 32

After Shao came out of his fever and delirium, he still needed a few days of rest, good food, and more antibiotics before he felt confident enough to make the trip to Shanghai. He stood at the prow of the freighter as it lurched its way through the waves, the muddy yellow stream of the Yangtze River merging with Hangchow Bay's darker waters. They were nearing the mouth of the Yangtze River and the wharves of Shanghai. He wore clothing borrowed from his brother's closet, a warm, fur-lined coat over a woolen sweater. A year ago, they'd been the same size. Now he was so thin he could've worn another padded tunic underneath and it would still have been loose. Shao leaned against the railing, ignoring the cold wind that scoured his face.

Before they left Wen-chou, his brother's mistress

had come into the room while Sparrow packed their bags for the journey to Shanghai. He still couldn't believe that she had stayed behind in Wen-chou while Tienming was in Shanghai. His brother must be thoroughly infatuated to indulge her preference of remaining in Wen-chou.

"I have a letter for your brother," she said, holding out an envelope to Shao. "Would you please give this to him?"

"Of course," he said. "I'm sure he'll be glad to hear from you. I'm sure he misses you."

Mrs. Deng paused at the door. "Shanghai's too noisy. Too bright. You can't see the stars at night." She smiled at Sparrow. There was wistfulness in Sparrow's returning smile, and something stirred in Shao's memory. A dream of two shimmering figures.

THE RIVERFRONT WAS utterly changed. The freighter passed Shanghai's industrial districts, once a hive of industriousness. Factories and mills, schools, shops, and temples. Tenements that were home to workers and their families. Now there were only ruins and an eerie silence. Closer to the city's wharves, within the safety of the International Settlement, the shores were lined with hundreds of shacks, a sea of straw-mat roofs.

A car waited for them at the wharf on the Bund. Shao recognized it at once, an American Ford motorcar his father had imported for his mother's use. Which she no longer used. The driver opened the door and a familiar figure stepped out. Shao felt a surge of warmth at seeing his father, but in the crush of the Bund and with so many curious eyes, all he did was greet his father with a formal bow. Then he climbed into the back seat of the car beside his father. Sparrow moved to sit at the front with the driver, but Liu Sanmu stopped her.

"Come sit in the back with us, Sparrow," he said. "I want to hear everything, your story as well as his."

But it was Shao's father who did most of the talking on the way home.

His mother had been losing weight for months. Their doctor believed her complaints were purely due to a nervous disposition and worries over her sons. Even though she obediently drank nourishing broths and soothing herbal teas, she grew thinner and weaker. She complained of being in constant pain.

"For your mother's sake, it's good that you're home," his father said. "Once she worries less, she'll get better."

The car turned down a treelined street. The gates to the Liu estate opened and the car entered the gardens Shao had known all his life. After months of winter in central China, he'd forgotten that coastal Shanghai's climate was so much warmer, more temperate. He had traveled into spring. Trees and shrubs bursting with new growth lined the long arc of the circular driveway that swept past all eight mansions. The fresh greens of emerging leaves, the creamy white of flower buds tinged with colors yet to be revealed.

The car's tires crunched along the pea gravel drive to the accompaniment of shouts from their head gardener. "Third Young Master is home! Third Young Master is home!"

Stepping inside his house, a cluster of servants welcomed him, including Amah Fu, who pinched his cheeks as though he was still five years old. She left only after he promised to visit her next door, where she was now *amah* to his cousin's new baby.

Upstairs, the door to his mother's room was slightly ajar. When she was awake, his father explained, she liked listening to what was going on in the house. Even before Shao entered the room he could smell the faint fragrance of her perfume, freesia and bergamot. The drapes were open. He couldn't recall the last time he had seen this room so bright with daylight. The nurse sitting at his mother's bedside stood up when he and his father entered. The trolley beside the nurse held a jug of water, folded white towels, small brown glass bottles.

Shao took the chair beside the bed while his father and the nurse whispered in conversation. His mother was beyond thin. If not for her clean face and hair, the fine cotton nightgown, she could've been one of the emaciated refugees they had seen on their travels. He took her hand and she opened her eyes briefly. Her eyes were unfocused, her smile merely polite, devoid of recognition.

"Let's go down for lunch and you can come back," his father said. "Your mother will be awake by then."

The smells in the dining room, so familiar, almost made him swoon with hunger. After months of eating all his food piled into a single bowl of chipped enamel, the table's place settings seemed extravagant. Linen napkins, ivory and silver chopsticks, porcelain spoons and bowls glazed in a design made exclusively for his family.

The head cook personally carried in a huge tureen. "Welcome home, Third Young Master!" he said, beaming.

Throughout lunch, family members from the other houses came by and put their heads in the door to greet him. Some stayed to eat and chat, their faces familiar and comforting. Here, it was easy pushing sad memories to the back of his mind. The numbing cold of the open road. The destruction after an air raid. Shao wanted to leave those memories behind, if only for a day.

His brother Tienming sat down briefly for some soup, then excused himself as soon as Shao gave him the letter from Mrs. Deng.

"Third Son," his father said, at the end of the meal, "you've just recovered from fever. Stay at home and rest for a few days. Spend time with your mother." It was a command, not a request.

He couldn't go out now. He would have to send Sparrow to check on Lian.

After his father left to return to work at *Xinwen Bao*, Shao sought out his brother. Tienming sat upstairs in their childhood playroom, his tall frame doubled up in a small chair by the window, as if he'd dropped into the seat forgetting he was no longer a boy. His hand clutched the letter from Mrs. Deng, his expression blank.

"She's left me," his brother said. Grief and bewilderment seeped into his features. "By now she'll be gone from our house in Wen-chou." His voice choked slightly. Shao had never seen his brother show so much emotion. He'd always been the most reserved of the three. The most self-sufficient.

"How did Mrs. Deng seem to you?" he said.

"Very pleasant, very calm," Shao said, "although I did wonder why she wasn't in Shanghai with you, since you've been here such a long time."

"I met her only a short while ago, you know." His brother blinked and looked at the paper in his hand, smoothed it out carefully. "At some restaurant. It's so hard to remember now. I thought she was the most beautiful woman I'd ever seen. She never asked me for anything. But she liked it when I did anything nice for her. Clothes, jewelry, the flat."

He'd been so happy when she agreed to live in Wen-chou with him. There, he could pretend they were married. It was like living in a dream.

"And now she's gone," he said, looking down at the paper in his hand. "Back to her family, she says. But I know nothing about her family or where she's from. I never thought to ask. Why didn't I ask?"

Tienming pulled out his wallet and looked at a small photograph before handing it to Shao. The face that looked out from the photograph was pretty, but not exceptionally so. It was a poor likeness of Mrs. Deng. It barely hinted at her heart-stopping beauty.

An image flashed through Shao's memory. Mrs. Deng and Sparrow sitting together, bright as moonlight, their faces so similar, so lovely. A fever dream. He dismissed it from his thoughts.

"In fact," Tienming said, "I didn't really know her at all, did I?"

But at that moment the nurse rapped on the open door and beckoned to Shao. His mother was asking for him.

HIS MOTHER HAD made an effort to dress up for him. Her nightdress was different, one with ruffles around the neckline that hid the gauntness of her throat. Her skin was dry and papery, but her face lit up when she saw her son. This time, when Shao took her hand, she squeezed back.

"You look thin," she said, her voice barely above a whisper. "I will tell Old Zhao to make that pork belly dish you like so much."

"How do you feel today?" he said. Her hand was as light as a sheet of paper, her hair brittle, no longer lustrous.

"I'm happy you're home," she said, "but that's not what you meant, is it?" She struggled to sit up. "It's frustrating, Third Son. No one believes me when I say something's wrong. But never mind that. I got your first letter from Changsha but nothing since. Tell me everything."

He didn't tell her anything that would make her worry. Nothing about his own illness. He made light of the hardships and the long miles, the tragic sights along the way. He didn't mention Lian. His mother listened but soon she grew restless and distracted, her eyes darting around the room. Then she gestured to the nurse.

"Just a small amount," the nurse said, holding out a spoonful of brown liquid. Shao's mother swallowed eagerly, then leaned back on the pillows, her face pale, all strength spent. Her eyes closed but she held on to his hand.

"Will you send Sparrow to see me later," she murmured. "She's such a good girl. A good servant."

The rest of her words were inaudible. He sat beside his mother until she sank into sleep.

SHAO'S FATHER INVITED him for lunch downtown, a signal that he considered Shao sufficiently recovered to go out again. Rather than take one of the family cars, Shao had the gatekeeper call him a rickshaw. All the way to his father's office, he took in the streets of Shanghai. So familiar, yet completely changed.

At exit points where Shanghai's residents were allowed to cross in and out of the Settlement stood unsightly and intimidating barbed-wire barricades, the guardhouses were manned by Japanese soldiers. Refugees from outlying areas struggled to enter the safety of the Settlement. They feared the Japanese guards but lined up anyway. One man carried a birdcage, his only possession.

At the barriers, the backdrop behind the anxious crowds was one Shao had only seen so far in news photos. The bombed-out buildings of Greater Shanghai, blackened and bullet-ridden.

"Go some other way," Shao called out to the rickshaw puller. "I don't care if it takes longer. I don't want to see those barricades."

The staff at the newspaper office, most of whom Shao had known since he was a boy, greeted him enthusiastically. They wanted firsthand accounts of his evacuation, the conditions China's schools faced during their evacuation. He recounted a few stories about Minghua 123's long journey. After repeating them so often to his own family over the past few days, the narrative was now so familiar he felt as though he read from a script, his memories replaced by the words he spoke.

The long nighttime journeys and walking on moonless nights to avoid aerial attacks. The duty of transporting the Library of Legends, a heavy responsibility that also lifted their spirits. The day they learned the secret of tying straw sandals over cloth shoes. The never-ending pain of blisters. With each retelling, he'd made the experiences sound more amusing, the horrors he'd witnessed less unnerving. He even made their constant battles against vermin entertaining, small enemies they had to outwit. And all the time, west, to the west.

He didn't mention Jenmei, only Mr. Shen, when asked whether Minghua 123 had lost any of its members to enemy attacks.

"Weren't you afraid?" a junior reporter asked. The young man had been scribbling madly in his notebook while Shao talked.

He paused. "It's strange, but I always knew I'd be safe as long as I followed the university and did as our professors instructed." Then he realized the truth of his words. "This may sound ridiculous, but even after Mr. Shen was killed, we all believed we would get to Chengtu unscathed, as long as we carried the Library of Legends. How could fate be so cruel as to destroy the Library and those entrusted with its safe passage?"

And afterward, on the journey east, why had he been so confident? Even through his bouts of fever, he had been sure they'd reach Wen-chou. He had been a burden to Lian and to Sparrow, but he'd never doubted. As though he were exempt from catastrophe.

The restaurant they went to for lunch was one his father often patronized near *Xinwen Bao*'s office, just around the corner. It served Western food and was also inexpensive and quick. After ordering, they talked about the war, his father asking his opinions, listening to him as though he were another adult.

"What's been going on in Nanking is far worse than anyone knew," his father said. "The Japanese won't let journalists into the city and they censor heavily. But there were foreign reporters in Nanking when the Japanese marched in. They got out of China and the stories they filed are now being published."

"But no one outside China seems to know or care," Shao said.

His father nodded. They were both thinking of the USS *Panay*. The Japanese air force had mistakenly sunk the American ship and foreign newspapers devoted more coverage to the *Panay* than the fall of Nanking.

When their food arrived, his father leaned back in his chair and crossed his arms, a sure sign that a serious topic was imminent.

"I received a letter from Minghua University yesterday," Liu Sanmu said. He handed Shao an envelope. "The town of Shangtan was bombed. The university is very sorry to inform me that you are missing, presumed dead. You didn't think to tell the school before you left? What if your Miss Hu hadn't come to see me until after this letter arrived?"

The envelope was postmarked Chengtu. So Minghua had finally reached its wartime campus. The stationery was Minghua letterhead, signed by the new director of student services. Mr. Lee's replacement.

> *Many students were in town and able to hide in air-raid shelters. At first, we hoped your son was one of these. But he is still missing, so we must reluctantly accept that he was killed.*

The letter didn't mention whether any other students had been killed. Nothing about Sparrow.

"And your friend Miss Hu," his father said. "Does the university know she left with you before the air raid?"

Shao looked down at his omelet. He knew Lian had hoped the university—and Wendian especially—would believe she had died, a victim of the air raid. He had to protect this fiction, keep her trust. He didn't know how much Lian was willing to reveal about her mother and it wasn't his story to tell.

He couldn't lie to his father. But he didn't have to tell him everything either.

"The three of us left without saying anything," he said. "Lian was afraid they'd stop us from leaving. That's why we escaped in secret."

"I hope her parents don't get a letter before she reunites with them." His father's expression remained grim. "You realize I'll have to write the university so they know that you're alive and in Shanghai."

"Father, please don't mention Lian when you write the university," Shao said. "When I see Lian, I'll tell her you got a letter from Minghua. That her . . . family will be getting one."

There was a long silence as his father sliced into a piece of fish. He tapped his finger on the table and a waiter rushed over to refill their tea.

"Well, her family is none of our business," he said, finally. "If her parents get a letter of condolence, that's for her to deal with. But it was irresponsible, not well thought out at all."

His father signaled the waiter for a chit. "I've made some inquiries regarding your classmate Yee Meirong," he said. "All we can do is wait for news."

"Thank you, Father," Shao said.

"In the meantime, you can't sit around Shanghai," Liu Sanmu said. "I've had you enrolled at Jiao Tong University for the summer semester."

And just like that, Shao was the youngest son again. His father making decisions for him again.

"You need to register for classes before June," his father said. "I have no preferences, just sign up for whatever will complete your degree."

"Yes, Father," Shao replied, quelling resentment. He had to speak to his father about another issue. "Father, Sparrow has changed. She's more restless now, impatient."

Now that he was well enough to notice, Shao perceived her frequent absences. No one in the Liu household expected her to resume her previous duties as a house servant right away. She did a little housekeeping then went out. Exploring Shanghai, she said, getting to know it again. Although Shao told himself it wasn't any of his business, it did bother him.

"What she's seen, what she's had to endure, it changes people," Liu Sanmu said. "China itself has changed, Third Son."

"She can't work just as a house servant anymore."

"You're right. Sparrow deserves more," his father said. "Perhaps Second Aunt can find a husband for her. A small merchant who'd like closer connections to our family. It's time she got married, started her own family."

Shao put his cutlery down. Sparrow, married. He stared at his father, who continued talking.

"This is your last year of university, Third Son. Once you're back taking classes again, look around for a young woman. All I ask is that she come from a good family."

Some families put their daughters through university to prove they were rich enough to waste their money educating girls. Others did it to improve their daughters' marriage prospects. There were girls in Shao's social circle who regarded university as a sort of finishing school.

But not Lian. Lian's pursuit of knowledge was pure and un-complicated. Sincere. She was going to write her term paper on the legend of the Willow Star despite all that had happened, she'd told him. Her rucksack had been heavier than his because she'd brought all her notebooks. She'd never once complained about their weight.

He cleared his throat. "About Mother," he said, changing the subject. "Is our doctor doing everything possible?"

"I'm having doubts," his father said. The waiter brought the chit, and Sanmu signed it. "I've been slow to act because Dr. Wu has been our doctor for decades. He'll lose face if we change doctors but I'm going to ask some of our friends for a recommendation."

"Mother's health matters more than Dr. Wu losing face," Shao said. "We should get in touch with Dr. Mao, who looked after me when we were in Wen-chou. I have his card."

"I'm not sure," his father said. "A small-town doctor? A refugee?"

"A doctor," Shao said. "A doctor who had to flee his home."

On the sidewalk, they went their separate ways. Shao got in one of the many rickshaws lined up along the street to go back home, still pondering his father's words.

Sparrow, married.

EVEN THOUGH MEMBERS of the Liu clan from three different cities had come to sit out the war in Shanghai, the Lius weren't suffer-ing or even inconvenienced much. Other, less favored households squeezed a dozen people into three-room flats, sharing incomes and even garments with relatives who had fled with only the clothes on their backs. But a number of Liu relatives from out of town already owned property in Shanghai and simply moved into those homes. The rest installed themselves with varying degrees

of comfort inside the eight-mansion estate, living in guest quarters and spare rooms. Servants grumbled at having to make room
for their guests' servants, but their complaints remained behind
closed doors.

Each household took turns hosting dinners for their guests.
Shao braced himself the night his least-favorite great-uncle came
to dinner. Judge Liu and his extended family had left Changchow
as soon as the Japanese began marching down from Manchuria.
Although the judge's only son lived in a palatial flat, the judge
refused to stay with him. His son's notoriously beautiful wife had
left him for a Hong Kong film director. She was now an actress,
living in Hong Kong. It was a scandal for the conservative judge,
but Shao couldn't blame the wife. The judge's son was about as
intelligent as a houseplant, with a personality to match. And he
was an opium addict.

Judge Liu generally held a low opinion of the younger genera-
tion, especially his nieces and nephews in Shanghai, but for once,
he spoke approvingly to Shao.

"That you valued your education enough to follow Minghua
University through so much hardship is admirable," his elderly
relative said. "That you risked your own safety to give your mother
peace of mind during her illness is even more commendable."

Shao bowed his head to hide his smile at this unexpected
praise. "Thank you, Great-Uncle."

"How is your wife?" the judge said, turning to Liu Sanmu.
"Has your doctor any new insights?"

"I'm going to find a new doctor for my wife even though my
mother is against it," Shao's father said. "She is loyal to Dr. Wu
and thinks it will make him lose face. But it's been months and
my wife is no better."

"Have you a doctor in mind?" the judge asked.

"Fifth Uncle suggests a British doctor," Sanmu said. He reached into his jacket and pulled out a card. "But my son wants me to get this doctor, a refugee. Dr. Mao Ba, the one who looked after Shao during his bout of relapsing fever."

"Dr. Mao! Can it be?" the judge exclaimed, taking the card. "Physician and surgeon. Yes, the same. So, he's here in Shanghai. I must pay my respects."

When Judge Liu first heard of the doctor, it was because of rumors that Dr. Mao had developed a cure for opium addiction. The judge traveled to the small town where the doctor lived to see for himself. He'd done this without expecting much, but where his son was concerned, he had to explore every avenue. He had found, most improbably, a modern clinic and a physician qualified in both Chinese and Western medicine. Dr. Mao was also cultured and well-read, a scholar of the classics. This was the deciding factor for the judge. He put his son into the clinic for two months and the man hadn't taken opium since.

"Dr. Mao is no simple country doctor," Judge Liu said. "When word gets around that a physician of such excellence is in Shanghai, you'll have to stand in line for days."

"If you recommend him, Uncle, then there's no question," Sanmu said. "I'll send for the man first thing tomorrow."

CHAPTER 33

Minghua University left Shangtan a few days after the last bombing. Officially, six members of Minghua University were reported as missing, presumed killed, a list that included Liu Shaoming, Hu Lian, and Sparrow Chen. Professor Kang consoled himself in the secret knowledge that the three had already left town when the bombs fell. Perhaps by now they had reached Shanghai.

But there were three other young lives to mourn and the next leg of Minghua's evacuation would be hard enough already without the memory of lost comrades weighing down upon them all. They were making the final push for Chengtu, more than a month of walking, the longest continuous journey they had ever faced. They would stop only to rest and sleep.

The professor, however, had another duty to fulfill and would not be with the main group. Colonel Chung, their liaison officer in Changsha, had loaned him a truck and driver. The purpose was to deliver the Library of Legends as quickly and safely as possible to the caves near Zunyi. Both Minghua University and the government were in complete agreement on this.

Riding up front beside the truck driver, Professor Kang decided he would not think of this as one of the saddest days of his life, the day he relinquished his last link to the celestial. Instead, he would remember this as the day he guaranteed the safety of a national treasure. He glanced behind him, where Old Fan, the laborer, and Bantien, the cook's assistant, rode on the truck bed, steadying the stacked crates whenever the vehicle jolted out of a pothole.

The ride from Changsha to the caves near Zunyi, with an overnight stay at an inn, felt too short a journey to the professor. The truck pulled off the main road, tires grinding as they came off hard-packed earth and began scrabbling along a stony single-track road. Through the sparse undergrowth he caught glimpses of a creek. The professor hoped the gentle stream was all that remained of any water that eroded caverns into the limestone, that the caves no longer dripped with moisture.

"This isn't a road," the driver growled, shifting gears to climb uphill. "It's barely a trail."

"Please bring the truck as close as possible to the caves," Professor Kang said. "The boxes are heavy."

He ignored the driver's muttered complaints as the truck lurched its way along. Another ten minutes and the driver stopped.

"This is as close as we can get to the caves," he announced.

"You've done your best," the professor said. "Thank you."

The driver got out and lit a cigarette, idly standing by while the two servants carried the crates up to the cave entrance.

The cave entrance stood just a few feet above the track, but high enough on the hillside to be safe from floods. Professor Kang directed the two servants in stacking the crates of books against cave walls. The watertight boxes rested on wooden pallets that kept them from directly touching the cave floor. Then they threw a large tarp over the stacks.

Old Fan and Bantien had offered to stay in the cave. They would be caretakers for the Library. They would make the cave their home until the end of the war. They had brought supplies of food, a few pieces of furniture, and kitchenware. The cook's assistant planned on growing vegetables and there was a village halfway to Zunyi where they could buy other necessities. Zunyi itself was only four hours away.

"Remember to check every day for rodent droppings," the professor said. "Get a cat if you must. And be discreet. If anyone sees these books, they mustn't know how valuable they are."

"Don't worry, Professor," Old Fan said. "We're just one of the many who lost our homes, living in a cave until the war ends."

"Your wages will be sent to the bank at Zunyi," Professor Kang said, "and I'll do my best to come by every so often to see how you're doing."

Old Fan chuckled. "Ah, we're not fooled," he said. "You want to see how the Library of Legends is doing, and fair enough."

"Next time you come, we'll serve you a meal," Bantien said. "There'll be a proper latrine and a vegetable garden. Running water, even. I'll find a way to divert that stream."

The two had been happy to volunteer for this role. Living in the caves, they were safer from air raids than the students or any townspeople. With no one to look after but each other, their daily lives would certainly be more leisurely. And they believed that in return for protecting the Library of Legends, the gods would protect them.

"Mothballs," Kang said. "You have the mothballs?"

The servants laughed. "Professor, you sound as though you're leaving your firstborn grandson behind," Old Fan said. "Don't worry."

Professor Kang knew he was delaying. He shook their hands, the men suddenly shy but pleased at this gesture, more accustomed to bowing than being treated as equals by an employer.

"You're following in the footsteps of a great philosopher of the Ming Dynasty who made his home in a cave, right here in this county," he said, climbing back on the truck. "Also, the feng shui here is very good. Farewell."

"May favorable winds attend your journey," Old Fan called out.

The truck started up and the professor turned to look behind. The two servants stood on the road, waving until the truck dipped around the bend, out of view.

As soon as they were off the stony track, the driver pushed down on the gas pedal, eager to get back to civilization. Minghua was setting out for Chengtu the next day. Thanks to the truck, the professor would get there ahead of the main group, but he had to. There was work to do at the new campus, making sure all the arrangements would be ready. Some of the administrative staff were there already, meeting with banks and government officials.

Professor Kang did his best to get comfortable on the hard seat and ignored the smoke from the driver's cigarette. From the pocket inside his tunic he pulled out a small notebook to review the notes he had been jotting down since he first met the Star. He turned to the question he had been pondering most recently.

The exodus of immortals. "Long overdue." Why are they leaving? When should they have gone?

The truck bounced in and out of a pothole, making him wince. His spine might not survive the trip. It made writing difficult, but he penciled his thoughts.

Hypothesis based on hierarchy of the universe. The gods in heaven, the emperor here on Earth. Emperors sacrifice to heaven to mediate on behalf of the common people. Fall of the Qing Dynasty 1912. No more sacrifices by an emperor. Gods were therefore freed from their obligation to hear our prayers.

Another jolt. He sighed and waited for a clear stretch of road. The road showed no signs of getting any less bumpy. The professor gave up, put away the notebook and pencil. Closed his eyes. Closed off his sadness at parting from the Library of Legends. Stopped thinking about the Willow Star. Concentrated on his responsibilities to the students, to the university.

IN CHENGTU, IT didn't take long for Professor Kang to realize how much he disliked the new director of student services. Mr. Lao's lanky frame, long face, and large teeth gave him a horsey look. He was austere in his habits and drank only hot water, as far as the professor could tell. Kang had yet to hear him laugh. He contrasted this with Mr. Lee, who had enjoyed a good joke and a mug of fine tea. Lee had been genuinely fond of the students. A director of student services appointed during a simpler political climate.

Supposedly Mr. Lao had been working with the rest of Minghua's administrators to get their offices organized. But mostly, he read student files and took charge of the mail. Letters were beginning to arrive in Chengtu for students and faculty.

"There is nothing quite so good for morale as word from home," Professor Kang said, when he poked his head into Lao's office. "Anything for me?"

Mr. Lao was working his way through a small pile of envelopes. Lao pointed to a stack at the corner of his desk. "I believe so. Letters for faculty."

Kang wondered whether Lao opened staff mail or just the ones for students. Perhaps some other unknown person was tasked with spying on the professors.

"Hmm." Lao frowned and slit open an envelope with a razor-sharp letter opener. "This one is for that girl who was killed. Hu Lian. From her mother. With a return address. Now I know where to send the official letter of condolence."

"I hope that letter takes its time arriving," the professor said, "although mail to and from Chengtu has been relatively quick. The postal service seems nearly back to normal."

"It helps that our campus address is now fixed," Lao said. "And, of course, we benefit from the fact that many high-ranking officials have moved their families here. Did you know this Hu Lian well?"

Lao held the letter out to Kang.

My dearest daughter, good news. I am working at the Southern Baptist Mission refugee camp in exchange for meals and a place to sleep. Perhaps even some small

wages soon. Such good fortune! Send mail to this address.
I want to know all about your adventures. It's such a com-
fort to know that by now you must be safely in Chengtu
with your university . . .

Lao opened his desk drawer, took out some newly printed letterhead, and began to write. He copied the words from a draft, the same words he'd used before to the parents of other students killed in Shangtan. If nothing else, the man was conscientious when it came to duty. The professor took his small bundle of mail and hoped the letter to Lian's mother would end up lost in a post office, abandoned at the bottom of some mailbag. At least until Lian had found her mother.

CHAPTER 34

The spring of 1938 arrived gently, mild and sunny, as if to apologize for the vicious cold that had gripped the city earlier. Green buds on sycamore trees that had resisted opening now unfurled into leaves the size of Lian's palm. In gardens and parks, bright yellow shrubs of forsythia and the flutter of foliage gave back to Shanghai some of its charm and the illusion of peace.

Lian had been in Shanghai just over a week now and had gone to the *Xinwen Bao* office once to check for news of Meirong. She trudged up the apartment staircase, which echoed with muffled sounds of conversation, shouts, and arguments that drifted up from each floor as she climbed. There was hardly a family in Shanghai without friends or relatives squeezed into their homes. In private, behind closed doors and shuttered windows, people voiced the annoyance of sharing a home for months, the embarrassment of having nowhere else to go, the despair and worry over what was yet to come.

On her best day Lian had visited three camps and returned to the flat before sunset. Most days she only managed two. When the gaudy neon signs of Shanghai blazed on, it was time to get off the streets. She entered the apartment each evening despondent and weary. More tired than she had ever believed possible, even when she had been on the road.

But perhaps tomorrow someone would say to her *Yes, we know your mother, she's right inside!*

But Lian knew, after her first day of searching, that the camps couldn't even keep accurate records, it simply wasn't possible. The only way she could be certain was to walk through each camp, between rows of straw-mat tents, looking and questioning, both hoping and dreading that she would find her mother there among the dejected homeless. There were so many orphaned children, so many women. Young teenagers. Very few elderly.

When she reached the third floor and entered the flat, Lian found a letter that had been slipped under the door. On the envelope, Sparrow had written she would come by again later. Inside was a note from Shao.

> *I'd come see you, but I want to stay close to my mother right now. Sparrow will take you out for a meal. My brother Tienming knows you're at the apartment and says you're welcome to stay until someone else needs it. I delivered him a letter from Mrs. Deng. She's left him. Did you have any inkling when you were in Wen-chou?*
>
> *Minghua University's new director of student services wrote to my father saying I was missing, presumed dead*

after that air raid on Shangtan. They probably think you were killed too. I had to explain to my father why we left Minghua without telling anyone. Sparrow will fill you in on what I said, but rest assured it was minimal and my father has promised not to mention your name when he writes back to Minghua. If there's anything you need, just tell Sparrow. I'll come see you soon.

Lian put the note on the windowsill and sat down on an elm wood chair. It was a beautiful piece of furniture, the arms smooth and polished, a pleasure to touch. She leaned against the curved back. All she wanted was to sleep. When she shut the door to the flat, she told herself she was shutting out the world. Then she would heat up some rice and boil water for tea. She worried about her mother and cried herself to sleep over Shao. When she slept, she often dreamed about Sparrow, the Star looking at her out of eyes like pools of night, sometimes amused, sometimes contemptuous.

Then in the morning, Lian would eat quickly after getting up and pack a steamed bun for lunch, sometimes a boiled egg, slipping it in her cloth tote with her list and the map. She made sure the apartment key was hanging securely on a cord around her neck, tucked under her clothing. Only then would she take the stairs down to the foyer, praying that this would be the day.

She started when the doorbell rang and realized she had been dozing. She opened the door to Sparrow, in a wool coat over a high-necked *qipao* dress. A dress of good quality.

"I've never seen you in ordinary clothes," Lian said. "You look so . . ."

"So ordinary?" Sparrow said. She dropped the coat on a chair. "Shao's second aunt gave me some of her clothes."

Lian thought Sparrow looked tired, somehow diminished, and not for the first time she remembered that the Star had no special powers. Except for being immortal. Sparrow looked around the room, at the polished parquet floor, the tall French windows.

"I can't imagine my sister living here," she said. "No courtyard, no view of the sky without leaning out that small false balcony. Let's go for dinner."

After hot soup followed by a dish of freshwater crabs steamed with ginger and garlic, Lian felt less despondent.

"But I don't know why I get so tired, Sparrow," she said. "After all that time on the road, all those miles of walking, stumbling around in the dark and the cold, I thought walking through Shanghai would be easy. But I just want to fall over as soon as I close the door."

"It's not the walking," Sparrow said. "It's the sight of so much tragedy concentrated in such a small area. The Settlement is only thirteen square miles' worth of Greater Shanghai. They say more than a million displaced now live here."

"And my mother's here somewhere," Lian said. Despair returned. "Among the million."

"You'll find your mother," Sparrow said.

"I have a routine now," Lian said, trying to sound cheerful. She pulled her list out of the tote bag. "Every night, I take out this list and cross off the names of the camps I've visited. Then I take out the map and circle two or three more locations for the next day. I began by going to the camps closest to the apartment and now I walk farther each day."

Sparrow looked at the list. "Let me make a copy. The External Roads district is a long walk from here, but not as far from the Liu residence. I can search the camps on the western side of the city."

"Oh, Sparrow, that would be such a help," Lian said. Relief washed over her. Then hesitation. "But you must have duties that keep you busy."

"No one seems to care whether I work or not right now," Sparrow said, "because I brought Shao home. They say I should rest for a while. So let me help."

"Shao's letter says Mrs. Deng has left Wen-chou," Lian said. How did one make small talk with a celestial being? Sometimes she thought she had dreamed the night with the *qilin*, the evening she had sat with the Star and her sister, a gleaming pair of lights.

"Yes, as soon as Shao and I got on the freighter, my sister vanished," Sparrow said. "Shao's brother is taking it hard. It will pass. Men forget."

"What about Shao's mother?" she asked. "He didn't mention anything in his letter. Is she better now that he's home?"

"She's not improving," Sparrow said, "but Shao's father has agreed to bring in Dr. Mao, the one who treated Shao."

IT WAS THURSDAY again. This would be Lian's second visit to *Xinwen Bao* for news of Meirong. Her steps took her past an alley lined with flimsy shelters, bamboo sticks propping up roofs of cardboard. The weather was still cool but the reek of urine and rot drifted out to the sidewalks. It would be much worse once the hot weather arrived.

The clerk at *Xinwen Bao* was busy on the telephone, evidently not happy with the conversation, jabbing his finger at a sheet of paper in front of him, a gesture entirely wasted on the person at the other end of the phone. He recognized Lian and gestured for her to wait. On her last visit he had just shrugged and given her a quick shake of the head to indicate there was nothing for her. Finally, he slammed down the receiver.

"The boss has something for you today," he said, still scowling. He swiveled his chair to the pigeonhole bookcase behind him and pulled out a folded square of paper.

Miss Hu, please come up. I have news.

The Liu family connections had done their work. Lian flew up the staircase and knocked on the door to Liu Sanmu's office. The handle unlatched and Shao held open the door for her.

"How wonderful to see you!" she cried, too happy to feel awkward about hugging him in front of his father. "So you know the news about Meirong!"

He gave her a crooked smile and leaned against the wall beside his father's desk. Liu Sanmu remained sitting and pointed at the chair facing him. Lian sat, leaning forward in anticipation. Large windows behind the desk overlooked a peaceful green square. Unlike other open spaces in Shanghai, the lawns of this park were not crammed full of tents and crude shacks.

Liu Sanmu cleared his throat. "I'm sorry, Miss Hu. My contacts managed to get release documents for Yee Meirong, but I have bad news."

Her exhilaration died away, replaced by anxiety. "What's wrong? Is she ill?"

"The authorities in Changsha sent instructions to the camp," he said. "Instructions to free Yee Meirong. But it was too late."

Meirong and two others had escaped from the camp, but they were in a remote area, far away from any farms or villages. There was nowhere to hide, and few landmarks to help them find their way. The guards had caught them easily. As punishment for trying to escape, Meirong and her fellow fugitives were executed.

Lian stood up slowly and walked to the window. She heard

floorboards squeak, felt Shao's hand on her shoulder. Her eyes focused on the park across the road. Grass, trees, and paths. Blocks of white stone and sculpture arranged in rows. It wasn't a park, it was a cemetery for foreigners. No wonder the square of green was empty. Even the most desperate would not sleep with foreign ghosts.

LIAN COULDN'T RECALL exactly how she got back to the apartment. It was in an automobile, Shao beside her, his voice sympathetic, his arm around her clumsy and uncomfortable as he tried to comfort her. She didn't remember his words, had barely been aware of them as a hundred pointless scenarios flitted through her mind.

Should she have begged Cook Tam to intervene? Should they have run away from Shangtan sooner? Why hadn't she sent Meirong a letter before they left, to give her hope, to say they were going to get Shao's father to help?

Shao led her into the elevator, then to the door of the flat. She felt his steadying hand on her arm. Inside, she dropped her cloth bag on the floor and went to the kitchen.

"Do you want tea?" she asked. "I can boil water." She said this automatically, out of habit.

She didn't know whether she made the tea or whether it was Shao who did it. She was mired in regrets. She hadn't saved Meirong. No, that wasn't true. She *had* saved Meirong, could have saved her. But her stubborn, willful friend had been too impatient. Surely Meirong must've known what would happen if she tried to escape. Had she escaped out of defiance? Or because she had been beaten and tortured during her "reeducation"?

Whenever Shao left, Lian didn't notice. Nor did she remember eating anything for dinner.

In the morning, she pulled open the soft velvet drapes and looked down at the street. It was still early but Shanghai had been awake for hours. There were cars and rickshaws jostling along the road, handbarrows loaded with goods pushing their way between the lanes. A gleaming black sedan stopped and two young men got out, neckties loosened about their collars, laughing as they staggered into the apartment building opposite. A woman paused to smooth down her hair before hurrying into the florist shop, late for work.

It was all so busy and lively, so normal. Meirong would've made up a story to tell about the young men, about the florist shop assistant. But there was no Meirong, and now the only person Lian wanted was her mother. Not Shao, not Sparrow. Her mother. Her mother would've told her that the hard knot of pain in her chest wasn't just because of Meirong. That it was all the tears she had been holding back since leaving Nanking, tears she had not allowed herself to cry over all the tragedies she had witnessed.

But if she started crying, she never would've stopped. Not for days.

Below, traffic moved and pedestrians filled sidewalks, the hundred small dramas of life on the street continued. Lian stood at the window until she was cold then moved stiffly into the kitchen, where she ran water into the kettle. She wasn't hungry but she wanted to warm her hands around a bowl of hot water.

When the doorbell rang she considered not answering. It was probably Shao, checking on her. But she was living in property his family owned, so she couldn't refuse. She opened the door to Sparrow, glowing in the dim light of the hallway.

"I heard about Meirong. How terrible," Sparrow said. "I'm so sorry. Are you all right?" There was something in her voice that frightened Lian.

She came inside and gently led Lian to the couch. "I have news, Lian. It's good news, but you must be strong." Her hands pressed tightly around Lian's. "I found your mother."

Lian gave a little cry. "Where? Where is she?"

"She's at West Gate Hospital on Siccawei Road," Sparrow said. "Lian, she thought you were dead. She tried to kill herself."

CHAPTER 35

Shao rushed to West Gate Hospital after reading the note Sparrow left him. She had found Lian's mother at the Southern Baptist Mission's refugee camp. Or rather, she learned that Lian's mother had been working in their administrative office but was now in the hospital. She was taking Lian to see her mother.

He found Sparrow waiting in the corridor outside the ward.

"How is her mother?" he said, instinctively lowering his voice to a whisper. "What happened?"

"A letter of condolence from Minghua," Sparrow said. Shao groaned.

Before anyone realized her intentions, Lian's mother had run up to the second floor of the Mission's offices, the highest building on the property, then thrown herself out a window. From such a height, she had broken her leg and briefly lost consciousness. And now she was in the hospital, lying in one of seven beds crammed into a room meant to sleep four patients.

"What can I do?" he said. "Does the hospital need payment?"

"No, this hospital is jointly run by several foreign missions," Sparrow said. "But the problem is that they've lost one of their surgeons and the one who's here is already working far too many hours. Lian's mother is on a very long list."

"Have you seen her mother? What's she like?"

"I didn't want to intrude on their reunion," Sparrow said, "so I haven't actually met her. I just took Lian to the room and looked in. There's a strong resemblance. A small chin, eyes like smoky brown topaz. Beautiful."

Lian came out, her face pale and her expression strained, but she managed a smile. Sparrow was right. Lian was beautiful.

"How's your mother?" Shao said. He held his hand out to her but she didn't take it, just leaned her back on the wall beside him. Her blunt-cut hair was growing out and hung over her face, like curtains closing her off to him.

"She's happy I'm not dead," Lian said, "and I had so much explaining to do. But she's in pain. A broken leg, you don't even need X-rays to see that. The nurse says it should be set quickly, but how long a wait, she can't tell. And there's some chance of infection."

Shao looked around. The hospital was cleaner than the one in Changsha, but that wasn't saying much. Patients sat on benches and corridor floors waiting for care, some with open, weeping sores. There were children with eye infections, adults with large, visible tumors. Too many were wounded.

"There's so many urgent cases ahead of her," Lian said. "I understand that. I just want her to come home." The catch in her voice pinched his heart, a sharp twinge.

"Have you eaten at all today?" Sparrow said. "Can your mother eat? I'll get something and bring it back."

"I'd be so grateful," Lian said. She straightened up. "I'm going to sit with my mother and watch her in case she starts running a fever. Apparently, that's the first sign of infection." Lian returned to her mother's room.

"She looks so fragile and so . . . young," Shao said. "She makes me feel protective. As though she needs my help."

"Lian isn't fragile," Sparrow said. "Think of what she's had to deal with on top of the hardships we all faced with Minghua 123."

Shao mused on all Lian had been through. That business with Mr. Lee. Then being threatened by Wendian. Not knowing where her mother was the entire time they were on the road. That moment in the air-raid shelter when he'd caught a glimpse of the steel in her. With or without him, she would've come to Shanghai for her mother, for Meirong.

"No, she doesn't need protection, but she makes me feel worthwhile." He leaned against the corridor wall. "As though I'm someone who can make a difference."

"Don't I make you feel worthwhile, Young Master?" Sparrow asked. He couldn't tell whether she was teasing.

"You take care of me, Sparrow. You're so competent it makes me feel useless," he said. "Everyone just thinks of me as the youngest son. They see my family's money and think I won't ever amount to much."

"You've done well at Minghua," Sparrow said. "Good grades, a tutorial leader."

"But now I'm back in Shanghai, doing what my father wants," he said. "He's enrolled me at Jiao Tong University. I'm not like my brothers. They've always been decisive. All I've ever done is follow along. I have no initiative of my own."

"You thought of getting your father to help Meirong," Sparrow said. "You helped Lian escape to Shanghai."

"I got sick," he said. "It would've been a lot faster if you hadn't had to look after me most of the way."

"It's not your fault for getting sick," Sparrow said. "And all you really needed was some rest, good food, and Dr. Mao."

WHILE ON THE road, trudging behind a cart, Shao had tried not to think too much about his hometown. Now he could admit how much he had missed its noisy sophistication, brightly lit streets where music blared out from nightclubs and delicious smells escaped through restaurant doors. He'd missed the gleam of polished automobiles and the gaudy flashes of neon signs. It was easy to take a route that avoided the edges of the Settlement, so that he wouldn't have to look at the ugly barbed-wire barricades. He enjoyed walking its streets, pretending that war had never touched the city.

But today he took a rickshaw, promising the puller a silver coin if he ran fast. Shao checked the address on the business card one more time as the rickshaw rushed through traffic, cutting off other vehicles and taking shortcuts through alleys too narrow for cars. Shao got off on Nanho Road, a street of modest shops and apartments. He took the stairs two at a time to the building's third floor hoping he wasn't too late, that Dr. Mao's office hours were not yet over. When he reached the landing, it was immediately obvious which flat contained the doctor's office. A handwritten sign pasted on the door read DR. MAO BA. PHYSICIAN AND SURGEON.

Shao rapped on the door. When there was no reply, he pushed it open. An empty desk and chair, a tall filing cabinet, the pale green walls bare except for a pair of calligraphy scrolls. A folding screen of green fabric divided the room in half. The murmur of conversation came from behind the screen.

He called a greeting and a voice from behind the screen, cheerful and familiar, called back. "Please sit and wait. Two minutes."

While he waited, Shao took a closer look at the scrolls. Two lines of poetry by the Tang Dynasty poet Zhang Jiuling. The calligraphy was exceptional, the brushstrokes expressive yet still within the bounds of classical style. If this was Dr. Mao's own calligraphy, no wonder Judge Liu had been impressed. The doctor possessed the gentlemanly accomplishments of a scholar as well as a medical degree.

"You're better off spending your money on nutritious fresh fruits and vegetables." Dr. Mao came out from behind the screen with his patient, a pregnant woman. "Those herbal remedies are of questionable benefit."

The doctor closed the door after the woman, then turned to shake Shao's hand. "Mr. Liu, are you unwell again? Or are you here because of your mother?"

"I'm fine," Shao said, "and my mother is as well as can be expected. No, I'm here on behalf of my friend Lian. Her mother needs someone to set her broken leg."

West Gate Hospital for Women and Children was staffed entirely by women, its charter drawn up during a time when Chinese women, especially those of good family, were forbidden to be seen by men who were not relatives, let alone foreign men. But these were extraordinary times and the hospital was desperate. Shao could only hope they were desperate enough to agree to his idea.

He accompanied Dr. Mao to meet the head of surgery, an American woman. She was polite but wary, obviously skeptical. Shao moved out of earshot, watched the woman's gestures grow animated, her body shifting closer to Dr. Mao. Then she shook

Dr. Mao's hand, holding it in both of hers as though his presence was a miracle.

In exchange for the use of an operating theater and assistants, Dr. Mao agreed to perform two other surgeries. Furthermore, he would fill in as a visiting doctor two days a week.

"I'm sorry, Doctor," Shao said. "I didn't mean to add more to your workload."

"Nonsense, I should thank you," the doctor said. "It's good for my practice to be affiliated with a hospital. There's only so much I can do from an office. As for workload, I've hardly got any patients. I'm too new. I have no reputation yet in Shanghai."

"But now you're the Liu family doctor," Sparrow said. "When word gets around, all of Shanghai society will be at your door."

"Maybe, maybe," he replied amiably and picked up his bag. "Now let's go see my new patient."

Shao followed the doctor, who strode along the corridor, absentmindedly tugging at the stethoscope around his neck. There was something incongruous about the shiny instrument dangling down the front of his long scholar's gown.

Lian's face transformed when Shao explained that Dr. Mao would operate on her mother. There was a small glimmer at first, like the flame from a matchstick. Then a smile that made her face glow like lamplight. She'd looked up at Shao as though he had performed a miracle. As though Shao were the one who would set her mother's leg. For a moment, he thought she was going to fling her arms around him, and he braced himself in smiling anticipation. But instead she took a step back.

"You're wonderful, Shao," Lian said. "I can't thank you enough." Then she disappeared through the swinging doors back into the ward, leaving him alone with Sparrow.

Sparrow's expression could only be described as appraising. "That was very kind of you, Young Master. And quick thinking."

"Dr. Mao is the kind one," he said. "He's not going to charge Lian for the operation. He says his patients pay according to their means. No wonder he lives and works out of a tiny flat."

"That will change when patients of means begin coming to him," Sparrow said. "Why don't you go home, Young Master? You should go see your mother. I'll wait here in case Miss Hu or her mother needs anything."

He nodded. "I'll go home now. Let's talk when you're back home too. We haven't spent much time together lately, have we?"

"If you have any spare time, you need to spend it with your mother, Young Master," Sparrow said. "It matters to her and it matters to you. Once she's gone, you'll be sorry for every minute you weren't by her side."

"Sparrow, please don't call me 'Young Master' anymore," he said. "No one thinks of you as a servant. Once Second Aunt arranges a marriage for you, you'll be mistress of your own household."

Marriages and jobs. Gifts of money for the birth of a child and for funeral arrangements. The family servants could count on the Lius to take care of these things. But Sparrow didn't respond. The silence between them grew.

"It seems so feudal, doesn't it?" Shao said. Now he wished he hadn't brought up the subject. "But Second Aunt will find a few suitable candidates. And you'll get a good dowry."

"I'm grateful to your father and Second Aunt," Sparrow said. Her words were pleasant, yet unaccountably he felt reprimanded. "You should go home now."

CHAPTER 36

Lian had spoken to Shao just once since West Gate Hospital. The day after her mother came home, there was a quiet knock on the apartment door, Shao and Sparrow. Lian put a finger to her lips. Her mother was sleeping.

"We came to drop off your mother's belongings," Sparrow said. She held a small wicker suitcase. "I went to the Southern Baptist Mission refugee camp. The ladies said to tell your mother they're praying for a quick recovery."

"We'll go now," Shao said. "We won't bother you."

"No, no," Lian said quickly. "Let's have some tea. Tell me about your mother, Shao."

"I'll make the tea," Sparrow said. "And Old Zhao sent some pastries."

Shao opened the French doors, letting in light and

noise. He was casually and beautifully dressed, a cardigan of fine wool that matched the blue pinstripe of his Oxford shirt. He'd had a haircut and there was no longer any evidence of the windburn that had roughened his face. Lian resisted the impulse to touch his cheek.

"How is your mother—" she began.

But he interrupted her, speaking quickly, almost as if reciting. His father had sent for Dr. Mao, who diagnosed his mother's various ailments as symptoms of cancer. The doctor had given them the news with kindness and tact. Then his father had called their longtime physician, Dr. Wu, to the house and asked whether his wife's symptoms could be those of cancer. After another examination Dr. Wu admitted the possibility, then tried to blame his negligence on Mrs. Liu's long history of nervous complaints.

Dr. Mao was now their family doctor, but Shao still held his father responsible for taking so long to consult a different doctor.

"He's always been dismissive of my mother's health," Shao said. He leaned against the wrought-iron railing and lit a cigarette. Lian didn't remember him smoking before. "My father thought she was going through one of her moods and said as much to Dr. Wu, who was happy to do as little as possible. So neither of them took her seriously."

Lian almost reached over to take his hand. She wanted to take his hand but knew she should keep her distance. She gripped the balcony railing instead. "So what does Dr. Mao prescribe?" she said.

"According to him, it's too late," Shao said. He savagely stubbed out his half-smoked cigarette and threw it over the balcony. "He says it would've been too late even six months ago. My mother won't see the end of summer. His work now is to keep her comfortable."

"I'm so sorry," Lian said. She'd spent months worrying about her own mother but even in her most overwrought moments there had only been uncertainty, and therefore, hope. Shao had none.

"It's all right in a way," Shao said, "at least according to Mother. She says it's a relief not having to wonder anymore if she's been going mad with imagined ailments."

Sparrow brought out a tray with tea and pastries and set it down.

"There's some happier news," Shao said. "My father is giving Sparrow a dowry and Second Aunt is doing the matchmaking. She lives for this sort of thing, my second aunt."

Sparrow poured the tea, seemingly unperturbed and oblivious to Lian's gaping open mouth. After they left, Lian went to the bedroom to check on her mother. But for the first time in days, it wasn't her mother's health that preoccupied her.

Sparrow, married.

LIAN COULD TELL her mother was still afraid. How long would it take for all those years of mistrust to let go? Even in the flat, with just the two of them, her mother still clung to old habits. She looked out of windows from behind the drapes and paused the conversation if she heard voices coming up the staircase. If only her mother could enjoy their reunion, which for Lian was like a dream after so many months of worry. A dream where she and her mother lived in a beautiful flat. Where they spent hours each night talking until her mother laughingly and reluctantly told her it was time for bed, as though she were a little girl again. Where they slept in the same room, Lian on a layer of quilts on the floor, her mother on the bed with a pillow propped under her plaster-casted leg.

Lian woke to the fragrance of steaming rice and the sounds of crockery being set out. She dressed and hurried out to help but breakfast was already waiting on the table. Congee the way Lian remembered it, with salted duck egg crumbled on top of the soupy mix, a small dish of sliced cucumber and radishes pickled in soy and vinegar for sharing. Her mother moved around on crutches but always made their meals. It was a pleasure to be cooking for two again, she'd insisted.

Dr. Mao had urged her to eat as much as she could. Her body and bones were mending and she needed food. In the few weeks they'd been together, her mother's cheeks had plumped up and the shadows under her eyes were all but gone. Her face was more lined, her hair streaked with gray, but her hands moved gracefully as she poured hot tea for Lian. She listened with her head slightly tilted to one side. Lian's father used to say she reminded him of a blossom on its stem. Lian's mother did this because she was hard of hearing in one ear. But unless you knew this, it appeared merely a charming trait, one that suited her mother's name. *Beihua*, Northern Flower.

At the hospital, Lian had spent every waking moment at her mother's bedside, telling her everything that had happened since the bombing at the Nanking railway station. About the evacuation from Nanking, the long days of walking, the cold and hunger, always alert to the sound of airplanes. About the Library of Legends. About Mr. Shen, the first of them to fall. Mr. Lee's threats and Wang Jenmei's murder. About Meirong's arrest and execution. How Wendian had gotten Mr. Lee arrested. The escape from Shangtan, and the journey east with Shao and Sparrow.

Then she had told her mother about her fright when she'd seen Mr. Lee at the hospital in Changsha. And the completely unexpected news that her father's name had been cleared. That his file now showed he'd been an innocent victim.

"We don't need to be afraid anymore, Mother," Lian said, holding her mother's hand. "We can use our real names. You can be Jin Beihua again."

"All those years of hiding, the false identities." Her mother began to cry. "And all that time, they knew where we were, who we were. I was so foolish. I ruined your childhood."

"Don't worry about that, everything's worked out," Lian said. "What matters is that the authorities have cleared Father's name. Do you think his cousin knew, the one who got us the false papers? Why didn't he tell us everything was all right?"

"He died a few years after we moved to Peking," her mother said, wiping her eyes. "I saw the obituary."

Her mother's journey to Shanghai had been somewhat less eventful than Lian's. She'd attached herself to some foreigners, missionary families glad to have help with children and the elderly, having left their own servants behind in Peking. Beihua had entered the International Settlement as part of their group, posing as a member of the household, a humble Chinese servant.

And now her mother was restless, worried again.

"Lian, we need to make some changes," she said, looking around the beautiful room. "We can't go on taking advantage of the Liu family's generosity. Even though you helped bring their son home while he was so sick, it's not a debt of gratitude that goes on forever."

It wasn't just the flat either. Whenever Sparrow came by, she brought food sent by Old Zhao, the Lius' cook. When Lian's mother had to return to the hospital for a follow-up visit, Shao sent a car and driver to take them.

When her mother had fled Peking, she had taken a large sum of money with her, almost all her savings. But the journey had depleted those funds. Transportation was expensive and so were the bribes that allowed her to get on trains and trucks as she followed the missionary families to safety. She'd added what was left to Lian's small cache and it was clear they would soon run out of money. The pantry was emptying at an alarming speed. Rice, flour, soy sauce, even salt.

"I must get back to the Southern Baptist Mission," her mother said, struggling onto her crutches. "It pays a pittance but it's better than nothing. Work is nearly impossible to find in Shanghai. Even if it's only a cot at the Mission office, we'll need somewhere to live when we lose this flat."

When, not if. Rents in Shanghai were increasingly exorbitant. Even the Liu family would take notice soon and want to make the most of the opportunity.

"But not yet, Mother," she said. "You're still on crutches. You can't walk to the Mission every day."

"I don't need crutches to type," her mother said, sitting down again. Her hands clenched tightly around a teacup. "I can take a rickshaw. It's worth the expense just to hold my place there. You could come with me. You can bring me documents from the filing cabinets, run errands so I don't have to get up and walk. You should meet the Mission staff. You'll make a good impression. Who knows, they might give you a job too. I must get back, let them know I'm ready to work again."

Lian had to calm her down. She put her hand over her mother's. "You still need to rest. Let me go to the Mission office and tell the staff you're coming back. I'll ask them to hold your job for you."

Slowly, her mother's fingers eased their grip and let go of the cup. Lian felt her shoulders tense, recognizing that once again, she needed to look after the two of them.

"Remember, we invited Shao and Sparrow tonight for dumplings," Lian said. "And Dr. Mao. Do you need anything from the market while I'm out?"

THE SOUTHERN BAPTIST Mission refugee camp was only a forty-minute walk from the apartment. Lian felt relief for this time on her own, to think on her own. She and her mother had been apart for only two years, yet so much had befallen them during that time. They had been living as normally as they could, creating a home in rooms that were not theirs, in a city that was trying to do the same amid misery, chaos, and political unrest. They made plans. Plans that depended on a quick end to the war, others that assumed the war would go on for years. Plans for what to do when they had to leave the luxurious flat.

Her mother still had a few gold coins hidden away, sewn into the lining of her wicker suitcase. But those were for emergencies. And even if they used the gold, it wouldn't last long once they had to pay rent. Even a single room cost a fortune these days. They might have to share with strangers. Their best and cheapest option was to share the cot at the Mission office, if they were allowed. Lian hoped her mother's attempted suicide hadn't frightened off the missionaries.

It was clear to Lian that she needed to find a job, to start earning something, whether or not her mother went back to work at the Mission. But every refugee in Shanghai was hoping to find work, even those lucky enough to have family connections. The only connection she had was Shao. She didn't want to ask him, didn't want to owe him more. But there was also Sparrow.

She hadn't told her mother about the Willow Star except as a legend. A topic for the term paper she still wanted to write. Nor did she mention her feelings for Shao since there was no point. Even if her mother had advice to offer, what good would it do?

Lian could dream all she wanted but Shao would never love anyone but the Star.

No, he couldn't even love the Star. The Star had forfeited that
when she bargained it away, because she'd wanted her Prince to
live comfortably in every one of his reincarnations.

How could she resent Sparrow, who had loved and endured
without reward for centuries? It was far better to marvel at the
presence of an immortal in her life. An immortal she could call
friend. An immortal who seemed to be going along with the no-
tion of a marriage arranged by Shao's second aunt.

WHEN THE MISSIONARIES and workers learned who Lian was, they
gathered around her, clucking sympathetically and asking about
her mother's recovery. They didn't utter a word of condemnation
about her mother trying to take her own life.

"This war has pushed people to the limits of physical and
emotional endurance," a woman said, shaking her head. "Your
mother had suffered so much, seen so much suffering. And then
she thought she'd lost the one person she loved. If only she had
trusted in the Lord."

"Miss Mason is the one who hired your mother," another said.
"You need to speak with her. She's busy doing her rounds. Can
you wait for about an hour?"

"Of course," Lian said. "But please, let me do something in the
meantime to help."

They put her to work cleaning the office and small porch outside. A trio of girls who sat huddled on the porch steps edged away
as she swept, then drifted back once she'd finished sweeping the
steps, moving like flotsam carried by the tide's ebb and swell. Lian
recognized their furtive determination. They were staking out
their place.

A plump foreign woman entered as Lian finished wiping down the furniture. She had wisps of gray-blond hair falling out from the roll pinned to the top of her head, a style outmoded for at least twenty years. Her blue eyes crinkled in a smile upon seeing Lian.

"I heard the news," she said, opening her arms to pull Lian into a talcum-powder-scented embrace. Her Chinese was excellent. "You're Lian. And your mother is on the mend. We've been so worried."

Lian tried not to look startled. Were all foreigners this effusive?

"Thank you for your concern, Miss Mason," Lian said. "My mother is hoping to come back to her typing job soon. And I'd like to do something to help also. As a volunteer, of course. I did learn some first aid, simple wound care, bathing invalids."

"How I've missed your mother," Miss Mason said. "She's fast and accurate, and she could decipher the worst handwriting. I'd be happy for her to come back anytime, but only if she feels strong enough."

"She'll be on crutches for a long while yet," Lian said, "but she doesn't need crutches to type. And I can run her errands around the camp if need be."

"Perfect, perfect," the foreign woman said, clasping her hands to her heart. "I can't ask for more. I think we could use you, Lian. As a letter writer. Many of the refugees are illiterate. They need to get in touch with their families."

"I can start right now, if you like," Lian said. "Perhaps just for a few hours?" She wanted to make a good impression on this woman.

At the end of a few hours, Lian returned to the office with a shoebox full of letters she had written. Miss Mason was typing, her fingers pecking determinedly on the keys. She paused to hand

Lian a small box of stamps and a tin can for coins. Lian dropped in the coins she had collected. She had written letters only for those who had money for postage. The Mission simply couldn't afford to give them stamps as well as stationery.

"Although there are emergency situations where we do," Miss Mason quickly added when explaining.

Lian began pasting stamps on envelopes, conversations with the people who had dictated their letters coming back to her as she handled each one. The young man now responsible for his sister's children as well as his own. A haggard face, haunted eyes. A baby under one arm, hungry toddlers beating on his back. *We are in Shanghai. Tell our parents Second Sister died.* The middle-aged woman, her elderly in-laws seated listlessly on the ground behind her. Her husband too injured to move. A pleading letter to siblings. *We are in Shanghai. Send money.* The young mother with two children, her face impassive, impossible to read. Forbidding Lian to ask. *We are in Shanghai. Is it safe to come home?*

"Sometimes I feel as though the world is ending," Lian said. "How much more tragedy can these people survive?"

"It can be overwhelming." Miss Mason looked up. "No, it *is* overwhelming, no denying that. Thank goodness we got through the cholera epidemic."

"Miss Mason," Lian said, "does anyone outside China know how bad conditions are?"

"Oh yes, yes," she replied. "All our churches get regular bulletins. Your mother types up those reports." She studied Lian for a moment. "But what you want to know is whether other nations will help."

Lian nodded. "Yes. Or are we on our own?"

"I don't know, my dear," Miss Mason said. "I don't know enough about politics. I can't even say how much my own church is able to help. I only know that with something as big as this war, the best I can do is make a difference for a few people. Or even just one person, Lian. If each of us could make a difference to just one person."

"You've made a difference to my mother," she said. "Thank you for taking her in. Giving her work."

Miss Mason made a dismissive noise, inserted another sheet of paper into the typewriter.

"Miss Mason, there's something I need to tell you," Lian said. "My mother and I may need to live here soon. We can both sleep in this office as she used to. If it's all right with you."

"Oh. Oh dear." Miss Mason blinked. "I'm so sorry, but those girls on the front porch sleep here now at night. When we heard your mother was living with you, we thought she didn't need a bed anymore. And there are so many others in need."

CHAPTER 37

The evening was pleasant, cool but not windy. Rather than hail a rickshaw, Shao walked. Sparrow had gone to the flat ahead of him, to help Lian and her mother with the cooking. He strolled up Rue Joffre, not minding its congested sidewalks. Restaurants were lively with diners and music, touts beside nightclub entrances called out to Shao. In his neatly pressed wool slacks and silk tie, a new cashmere coat, he looked exactly like what he was, a princeling, one of Shanghai society's elite.

He'd meant to see Lian more often but he didn't know what to make of her anymore. It was as though she didn't want him around. Perhaps he just needed to wait until she and her mother had spent more time together. And then . . . and then what?

Anyway, his social life wasn't suffering. When

word got around that Shao was back in Shanghai, he'd been invited to round after round of parties. Sammy Chung, never seen without a bowler on his head, was especially insistent. Resplendent in flannel suit and loud paisley tie, Sammy had pulled a card out of his wallet and jotted down the date and time of a party at the Majestic Hotel.

"This weekend, the biggest party of the season," Sammy said, pressing the card into Shao's hands. "For men only, if you catch my meaning. A little gambling, good dance music. Pretty hostesses, a few foreign ones. Russians. Promise you'll come. We all want to hear about your adventures."

Shao knew these weren't his friends, not really. They had no interest in listening to his tales of life on the road, didn't want to know what he'd seen of rural China. Before the war, Sammy and his friends had fluttered at the periphery of his and Pao's circle. Pao had dismissed them as shallow. But Pao wasn't in Shanghai anymore and neither was the rest of the Zhu family. The day after he arrived home, Shao had gone across the street to pay his respects. But the gatekeeper told him the Zhus had left Shanghai and moved south, to their summer home in Kunming. Pao had transferred to the University of Hong Kong and now lived there. Sammy and his friends merely filled a vacancy.

Sparrow didn't hide her dislike of Sammy. "Mr. Chung is a waste of your time, Young Master," she said.

"I have nothing but time these days," he snapped, annoyed that Sparrow would judge his choice of friends.

He told Sparrow very little about what he did when he was out with Sammy. But he knew Sparrow could tell. She still looked after Shao's wardrobe and these days the suits she hung to air out reeked of cigarettes. Sometimes, there was lipstick on a collar, wine stains on a necktie. When she found gambling chits in trouser pockets, Sparrow put them in the lacquer tray on his chest of drawers. All without saying a word.

Shao regretted losing his temper with her. He didn't understand his restlessness, the impatience. The drifting, untethered feeling, as though waiting for something to happen. Something beyond his control. It had seemed so heroic, traveling to Shanghai in the middle of a war to see his dying mother. Offering Lian the protection of his company. He'd done the right thing, he knew that. Even though he'd ended up sick and a burden, it had been better for Lian to travel with him and Sparrow than run away on her own.

But now, he found himself quelling resentment. Sitting beside his mother day after day had proved a thankless duty. The opiates from Dr. Mao clouded her mind. Her words were incoherent, ramblings that made no sense, questions he couldn't answer. On the occasions when she was lucid, she was also in pain, suffering with every movement, even the slide of silk sheets over her skin could make her cry out.

"It's as though I have powdered glass in my joints," she said, closing her eyes as the nurse put the needle in her arm.

Shao felt useless. There were times he stayed out so late he slept through the morning then woke up filled with guilt for missing breakfast with his mother. But it didn't matter. Dr. Mao was steadily increasing her dosage and she slept most of the time now. All Shao could do was hold her hand while she gazed at him, her vague smile still lovely. He couldn't be sure she even knew him. Or his brothers or father when they came into the sickroom.

"She knows someone she loves is with her," Dr. Mao said. "That's what matters."

Now Shao hardly went to her room except for short, token visits. It was too easy sliding into the life he had always known, giving in to people like Sammy Chung. He told himself he needed the distraction, deserved some fun.

He wondered if everyone at Minghua had reached Chengtu safely. He couldn't help wishing he were still with his classmates. At least at Minghua, he'd been part of something important, something worthwhile. He wrote to Shorty Ho, addressing the letter to the Chengtu campus.

He hoped Shorty would write back, the lazy ass. He really missed Shorty.

SPARROW HAD ARRIVED at the flat on her own, bringing vegetables from Old Zhao's kitchen garden to add to the dumpling feast. Dr. Mao was also there. The older man's cheerful greeting immediately lifted Shao's mood.

"I heard there were dumplings for dinner so I came," the doctor said, shaking Shao's hand with real warmth. "It's been so long since I tasted homemade dumplings."

"Dr. Mao has been very kind," Lian said. "He's been coming here to check on my mother's recovery, so we haven't had to make the trip to the hospital."

The two men chatted while dinner cooked. It was the first time Shao had spoken with the doctor about anything other than his mother's health. Dr. Mao was a scholar of the classics and only too happy to discuss literature. He knew about the Library of Legends and shook his head in admiration at Minghua 123's role safeguarding the books.

Lian's mother called them to dinner. She had put on weight since coming back from the hospital. Her cheeks glowed from the warmth of the kitchen and her eyes were bright. Shao could see in her an older Lian. The conversation shifted as Lian told them about her day at the Mission with the refugees.

"A lot of them were peasant farmers hoping to return to their land," she said, "but Miss Mason says there's also teachers and domestic servants, merchants, handicraft workers. Useful trades, but even though some of the factories are starting up again, there are more willing workers than jobs."

"It's not easy to reestablish yourself when you're a refugee," Dr. Mao said. "I see this with some of my patients. Carpenters, bookkeepers, artists. People with skills, educated people. Now it's as though they've been stripped of those qualifications. Reduced to the category of 'refugee' and treated as members of a needy multitude."

"I hope your practice is growing, Dr. Mao," Sparrow said.

"Indeed, it is," the doctor said. "Last month I barely made the rent for my single room. But this month's rent won't be a problem. And soon, two rooms!"

He slapped his knee and burst into laughter so infectious they all joined in. Shao had never met anyone so willing to be happy, whose mere presence could make others so happy. He looked at Lian's mother, giggling behind her napkin, her eyes on the doctor. And Dr. Mao gazing back.

"There's something going on down in the street," Shao said, getting up. "Hear that music? Let's open the balcony door, Lian."

On the street below, a long line of convertibles filled with musicians and revelers moved with deliberate slowness, creating a traffic jam in the westbound lane. Trombones and trumpets, saxophones and clarinets, snare drums, even a double bass. There must've been two dozen musicians and as many passengers riding in the cars. Women in evening gowns sparkled with jewels that reflected back the streetlights. The men riding with them were impeccably turned out in tuxedos. Shao guessed they were enter-tainers, promoting a new club.

The cavalcade approached slowly, ignoring irate shouts and tooting horns. The musicians played a jaunty tune. A tune Shao recognized as one Shorty Ho used to whistle all the time while walking, but he couldn't remember its name.

"Young Mr. Liu," the doctor called from the dining room. "Do you know how to wash dishes? I think it's the least we can do for our hostesses."

Shao turned to go back inside, then stopped. He reached inside his jacket and gave Lian an envelope. "Before I forget," he said. "From my brother."

LIAN TOOK THE note and put it in her apron pocket. Whatever was in the note, it could wait. The parade below was too interesting to miss. She leaned over the balcony to watch the procession, the cars and musicians, passengers in evening attire.

Then Sparrow came to stand beside her and it all changed.

The shiny black convertible leading the parade was no longer a convertible. A handsome bearded man led the procession, robes of heavy silk fluttering against the flanks of the tall black horse he was riding.

Sparrow waved at the bearded man, who bowed gravely in return.

Open horse-drawn litters carried his entourage, men and women dressed in ancient garb. The women's diaphanous gowns were rich with embroidery, the men's robes bright as jewels. They were all, every single one, male and female, scandalously, seductively beautiful. One of the women looked up at the balcony and winked at Lian. A slow, lascivious wink. Then she raised her bamboo flute and continued playing. The music hadn't changed, a lively familiar tune from some Hollywood movie.

"Who are they?" Lian asked, fascinated.

"Ba Meishen, the guardian of prostitutes, and his assistants," Sparrow said. "Shanghai has been a good home base for them. Leaving was a hard decision."

The end of the procession passed below them, and gradually Lian heard only music, the lively tune above the noises of traffic, the shouts of sidewalk vendors. From inside the flat, the sound of spirited conversation, Shao and the doctor discussing literature, their voices raised, the dishes forgotten. Outside on the balcony, Lian could've done fine embroidery by the light of the Star.

"It's nearly over," Sparrow said. "Almost everyone is on their way. The Shanghai City God has promised me he'll be the next to go."

"How will we manage," Lian said, "without help from the gods?"

But Sparrow wasn't listening to her. The conversation inside now held her attention, the words drifting out clearly to the balcony as both men's voices grew louder in their enthusiasm.

"But that one word *shen* carries multiple meanings," the doctor said, "making interpretation quite a problem."

"But the poem must offer context," Shao said, "to indicate whether *shen* means the human spirit, supernatural spirits, or something spiritual and unfathomable to human minds."

Shao loved this sort of discussion, picking apart words and debating nuances of meaning. It was the most animated he'd been all evening. When he first arrived, Lian thought he looked as though he wished he were somewhere else.

"In this case, I feel the poet offers room for all three meanings," the doctor said. "He's asserting that the gap between humans and gods can be bridged through enlightenment. That mortals hold within us the capacity to advance, and as we advance with each reincarnation, we have the potential to achieve spiritual enlightenment, which in turn achieves immortality. Thus, a mortal can become an immortal, even a deity."

Lian heard Sparrow's small gasp. The Star's eyes were fixed on the doctor as the two men finally began taking dishes to the kitchen. And from far away, up the street, the faintest echoes of a tune came to Lian's ears. A tune she could finally name, "Pennies from Heaven."

LIAN'S MOTHER EXCUSED herself from the party. She had to lie down.

"Your body is hard at work repairing damage," Dr. Mao had said. "You need lots of sleep, lots of food. Go, go. No apologies necessary."

Lian had noticed all evening how often Dr. Mao's gaze rested on her mother's face, how he leaned closer when speaking to her. And all evening, soft color had bloomed in her mother's cheeks whenever he addressed her. She'd laughed at his jokes, her eyes bright and alert. But he was at least fifty, more than ten years older than her mother. With a plain, square face, he was not at all like her father, who had been as handsome as a film star. Her parents had been the most beautiful couple at any gathering.

Their guests left shortly after her mother went to bed, first Shao then Dr. Mao. Shao, to meet some friends at the Majestic Hotel. The doctor, because he had patients in the morning. They'd left half the dishes unwashed, a chore neglected when they'd become absorbed again in conversation. Lian shook her head and shrugged. She finished the washing up then sat at the dining table for a final cup of tea with Sparrow, who seemed preoccupied with her own thoughts.

"Shao seemed unhappy when he first arrived," Lian said, clearing her throat. "But I suppose it's because of his mother."

"He's hardly ever home now," Sparrow said. She shook her head, a sign of disapproval. "He's out all day to avoid spending time with her."

"I don't understand," Lian said. "All those hardships, all that risk. He wanted to be at his mother's side."

"It's hard for him to watch her fade away," Sparrow said, "especially now that she's unconscious most of the time. But Shao isn't avoiding his mother. He's avoiding the person he turns into when he's with her. Helpless, impatient, angry."

Sparrow knew Shao so well, understood his moods and what he needed. No one else could love him as she did. As she had for centuries. All of Lian's lovelorn yearnings, all her heartache, they were minor inconveniences compared to what Sparrow had endured.

"He cares about you, Lian," Sparrow said, pouring herself more tea. "More than any other mortal he's encountered in all his lives. You should know this. If not for my presence here on Earth, he would've recognized his feelings long ago."

Lian didn't know what to say or what Sparrow meant by telling her all this.

"It's a game to the gods, a cruel and not very good one," Sparrow said. She looked sad. Resigned. But she managed a wry smile. "All will be revealed, as they say in those foreign films."

She finished her tea, then looked at Lian. "Minghua University is in Chengtu by now. The Library of Legends should be safely stored away. I have no more obligations."

"What does that mean?" Lian said. "You don't need to stay in our world anymore?"

"Strangely enough," Sparrow said, "I've never had to stay at all until this life. I could've given up the Prince at any time. This life has been different. I was given responsibilities. Seeing to the safety of the Library of Legends. Rousing the guardians and spirits to leave."

"And now, what will you do?" Lian said.

"My sister says being mortal through so many lifetimes has finally affected me," Sparrow said, "and she must be right because I look at things differently now." She blew on her tea and sipped it. "I think I should write to Professor Kang."

FOR THE SECOND time that night Lian stood at the balcony. She watched Sparrow's glowing form cross the street, followed her light as it moved farther away into the darkness until it vanished around the corner. Then she sat in an armchair and took out the envelope that had been in her apron pocket for the past hour. A letter from Liu Tienming. Who she supposed was their landlord.

> *Miss Hu, our property manager has decided all our vacant properties should be rented. I've told him that you are occupying the flat until the end of July, after which he will offer it to you at a discount. It's the best I can do.*

Even at half the price, they could never afford this beautiful, luxurious flat. They had another two months. Two months to find an affordable place to live, in a city where a single room might house a family of nine. Two months for her to find work, in a city where businesses had their pick of desperate workers. She would have to tell her mother about this in the morning. And also the news that they had lost the cot at the Southern Baptist Mission office.

CHAPTER 38

Shao's mother died at the end of June. The family had been planning her funeral for months.

Shao didn't feel like talking to anyone but Sparrow, but she was not her usual self. She'd never been talkative, but she was even quieter than usual lately, more withdrawn. Distracted. She lingered about doing pointless housework, wiping dust off an already spotless side table, sweeping floors that had just been cleaned. Most incomprehensibly, she had taken to chatting with the gatekeeper, then bringing in the mail. This had been going on for days. Weeks.

"What's the matter, Sparrow? Are you worried about Second Aunt?" he asked, picking up the gold and onyx cuff links he would wear that evening. "You know she takes her matchmaking very seriously. She's always made good choices."

"I'm not worried about that," she said, giving his suit a final pass with the clothes brush. "It's your choices I worry about."

"No need," he said, trying to quell his irritation. "When I'm back at university, I won't have time for Sammy Chung."

Shao and his father had discussed whether he should attend classes for the next few weeks while the family observed mourning. After his father spoke to the chancellor of Jiao Tong University, they decided he would stay home but do the assignments. Shao's professors would send them to the house.

But Sparrow didn't respond, just gazed out the window at the gate. He'd finally grown accustomed to seeing her in a *qipao* instead of a maidservant's tunic and trousers. Today she wore a *qipao* of deep blue, blue as the night sky. Second Aunt had given Sparrow a new wardrobe in anticipation of meetings with prospective in-laws. To the best of Shao's knowledge, Sparrow had only met one family so far.

"What's wrong, Sparrow?" he said. "You can tell me anything."

She shook her head. "I'm just waiting for news."

"I was right. The matchmaking," he said. At this, she made a scoffing noise and left the room. A moment later, her slight figure appeared below his window, walking toward the front gate. She greeted the gatekeeper, who gave her a bundle of mail.

Then the old man rushed to open the gates. The relatives were arriving. Shao quickly finished dressing. His father and brothers were already downstairs, ready to greet guests.

THE LIU FAMILY burial grounds were to the west of Shanghai, outside city limits, at a location deemed to have good feng shui.

A long procession, suitable to the family's standing, wound its way through the streets of Shanghai. It was an expensive funeral, made even more expensive by bribes his family paid to ensure the funeral rites wouldn't be interrupted by Japanese soldiers or gang-related violence.

The entire clan attended, a line of automobiles following slowly behind the hired mourners. Shao rode in the car his mother had used, chatted politely to the relatives beside him, his mother's cousins. Every so often he caught the scent of freesia and bergamot, and it made him close his eyes with painful regret. He wished he'd been a better son. More loving. More patient.

After the funeral banquet, he moped in the back garden for a while, sitting in the pavilion built over the artificial lake. Then his cousins joined him, carrying a bottle of cognac purloined from the dining room. Shao left them still drinking, went up to his room, and stripped off his jacket. He fell asleep on top of the covers.

In the morning, he saw the letter on his bedside tray. It was too early for the morning mail to have arrived, so it had to be from yesterday's post. The letter was from Shorty Ho. He tore it open. A page and a half of writing, a big effort coming from Shorty.

He expressed relief and astonishment that Shao was still alive. He passed on greetings from various classmates.

The military police came by the day after you went missing. They had Professor Kang call an assembly. We received a blistering lecture from a police captain on the evils of wasting their time with false accusations when they have so many real problems to deal with. Then they drove away. Tan Wendian was expelled. Apparently, she was the troublemaker behind Mr. Lee's arrest.

So the police cars they saw had been on their way to deliver a lecture, not make an arrest. This was good news for Lian. Wendian's accusations had gone nowhere.

Professor Kang didn't travel with us, he went to Zunyi with the Library of Legends, to store them in some caves. You remember Old Fan and Bantien? They're living in the caves to look after the Library of Legends. We held a small farewell ceremony as the truck drove away with crates of national treasure. I confess to being surprised at how sad I felt, as though the gods had abandoned us. Anyhow, between walking and the rides on army trucks we were able to get, Minghua University made Chengtu in only four weeks instead of five.

And your letter was waiting when we arrived. Chengtu itself is beautiful. Or maybe it's just because of springtime. But so much for the government's interim campus! We live in flimsy shacks with hard earthen floors. We've plastered over cracks in the walls with mud. Once your mother gets well, catch an airplane to Chengtu and join us. Our numbers are growing. Now that the universities have settled in for the duration of the war, students from all over China are making their way here to enroll. Some of our old classmates showed up the other day.

When Shao turned over the page to read the last few lines of Shorty's letter, his heart sank. Another bit of news he'd have to tell Lian. Perhaps Sparrow could go with him to visit Lian.

Shao asked everyone, the servants, the gatekeeper, but no one had seen Sparrow since the day before. The gatekeeper thought he saw her walking out to the street, but he couldn't be sure. He had been busy opening and closing the double gates.

Shao waited until the evening, then went to see Lian on his own. He wanted to see her very badly. And he was worried about Sparrow.

SHAO WAS THE last person Lian expected to see. It was only the day after his mother's funeral, his family still in mourning. He hung back, his expression both stern and miserable, but then Lian's mother limped up to the door on crutches and took Shao's hands in both of hers.

"We are so very sorry about your mother," she said. "Sometimes we prepare ourselves for the inevitable and when it happens, we realize we were really not prepared at all."

"Thank you, Mrs. Hu." His shoulders sagged imperceptibly. "Lian, I have a letter from Shorty that you should read."

Lian read Shorty's words, then looked up from the letter to her mother. "Wendian didn't accuse me of being a Japanese spy. Or else she did and no one believed her. Mother, do you know what this means?"

That there were no more shadows in their lives. Her father was blameless and now she was too. There was nothing left to fear.

"It means you can go back to Minghua!" her mother exclaimed. "I've been so worried about your education. I didn't know how we could afford it. But you have a full scholarship at Minghua. You can still go back."

A small wave of excitement rippled through Lian. Hope. That there might be a chance to finish her studies. Perhaps after the war. Not right now.

"Go back?" She shook her head. "I'm not leaving you again, Mother. Shao, this is wonderful news. This is such a relief. Thank you. You must be so very busy right now, but you came to show me this."

But he still looked morose. "Read the other side," he said. "There's more news."

Perhaps you've heard already. Wei Daming was killed only a few days after he returned to the front.

Lian closed her eyes for a moment, then read Shorty's words again. Daming was dead. She offered up a silent prayer to the gods. Before remembering it was no use anymore.

"Poor, dear Daming." Lian sighed, sinking back on the settee. "We would never have made it back without his help."

"Was he the young army doctor?" her mother said. "The one who was your classmate?"

"He never claimed to be a doctor," Shao said, "but he did the job as best he could. Before he was expelled and joined the army, he was even more useless than Shorty. The war changed him completely."

"I liked him," Lian said sadly. "He had a good heart."

"I should get back home, but I wanted you to know the news," Shao said, lighting a cigarette. "The good and the bad. By the way, I don't suppose you've seen Sparrow? She hasn't been around all day."

Lian had to resist putting her hand in her pocket to touch the note from Sparrow. Slipped under the door the day before. A note Shao couldn't know she had.

LIAN HAD NO luck finding work in Shanghai. She had walked up and down the streets for the past few weeks, scanning signs for the names of businesses, climbing staircases to knock on door after

door. If she saw a typewriter, she mentioned her mother's qualifications. Any secretarial work was bound to pay better than the
Mission.

Some factories had relocated inside the Settlement. Others in
bombed-out districts were rebuilding, getting back into produc-
tion. Even war could only put a temporary damper on Shanghai's
enterprising spirit. If she had to, Lian would do factory work.
Hopefully somewhere inside the Settlement so she wouldn't have
to cross the gauntlet of Japanese soldiers and barbed wire each
day. But the situation had become truly pressing. Right now, she'd
be willing to take any job, inside or out.

She gave up for the day, walking home on a route that would
take her past some stores. She had to get a block of tofu. Her string
bag was rolled up in one pocket. Her hand reached inside the
other pocket and touched the edges of Sparrow's note. She had
memorized the words, could see them in her mind's eye, Sparrow's neat, exquisite handwriting.

> Lian, I will be leaving soon. Don't tell Shao. I can wait
> for him. I have the advantage of eternity. You only have
> this life. You will know when I am gone.

Sparrow had decided to leave. Leave the Liu household? Leave
Shanghai? Or was she going to the Kunlun Mountains? Lian
couldn't help but worry. Although Sparrow was immortal, she
had no powers. She was as vulnerable as Lian to hunger and cold.
To injuries and violence. The only part of the note she understood
was that she shouldn't tell Shao. And by inference, no one else
either.

When Lian opened the door to the elevator lobby, her mother
called down the staircase. "Don't come up yet! Go around the

corner and buy a yellow croaker fish. I'm making fish soup with noodles. Dr. Mao is coming for dinner."

Lian sighed and went down to the street again.

Much as she liked Dr. Mao, Lian didn't like opening up the small, safe circle that was her two-person family. Her happiness was still too precarious, her mother still too fragile to trust an outsider. But whenever Dr. Mao's cheerful voice filled the flat, she saw her mother brighten, then blush with pleasure at the small gifts he always brought. A bunch of irises, a small basket of oranges.

In his traditional long gown and with his plain, honest face, Dr. Mao looked exactly like what he was, a country doctor. Lian couldn't deny his gentle manner had a calming effect on her mother. Or that his stories made her mother laugh, loud whooping hoots Lian hadn't heard in years. Since Harbin.

THE DOCTOR SIGHED contentedly upon finishing the last of the noodles in fish broth.

"Eating fish always reminds me of the tale of Old Quan the Miser," he said. "A classic. Old Quan was too stingy to buy a real fish for the family New Year's dinner. So he hung a painting of a fish on the dining room wall and told them to look at the picture instead. There it was, a plump, whole fish laid out on a bed of watercress, slivers of ginger arranged just so over its body, the eyeballs glistening and lifelike.

"So lifelike that Quan's youngest grandson couldn't stop staring up at the fish. Whereupon Old Quan landed a sharp slap on the side of the boy's head, shouting, 'You greedy brat! Do you think we're so rich that you can look *twice*?'"

Lian's mother laughed until she had to wipe the tears from her eyes. Lian brought out the pastries, egg tarts the doctor had brought. Her mother hobbled to the kitchen to boil water for tea. Dr. Mao cleared his throat.

"My practice has grown very quickly, Lian," he said. "The Liu family has referred so many people my way I hardly have time to see patients and also keep my appointment diary and patient files organized. I can't pay very much yet, but would you be willing to work for me?"

"Yes, Doctor," Lian said. "More than willing." Then bit her lip at those last words. Had she sounded too eager? Did she really want their lives more closely entangled with his?

When the doctor left, her mother lingered at the door and didn't shut it until he had descended the staircase.

"He's here for dinner so often, Mother," Lian said.

"We need to build our connections," her mother said, looking flustered. "It's how the world works."

A loud pounding interrupted what Lian was going to say. Shao's voice called her name and when she opened the door he almost fell inside. He looked disheveled and frantic, as though he hadn't slept all night.

"Is she here? Have you seen Sparrow?" he asked. His eyes darted in all directions about the room as though Sparrow might be hiding from him.

"Not recently," she said. "What's wrong?"

"It's been days and she's still missing," Shao said, collapsing into a chair. "She's been very quiet, maybe even troubled. I hoped she had come to see you. That she might be here."

Sparrow's room in the servants' quarters was tidy, the bed neatly made. He'd searched the drawers, the trunk at the foot of her bed, but not knowing what she owned, he couldn't tell what was missing. Neither could anyone else.

"But I found this." He pulled a letter from his jacket, gave it to Lian. "It's to Sparrow from Professor Kang, of all people. I think it must've arrived the same time as the letter from Shorty, both mailed from Chengtu."

I agree with your assessment. Each advancement brings us closer to enlightenment and with enlightenment comes the possibility of immortality. A man who lives a passive existence without purpose cannot advance to a better state in the next life. Perhaps the best choice is to let go and wait. Trust in the Wheel of Rebirth, whose purpose is to bring worthy souls closer to enlightenment with each reincarnation. The advantage of immortality is that one can wait.

"It sounds as though they were carrying on a discussion about spiritual beliefs," he said. "It couldn't possibly be anything to do with her disappearance."

The advantage of immortality is that one can wait. Lian handed back the letter. "What will you do next?"

"My father has called the police." He put his head in his hands. "Tomorrow there'll be a missing persons notice in the newspaper. I knew she wasn't happy about an arranged marriage, but she should've said something. No one was going to force her."

"Will you stay for something to eat?" Lian's mother asked.

"No. I've a car outside. I'm going to drive up and down some of the streets, ask if anyone's seen her." He paused at the door. "Shanghai has always been dangerous, the way any big city is dangerous. But now with the war, different factions, gangs fighting each other—innocent people can get hurt. That's what really worries me."

You will know when I am gone.

Trust in the Wheel of Rebirth.

THAT NIGHT LIAN dreamed there was a procession on the street below. She stood on the balcony watching it go by. The Shanghai City God was leaving and the entire city had turned out to mourn his departure. Dressed in the court robes of a high-ranking Ming Dynasty official, his long black beard hung down to his belt and beaded strings of jade and coral hung from his hat. He sat in a magnificent sedan chair carried by giants. There was music, flutes and drums, cymbals and horns.

And in the entourage walking behind the City God, she recognized Sparrow. She gleamed more brightly than Lian had ever seen her shine. When the procession passed under the balcony, Sparrow didn't look up. Lian kept watching the procession move along the street, to the next block and beyond, until she could no longer see Sparrow's light.

CHAPTER 39

The Shanghai Municipal Police were too stretched to search for a servant, even one valued by the Liu family. The private detective firm Shao's father hired to search for Sparrow hadn't found a single clue. The missing persons notice in *Xinwen Bao* attracted only fraudsters and cases of mistaken identity, and finally ceased appearing.

Shao came to the flat nearly every evening. Morose and restless, he seemed to take comfort in the company of Lian and her mother.

"I should've spent more time with my mother before she died," he said. "Even just to hold her hand a little longer. But I couldn't face it, Lian. So I went out all the time."

"No one blames you," she said. And then, because she knew he needed to hear it, "Sparrow understood."

"She was a good friend," he said. "She was like a sister and knew me better than I knew myself. And I never appreciated her as much as I should've. My father says we'll have to give up the search soon, tell the private detectives to quit. Either she's run away or it's too late to do anything."

You will know when I am gone.

What did Sparrow mean by that? There had been a dream, Sparrow leaving for the Kunlun Mountains in the company of the Shanghai City God and his assistants. It had been so vivid and intense, but was it only a dream or had it been Sparrow's way of saying farewell? How long would it take for the City God and his entourage to reach the Kunlun Mountains?

"I feel so . . . like a boat that's drifted off its moorings." He paced up and down the room. "Do you need a car to help you move? Is there anything you want to take from this flat? No one will miss it. If they do, I'll say I gave it to you."

When Dr. Mao learned about Lian and her mother's predicament, he made a suggestion. His practice had grown to the point where he could afford larger quarters.

"Beihua, let's just hurry up and get married," he said. "Life is precarious, happiness fleeting. Come live with me. Let's be a family."

Family. The word made Lian catch her breath, chopsticks halfway to her mouth.

"Lian and I will talk it over," her mother said, fixing Lian with a look that made her close her mouth.

"Of course," Dr. Mao said. He looked very humble and hopeful. "It should be a family decision."

When Dr. Mao left, Lian turned to her mother. "Why doesn't a man like Dr. Mao already have a family?"

"But he did, didn't I tell you?" Her mother looked perplexed.

"He had a wife and two sons. They were staying with his parents in Tongxiang when a cholera epidemic swept through. He lost his whole family."

"But he seems so cheerful," Lian said. "Not at all like someone who has suffered so much tragedy."

"He's so willing, no, determined to be happy again," her mother said. "It's one of the reasons I admire him. He still manages to be kind and generous despite such tragedy. He doesn't drag around the sorrows of his past."

THEY MOVED INTO a flat, two small rooms, but it had its own kitchen and bathroom. They were lucky to have a space that could accommodate both clinic and home in a single apartment. A folding screen partitioned the larger front room to create a cramped consulting area where Dr. Mao examined patients. Lian worked at a desk facing the door. After hours, the desk doubled as their dining table and at night Lian slept in the outer room, on the examining table.

Her mother no longer worked at the Mission, laughed more often, and the few times when she was overcome with fear, it was Dr. Mao who soothed her. Not Lian. Not anymore. The tightness in Lian's shoulders eased and, in less time than she thought it would take, she began thinking of him as her stepfather. Her two-person family circle widened.

And there was Shao. Her mother invited him to supper often. Lian sometimes glanced over and caught him watching the three of them rather wistfully.

"You need friends your own age," her mother said to Lian. "You're not at school anymore and he's a former classmate. And you're fond of each other, so you should keep up the friendship."

By now she had confessed to her mother her feelings for Shao.

"It's hopeless and it will pass," she said. "He belongs to the wealthiest, most influential family in Shanghai."

"Your stepfather is a well-respected physician," her mother retorted. "Don't think so little of yourself. And of us."

How could she tell her mother that a thousand-year-old celestial agreement stood between her and Shao? Between Shao and anyone on this earth?

At first hesitant to intrude after the three of them moved into their new home, Shao became a regular visitor, bringing books for the doctor, poetry and literary journals. Some of their debates lasted long into the night, loud and enthusiastic. But those were the pleasant visits.

There were times when he dropped by, unshaven and reeking of cigarette smoke, his handsome features haggard from lack of sleep. So restive he stayed only a few minutes. He complained of boredom.

Finally, Lian could take no more. "You're attending university, Shao. How dare you grumble while our Minghua classmates are living in shacks and eating millet porridge?"

"I didn't mean bored of university," he muttered, looking embarrassed.

"Of course not," she said. "You can't be bored with classes you never attend."

"If you're bored, come with us tomorrow night to the Lutheran Mission," Dr. Mao said. "They're holding a charity auction for the orphanage. If nothing else, the missionaries serve excellent coffee."

After a moment's hesitation, Shao agreed. Then after some more cajoling from the doctor, he even promised to round up some family and friends.

Dr. Mao beamed. "You'll have a good time. All sorts of interesting people attend this annual auction. It's quite the thing, I've been told."

LIAN AND HER mother had promised to arrive early and help with refreshments, so Dr. Mao said he would go early as well and look in on some of the children he'd been treating. The skies had clouded over, and on the Lutheran Mission's lawn, workers were putting up a large marquee where the auction would take place. As soon as the three of them entered the wrought-iron gates a woman hurried over to greet them. She looked haggard, as though she hadn't slept in days.

"Dr. Mao, you couldn't be more welcome," she said. "Missionaries from Henan arrived an hour ago with a truckload of orphans. The poor children need to be examined for infections, lice, malnutrition, the usual."

The Lutheran missionaries had stayed in Henan as long as they could to help the city's victims, but in the end, they'd had to leave. The front lines were getting too close. Henan was a name to make them all wince. In the long list of battles since the war began, Henan was proving one of the bloodiest.

"The poor little creatures," Lian's mother said. "May we help? Perhaps with their bathing and feeding."

Wearing a borrowed pinafore, Lian carried buckets of hot water from the kitchen to the hut where the orphans were being washed. Her mother sat on a low stool beside a wooden tub, briskly scrubbing a small girl's feet. All around them, the hum of conversation in several Chinese dialects, German, and occasionally, English.

Lian counted two dozen children, all girls. Some had been at the Henan orphanage for years and looked healthy, reasonably clean, and calm after their harrowing journey through a war zone. Most, however, were recent casualties of war, orphaned or abandoned, seized from harm. These children were silent and thin, confused and timid. She caught snatches of conversation as she walked back and forth between kitchen and hut.

"The difficult part was how to bring the children," said one of the women. "The army ordered us to evacuate, but the missionary ladies refused unless they provided enough transportation for all the orphans. *Waah*, those army officers were so eager to be rid of the foreigners, two large trucks appeared at our door the very next day!"

Lian carried a tub outside, tipped the dirty water into a flower bed. She took the wooden tub back to her mother and together they filled it with warm water. An orphanage worker brought another toddler over to the tub and began removing the little girl's rags.

"Let go of that ribbon," Lian's mother coaxed. "I'll put it down here and you can have it back later, after your nice, warm bath."

The child gripped the dirty strip of red closer to her chest. A red crocheted ribbon. Lian's breath caught in her throat. She looked more carefully at the girl's face. Dirty and thin, unsmiling. The cheeks no longer plump, the eyes no longer bright.

"Duckling?" she said, kneeling beside the child.

At the sound of her name, the girl looked up and around. "Baba?" she said, in a plaintive, uncertain voice. Father. She was looking for her father. Private Fung, whose wide smile she had inherited. A father who couldn't have been prouder of his little daughter.

"Do you know this child?" the worker asked.

"Yes, her name is Duckling," Lian said. "Family name Fung. From Shaanxi Province. Her father . . ."

Her father. Young Private Fung was probably dead on a Henan battlefield. Or dying in an understaffed hospital. Lian didn't want to think about the horrors Duckling must've survived if her father had actually taken her to the front. Surely by then he would've understood the danger. Surely he had changed his mind, left his daughter behind in a safe place. A place where the missionaries had found her. She prayed this was what he'd done.

She held her arms out but Duckling shrank away, small fists clenched tighter than ever.

Little Duck, Little Duck,
Sing the moon, dance the stars!

Lian clapped her hands softly as she sang. Duckling's lips moved hesitantly, forming the words in silence. The tiny hands, one still clutching the ribbon, began to clap. Then finally a breathy childish voice joined Lian's.

The skies shine out from the pond tonight,
Come with us, Little Duck!

Inside Lian's heart, locks and latches fell open. She began crying, a silent deluge. She held the little girl to her chest, rocking back and forth as she held back her sobs so as not to frighten Duckling. She cried for Private Fung and his comrades, for their awkward friendly grins and naïve confidence as they'd marched off to battle. For Wei Daming and the soldiers he tried to save. For Meirong, whom she couldn't save. For Mr. Shen and Wang Jenmei, on opposite sides of China's politics but each a patriot. She cried for all the sorrows she had seen.

She cried because she would never see Sparrow again.

Gradually, Lian became aware of her mother's arms around her, enclosing Duckling in their circle. "We're not leaving her, Mother," she said, choking back tears. "We're taking her home with us. She won't be abandoned again. I won't have it."

Even just one person, Miss Mason had said. *If each of us could make a difference to just one person.* Why couldn't her one person be Duckling? Lian stifled her sobs and finished undressing Duckling. All around her, there was more talk, murmured discussions in both Chinese and German, between the foreigners, her mother, and Dr. Mao.

Then a woman's voice, her words authoritative and oddly inflected.

"We would rather she went to a family that cares about her than someone who will raise her to be a servant," the woman said. One of the German missionaries.

There was more conversation, then Lian heard Dr. Mao say, "My wife and I will adopt her. I've heard about this little girl."

"Thank you, Stepfather," Lian said and closed her eyes for a moment in relief. The sorrows she'd witnessed still continued. There was still brutality and darkness. But also a small shining point of light. Duckling squirmed, then giggled as Lian splashed warm water over her.

Together, Lian and her mother bathed Duckling, who now seemed quite content to let go of the red ribbon. They dressed her in clean clothes and socks, then took her to the orphanage dining room. The orphans had been given a snack when they'd arrived so unexpectedly, but now a real dinner was ready for them. Already charmed by the toddler, her mother walked ahead, carrying Duckling over her shoulder. Lian walked behind, making silly faces to coax a smile from Duckling.

A hand tapped her on the shoulder and she turned to see Shao smiling down at her. She caught her breath at the sight of him. He seemed different somehow. There was a lightness to him, a new clarity in his eyes.

"I hear you have a new sister," he said. "That little girl from the riverboat."

"It's a miracle, but it really is Duckling," she said. "Come meet her. My mother's just taken her to the orphanage dining room."

"Not yet," he said. "There's something I want to show you."

The skies were dark now but the marquee on the Mission's front lawn glowed with strings of lights. The charity auction was in full swing, the auctioneer's voice bellowing out from a megaphone, "Dinner for ten at the Cathay Hotel, a selection of fine wines included!"

At a long table under an awning, volunteers outside the marquee were packing away auction items that had been sold. Shao walked to the end of the table where a set of books was being put into boxes. He picked one up and held it out to her. The bindings were beautiful leather, custom-made for a private collection.

THE LIBRARY OF LEGENDS
A Collection of Myths and Folklore
from the Jingtai Encyclopedia
Minghua University Press

"I asked my father to donate these to the auction," he said. "He's here somewhere with my brother. Turns out this is one of the charity events he attends every year."

"This is so generous of him," Lian said, stroking the leather binding. "If I owned these, I could never bear to give them up."

"Oh, don't worry," Shao said. "We've another set at our summer home in the Moganshan Mountains."

"And someone has bought them," she said. "I hope they go to a good home. And that the Mission got a good price."

"The Mission did very well," he said. "I bought them for you. They're yours now, Lian. Fortunately, on a modern printing press, you don't need 147 volumes to contain all the stories, just 20."

She gasped. "Shao! That's too generous! I can't accept."

"Well, if you don't take them, then I'll give them to your step-father," he said with a grin. "I look forward to many interesting discussions with him—with both of you—about the Legends."

She touched the embossed covers, the gilded characters along the spines. *Tales of the City Gods. Tales of Dragon Lords. Tales of Fox Spirits Volumes 1–3. Tales of Celestial Deities.* A record of all that had been wondrous in China. A record protected by the gods so they would be remembered even after they were no longer worshipped, no longer needed. A record the gods now depended on mortals to preserve. Mortals who had never seen a herd of *qilin* awaken spring as they dashed into the woods. Or watched a Star live out her lonely, patient quest.

"I don't know what to make of a gift like this," she said, finally. "But thank you."

"This," he said, taking her hand and kissing it. "This is what to make of it."

They walked away from the marquee, as far away as possible from its glaring artificial lights. He pulled her under the shadows of a tall maple. When he held her close, his heart was beating as rapidly as hers. This time he kissed her on the lips, and her arms tightened around his shoulders, felt his muscles tense in response.

Then she pulled away from him. "The front of my pinafore is wet," she said in dismay. "And now so is your shirt." Shao laughed and she looked at him, searching his face.

"There's something different," she said. "Have you stopped drinking?"

"I don't know what it is," he said. Even his voice was different. Joyous. "I do feel different. Perhaps I'm doing better at putting away grief over my mother and Sparrow."

"You seem happier," she said. More alive, she wanted to say.

"It's as though a veil has been lifted from my mind and my heart," Shao said. "My feelings aren't muddled or muted anymore. Lian, I was confused before. But I can't pretend you're just a friend anymore."

She closed her eyes, allowing her other senses to recognize him. The scent of his skin, its slightly salty taste. The lean strength of his arms. She moved her hand to his chest, felt the quickening beat of his heart, heard the soft impatience of his breath against her neck. And then his lips were against hers again.

If not for my presence here on Earth, he would've recognized his feelings long ago.

I can wait for him. I have the advantage of eternity. You only have this life. You will know when I am gone.

Lian rested her head on his shoulder, contented. Comforted.

"My mother will be wondering where I am," she murmured, but without any conviction. In reply, Shao lifted her face to his and kissed her again, his lips lingering on hers before kissing her throat.

They stood quietly under the maple, arms around each other, until the auctioneer's calls ceased and they could see people in evening dress emerge from the marquee. Taking his hand, Lian led Shao across the lawn toward the orphanage, to her family. Dr. Mao and her mother came out to stand on the veranda, the doctor carrying Duckling in his arms, the little girl now asleep.

It was a clear night, all threat of rain had passed. Lian's eyes moved across the sky, searching until she found the Purple Forbidden Enclosure constellation and inside it, a cluster of stars, the Four Maids-in-Waiting.

She lifted her hand in greeting.

AUTHOR'S NOTES

The exodus of Chinese universities and middle schools began in 1937, the official start of the Second Sino-Japanese War, which many also regard as the start of China's World War II. I've been fascinated by this migration ever since my father first recounted his experiences as a *liuwang* (refugee, nomadic) student, not only for the bold spirit of those who embarked on these journeys, but also for the symbolism of such an effort. By 1941, seventy-seven colleges and universities had relocated to China's interior. In protecting China's "last drop of blood," as one of China's generals called the students, the Chinese government was safeguarding the nation's intellectual legacy, so necessary for building the future. But I didn't know how to even begin weaving a story around such an epic.

Then my friend Ray Wang (who reads Chinese, and alas I do not) told me about a memoir by one of the refugee students. In it was an unforgettable scene: a teacher who walked ahead of his students carrying on his back a chalkboard with the day's lessons written on it. The image was so powerful and moving.

It spoke of reverence for education, a cornerstone of traditional Chinese values, and I knew that if I wrote a story, it would include such a scene.

Then I read *Race the Rising Sun*, memoirs of Zhejiang University alumni who trekked a thousand miles from coastal Hangzhou to Zunyi in the interior of China. The university also brought with it a treasure from the Qing Dynasty: a seventy-thousand-volume encyclopedia of Chinese literature known as the *Siku Quanshu*. Zhejiang University moved the books inland to safety by boat and automobile, by train and truck, and on the backs of students. Stored in caves outside the town of Guiyang in Guizhou Province, the encyclopedia survived the war in good condition under the care of two university servants who stayed behind in the caves. This was the thread I needed to pull the story together.

In the novel, the *Siku Quanshu* became the *Jingtai Encyclopedia* and its only surviving volumes the Library of Legends, which traveled across China awakening the supernatural beings described in their pages. For anyone interested in reading Professor Kang's (fictional) pamphlet on the Library and how it survived the centuries, please see my website www.janiechang.com. Click on the Books tab, where I stash bonus materials for each novel, and see what's available for *The Library of Legends*.

Minghua University is fictional, but my father did attend university in Nanking and walked all the way to Chongqing when the school had to evacuate. The majority of *liuwang* students miraculously reached their destinations, although many were malnourished by then and suffered a range of illnesses from eye infections to malaria.

The legend of the Willow Star is my own invention, a riff on the popular Chinese myth of the Cowherd and the Celestial Weaver Girl. Their love story is celebrated every year on the seventh day of the seventh lunar month in a festival that's been branded as "Chinese Valentine's Day."

Chinese constellations do not map to Western star charts. The Purple Forbidden Enclosure where the Willow Star and her sisters live consists of constellations surrounding the North Celestial Pole, or Polaris the Northern Star. The Four Maids-in-Waiting, the stars representing the Willow Star and her sisters, correlate roughly to the constellation Draco.

Minghua 123's route through China is an amalgam of several journeys described by various survivors of mobile campuses. Some of them took circuitous routes because the Japanese did not roll across China in a single, unbroken wave. A time-lapse map of the invasion would look more like splotches of amoeba-shaped territories, advancing and retreating. There was no one safe route and it was impossible for refugees to predict from one day to the next whether an area was still part of Free China or occupied by the Japanese.

The spelling of place names (Nanking, Peking, Chengtu, etc.) is according to Chinese postal romanization, a form of Wade-Giles romanization that persisted in common use even after it was abolished by the Chinese Communists in 1964.

And finally, readers of *Three Souls* and *Dragon Springs Road* may recognize some of the minor characters in this novel.

RESOURCES

For those interested in learning more about the *liuwang* students as well as the refugee situation in China during the Second Sino-Japanese War, the following books are very worthwhile:

The Great Flowing River: A Memoir of China, from Manchuria to Taiwan, by Bangyuan Qi, John Balcom (translator). Columbia University Press (2018)

Shanghai 1937: Stalingrad on the Yangtze, by Peter Harmsen. Casemate Publishing (2013)

In a Sea of Bitterness: Refugees During the Sino-Japanese War, by R. Keith Schoppa. Harvard University Press (2011)

Race the Rising Sun, by Chao-Min Hsieh, Jean Kan Hsieh. Hamilton Books (2009)

Wuhan, 1938: War, Refugees, and the Making of Modern China, by Stephen R. MacKinnon. University of California Press (2008)

Lianda, A Chinese University in War and Revolution, by John Israel. Stanford University Press (1998)

Teaching in Wartime China, by Edward Gulick. University of Massachusetts Press (1995)

In the Shadow of the Rising Sun: Shanghai Under Japanese Occupation, by Christian Henriot. Cambridge University Press (2004)

Some online information about the real encyclopedias:

"The C. V. Starr East Asian Library Receives Monumental Gift": https://ieas.berkeley.edu/news/c-v-starr-east-asian-library -receives-monumental-gift

The Yongle Dadian: http://www.chinaknowledge.de/Literature /Science/yongledadian.html

ACKNOWLEDGMENTS

I t's pretty clear to me by now that authors only get through the trauma of writing a book because we are blessed with friends and professional colleagues who tolerate us with great indulgence despite our strange hours and even stranger behavior.

During my initial research on refugee students, *The Great Flowing River*, a memoir by Bangyuan Qi, was only available in Chinese and German, neither of which I can read. Thank you to Dr. Hui-wen Von Groeling-Che, responsible for the German translation, for answering my questions so generously. Thank you also to my sister-in-law, Alice, whose network of amazing friends put me in touch with Dr. Von Groeling-Che. Big thanks to my friend Dr. Helena Swinkels, who never got annoyed at my questions and even lent me her handbook of infectious tropical diseases.

I'm immensely grateful to some wonderful people who were willing to read the early and ugly versions of the manuscript. To my secret weapon Jennifer Pooley, who has helped on all three of my novels; the beautiful and talented Claire Mulligan; and the incomparable

Kate Quinn. Thank you, thank you for your patience and your astute comments, all of which helped shape the book.

There are so many authors whose friendship I treasure. You may not realize it but sometimes your words and support have made the difference between giving up and staying with the job of writing. There are too many to list, but thank you: Caroline Adderson, Matthew Boroson, Kate Hilton, June Hutton, Julia Claiborne Johnson, Shaena Lambert, Evelyn Lau, Mary Novik, Roberta Rich, Jennifer Robson, and Sam Wiebe. And of course, each and every one of the Tall Poppy Writers, for providing moral support, professional advice, and plenty of laughs.

A very big thank-you to the Canada Council for the Arts. I could not have written this novel without your support. It felt very meaningful to receive assistance from an organization dedicated to advancing Canada's cultural identity while I was writing a novel about a government's wartime efforts to preserve a country's culture.

So many thanks and hugs to "my" team at HarperCollins Canada and William Morrow, especially Iris Tupholme and Jennifer Brehl. Thank you yet again for believing in me and in this story. Janice Zawerbny, bless you and your editorial insights, and thank you for not laughing at my struggles with close third-person POV. Also much gratitude to Cory Beatty, Michael Guy-Haddock, Michael Millar, Lauren Morocco, Amelia Wood, Camille Collins, Shelby Peak, Laurie McGee, Elsie Lyons, and Diahann Sturge. To Jill Marr, my agent, and everyone at the Sandra Dijkstra Literary Agency: a third book! Sometimes it's still hard to believe I'm a published author. Thank you for helping me in this adventure.

Last but never least—thank you, Geoffrey. Your support matters more than any other.

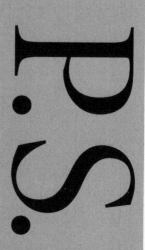

About the author

About the book

Read on

Insights,
Interviews
& More . . .

Meet Janie Chang

Ayelet Tsabari

JANIE CHANG is a Canadian novelist who draws upon family history for her writing. She grew up listening to stories about ancestors who encountered dragons, ghosts, and immortals and about family life in a small Chinese town in the years before the Second World War. She has a degree in computing science and is a graduate of The Writer's Studio at Simon Fraser University.

She is the author of *Three Souls* and *Dragon Springs Road*, both of which were longlisted for the International Dublin Literary Award. *Dragon Springs Road* has been a Globe and Mail National

Bestseller. Born in Taiwan, Janie has lived in the Philippines, Iran, Thailand, and New Zealand. She now lives in beautiful Vancouver, Canada, with her husband and Mischa, a rescue cat who thinks the staff could be doing a better job. ∾

Reading Group Guide

1. The majority of English-language novels set during World War II take place in Europe. What did you know about World War II in Asia before reading *The Library of Legends* and how did you learn? In school? Through books? TV and movies?

2. *The Library of Legends* is set during a time of great political and social change. What sorts of situations do the educated young adults of Minghua University encounter to make them question their assumptions?

3. Chinese culture has honored education and teachers for thousands of years. Discuss how this is reflected in the novel.

4. When reading historical novels, especially those set in foreign places, it can be hard to set aside our modern sensibilities. What situations in the book did you find hard to relate to and why?

5. What were the situations you empathized with and why?

6. At the beginning of the novel, Lian is aloof and cautious about forming attachments. How does she change over the course of the story and what are the factors that contribute to her change?

7. The Second Sino-Japanese War displaced an estimated eighty to one hundred million Chinese. How relevant do you feel the themes in this novel are compared to current world events?

8. The students of Minghua University endured a great deal of suffering on their evacuation, both physical and mental. Which of the hardships experienced by the characters would you find most difficult to bear?

9. In the novel, it's not just people but also the gods and guardian spirits of China who are leaving their homes. What do you think the author means to say about the impact this war had on China?

10. The author was inspired to write *The Library of Legends* because of her father's stories about his life as a refugee student traveling with his university during the years of war between China and Japan. The Author's Notes highlight some (not all) of the incidents and characters that were based on real life. Which of these affected you the most once you knew they were true events?

11. There are many categories of historical fiction. *The Library of Legends* adds an element of fantasy to an otherwise traditional historical novel (one that stays true ▶

About the book

to events of the past). How do you feel about historical fiction that crosses genres to incorporate fantasy, alternative history, romance, mystery, and so on?

12. If the author were to write a sequel to *The Library of Legends*, which of the characters would you want the story to follow? ᴄᴡ

Behind the Book:
The Years of War

Readers always ask which incidents
in the novel are based on true events.
There is so much in this book drawn
from my own family history and family
connections.

My father was only fourteen when
he left home for boarding school.
After high school, he went on to
Nanking University. When war broke
out, students who were able to return
home did so, but by then many could
not even contact their families. Father
felt he had to stay with his professors
and school no matter what. A university
education was his sworn duty to his
family. And so when Nanking University
evacuated, he left with them.

He traveled with classmates,
professors, school administrators,
and servants. They walked beside
donkey carts piled high with luggage,
lab equipment, library books, and
kitchenware. They traveled in a less-
than-organized manner, often breaking
off into smaller groups depending on
what transportation they could find.
Sometimes they split up with plans no
more definite than to meet at a certain
town in a few days' time. Some students
hitched rides, others climbed on trains,
but most walked. They stopped wherever
it seemed they might be safe for a few
days and always tried to carry on with
classes. ▶

Behind the Book: The Years of War
(continued)

Buddhist and Daoist temples could be found in every village and throughout the countryside. They were the most suitable accommodations since temple halls could be used as both classrooms and sleeping quarters. After long hours of walking, the students would sling off their heavy canvas backpacks, unroll straw mats and blankets onto cold stone floors, and settle down to sleep. My father dreaded the Daoist temples because of their giant demon statues, deities with protruding eyes and enormous fangs, painted in bright colors. Sometimes when he woke in the early hours of the morning, my father would open his eyes to a red-painted guardian from the gates of hell glaring down at him. Decades later, he still suffered nightmares of demons trying to drag him into the underworld.

When he thought back to those days on the road, my father said that to describe what they did as "fleeing" was ridiculous. He estimated they probably covered no more than eight or ten miles a day, a small distance to put between them and an invading army. But somehow through all this, my father never felt as though he was truly in danger. Since he and his classmates all suffered the same hardships, he simply accepted the constant hunger and fatigue. With the self-centered optimism of youth, he believed he and his classmates were safe as long as they obeyed their teachers.

But from time to time, a student would disappear and there would be rumors that they had slipped away to enlist or had been murdered by the opposing side. The character of the bold and beautiful Wang Jenmei is based on one of my father's classmates, a young man who was murdered during the journey, drowned in a lake. Decades later, my father still suffered nightmares in which he had been captured by Communist spies (in his dreams it was always the Communists) who were going to murder him.

The young field medic Daming is based on the wartime experiences of a dear friend of the family, Chi-Han Chou, our uncle Chou. Like Daming, Uncle Chou was not a very good student and thought that going to war would be an adventure. So he and a classmate dropped out and made their way to the front lines to look for the classmate's uncle, a general. The two young men were only about nineteen at the time, with no real skills, but they could read. So they were given medical manuals and pressed into service. Unlike Daming, Uncle Chou survived the war. He married my mother's dearest friend, moved to Taiwan, then Seattle, and lived a long and blessed life.

The story of Duckling is heart-wrenching and sadly true. A friend of the family, James Oliver Bennington, served during World War II as a water tender second class in the US Navy. ▶

Behind the Book: The Years of War
(continued)

On one trip, they transported a troop of Chinese soldiers. One of the soldiers brought his daughter with him. She was "the most be-yoo-tiful little girl," James recalled. The Americans spoiled the child terribly while she was on board, but in the end there was nothing they could do but watch the young soldier march off to war, his daughter riding on his shoulders. I wrote a better fate for Duckling.

For the chapters set in Shanghai, I drew upon my mother's stories. She was fifteen and at boarding school in Nanking when war broke out. Her father (the real Dr. Mao) rushed there to bring her home. The family of nine (my grandparents, my grandfather's concubine, four children, his intern, and a maidservant) traveled by riverboat from their hometown of Pinghu to Shanghai's International Settlement. They were luckier than most because as a doctor, my grandfather could support them. For the next eight years they lived in a two-room flat. My grandfather used the front room as his clinic and at night the family spread out over the two rooms to sleep. My mother slept on the examining table.

My grandfather had developed a cure for opium addiction, and a bank manager in Shanghai heard about this and sought him out. After my grandfather cured him, the manager began referring all his wealthy friends to my grandfather, whose practice thrived until the war ended and the family could return to their hometown of Pinghu.

As for my father, he was twenty-eight years old before he saw his family and his hometown again. ᴄ᙭

An Excerpt from
Dragon Springs Road
by Janie Chang

CHAPTER 1

November 1908, Year of the Monkey

The morning my mother went away, she burned incense in front of the Fox altar.

The emperor Guangxu and the dowager empress had both died that week. My mother told me our new emperor was a little boy of almost three called Puyi. A child less than half my age now ruled China and she was praying for him. And for us.

My mother knelt, eyes shut, rocking back and forth with clasped hands. I couldn't hear the prayers she murmured and did my best to imitate her, but I couldn't help lifting my eyes to steal glances at the picture pasted on the brick wall, a colorful print of a woman dressed in flowing silks, her face sweetly bland, one hand lifted in blessing. A large red fox sat by her feet. A Fox spirit, pictured in her human and animal forms.

The altar was just a low table placed against the back wall of the kitchen. Its cracked wooden surface held an earthenware jar filled with sand. My mother had let me poke our last

Read on

handful of incense sticks into the sand and even let me strike a match to light them. We had no food to offer that morning except a few withered plums.

The Fox gazed down at me with its painted smile.

After we prayed, my mother dressed me in my new winter tunic.

"Stay here, Jialing," she said, pushing the last knot button through its loop. "Be quiet and don't let anyone know you're here. Stay inside the Western Residence until Mama comes back."

But three days passed and she didn't come back.

WE LIVED BY OURSELVES, just the two of us, in the main house of the Western Residence. I usually slept with my mother in her bed, but I was just as used to spending nights in my playroom. It was out in the *erfang,* a single-story row of five connected rooms, each with a door that opened onto the veranda that wrapped around the front of the building, steps leading down to a paved courtyard. There were two *erfang* that faced each other across the courtyard, but the other was derelict, its roof fallen in.

Whenever Noble Uncle came to visit my mother, I had to leave the main house. She would send me to my playroom and fetch me the next morning after he left. Then our placid life would resume. ▶

An Excerpt from *Dragon Springs Road* by Janie Chang *(continued)*

Sometimes Noble Uncle took her away for a day or two, but never for this long.

ON THE FIRST day of my mother's absence, I paged through the few books in my playroom, then wandered out to the courtyard to shake more plums from the fruit trees. I pulled off their desiccated flesh and put the pits in my pocket. Using the charred end of a stick from the kitchen stove I drew a checkers board on the paving stones and placed pits in the squares. Morning and afternoon I shook the trees, hoping more fruit would fall so that I could have more pieces for my game.

After two days, I began eating the plums despite their moldy taste.

But mostly, I watched and waited for my mother to return.

The smaller front courtyard had gates that opened out to Dragon Springs Road. Years ago my mother had pushed broken furniture against one corner of the courtyard's walls, tying wooden legs and chair backs together to steady the stack into a platform we could climb. From this perch we had spied on the world outside.

The honeysuckle that clambered across the top of the wall was bare of leaves, but the tangle of vines was still thick enough for concealment. Looking down to the left, I could see the front courtyard of the Central Residence, the home where Noble Uncle and his family lived. There was a door in the wall between the two front courtyards, but the only one who ever used it had been Noble Uncle.

To the right was the street. Standing on tiptoe I peered through the vines, hoping to see my mother's figure alight from a sedan chair or rickshaw, but all I saw were our neighbors, unwitting and uncaring of my presence.

Back at the Fox altar I knelt down to pray, rocking on my haunches, gaze fixed on the picture pasted to the wall. My nostrils prickled with the musty fragrance of incense. *Please, bring back my mama.* But the Fox woman looked into the distance, and the Fox merely smiled.

"Fox spirits are almost always female," my mother had said. "They can appear in Fox shape or as beautiful women. They help those who befriend them. Some are especially sympathetic to unfortunate women."

Now I wondered at my mother's words. Did she pray to a Fox because she was an unfortunate woman?

That night I dreamed that I had wandered out to Dragon Springs Road all on my own, when a dreadful knowledge seized me that my mother had gone away never to return. Fear jolted me out of sleep and into the gray light of early morning. I was utterly alone. I cried and cried, but my forlorn wails went unheeded. Curling up under the quilt, I sobbed myself back to sleep.

The next morning, I lay on the ▶

An Excerpt from *Dragon Springs Road* by Janie Chang *(continued)*

pallet bed with all my clothes on, quilt pulled over my head, trying to keep warm. The plate on the floor taunted me with reminders of chicken and sticky rice steamed in lotus leaf packets, the scent of garlic and sesame oil still clinging to the leaves. My stomach ached, a harsh kneading that twisted my insides. I tried chewing on a lotus leaf, but when I tried to swallow, the tough fibers made me retch and I spat them out.

Finally, I went outside to get a drink from the well in the courtyard. I knelt beside its low stone wall and pushed aside the wooden lid. I tossed in my tin cup, heard it splash in the dark depths, and pulled on the rope, hand over hand as my mother had taught me. I took care not to lean too far over the stone rim, as she'd always cautioned, and replaced the lid. I didn't want to end up as the ghost of a drowned girl, dank hair hanging over my face, luring victims to share my fate.

It won't be long now, a voice behind me said. People are coming. I can hear them up the road. The voice was high pitched, the words pronounced precisely.

I swung around. An animal with tawny red fur yawned, showing a pink tongue and sharp white teeth. It looked like one of the stray dogs that sometimes came into Dragon Springs Road, but it was sleek, not mangy, with a plume of a tail. A fox. Its eyes shone amber yellow, dark centers with flecks of green in their depths. Its snout was long and elegant, its paws neat and stockinged in black. Then it vanished.

Startled, I dropped my cup and toppled over, my back against the well. Had I fallen asleep and dreamed the creature?

Then I heard voices. Unfamiliar voices. Voices shouting commands, voices shouting in reply.

I hurried through the bamboo grove to the front courtyard and climbed up the pile of furniture. Next door, the gates stood wide open. There was excited laughter and chatter from the street, and then a woman's voice called out in stern tones.

"Silence! Show respect for the spirits in our new home!"

The chatter ceased immediately.

"All the doors and windows are open, Old Mistress." A sturdy man in plain blue servant's garb came out from the main courtyard to face the entrance gate. "Any spirits who wanted to leave should be gone now."

"Does everyone have something to carry?" A male voice, deep and jovial. "We mustn't enter our new home empty-handed."

A man stepped over the threshold of the entrance gate. An exuberant smile lit his round face. His long queue gleamed with the same dark shine as his satin skullcap, and he carried a bundle of books under his arm.

The old woman by his side wore her ▶

An Excerpt from *Dragon Springs Road* by Janie Chang *(continued)*

white hair scraped severely into a bun, her forehead covered by a wide band of black silk. She carried a pair of scrolls and tottered in on tiny feet. Then two younger women stepped into the entrance courtyard. One had a rounded, smiling face and a rounded belly; she held a basket of fruit against her hip. The other was tall and pale, with pursed lips that gave her a dour expression; a panel of embroidered fabric hung over one thin arm.

A young man and a girl followed. The young man carried a small lacquerware box, the girl a covered basket. She was tall, nearly as tall as my mother, with hair dressed in two heavy braids looped with ribbons on either side of her head, glossy and thick. Her padded winter tunic of dark blue flannel just reached her ankles.

Then came a female servant holding a little boy by the hand. Two more female servants entered, gazing around and up, but they didn't see my face peering from behind the vines.

"Lao-er, where's our lucky orange tree?" The jovial voice belonged to the round-faced man. He stood at the threshold of the inner gate, ready to enter the main courtyard. "Go, go. Plant it!"

The servant who had first spoken pushed the entrance gate open wide and wheeled in a barrow. On the barrow were gardening tools and a small orange tree, its root ball bound inside a muddy burlap bag. The small procession crossed through the inner gate and into the main courtyard. More handbarrows and workers followed, loaded down with furniture and belongings.

My mother wasn't among those parading in and out.

Back in the courtyard, I shook one of the plum trees at the edge of the bamboo garden. Four aged fruits fell from its branches. I scooped what I could into my hands and ate it all, not caring about the grit that covered the plums. I spat out the pits and arranged them on my checkerboard.

A scraping noise sent me scuttling into the playroom, the sound of the gate between the two front courtyards opening. I waited, kneeling by the window. Through the carved latticework of the window shutters, I saw a figure enter the courtyard. It was the girl.

For a moment she vanished from sight as the path took her through the bamboo trees, then she appeared again, following the path through the rockery and under the garden arch. She took her time, pausing to look at a rock, a striped bamboo trunk, the carved stone of the arch. She gazed around the courtyard and the buildings that enclosed it, the two-level main house at the far end of the courtyard, the *erfang* where I was hiding, the derelict *erfang* opposite, the bamboo garden she had just come through. She climbed the steps to the veranda of the main house and peered ▶

An Excerpt from *Dragon Springs Road* by Janie Chang *(continued)*

through the carved lattice windows, into the rooms where my mother and I had lived. Then she walked back down the veranda steps and paused to look down at the plum pits lying on the makeshift checkerboard.

Show yourself to her, the voice said.

I blinked at the Fox who had appeared beside me. I reached my hand out to touch, to feel whether it was real. The creature gave me a small lick, a raspy warm sensation that gave me courage.

"Who are you?" I whispered.

Your mother burned incense to a Fox spirit, it said. Don't you remember?

My mother had been fond of telling stories about Fox spirits. "Are you a good spirit or an evil one?"

She gave a small bark of disdain. How can you tell whether anyone is truly good or evil? I've been a Fox for hundreds of years and from what I've seen it takes generations before consequences truly run their course.

This answer made no sense to me, but her next suggestion did. Go to that girl. She'll give you something to eat.

"My mother said not to let anyone know I was here," I said, but my words of protest were feeble. The hollowness in my stomach mattered more.

In response, the Fox nudged me toward the door.

CLOSER, THE GIRL'S eyes were the first thing I noticed. Her looks were unremarkable, smooth flat features on a plain face. But her eyes were large and deep-set, solemn and serene.

She spoke first. "The neighbors outside said they've heard crying for the last two nights since the Fong family moved away. They say it's the ghost of a concubine who committed suicide. Have you seen such a ghost?"

I shook my head. My mother had never mentioned any ghost.

"You were the one crying, weren't you?" she said. "I thought so. I knew there was someone here when I saw those plum pits. They were still damp."

"Have you seen my mother?" The question tumbled out, more important than food.

"Who's your mother?"

"Her name is Mama." What other name could she have? The girl looked at me, as if expecting more. "She went away with everyone else. But she's coming back."

"Why didn't you go away with her?" the girl asked.

I had asked myself this question for days and could only look away, unable to answer.

"What's your name?"

"Jialing."

"My family name is Yang," she said. "Yang Anjuin. What's your family name?"

"Zhu. I think." How could I have been uncertain of my own name? My mother had never made a family name seem important. She only ever ▶

An Excerpt from *Dragon Springs Road* by Janie Chang *(continued)*

called me Jialing. *My little Ling-ling,* she sometimes teased, like the sound of a bell.

"Let's go talk to my grandmother, Jialing."

Anjuin held her hand out and I took it. My fingers were cold and rather sticky, but Anjuin's grip was firm, and her eyes as she looked down were clear and kind. My wariness dissolved, and when she squeezed my hand, I squeezed back.

As we left, I heard a rustle in the bamboos. A small note of caution from Fox sounded in my mind, warning me not to mention anything about a Fox spirit to anyone.

And behave yourself, the voice added. Be good and make it easier for them to let you stay. ᘓ

D iscover great authors, exclusive offers, and more at hc.com.